PENGUIN CLASSICS

TALES FROM THE *DECAMERON*

GIOVANNI BOCCACCIO was born in 1313, either in Florence or in nearby Certaldo, and was the illegitimate son of an employee of the prestigious Bardi bank. His father became manager of the Bardi branch in Naples around 1327, and took his son with him to be trained as a banker. Instead Boccaccio found his way into literary and intellectual circles connected with the Neapolitan court, and began to write narrative poems and prose. He returned to Florence, probably for economic reasons, in 1340–41. The experience of the devastating plague of 1348 led to his greatest work, the *Decameron*, which he completed in the early 1350s. He then turned his energies primarily to Latin and Greek. Boccaccio acquired a reading knowledge of ancient Greek and wrote highly influential encyclopaedic works in Latin. Now a respected figure in Florence, he was sent on various diplomatic missions. He spent most of his later years in Certaldo and died in 1375.

PETER HAINSWORTH has been a lecturer in Italian at the universities of Hull, Kent and Oxford, from where he retired in 2003. He is now an Emeritus Fellow of Lady Margaret Hall. He co-edited with David Robey *The Oxford Companion to Italian Literature* (2002) and, again with David Robey, co-authored *A Very Short Introduction to Italian Literature* (2012) and *A Very Short Introduction to Dante* (2015). His translations of a selection of Petrarch's poems and prose appeared as *The Essential Petrarch* in 2010.

GIOVANNI BOCCACCIO

Tales from the *Decameron*

Translated, Introduced and with Notes by
PETER HAINSWORTH

PENGUIN BOOKS

PENGUIN CLASSICS

UK | USA | Canada | Ireland | Australia
India | New Zealand | South Africa

Penguin Books is part of the Penguin Random House group of companies
whose addresses can be found at global.penguinrandomhouse.com.

This translation first published in Penguin Classics 2015

001

Set in 10.25/12.25 pt Adobe Sabon
Typeset by Jouve (UK), Milton Keynes
Printed in Great Britain by Clays Ltd, St Ives plc

ISBN: 978-0-141-19133-1

www.greenpenguin.co.uk

MIX
Paper from
responsible sources
FSC   FSC® C018179
www.fsc.org

Penguin Random House is committed to a
sustainable future for our business, our readers
and our planet. This book is made from Forest
Stewardship Council® certified paper.

Contents

TALES FROM THE
DECAMERON

DAY ONE

DAY TWO

DAY THREE

DAY FOUR

DAY FIVE

DAY SIX

DAY SEVEN

DAY EIGHT

DAY NINE

DAY TEN

*Note: The story titles are not in
the original and are intended solely
to help the modern reader.*

Chronology

1313 Giovanni Boccaccio born either in Florence or in nearby Certaldo, the illegitimate son of an unknown woman and Boccaccio di Chellino, an agent of the important Bardi bank.

1313–25 Spends his childhood mostly in Florence.

1327 (or thereabouts) Goes to work and train at the Bardi branch in Naples, which is managed by his father, who enjoys a position of some prominence in the city and court.

1330/31–4 Studies canon law at Naples University.

1330s Has access to the court of Robert of Anjou, the ruler of Naples, and joins its intellectual and literary circles, leading to his enthusiastic immersion in Latin and French literature. Writes first poetic works: *La caccia di Diana* (1334?) and *Filostrato* (1335?), and his first prose narrative, the *Filocolo* (1336?). Invents the story of his affair with Fiammetta, which figures in most of his work in Italian before the *Decameron*.

1340–44 Returns to Florence (1340–41). Writes various works in verse and prose: *Teseida* (1340–41?), *Comedìa delle ninfe* (or *Ameto*) (1341–2?), *Amorosa visione* (1342–3?), *Elegia di Madonna Fiammetta* (1343–4?). He also writes lyric poems, many of which he may later have destroyed.

1345–7 Travels to various Northern Italian courts and may have been employed briefly in one or more of them. Writes his last narrative poem, the *Ninfale fiesolano* (1344–6?), translates part of Livy's histories into Italian (1346?), and exchanges Latin verse letters with the humanist Checco di Meletto Rossi. Writes also a Latin biography of the poet Petrarch.

1346 Collapse of the Bardi bank when Edward III of England reneges on his debts. Boccaccio's finances are fragile from now onwards, if not before.

1348 Witnesses the Black Death in Florence.

1349–51? Writes the *Decameron*.

1349 Death of father.

1350–51 Elected Chamberlain of the Commune of Florence. Goes on largely honorific ambassadorial missions, to the lords of Romagna in 1350, and in 1351 first to Queen Giovanna of Naples and then to King Ludwig of Bavaria.

1350 Meets Petrarch and entertains him as his guest in Florence. Their friendship will continue until Petrarch's death in 1374, conducted mostly through letters in Latin. There will also be visits to see Petrarch in various places where he is living: Milan in 1359, Venice in 1363 and Padua in 1367.

1354 Ambassadorial mission to Pope Innocent VI in Avignon.

1355 (and again in 1362) Attempts to re-establish himself in Naples, but fails.

1358 Death of his (illegitimate) daughter Violante.

1350–75 Writes encyclopaedic Latin works: *Genealogia deorum gentilium*, *De casibus virorum illustrium*, *De mulieribus claris*, *De montibus, silvis, fontibus*, etc., plus the pastoral *Buccolicum carmen*.

1361 Takes minor orders in the Church, and largely withdraws from Florence to Certaldo.

Early 1360s Studies Greek with the Italo-Greek Calabrian Leonzio Pilato and collects and copies works by Homer and other ancient Greek and Latin writers.

Later 1360s and early 1370s Writes the misogynistic *Corbaccio*, twice revises and expands his celebratory life of Dante, *Trattatello in laude di Dante* (originally 1351), revises the *Amorosa visione* and makes a definitive copy of the *Decameron*.

1365 Ambassadorial mission to Pope Urban V in Avignon and again in 1367 in Rome.

1370–01 Final visit to Naples.

1373–4 Delivers lecture-commentaries (*Esposizioni*) on Dante's *Divine Comedy* in the church of S. Stefano della Badia in Florence, stopping after the first seventeen cantos of the *Inferno*.

1374 Death of Petrarch, who leaves Boccaccio in his will an ermine robe to keep him warm when studying on winter nights.

21 **December** 1375 Dies, probably in Certaldo.

Introduction

When he finished the *Decameron*, sometime between 1349 and 1351, Boccaccio was in his late thirties and living in or near Florence. His previous works had all broken new ground in different ways and some were already well known. But this collection of a hundred stories quickly became his most popular work in Florence and beyond. The *Decameron* offered a blueprint for subsequent collections throughout Europe and in sixteenth-century Italy was granted the same sort of status as the ancient classics.

Modern readers are likely to be impressed first by the sheer readability of these stories, their narrative verve and pace, and the surprises they seem always to have in store. Then there is the range of characters and settings, the humour (sometimes but not always bawdy) and of course the sex, which gives as much scope to female as to male desire.

All of this can seem fairly simple on first reading. But the *Decameron* is a rich and complex work, which deploys ambiguities in ways a modern author might envy and yet has the easy grace and balance that we associate with classical literature. None of Boccaccio's earlier works reaches this level, nor does anything he wrote later, when his interests were much more overtly learned and he was writing principally in Latin, not Italian.

BEFORE THE *DECAMERON*

Boccaccio sometimes alludes to being the illegitimate son of a French princess with whom his father had an affair during a business visit to Paris. He was indeed illegitimate, but born in 1313 to an unknown mother either in Florence or in the small town of Certaldo a little to the south-west, where his family was from, and which is depicted in the story of Friar Cipolla in the *Decameron* (6.10) as populated mainly by gullible yokels. His father was employed by the Bardi, one of the most important Florentine banking families, with Europe-wide operations.

Some time in his early teens Boccaccio went to work for the Bardi in Naples. He was no more cut out for commerce than he was for law, which he began to study at Naples University. But Naples was the capital city of the Angevin dynasty, which had been ruling southern Italy since the late 1260s, and the court of Robert of Anjou was a vibrant intellectual and literary centre, into which the young Boccaccio found his way and flourished. He became friends with some of the court's leading intellectuals and was able to gain a knowledge of French romances and poems, as well as of Latin literature, both medieval and classical. Perhaps he also had the prolonged and passionate love affair which he mentions in the Prologue to the *Decameron*. However, the Fiammetta who appears intermittently in his work is a literary construction and not, as was long believed, an otherwise unknown illegitimate daughter of King Robert named Maria d'Aquino.

Boccaccio soon began writing narrative poems and prose romances in Italian, all centred on the theme of love. From the beginning it was love with a resolutely sensual side, unlike the sort of transcendental love for Beatrice that Dante (who died when Boccaccio was eight) celebrated in the *Divine Comedy*; and also without the spiritual torments and uncertainties that figure in the lyric poetry of his slightly older contemporary Petrarch, who later became his much-admired friend.

A first poem, *La caccia di Diana*, is a homage to a string of Neapolitan ladies, who hunt down stags, only to find to their delight that Venus brings their kill back to life as delectably handsome young men. A second, the *Filostrato*, is Boccaccio's first real narrative, telling the story of Troilus and Cressida that would be taken up by Chaucer and then by Shakespeare. Though formally set in ancient Troy, the atmosphere and attitudes of the *Filostrato* are those of a contemporary, rather down-to-earth romance. Another, more serious narrative poem, the *Teseida*, aims at something more like ancient epic, and is divided into twelve books after the model of Virgil's *Aeneid*. But it is really another romance, which, not so many years later, was recast by Chaucer as 'The Knight's Tale'. All of these poems are fluent, straightforward and even popular in tone, as is the case even in the *Amorosa visione*, where Boccaccio has a go at visionary (but still not transcendental) allegory in the Dantesque manner.

Boccaccio's prose writing is patently more elaborate, deploying abundant references to classical myth and history, and raising the rhetorical level with the tricks and tropes listed in medieval handbooks, and an abstract vocabulary freely plundered from contemporary Latin practice. The rhetoric of the early *Filocolo* almost buries the French romance of *Floire et Blanceflor* on which it is based, although one episode, in which characters tell stories during a debate about 'questions of love', does look forward to the *Decameron*. The much shorter *Elegia di Madonna Fiammetta* is a first-person account by a Neapolitan noble lady (Boccaccio's beloved?) of being jilted by her lover Panfilo (Boccaccio?) when he leaves Naples. In some ways an early psychological novel, the *Fiammetta* actually stitches together material from the laments of abandoned heroines from Greek mythology that make up Ovid's *Heroides*.

Boccaccio left Naples for Florence in the early 1340s; the *Fiammetta* – and perhaps the *Teseida* – may have been written or completed after his return. Two other works followed before the *Decameron*. The *Ameto* (known later as the *Comedìa delle ninfe*) is an account, with verse interludes, of the education in love given to a Tuscan shepherd by seven nymphs, each of whom tells him the story of her initiation into passion. The nymphs are said to symbolize the seven virtues and their lovers the seven vices, though quite what this adds up to is unclear. The framing narrative is another anticipation of the *Decameron*, and the whole work looks forward to the Renaissance pastoral romances of Sannazaro, Sir Philip Sidney and others. The second work, the *Ninfale fiesolano*, is (if genuine) Boccaccio's last and arguably best narrative poem, a faux naïf metamorphosis story along Ovidian lines about the love of Africo and Mensola, who are in the end transformed into the two Tuscan streams that bear their names.

THE *DECAMERON*

The 1340s were a difficult decade for Florence. The Bardi and the other major Florentine bank, the Peruzzi, had probably over-extended themselves. When the English king Edward III reneged on his debts, both banks were thrown into crisis and eventually collapsed, sending shock waves throughout the banking industry in the city. It may be that Boccaccio's return was related in some way to the crisis, and there are signs that he was unhappy to be back. However, his own troubles and those of his city were soon enormously increased when, after two less serious incursions in the earlier 1340s, the plague (what we call the Black Death) arrived in 1348, killing up to half of Florence's population.

Though some of the stories in the first five days of the *Decameron* may go back to Boccaccio's time in Naples, most of the book was written in the wake of the Black Death. The Introduction to Day One exaggerates the number of dead and the social disruption caused, and probably draws on an account of plague by the eighth-century Latin chronicler Paulus Diaconus, as well as on direct observation and first-hand reports. But the fact that Boccaccio chooses to begin a literary work with a lengthy description and analysis of a historical disaster is an indication of the plague's impact, as well as being a new and unique departure for him.

Boccaccio's justification is that he wants to lay the foundations for the stories that follow. To escape the plague, his ten young people retreat to the country, discounting the fact that it is there too, on the grounds that in the countryside there are fewer people and therefore fewer dead and dying immediately before their eyes. The country provides an idealized, idyllic environment which echoes the *Ameto* and the storytelling part of the *Filocolo*, for there is nothing to do there except find pleasant ways of passing the time, of which telling stories becomes the most agreeable and important.

Yet the plague does not simply get the storytelling moving. The chaos it causes is moral and existential. The plague might be a punishment from God or the result of malign astrological influences or neither of these. Measures to deal with it sometimes work, but usually don't. Most infected people die, but some survive, for no discernible reason. It is little wonder then that morality and the social order break down. The world created by and for the narrators sets a form of order against this chaos – an order that is fragile, arbitrary and beautiful, and sustained by nothing but the desires of the party, their pleasure in each other's company, and their determination not to succumb to the despairing and disorderly immorality which they witness around them, principally in the form of sexual licence.

Once he introduces the seven young women of noble birth who meet one Tuesday morning in spring 1348 in the church of Santa Maria Novella, Boccaccio begins to edge away from realistic depiction. They are said to be real people whose identities he conceals out of concern for their good names, given the kind of stories they will hear and tell, not to mention the fact that most contemporaries would consider their going into the country with a group of young men to be grossly indecent and immoral, however much Boccaccio insists that nothing untoward occurred.

He then declares that the names he gives them say something about their characters. Pampinea is the most defined of the women, as also the most mature and decisive, and the one who first voices the idea of leaving Florence. Her name comes from the *Ameto* and means 'flourishing or in full bloom'. At the opposite extreme, Neifile, the youngest and shyest, has a name that means 'young in love'. The rest may have moments of individuality, but little more. Filomena at first objects to Pampinea's proposal on the grounds that they need male guidance, but after that she is hidden behind her name, which is taken from the myth of Tereus and Philomel. Emilia is the heroine of the *Teseida*, Lauretta a nod perhaps to Petrarch's Laura, while Elissa is an alternative name for Virgil's Dido. Fiammetta is Boccaccio's fictitious Neapolitan beloved, now made Florentine.

The literariness continues with the three young men who opportunely turn up in the church. Panfilo ('all loving') is the name of the unfaithful lover in the *Fiammetta*; Filostrato is a Greek name which we know, from the earlier poem, Boccaccio took to mean 'laid low by love'; Dioneo is 'given over to love', from Dione, the mother of Venus. The names of the servants – cited later by Pampinea in her speech on practical arrangements when the party arrives at the country house – are all taken from the plays of the Roman dramatists Plautus and Terence.

Three men, seven ladies, ten people altogether: ten stories a day, ten days of storytelling – hence the title the *Decameron*, which is derived from a slightly shaky Greek 'deka hemeron' or ten days – and a hundred stories in total. The numbers are talismanic, with perhaps echoes of the hundred canti of the *Divine Comedy*. But they seem to have no specific symbolic meanings.

A similar aura of uncertainty hovers over relationships in the *Decameron*. Boccaccio says that the three men are in love with three of the ladies, unhappily in the case of Filostrato, as it later emerges. Neifile at least seems to be in love with one of the men. Of possible pairings Fiammetta and Dioneo might go together, if Fiammetta is a version of Boccaccio's beloved and Dioneo represents Boccaccio himself. The grounds for that last supposition are that Dioneo is the liveliest and wittiest person in the party, the one who tells the most risqué stories, and who, as king for Day Seven, pushes the ladies into agreeing, after some initial reservations, that the subject should be wives playing tricks on their husbands. He is also the one who frequently strikes something like the same note as Boccaccio himself in his own ironically disingenuous interventions.

The day after meeting, the party leave Florence on foot with their servants and walk out only about two miles to what will be the first of two beautiful and well-appointed residences. Each is set on a hill and surrounded by delightful gardens, their mixture of natural growth and cultivated artifice reflecting the easy but orderly society the visitors create for themselves. This first villa has traditionally been located near Fiesole, although Boccaccio is as vague about this as he is about his narrators' identities. The second villa, even more beautiful than the first, is further out into the countryside, suggesting a greater remoteness from the plague and also from normality and normal restraints. Not far from it is the lovely Valley of the Ladies, complete with a pool in which the women bathe and later the men. It seems at this stage that boundaries might be crossed, but decorum is maintained, although the valley does become the setting for the more daring storytelling of Days Seven to Nine.

Telling stories is of course the most important activity of the 'happy band', but it is not the only one. Pampinea proposes there should be a head of the party for each day they are there. She is elected queen for the first day and establishes the basic routine, although other details emerge later. Mornings are free, and then, after a late morning meal and siesta, the party reassembles in a shaded spot in the garden to tell stories. Once the stories for the day are finished, the queen or king for the day designates a successor, who announces the subject of the stories for the following day. The party then relax until the evening meal, after which there is music, dancing and a song (a different member of the party singing each evening), before everyone finally retires for the night.

This routine will go on every day except for Fridays (for religious reasons) and Saturdays (when the ladies like to wash their hair). This means that while there are ten days of storytelling, the party in fact spend fifteen days away from Florence. Eventually they accept the proposal of the last king, Panfilo, that they should return: everyone has been king or queen for a day, there is the risk that others might break in on them, and, although their behaviour has been irreproachable in spite of some of the risqué stories they have told, people might begin to talk, so it is time to go.

The king or queen selects tellers as the storytelling proceeds, and in no particular order. The sole restrictions, which are established at the end of Day One, are that the monarch should tell the penultimate story and that Dioneo should have the privilege of telling the last and of departing from the set subject of the day. The expectation is that he will tell a story that will make them all laugh, whatever the other stories have been like.

The overall result is a blend of order and variety. In a given day stories may contrast with each other, pick up another story or simply give an alternative perspective on the set subject. Nor does Dioneo's privilege necessarily mean going off in a different direction. The first nine short stories of Day Six, for instance, are all about pithy or witty remarks that individuals come up with to make a point or to get themselves out of trouble. Dioneo's story of Friar Cipolla is a much longer one about a friar getting himself out of trouble by improvising a (brilliantly funny) long speech.

Dioneo has a certain definition as a storyteller, although he goes against type in the very last story of the whole collection, with his account of the all but incredible patience with which Griselda bears the gratuitous sufferings inflicted on her by her husband. The other male storytellers also show some minimum individuality in so far as they direct the course of the storytelling more than any of the women, apart from perhaps Pampinea, who sets the whole business going.

Filostrato lives up to the dejection signified by his name, when he is designated king for Day Four, and decrees, much to the distress of the ladies, that the subject will be unhappy love. This departure from the general tone of the storytelling is then corrected in Day Five and the issue of Filostrato's misery retreats into the background.

The third man, Panfilo, also imposes his will on the party. On becoming king for the final day he declares that the subject will be generous or magnificent action, a marked shift away from the laxity of Days Seven, Eight and Nine, which means the collection can be read as ending on a note of high moral probity.

But neither Filostrato nor Panfilo nor really Dioneo has an individual voice; for most of the time they are indistinguishable as storytellers from each other and from the ladies, who as a group are somewhat wary of more salacious material during the earlier days, but otherwise tell stories in the same way as the men.

Unlike Chaucer, then, Boccaccio is obviously not much interested in the relationship between individual storyteller and the story told. For the purposes of the *Decameron*, storytelling is established as a conventional skill. Storytellers mark out beginnings and endings, move their tales along, sometimes comment on them, and, if need be, distance themselves from them. But the storyteller is usually pushed aside for the duration of the story itself, which asks to be read primarily as a story by Boccaccio, and not by Dioneo or whoever else may be the speaker, and a Boccaccio who is making radical innovations with respect to his earlier work.

A story in the *Decameron* may have a proem, reflecting on what are not always reliably declared to be its lessons or implications. Then comes an identification by name of the main character or characters, specifying where and when they lived (a large proportion of the stories are set in the recent past in an Italian town), their age, social class and occupation (if they have one). Both male and female protagonists are immediately characterized in terms of their marital status, looks, general behaviour and general alertness, and will conform to this initial characterization throughout the story, except when the whole point of the story is that they do something out of character. Already by this stage, a set of expectations has been set up. An attractive young woman must be an object of desire and feel desire; a young man similarly; but an old husband with a young wife is bound to be a figure of ridicule, because he cannot satisfy her sexual needs.

That situation generally suggests comedy, though what kind of comedy depends on issues of class. The further up the social scale the protagonist, the more likely a story is to be serious. Kings, princes and lords of one kind or another may make mistakes, but they are not to be laughed at or drawn into risible situations, unless they are geographically or temporally remote. Conversely, the lower the class the more likely the story is to be farcical, the desires more crudely physical, and the humour and language to have colloquial or bawdy elements.

All the same there is a good measure of unpredictability. A large proportion of Boccaccio's protagonists are drawn from the merchant classes that dominated Florence and other cities and are presented in force for the first time in his work. With these figures the story tends towards comedy, although the further up the ranks of the merchant aristocracy we go, the more courtly elements are introduced and the more elevated the story becomes, as, for instance, in the stories of Federigo's falcon (5.9) and Nastagio degli Onesti and the infernal chase (5.8).

Once the situation and characters have been set up, an issue is identified that the story will resolve. In many stories it is how to satisfy desire in the face of social or marital obstacles. In others it is how to deal with some unpredictable action of other people or Fortune. Or else, for one reason or another, someone initiates a course of action – say, playing a trick for the sake of it, as happens in Days Eight and Nine. From this initial situation the story moves insistently forwards, pausing only to prepare the ground for the next step and with only rare moments of retrospection. Though characters think and plan and may react with strong feelings to events, Boccaccio summarizes in quite cursory terms what is going on in their hearts and minds and focuses more on what they say and do.

Whereas the framing story contains detailed descriptions of the countryside, little attention is given in the stories to the evocation of particular places beyond simply naming them. So night-time Naples in the story of Andreuccio da Perugia (2.5), and the magic garden which causes Madonna Dianora such distress (10.5), are economically dealt with, as if they are of interest only in relation to the actions of the protagonists.

Conversation in the comic stories often has a natural air, but characters also make substantial speeches that follow accepted rhetorical principles. Ghismonda's response to her father (4.1) just before she drinks poison and dies is probably the most powerful example, but there are many others in which characters lay out what they are feeling or deploy rhetoric to manipulate

others. In such speeches and in his emphasis on action, as well
perhaps in his choice of subjects, Boccaccio is close to theatre.
Perhaps unsurprisingly some stories from the *Decameron* were
eventually turned into comedies during the Renaissance.

Taken as a whole, however, the style of storytelling is
quite elaborate. Here again Boccaccio was strikingly innova-
tive. The tradition with which he was working was a popular
one, not that of high literature. Many stories, perhaps the
majority, probably have an oral origin. Fiammetta says she
heard the story of Federigo and his falcon (5.9) from an old
Florentine gentleman, though that may be an invention, but
certainly many go back further in time. Written precedents
have been identified (not always convincingly) for about a third
of Boccaccio's plots. Barring a few taken from Apuleius and
other late Latin authors, almost all appear in collections written in unpretentious, straightforward language, whether in
Latin or the Tuscan vernacular. However, Boccaccio fills out
what his sources often supply in rather summary form and at
the same time raises the stylistic level enormously.

Here, for example, is a literal translation of a story (probably of Indian origin) which appears as the fourteenth story in
the *Novellino*, an anonymous collection of one hundred stories
put together in Florence in the late thirteenth century, only
about sixty years before the *Decameron*.

> A son was born to a king. The wise astrologers foresaw that
> unless he went for ten years without seeing the sun, he would lose
> his sight. So the king had him nourished and guarded in dark
> caves. After the time said, he had him brought out and had set
> before him many lovely jewels and many lovely maidens, naming
> all the things by name, but telling him that the maidens were
> demons. Then they asked him which he found most pleasing. He
> replied, 'The demons.' Then the king was much amazed at this,
> saying, 'What a thing is the tyranny and beauty of women!'

This looks very much like Boccaccio's source for the story of
Filippo Balducci in the Introduction to Day Four. But, leaving
aside the inversion of the moral, his narrative has a particularity

and fullness that is quite absent from the *Novellino* and from the medieval storytelling tradition as a whole. Not only that, but in Boccaccio's original at least, the sentences have expanded, becoming something like Latin periods with a high degree of subordination and a careful attention to rhythm and balance of the parts.

This is the *Decameron*'s characteristic narrative manner. It obviously continues from the elaborate prose of Boccaccio's earlier work, but there are novelties. In a way he had barely done before, Boccaccio incorporates conversational elements too, now and then slipping into syntactic non sequiturs and making free use of common words or phrases, as well as more elevated vocabulary taken from Latin or courtly literature. The level drops with the double entendres of comic stories, although as Boccaccio says in his Conclusion, he avoids crudity. Conversely the rhetoric is heightened in certain speeches (such as that by Ghismonda), as well as in Boccaccio's more or less playful interventions in his own voice. Generally the framing story preserves an even tone and rhythm somewhat above that of the stories themselves. All this presents considerable difficulties for a translator, as I shall discuss below.

Events are almost always brought to a happy resolution, especially for lovers. If they are unmarried (as they all are in Day Five) they finally marry and live happily ever after. If their affair is adulterous, some accommodation is reached whereby the liaison can continue, with or without the knowledge of others. An extreme point is reached with the story of Zeppa and Spinelloccio (8.8), in which the husband cuckolded by his friend pays back his friend in the same manner, and an arrangement is set up which satisfies all four people.

It is little wonder that Boccaccio so closely guarded the identities of his female storytellers, who at most express only the feeblest shock at what they hear. But there were precedents he might have appealed to. In the twelfth century, for instance, Andreas Capellanus stated baldly in his widely read *De amore* that marriage (to another person) was no obstacle to love, and most French romances took adulterous love as normal. From this perspective, the deceived husband is simply a fool who deserves all he gets, and whose best course of action, if he finds out about the affair, is to keep quiet.

The exceptions come in the tragic stories of Day Four, in which the resolution is brought about by the deaths of the lovers, through suicide, chance or at the hands of other people. However, the general consensus of the storytellers is that tales of this kind are a mistake, which threatens their project of laughter and amusement; so Boccaccio has Pampinea try to lighten the mood with her story of Friar Alberto pretending to be the Angel Gabriel (4.2). This not only displeases the king, Filostrato, who is set on enjoying being miserable, but proves exceptional in other ways: it is the one story in the *Decameron* which follows the common practice of French fabliaux in having its immoral protagonist punished, in spite of the laughter he has provided; and it is all but unique in tailing away, leaving it unclear quite how the friar met his end.

Non-love stories follow the rule in being firmly and clearly rounded off, although the modern reader may find some resolutions hard to accept. Calandrino, who has been made to believe in the power of the heliotrope to make him invisible (8.3), ends up bruised and battered, as well as giving his wife a bruising and battering too, without realizing he has been tricked. He is the victim of similar japes in another three stories I have not included. Simpletons, like deceived husbands, deserve no sympathy, as will be reiterated even more violently in a whole sub-tradition of Renaissance Tuscan storytelling following on from Boccaccio.

What does Boccaccio want his readers to make of all this? In his Prologue he claims to have written the *Decameron* for unoccupied, lovelorn ladies out of gratitude for the sympathy he received from them when he was himself suffering the pains of excessive passion, and makes no grand claims for the value of his 'fables, parables, histories or whatever we want to call them'.

He then expands on this in his Introduction to Day Four: these stories are modest efforts written in the Florentine vernacular for ladies without Latin, not scholars, and should be treated as such. He declares (with questionable seriousness) that he writes about love out of a fascination with the beauty of women and a desire to possess them that is natural in men. He then tells the comic story of Filippo Balducci and his son, ostensibly to bring the reader round to his way of thinking. Perhaps he really is proposing that natural human desires should be followed rather than disciplined. However, in his final defence of himself and his work in the Conclusion, the arguments become more and more inconsequential and seem ultimately to dissolve in laughter.

It may be that this is all comic pretence and that underneath the surface there is a serious medieval moralist at work. Vittore Branca, the greatest of twentieth-century Boccaccio scholars, argued that there was a progression from the denunciation of vice in Day One to the celebration of virtue in Day Ten. The problem with this argument is first that it is very hard to identify the stages of the progression, either within days or from day to day, beyond the general loosening of constraints that occurs over Days Seven to Nine, and the obvious contrast between Day Ten and everything that has come before. Secondly, and more fundamentally, one of the reasons why Boccaccio is still so interesting is that he embraces contradictions and exceptions, rather than advancing a clear vision of what is right or wrong with the world. Even in Day Ten things are not so clear-cut as they might at first seem.

Take Boccaccio's position on the Church. From the story of Abraham (1.2) onwards there are repeated denunciations – some of them very fierce indeed – of the venality, sexual profligacy, hypocrisy and ignorance of the clergy, especially friars. In this respect Boccaccio comes close to Dante and some other medieval writers. However, the stories in which friars and priests play a leading role appear to relish the ways in which they satisfy their immoral desires or get themselves out of a tight corner; as in the tale of Mrs Rosie and the priest of Varlungo (8.2) or Friar Cipolla's absurdly inventive speech to the people of Certaldo (6.10). Though things go wrong for Friar Alberto eventually, we are much more likely to be on his side, rather than sympathize with the silly woman who believes he is the Angel Gabriel. As for nuns who feel the sexual itch or who fall in love, Boccaccio seems to have nothing but amused sympathy for their plight, an extreme example being the story of Masetto da Lamporecchio (3.1).

What is absent from the whole *Decameron* is any sense of Christianity as a system of belief expressing transcendental truths. In the very first story Ser Cepparello, 'perhaps the most terrible man who has ever been born', becomes a saint after his death, and the point is solemnly made that God continues to hear our prayers, despite being prayed to through this vile intermediary. However, the whole focus of the story is on the success of Ser Cepparello's ludicrous confession to a naive – not to say stupid – priest and the sheer comedy of his sanctification. There is also a sense that the traditional story of the three rings, which concludes a trio of ostensibly religious stories that open the *Decameron*, accords with the view of the plague's inexplicability as put forward in Boccaccio's Introduction. As the Jewish banker Melchisedek says, neither Jews nor Christians nor Arabs can prove they possess the truth.

Ambiguities also surround Boccaccio's attitude to women. There is the fact that what he says in their defence in the Introduction to Day Four and elsewhere has a definite tongue-in-cheek air. And, for all the apparent sympathy with the plight of women, the constant emphasis on female sexuality and desire shows an indifference to other aspects of their lives and might well be thought to have a misogynistic component. At times the reservations become explicit. In the first of the tragic stories of Day Four, for instance, Ghismonda makes the most powerful speech of any of Boccaccio's female characters – defending her right to satisfy her natural sexual desires, and her good sense and discretion in choosing Guiscardo as her lover. We might agree, but the narrator of the tale suggests that Ghismonda is perhaps too headstrong and independent, while a moralizing contemporary might consider her extensive, high-flown rhetoric inappropriate. Short and pithy speeches, like those in the stories of Day Six, were regarded as better suited to women.

Or rather to *donne*, a word I have almost always translated as 'ladies', because, following common usage of the time, Boccaccio emphasizes the difference between *donne* and *femine*, mere 'women'. *Donne* are superior in terms of beauty, good sense, manners and behaviour, and are usually members of the upper classes or at least are not from the labouring classes. *Femine* may be from any class, but are characteristically lower-born. They are women in a more negative aspect: instinctive, unreliable, limited, sexual, but without charm, not beautiful in any serious sense and frequently old and even ugly. Boccaccio is writing for and about ladies, not women. And the problem is that ladies may be women underneath, so that they may, for instance, be incapable of doing things without male guidance, as Filomena says when Pampinea first proposes that they leave the plague-ridden city and go off to the countryside. Exceptions such as Zinevra, who becomes the Sultan's foremost servant (2.9), and Gilette de Narbonne, who becomes the only doctor capable of curing the King of France and then runs her husband's dukedom better than it has been run before (3.9), are not cast as role models. They also do what they do to survive and for love, albeit love of men we are likely to find unsympathetic.

The underlying issues come to a head in the story of Griselda, the last tale in the *Decameron* and a surprising one. Not only is it a serious story from Dioneo, but it also seems to overturn so much that has gone before. Petrarch thought it was the one story in the book with any real substance to it, largely because it offered a lesson in constancy, which might apply to the reader's relationship with God; and his Latin version of the story was a great success in Europe, partly because it could be read in that light. In Boccaccio's original, Griselda, the herdsman's daughter, becomes to all intents and purposes an ideal *donna* when Gualtieri chooses her to be his wife; she then accepts every abuse and humiliation he inflicts upon her in order to test her love, and, after being cruelly rejected, is overjoyed when he eventually takes her back.

Boccaccio certainly depicts Gualtieri as a tyrannical neurotic, and he may regard Griselda as an ideal. The members of the party praise her wisdom and criticize her husband; Dioneo briefly celebrates her unique patience and condemns Gualtieri as better fitted to look after pigs than to rule over men. But his final crude observation undermines the general message of wifely obedience that the story seems to be proposing: it would perhaps have served Gualtieri right if she had 'let another man shake her muff when she was driven from home in her shift, and that way got herself a decent dress'. What might have been a corrective to the moral liberties of the earlier stories risks falling apart. Griselda may just be a freak and it would have been understandable if she had gone off and found someone else. Perhaps Boccaccio is having it both ways.

Nevertheless, Day Ten does mark a change. Arguably, most of the stories in the preceding days have reflected the merchant ethos of Florence, although Vittore Branca exaggerated when he called the *Decameron* a 'mercantile epic'. Now Boccaccio recovers and celebrates something of the aristocratic ethos of his Neapolitan works, as is perhaps indicated by the fact that two of the stories originally appeared in the *Filocolo*. Characters in earlier stories have won the sympathy or envy of members of the party, but there has been no sustained celebration of virtuous acts. Day Ten offers more explicit moral positives to bring the *Decameron* to a close. Generosity of spirit and generosity with money and gifts and a certain measure of self-denial come to the fore, and comedy is almost entirely absent. What might have been comic plots are treated seriously (or perhaps fantastically, since several stories involve magic), and the exceptional qualities of the protagonists are dwelt upon in rhetorically elaborate conclusions.

Nevertheless, a measure of ambiguity remains, and readers are left as uncertain as they were with the stories of the nine preceding days how to map them on to the real world. That need not disturb us. Boccaccio's claim to be writing for love-lorn ladies and his repeated refusals to be pinned down mark out the *Decameron* as a book to be read primarily for enjoyment, not directly for moral or intellectual profit, despite occasional nods in that direction. From this perspective love-lorn ladies are an image of any reader, male or female, who is drawn into the book. All but a very few stories open with an address to ladies ('gracious ladies', 'dearest ladies', etc.), seemingly ignoring the three men in the party; and perhaps that is a way of emphasizing the sort of unoccupied reader Boccaccio is writing for.

We may well argue, however, that this sort of enjoyment is a serious matter. Boccaccio articulates the preoccupations of his society (and to some degree our own) by telling stories, particularly comic stories, which address their contradictions and ambiguities in narrative form. However, this process is not a simple one: there are all sorts of stories to be told, about all sorts of people in many different situations, and no one could tell them all. The ten narrators and the ten days of storytelling are a way of selecting and organizing a hundred possibilities in a complex, perhaps ultimately arbitrary pattern. The stories offer a range of pleasures and puzzles, as well as moving us deeply at certain moments. Perhaps, as in life, there is a real conceptual and moral coherence underlying the collection, but if so, Boccaccio leaves us to find or construct it, and to do so for the most part in a cheerful if sceptical frame of mind.

AFTER THE *DECAMERON*

Boccaccio seems to have gained a certain standing quite soon after his return from Naples, although this was almost certainly because of his expertise in Latin and ancient culture, rather than his writings in Italian. Though there were serious tensions in his relations with the Florentine government, he was sent on various diplomatic missions to other Northern Italian states and to the papal court, twice when it was in Avignon and a third time when it was again in Rome.

After the *Decameron* he seems to have lost interest in writing imaginative prose and poetry in Italian. Apart from a few lyric poems, there is only the *Corbaccio*, a much shorter prose work, in which a husband, driven to his death by his wife, reappears to denounce the immorality and general horribleness of women. It is a splenetic tour de force in complete contrast with the *Decameron*, unless we are persuaded that the more liberal attitudes voiced there are in fact a pretence or are ultimately soundly rejected. However, Boccaccio seems to have retained some interest in his earlier work: he revised the *Amorosa visione* in the later 1360s and made a copy of the *Decameron* which is fundamental to all modern editions.

He had already written an admiring Latin biography of Petrarch before they met in 1350 and spent some time together in Florence. They remained friends, mostly at a distance, until Petrarch's death in 1374. They exchanged Latin letters, in which Petrarch plays the role of self-deprecating master and adviser, Boccaccio his dedicated disciple. Partly under Petrarch's influence, Boccaccio now wrote mainly in Latin, producing a number of large, learned works based chiefly on ancient literature: the *Genealogia deorum gentilium* (Genealogies of the Pagan Gods), on ancient mythology, a set of biographies of famous men, then another of famous women, plus an encyclopaedic geographical survey entitled *De montibus, silvis, fontibus, lacubus, fluminibus, stagnis seu paludibus, de nominibus maris* (On mountains, woods, springs, lakes, rivers, fens or bogs and the names given to the sea). These works became far more widely read throughout Europe than anything Boccaccio wrote in Italian. He also composed a collection of bucolic poems and made a great deal more progress with the study of ancient Greek than Petrarch ever did.

The defence of poetry in Books 14 and 15 of the *Genealogia* is usually regarded as marking the start of Renaissance theorizing about the divine nature of poetry and poetic inspiration. Boccaccio's thinking about poetry was in part influenced by his long-standing admiration for Dante and a desire to defend and publicize his work. This led to an Italian biography, the *Trattatello in laude di Dante* (Treatise in Praise of Dante), subsequently expanded and rewritten, in which some of the arguments laid out in the *Genealogia* reappear, with Dante as the prime example of what a great poet can be. Nor did Boccaccio stop there. Many commentaries on the *Divine Comedy* had already been written, but in 1373 Boccaccio began a series of official public lectures on the *Inferno* in the church of Santo Stefano di Badia in Florence. He stopped halfway through, however, it seems partly because of objections that he was laying bare the secrets of the Muses to an ignorant lay audience.

This is a pity. Though his *Esposizioni sopra la Comedia di Dante* follow traditional allegorical procedures, they offer a good deal of new information and to some extent new approaches to Dante's masterpiece.

Boccaccio eventually retired to Certaldo, where he spent his last years. He can never have been rich, given that in his will Petrarch (who was much more adept at obtaining patronage) left Boccaccio an ermine robe with which to keep himself warm when studying in the winter months. He died a year or so after Petrarch on 21 December 1375.

Note on the Translation

In his Conclusion to the *Decameron* Boccaccio says that the reader is free to pick and choose among one hundred stories. I have selected thirty-two, plus some of the framing parts. I have aimed both to be representative and to include the most famous and best stories. These are the principal stories picked up more or less indirectly by Chaucer, Shakespeare and Keats. *The Canterbury Tales* reworks (using my titles) 'Brother Puccio's Penance' ('The Miller's Tale'), 'Lydia, Nicostratos and a Pear Tree' ('The Merchant's Tale'), 'Mrs Rosie and the Priest' ('The Shipman's Tale'), 'Confusion in the Bedroom' ('The Reeve's Tale'), 'The Problem of the Magic Garden' ('The Franklin's Tale') and 'Patient Griselda' (cf. 'The Clerk's Tale'). Shakespeare's *Cymbeline* derives from 'The Trials of Madonna Zinevra', and *All's Well that Ends Well* from 'Gilette and Her Supercilious Husband'. 'Lisabetta and the Pot of Basil' was the basis for Keats's 'Isabella, or The Pot of Basil'.

My titles are invented for the convenience of modern readers. Boccaccio himself provides short summaries rather than titles, to help the reader. I have retained these at the head of each story, but unlike most editors and translators, I have not reproduced them in the table of contents.

I have included Boccaccio's Introduction, which, apart from its intrinsic interest, gives the essential context of the storytelling. Further pages on the life of the 'happy band' (not included here) depict more fully the contrast between their world and the world of the stories. I also include the Prologue, Introduction to Day Four and the Author's Conclusion. Anyone reading the

Decameron needs to take these into account, no matter how playful and ironic they might seem to be.

Boccaccio's language poses particular problems for the translator. Keeping anything like his complex syntax in modern English seems out of the question. The risks of losing the free, conversational elements embedded in it, and ending up with ponderous old-fashioned literary prose, are just too great. I decided that if the results were to be as readable as Boccaccio's original was to his Florentine contemporaries in the upper merchant class, the sentences needed to be broken down; and in places I was ready to opt for very short units indeed, although still syntactically and grammatically correct by the standards of 'good' contemporary English prose.

Some shadow of Boccaccio's easy, flexible idiom might survive, I thought, through the addition of a measure of conversational phrasing, but without resorting to slang or phrases that might be alive today but will most likely die tomorrow. There was obviously the risk of producing unremarkable, colourless prose that would do Boccaccio even less justice than was unavoidable; however, I hoped that some degree of variety would emerge through modestly raising the level in the more elaborate passages, and dropping it rather more in comical speeches and exchanges.

Verbal humour was less of a difficulty than might be expected. Although some double entendres have had to be sacrificed, others (Friar Cipolla's speech, for instance, or the speech of the priest in the Mrs Rosie story) can be reworked, if not literally translated. Besides, Boccaccio makes less play with real or invented idioms and turns of phrase than Shakespeare does in his comedies. He relies more on the comic effects of the syntactic and morphological peculiarities of popular speech. Some stab at these can be made in English, though again there is the risk that what has ease in the original will become ponderous in translation.

Rather more unmanageable are some areas of vocabulary, particularly those connected with love and courtliness. In almost always translating *donna* and *femina* as 'lady' and 'woman' respectively, I persuaded myself that – given modern English sensitivities about both words – at least in this respect I was keeping some small degree of the medieval otherness of Boccaccio's thought and culture. Words such as *piacevole* ('pleasing'), *savio* ('wise'), *costumato* ('well-mannered'), *senno* ('good sense'), *bello* ('beautiful'), *sollazzare* ('to amuse or console', used euphemistically of sexual pleasure), and other recurrent terms I recast in a variety of ways, partly on the grounds that English inherently prefers greater variety.

For the same reason I have adapted Boccaccio's almost constant use of *disse* ('he said' or 'she said') to introduce direct speech, usually placed before the speech itself begins. I have often, though not always, varied the verb ('replied', 'stated', 'declared', etc.), and I have regularly inserted 'he said', etc., after the opening phrase.

Overall, however, I have attempted to follow the order of Boccaccio's phrasing as closely as possible and also to avoid introducing words and phrases to improve the resonance and flow of the English. The overall result may be a relatively spare and relatively colloquial Boccaccio, but then he is in fact a good deal sparer and more colloquial than much subsequent literary prose that looked to him as a model.

Further Reading

Recent Complete Translations of the *Decameron*

Giovanni Boccaccio, *The Decameron*, translated by Guido Waldman; Introduction and Notes by Jonathan Usher (Oxford: Oxford University Press, 1993).

——, *The Decameron*, translated with an Introduction and Notes by G. H. McWilliam, 2nd edition (London: Penguin, 1995).

——, *Decameron*, a new English version by Cormac Ó Cuilleanáin, based on John Payne's 1886 translation (Ware: Wordsworth Classics, 2004).

——, *Decameron*, translated with an Introduction by J. G. Nichols (Oxford: Oneworld Classics, 2008).

These all contain helpful introductions and bibliographies.

Selected Studies in English

General Introductions

Thomas G. Bergin, *Boccaccio* (New York: Viking Press, 1981).

Vittore Branca, *Boccaccio: The Man and His Works*, translated by Richard Monges (New York: New York University Press, 1976).

Robert S. Dombroski (ed.), *Critical Perspectives on the Decameron* (London: Hodder & Stoughton, 1976).

Victoria Kirkham, Michael Sherberg and Janet Levarie Smarr (eds), *Boccaccio: A Critical Guide to the Complete Works* (Chicago, IL: University of Chicago Press, 2013).

David Wallace, *Boccaccio: Decameron* (Cambridge: Cambridge University Press, 1991).

Studies of Specific Aspects of the *Decameron*

Guido Almansi, *The Writer as Liar: Narrative Technique in the Decameron* (London: Routledge & Kegan Paul, 1975).

Guyda Armstrong, *The English Boccaccio: A History in Books* (Toronto: University of Toronto Press, 2013).

Marga Cottino-Jones, *Order from Chaos: Social and Aesthetic Harmonies in Boccaccio's Decameron* (Washington, DC: University Press of America, 1982).

Pier Massimo Forni, *Adventures in Speech: Rhetoric and Narration in Boccaccio's Decameron* (Philadelphia: University of Pennsylvania Press, 1996).

Robert Hastings, *Nature and Reason in the Decameron* (Manchester: Manchester University Press, 1975).

Giuseppe Mazzotta, *The World at Play in Boccaccio's Decameron* (Princeton, NJ: Princeton University Press, 1986).

Marilyn Migiel, *A Rhetoric of the Decameron* (Toronto: University of Toronto Press, 2003).

Cormac Ó Cuilleanáin, *Religion and the Clergy in Boccaccio's Decameron* (Rome: Edizioni di Storia e Letteratura, 1984).

Glending Olson, *Literature as Recreation in the Later Middle Ages* (London: Cornell University Press, 1982).

Joy Hambuechen Potter, *Five Frames for the Decameron: Communication and Social Systems in the Cornice* (Princeton, NJ: Princeton University Press, 1982).

Aldo D. Scaglione, *Nature and Love in the Late Middle Ages* (Berkeley and Los Angeles: University of California Press, 1963).

Italian Edition

I have used the text established by Vittore Branca for his final edition of the *Decameron* (Milan: Mondadori – I Meridiani, 1985). I am deeply indebted to Branca's notes to this and other editions.

TALES FROM THE
DECAMERON

Prologue

remember this

Here begins the book called the Decameron,[1] *also called* Prince Galahalt,[2] *which contains one hundred stories, told in the course of ten days by seven ladies and three young men.*

It is a mark of humanity to feel compassion for the afflicted. This is a desirable trait in everyone, but it is especially required from those who have needed comfort in the past and have received it from others. And if anyone ever did feel the need of comfort, appreciated it or found relief in it, it was myself. From my early youth until very recently I burned to excess with the fires of an exalted, noble love,[3] perhaps much more than you would expect from an undistinguished person like myself, although I was complimented by discerning people who heard about it, and thought all the better of me as a result. All the same it took a terrible effort to bear it, not because of any cruelty from the lady I loved, but because poorly controlled desire set off a turmoil in my mind that was simply too much to bear. Since I could not happily set myself any reasonable limit, it often caused me more distress than was necessary. However, I found occasional relief in the soothing conversation and laudable encouragement of certain friends, without which I am convinced I should have died. But He who is Himself infinite made it an unchangeable law that all things in this world should have an end. This love of mine was unique in its fervour and no resolve, no advice, no risk of public shame or danger was strong enough to break it down or redirect it. But gradually in the fullness of time it faded away of its own accord. Now all that it has left in my memory is that pleasurable feeling that love usually grants to those who do not sail too far out into its dark seas. Whereas it was once wearisome, now the pain has been taken away and I feel that only the enjoyable part is left.

But though my sufferings have ended, I hold still in my mind memories of the kindnesses received from those who were fond of me and were concerned at my troubles. These memories will fade, I am sure, only when I die. Gratitude, I firmly believe, is one of the virtues to be most highly commended, just as its opposite is unacceptable. In order not to appear at all ungrateful, I have decided, now that I can call myself a free man, to make such repayment as I can, and to use the very limited powers I have to provide some alleviation of suffering for those in need, though these do not include those who did actually help me, thanks to their good sense or their good fortune. My support or comforting, as we might call it, may well seem to the needy not to amount to much. All the same I think I must try to offer it where the need is greatest. It is there that it might be most helpful and also most appreciated.

Now who will deny that, however small it proves to be, help of this kind should much more appropriately be given to gentle ladies than to men? Through fear and shame they keep the flames of love hidden within their delicate breasts, and those who have experience of it know how much stronger are hidden flames than those which are blazing openly. What is more, ladies are constrained by the wishes, pleasures and orders of their fathers, mothers, brothers and husbands, spending most of their time cooped up in the small space of their chambers, sitting there with next to nothing to do, wanting and not wanting at the same time, with all sorts of thoughts going through their minds, which can't possibly always be cheerful ones. If a gloomy forlornness comes over them as a result of their passions being frustrated, it inevitably stays there to torment them and weigh them down, unless some novelty comes along to cancel it out. Besides, ladies in love are less resilient than men, to whom such a thing obviously doesn't happen. If men are miserable or depressed, they have many ways of finding relief or getting over their troubles. No one stops them going out and about if they feel like it and hearing and seeing lots of things, or stops them hawking, hunting, riding, gaming or trading. These are all ways any man can get a hold on himself, in part if not entirely, and distract himself from painful preoccupations for a while. Then afterwards, in one way or another, something turns up to console him or the pain just diminishes.

My aim, then, is to make some partial correction to this injustice of Fortune, which has most begrudged support just where there is least strength, that is, of course, among delicate ladies. Since the rest can manage well enough with needles, spindles and wool-winders, my wish is to provide assistance and refuge for those who are in love. I intend to tell a hundred stories – fables, parables, histories[4] or whatever we want to call them – which were recounted over ten days, in a way that will become clear, by an honourable party of seven ladies and three young men who met together during the recent deadly plague. I shall also include some of the songs sung by the ladies mentioned for the party's enjoyment. The stories will tell of a range of pleasing and distressing instances of love, and other events dictated by Fortune, that took place in both modern and ancient times. The ladies I mentioned who come to read them will be able to find enjoyment in the entertaining material displayed before them and, to an equal extent, to take away some useful advice, in so far as they will learn what courses of action are to be avoided and likewise which are to be pursued. I don't think any of this can come about without their troubles fading away. If that is what happens (and may God so will it), let them give thanks to Love, who, by freeing me from his bonds, has granted me power to attend to their pleasures.

DAY ONE

Here begins the First Day of the Decameron, *in which the author explains how it came about that the persons he describes came together to tell stories,*[1] *and then, under the rule of Pampinea, each speaks on whatever subject most appeals to them.*

Introduction

Every time, most gracious ladies, that I reflect on how natural feelings of pity are for you, I recognize that you will judge this work to have a wearisomely depressing beginning. What it thrusts before you is a painful re-evocation of the carnage caused by the recent plague, which cannot but be deeply hurtful and upsetting to everyone who witnessed the events or learned about them indirectly. But I don't want this to frighten you from reading any further, as if you were bound to be sighing and weeping all through the book. As you read this horrible opening, consider yourselves travellers climbing a steep, rough path up a mountain, behind which is hidden a delightful plain; it proves all the more pleasurable the harder the climb and the descent that follows.

If the extreme limit of happiness is pain,[1] wretchedness is similarly brought to an end by the onset of joy. This brief distress (I say brief, because it takes up only a few pages) will be quickly followed by sweetness and pleasure, as I promised initially, but which you might not expect from an opening of this sort. And truly, if I could have decently led you where I want by some other path than the unpleasant one that this will be, I would have done so. But without recalling those events, it would have been impossible to explain what lay behind what you will be reading later. So it is from a sense of necessity that I bring myself to write about them.

I declare then the years that had passed since the fruitful Incarnation of the Son of God had reached the number of one thousand three hundred and forty-eight, when the mortal plague reached the splendid city of Florence, the noblest of all in Italy. It may have been the workings of the stars above that inflicted it on mortal men or it may have been God's righteous anger punishing us for our iniquities. In any event it had begun some years earlier in the East and, after causing numberless deaths in that part of the world, had moved relentlessly from one region to another westwards, growing more distressingly powerful all the time. No expertise or human measures had any effect. Specially appointed officials made sure the city was cleansed of all refuse, anyone sick was refused entry, and advice was given in plenty about how best to stay healthy. Humble supplications to God to show mercy were repeatedly made by the pious, who organized processions and so on. But it was all fruitless: in the early spring of the year mentioned, the ravages of the plague began to be horribly evident and in a monstrous way.

It did not show itself in the manner it had done in the East, where bleeding from the nose was a manifest sign of inevitable death. Instead for both men and women it began with swellings either in the groin or under the arms, some of which grew to the size of a middle-sized apple, while others remained egg-sized, though there were bigger and smaller ones too. The people called them *gavoccioli* and within a short space of time these fatal *gavoccioli* would spread from the two parts of the body where they had begun and could appear and develop anywhere. At a second stage the infection began to change its character and show itself as black or livid rashes. These appeared on the arms and thighs, although in many cases everywhere else on the body too. Sometimes they were large and spaced out and sometimes tiny and close together. Previously, the *gavocciolo* had been a clear sign of death being imminent, as it still was; and so too were the rashes for anyone on whom they appeared.

Evidently no medical advice and no medicine could do anything to treat or affect the disease. It may be that it was a condition that was by nature untreatable, or perhaps those who tried to treat it were ignoramuses – the trained doctors were vastly outnumbered by people, women as well as men, who had never had any medical education whatsoever. In any event they had no idea what started the disease and hence no proper means of dealing with it. As a result not only did few recover, but in less than three days after the first appearance of the symptoms I have mentioned, or maybe a little more, most people simply died, for the most part without fever or any other further complication setting in.

What was particularly virulent about this plague was that it would leap from the sick to the healthy whenever they were together, much as fire catches hold of dry or oily material that's brought close to it. And that was not all. Not only did speaking with the sick and spending time with them infect the healthy or kill them off, but touching the clothes of the sick or handling anything they had touched seemed to pass on the infection.

I shall cite an amazing example. If I'd not been one of many people who saw it with their own eyes, I would scarcely dare to credit it, let alone write about it, even if I had it from a truly trustworthy source. I have to stress how contagious this plague was. It visibly did more than just pass from one person to another. In many cases if something belonging to a sick person or to someone who had died of the disease was touched by an animal rather than a human being, it did not just infect the animal, but almost immediately killed it. I actually saw this happen several times, as I have just said, and in one instance I saw two pigs come across some rags belonging to a poor man who had died of the disease which had been thrown into the street. They first poked them with their snouts as pigs do. Then they got them in their teeth and shook them this way and that against their cheeks. A short time later they both went into convulsions, as if they'd been poisoned, and collapsed dead on the rags they had unfortunately chewed over.

These things and many others just as bad or worse filled those who were still alive with all sorts of fears and fantasies. Almost everyone shunned or ran away from the sick and anything belonging to them with ruthless determination, believing that this way they would stay healthy.

Some people were of the opinion that living a temperate life, avoiding any kind of excess, was the best protection against the disease. So they formed small communities and lived separately from everyone else, shutting themselves away in houses where there were no sick people and where they could be comfortable. They put themselves on a controlled diet of refined food and quality wines, avoided any kind of overindulgence, allowed no one else to speak with them, refused to hear anything about deaths and sick people in the world outside and spent their time playing music and enjoying such pleasures as they could.

Others were drawn to the opposite view. They declared that the most effective medicine when things were as bad as this was to drink a lot, enjoy yourself and go round singing and having fun, doing everything you could to satisfy your urges and desires, and laughing and joking about what was happening. And they did all they could to put their ideas into action, going from tavern to tavern, day and night, on an endless spree of uncontrolled drinking. Other people's houses were an even greater attraction if they heard there were things in them they might fancy. They could get in easily, because everyone had the impression they wouldn't live much longer and had given up looking after their possessions as well as themselves. Hence most houses had become common property and strangers who happened along treated them much as their rightful owner would have done. Still, in spite of being set on behaving like mindless animals, these people were always careful to keep well away from those who were sick.

With our city reduced to such a wretched state, any respect for the authority of the laws of man and God had effectively broken down or disappeared, since its servants and agents were all themselves either dead or ill, like everyone else, or else they had so few staff left that they couldn't carry out any of their duties. As a result everyone had total licence to do what they liked.

Yet many people did try to keep a middle course between the two extremes I have described, not restricting their eating as much as the first group, nor giving themselves over to drunken and dissolute behaviour like the second, but aiming at moderate satisfaction of their needs and desires. Instead of shutting themselves away they would go around with flowers in their hands or sweet-smelling herbs or different sorts of spices. They would keep sniffing them, on the grounds that it was an excellent thing to refresh the brain with odours of this kind, since the air everywhere seemed thick and heavy with the stink from sick or dead bodies and from the medicaments being used.

Some people were more callous, although perhaps with some justification, arguing that there was no better or effective remedy against any sort of plague than running away before it got to you. On this basis, thinking only of themselves and nothing else, many men and women abandoned their native city and with it their houses and properties, together with their relatives and whatever they possessed, and set off for places in the Florentine countryside or beyond. No doubt they believed God's anger was not directed at punishing the iniquities of men with this plague wherever they were, but had been stirred up only against those who happened to be within the city-walls. Or else it may have been their opinion that nobody was going to be left in the city and that its last hour had come.

While not all these people with their various different stratagems died, not all of them survived. On the contrary, whatever their view, many people fell ill all over the city. When they were healthy, they had set an example for those who were still in good health, and now they were left to languish away everywhere. It wasn't just that citizens kept away from each other, that almost no one spared any thought for their neighbours, that people rarely visited their relatives, if at all, and kept their distance when they did. The disastrous course of events instilled such terror in both men and women that brothers abandoned each other, an uncle abandoned his nephew, a sister her brother, and very often a wife her husband. Worse still – in fact, almost incredible – was how fathers and mothers shrank from visiting and looking after their children, as if they weren't theirs at all.

Hence the only support for countless men and women who fell ill came from the charity of their friends (and there were few of these) or else from money-grasping servants, who would only work for outrageously high wages, and even then were in short supply. Those left were gross individuals of both sexes, mostly with no relevant experience, who served almost no purpose other than to pass the sick the things they asked for and to keep an eye on them as they died. Doing this kind of work often meant they lost their own lives, as well as losing any money they earned.

As a result of sick people being abandoned by their neighbours, relatives and friends, and of servants becoming so scarce, something unheard of before became normal. Any lady who fell ill, no matter how attractive, beautiful or noble she was, did not object to being looked after by a man, whatever he was like, and whether he was young or not, and would let him see any part of her body without any shame, just as she would have done with a woman, if the illness made it necessary. Perhaps that was the reason behind the less than chaste behaviour later on of those who recovered.

That aside, many people died who possibly might well have survived if they had been given proper assistance. Hence, what with the sick not being able to obtain the appropriate services and the sheer virulence of the plague, the numbers of those dying day and night in the city made shocking listening, as well as being awful to witness. The almost inevitable consequence was that the citizens who were still alive developed customs that were quite different from those they had previously followed.

It had been normal – as we see it is again today – for female relatives and neighbours to gather in the house of a dead man, together with others who were close to him, and weep over him there, while outside in front of the house male relatives were joined by neighbours and various other citizens. The number of clergy in attendance depended on the status of the deceased, who would be lifted on to the shoulders of his peers and carried in a funeral procession with candles and hymns to the church he had indicated before he died. When the ferocity of the plague began to intensify, this all fell into general or even total abeyance and new practices took over. Not only did people die without ladies gathering round them, but many left this life unwitnessed by anyone at all. Very few were granted the privilege of wails of pity and bitter tears from their nearest and dearest. Instead laughter, banter and festive jollity became the norm, with ladies largely putting aside the feelings of compassion characteristic of them and learning very well this new way to help the souls of the dead towards heavenly bliss.

It was only in rare instances that a body was accompanied to the church by more than ten or twelve friends of the deceased, and it wasn't his honoured and esteemed fellow citizens who bore him on their shoulders, but what we might call corpse-collectors who emerged from the lowest class of people and called themselves sextons. They would offer their services at a price, hoisting the coffin on to their shoulders and hurrying off with it, usually not to the church which the deceased had specified before dying, but to the one that was nearest, with four or six clerics in front holding just a few candles, or sometimes none at all. The priests wouldn't bother themselves with a lengthy, solemn rite and, with help from these sextons, would hurriedly stick the body in any tomb they found unoccupied.

Lower-class people and probably most of the middle classes too, were a far more wretched sight. Since empty hopes or poverty kept most of them in their houses and they didn't move out of their own neighbourhoods, thousands fell ill every day. Having no servants or any other help, there was almost no rescue for them and they all simply died. There were people dying in the streets day and night. While many others died inside their homes, the first sign their neighbours picked up that they were dead was the stench of their rotting bodies, rather than anything else. But everywhere was full of the stench from these and from all the others dying throughout the city.

Neighbours mostly followed a particular routine, as much out of fear of being infected by the decaying bodies as out of any concern they felt for the departed. They would drag the bodies of those who had died out of their homes, sometimes with the help of porters if they could find any, and put them down in front of the doors, where, especially of a morning, countless numbers lay on view for any passer-by to see. Then they would send for biers,[2] though there were shortages, and sometimes they just laid them out on a few boards. It wasn't unknown for a bier to have two or three bodies on it, and you could have counted up quite a few cases of a wife and her husband sharing the same bier, or two or three brothers or a father and son or some such combination. It also happened countless times that two priests carrying the cross before one dead person found three or four other biers, carried by their bearers, following on behind, and instead of having one body to bury, as they expected, they had six or eight and sometimes more. Even then there were no tears, candles or mourners to honour the dead. Things had reached such a point that as little respect was shown for people who had died as there might be now for dead goats.

All this made one thing very plain. The wisest of men do not learn patient acceptance of life from the small-scale, intermittent disasters that occur in the natural course of events, but the sheer scale of the current calamities taught even simple people how to bear things with stoical indifference.

Given the enormous number of bodies arriving at all the churches almost every hour of every day, there was not enough consecrated ground for all the burials, especially if, in accordance with tradition, each body was to have a separate grave. So, since everywhere was full, great trenches were dug in the church cemeteries and hundreds of bodies were put in them as they arrived. They were stacked up, just as merchandise is stacked in layers in ships, and covered over with thin layers of earth until the top of the trench was reached.

I want to avoid going into all the details of the miseries afflicting our city at this time. So let me say that the adversities raging through it did not spare the surrounding countryside in the slightest. In the fortified townships things were much as in the city on a smaller scale. But out in the scattered hamlets and fields the wretched labourers and their families were dying day and night, and more like animals than human beings. They met their end in the lanes or in their homes or among the crops they were growing, with no doctor trying to help them or servants to look after them. Thus they let things go just as people did in the city and stopped bothering with their possessions or with their normal tasks. It was as if they were expecting death to arrive any moment and saw no possible point in livestock or crops or any of the work they had done in the past, and instead put all their efforts into consuming whatever was there ready for them. As a result, oxen, asses, sheep, goats, pigs and chickens wandered about as they liked in the fields, where the grain harvest stood abandoned, waiting to be reaped, let alone gathered in. Even dogs, the animals most faithful to men, were chased out of the houses and did the same. And many of these animals behaved almost rationally: after feeding well during the day, they would come back home sated, with no shepherd prodding them along.

To leave the countryside and coming back to the city, there is one other thing to be added about the extent and nature of the cruelty of heaven and perhaps up to a point of men too. Between March and the following July – what with the sheer force of the pestilential disease itself and the way in which many infected people were poorly looked after or left completely to their own resources, because of the fears of those who remained healthy – more than one hundred thousand human beings are definitely thought to have lost their lives within the walls of the city of Florence. Before the plague's murderous onset, no one would have calculated that the city had so many people living in it.

How many grand palaces, how many fine houses, how many noble dwellings, once thronging households, each with its lord and lady, were emptied of their inhabitants down to the last servant boy! How many lineages of note, how many vast inheritances, how many famous fortunes were left with no rightful heir! How many stalwart men, how many ladies of great beauty, how many young beaux – that Galen, Hippocrates and Aesculapius[3] and anyone else would have judged to be in the best of health – ate their morning meal with their relatives, friends and companions, and that very evening dined with their ancestors in the next world?

I regret having to spend so much time going over these miseries and want now to let be those that I can decently avoid writing about. So, this was the desolate, almost depopulated state of our city, when (as I learned from a very trustworthy source) one Tuesday morning, seven young ladies, dressed in the sort of cheerless clothing appropriate to the times, heard Mass together in the venerable church of Santa Maria Novella, which was otherwise almost empty. They were all either friends or related to each other, or else they knew each other through living in the same neighbourhood. None was over twenty-seven or younger than eighteen, and each was a highly sensible young person of noble birth, lovely looking, stylish and charmingly moral.

I would give their real names, but for the fact that there is good reason for not doing so, namely that I do not want the stories that follow, which they either told or heard, to prove embarrassing for them in the future. The laws regarding pleasurable entertainment are somewhat tighter today, whereas at that time, for the reasons I have set out, they were extremely lax, and not just for people of their age but for those who were of much more mature years. I also do not wish to give the envious-minded who like to get their claws into anyone living a praiseworthy life some pretext for besmirching the honour of these upright ladies with their filthy gossip. In order to make it easy to understand later what each of them has to say, I intend to give them names that correspond wholly, or at least in part, with their characters. So I shall call the first Pampinea, the second Fiammetta, the third Filomena, the fourth Emilia, while I shall give the names of Lauretta to the fifth, and Neifile to the sixth, and then, not without reason, call the last Elissa.[4]

They had nothing particular in mind when they met up by chance in the same part of the church and seated themselves more or less in a ring. At a certain point they left off reciting their 'Our Fathers', and with a lot of sighing began talking about various aspects of the times they were living in. After a while they all fell quiet, except for Pampinea, who embarked on the following speech.

'My dear ladies, like me you are bound to have often heard it said that anyone who makes use of their reason in an honourable way commits no wrong against anyone else. And natural reason tells everyone born into this world to promote, preserve and defend their life as best they can. It is even granted that on occasion people have been killed in order to safeguard life with no question of blame arising. If that is permitted by the laws that are the basis for the well-being of all mortal men, how much more acceptable is it for us and for anyone else to take all the steps we can to preserve our lives, so long as no one is going to be harmed by what we do! The more often I take a good look at how we've been this morning and many others in the past, and think about our conversations together, the more I realize, as I'm sure you do too, that each of us cannot but be fearful for herself.

'That doesn't surprise me. But it does amaze me that while we all feel ourselves to be ladies, none of you are taking steps to counter what you are rightly afraid of. We stay here, in my opinion, just as if what we wanted or were forced to do was just to witness how many bodies are brought in to be buried or to check on whether the friars here, who are reduced to almost nothing, sing their offices at the proper times, or else simply to let anyone who turns up see from the clothes we are wearing the depth and extent of our miseries. If we go out of here we see dead or sick bodies being transported around the city. Or else we see men rightly condemned to exile by the civic authorities on account of their misdeeds almost jeering at the law, because they know its agents are either dead or sick, and going on disgusting rampages through the streets. And then the scum of the city are drunk on our blood, calling themselves sextons, and go careering and charging about to insult us, throwing our misfortunes in our faces with the obscene songs they sing. The only thing we hear is 'So-and-so is dead!' and 'So-and-so is on the point of dying!' If there was anybody left to weep, we'd hear dreadful weeping everywhere. And then, if we go home – I don't know if it's the same for you as it is for me – since the only person I find still there out of all the people in my household is my maid, I become nervous and feel almost every hair on my head starting to stand on end. Wherever I go in the house, in every room I stop in, I seem to see the shades of those who've passed away, and not with their familiar faces, but terrifying me with strange and horrible looks that they've got from who knows where.

'So I feel bad here and outside here and at home. What makes it worse is the sense that, apart from us, nobody is left here who has any means and somewhere to go to. If any of them do stay – so far as I can tell from what I've seen and heard – they lose all sense of the difference between what's proper and what's not. They just obey their urges and go round by themselves or with other people, whether it's day or night, indulging in whatever gives them most pleasure. And this doesn't just apply to people with no religious vows to hold them back. Those shut away in monasteries convince themselves that what goes for other people goes for them too. They've broken their rules of obedience, surrendered to pleasures of the flesh with the notion that they will survive that way, and become dissolute, lascivious beasts.

'Given that's the way things are – as it plainly is – what are we doing here? What are we waiting for? What are we dreaming of? Why are we being more sluggish and slovenly about our well-being than all the rest of our fellow citizens? Do we think we're worth less than every other lady here? Or do we think that our lives are more strongly bound to our bodies than those of anyone else, and so we don't have to bother about things that have the power to hurt them? We're mistaken, deluded, mindlessly stupid if we believe that. Every time we call to mind the young men and ladies who've been killed by this vicious epidemic and think who and what they were, we have all the proof we need of how stupid we are.

'So let's not be either so finicky or so sure of ourselves as to fall into a trap we might have escaped in one way or another if we'd had the will. I wonder if an idea that strikes me will strike you in the same way. I'd judge it an excellent thing to have done, if, female though we may be, we did what many people before us have done or are doing and left this city. We'd be escaping from the immoral behaviour of others as much as from death, and we'd leave with our honour unblemished, simply going off to spend time in places out in the country, which we all possess in abundance, where we could enjoy all the fun and merriment and pleasure we are capable of, without ever going beyond the limits of what our reason tells us.

'There you can listen to the birds singing and contemplate the changing greens of the hills and plains and the cornfields rippling like the sea, with all the different kinds of trees around you and the open sky above. Though heaven may be angry with us, it will not deny us its eternal beauties, which are a much lovelier sight than the empty walls of our city. Besides the air is much cooler there and there's a greater supply of those things needed to maintain life in these times and a smaller number of those that cause pain. Though peasants are dying in the same way as people in the city here, it causes less obvious distress, since the houses and their inhabitants are more scattered. If I'm right, we're not abandoning anyone here. It's more the case that we can truthfully say that we are the abandoned ones, since our families have either died or fled the prospect of dying and left us in the midst of all this affliction, as if we didn't exist for them. Hence no blame can attach itself to us for following this plan; whereas, if we don't follow it, we can expect pain, distress and perhaps death.

'So, if you are in agreement, let's take our maids with us, and with the things we'll need following on behind, let's stay one day in one place and the next in another, entertaining and amusing ourselves the best we can given the times, for that's what seems to me the best course of action. And let's go on like this until we see what end heaven is storing up for all this, assuming that death doesn't overtake us first. I remind you again that departing with our honour intact is no more a slur on us than is staying on dishonourably for most other women.'

Having heard Pampinea out, the other ladies not only praised her proposal but were eager to put it into practice. They at once began discussing detailed arrangements, as if they could immediately set off as soon as they got up from where they were sitting. But Filomena, who had a particularly fine sense of what was appropriate, had something to say.

'Ladies,' she said, 'what Pampinea is arguing is all very well, but we shouldn't rush into action as you seem to be doing. Remember that we are all women and none of us is so naive as not to know how rationally a bunch of women behave together and how capable they are of organizing themselves without the guiding hand of some man. We are fickle, wilful, suspicious, faint-hearted and fearful. I'm really concerned that if we don't find some guidance other than in ourselves, this company might dissolve all too quickly and with more risk to our good name than is necessary. We'll do well to see to this before we start.'

Elissa then joined in. 'It's true,' she said, 'the man is the woman's head[5] and without male direction anything we embark upon rarely reaches a laudable conclusion. But how can we come by these men? We all know our male family members are mostly dead and those that are left alive are in little scattered groups we don't know where, trying to escape the very thing that we're trying escape from. Having outsiders with us would not be appropriate. So if we want to do what is best for us, we should try to organize things in such a way that going after pleasure and recreation doesn't end up producing distress and discord.'

This discussion between the ladies was still going on when into the church came three young men, although even the youngest was not less than twenty-five years old. For all the perversity of the times, the loss of friends and family, and their fears for themselves, they were still passionate lovers whose ardour had not cooled in the slightest. One was called Panfilo, the second Filostrato and the last Dioneo, and all of them were agreeable, courteous company. They were going about in search of what would most console them in the current chaos, that is, the sight of the ladies they loved, all of whom happened to be among the seven mentioned above, while some of the others were close relatives of one or other of them. They had no sooner caught sight of the ladies than the ladies caught sight of them.

'Look,' Pampinea said, smiling, 'Fortune is being favourable to us from the start. She's put before us some discerning, capable young men, who'll be glad to be both our guides and servants, unless we're too snooty to offer them the posts.'

Neifile's modesty had made her whole face blush scarlet, since she was one of those who was loved by one of the young men. 'Pampinea,' she said, 'in God's name take care what you're saying. I'm absolutely sure that nothing but good can be said of any of these three, and I think they're capable of much more demanding tasks than this. I also think they would provide virtuous and respectful company, not just for us but for ladies who are much more beautiful and precious than we are. But since it's obvious that they are in love with some of the ladies present, I fear scandal and censure are going to follow if we take them with us, even though neither we nor they will do anything wrong.'

'That's irrelevant,' Filomena said. 'If I live a chaste life and my conscience is quite clear, let people say the opposite if they want. God and truth will take up arms on my behalf. Now if only they were ready to come with us, we really could say, as Pampinea said, that Fortune is looking on our departure with a favourable eye.'

When the others heard her say this, they raised no further objection and with one accord all declared that the young men should be invited over, the project explained to them and a plea put to them to be pleased to accompany them on this excursion. With no further ado, Pampinea, who was a blood relative of one of the young men (who were standing there, looking at the ladies) got up and went over to them. Greeting them with a happy face, she explained the project and begged them, on behalf of the whole group, to be so good as to accompany them in a spirit of pure, brotherly affection. The young men thought at first that they were being made fun of, but when they realized the lady was talking seriously, they happily replied that they were ready to act as requested. And without delaying things any further, before leaving the church, they planned out what they had to do to prepare for their departure.

Everything required was duly got ready and a message sent on to the place where they intended to go. Then, the following morning – that is, on the Wednesday – as day was dawning, they left the city and set off on their way, the ladies accompanied by some of their maids and the three young men by three servants. They had gone no more than two short miles when they reached the place they had agreed on beforehand.

It was some way back from any of our roads, on a low hill with bushes and trees of various kinds, all in full green leaf and very pleasing to the eye. There, on top of the hill, stood a palace with a large and beautiful courtyard in the middle and with loggias, reception rooms and sleeping chambers, all lovely in themselves and notable for the delightful pictures with which they were decorated. Around the palace were grassy lawns, wonderful gardens and wells of cool, fresh water. There were also vaulted cellars full of expensive wines, somewhat better suited to the taste of demanding drinkers than to that of chaste and sober ladies. On arrival the party found to its great pleasure that everywhere had been swept clean and the beds made up in the bedchambers, with seasonal flowers all around and rushes spread out on the floor.

Once they had arrived and sat themselves down, Dioneo, who was a particularly entertaining and witty young man, had something to say.

'Ladies, it's your innate good sense rather than any cleverness on our part that has guided us to this place. I don't know what you intend to do with your worries. I left my own inside the city gate when I walked out with you a short while ago. And so either you put yourselves in the right frame of mind for fun, laughter and song together with me (I mean as far as your dignity allows) or else you release me to go back to my worries and stay in the city with all its tribulations.'

Pampinea seemed likewise to have cast all her own worries aside.

'Dioneo,' she happily replied, 'you put it very well. It's a festive sort of life that we want, and there was no other motive behind our flight from all those miseries. But things that have no order to them cannot last for long. I initiated the discussions that led to the formation of this fine company and my mind is now on how to keep the happy mood going. My view is that it's necessary for us to choose one of us as our principal, whom we honour and obey as someone above the rest of us and who thinks of nothing but how to make our life here enjoyable. Each one of us should experience the burden of responsibility as well as the pleasure of command, and thus, since there will be two sides to the role, anyone as yet without the experience won't feel like complaining. So I propose that each one of us should be granted both the burden and the honour for a day. Who will be the first should be decided by all of us voting.

Then subsequent principals will be nominated each evening as the time for vespers[6] comes round: he or she who has been ruler for that day will select the lady or gentleman they wish, and this individual will have discretion over the period of his or her rule to decide how and where we are to spend our time together.'

Pampinea's speech met with full approval and they unanimously elected her to be their queen for the first day. Filomena ran over to a laurel tree, having often heard people talk of how highly its leaves deserve to be honoured and how deserving of honour they made anyone duly crowned with them. She picked a few fronds and wove them into a striking wreath of honour, which she placed on Pampinea's head. From then on, for as long as their company existed, the wreath acted as a manifest sign to all the others of royal power and authority.

Once crowned queen, Pampinea commanded everyone to be quiet, having already summoned before her the menservants of the three young men and the ladies' maids, who were four in number. When silence was established, she made the following speech.

'I first wish to set you all a good example in the hope that it will lead our company to a still better state than the one it is in already and enable it to live and last in an ordered, pleasurable and irreproachable way for as long as we want it to. So first of all I designate Parmeno, Dioneo's servant, as my head steward. I assign to him care and responsibility for our whole household and everything related to our meals in the hall. I wish Sirisco, the servant of Panfilo, to be in charge of expenditure and funds, under the supervision of Parmeno. Tindaro will attend to Filostrato and also to the other two young men in their chambers, if it should happen that their own servants are impeded from doing so by their other duties. My own maid Misia and Filomena's Licisca will be on permanent kitchen duty and will diligently prepare the dishes commanded of them by Parmeno. We desire Lauretta's Chimera and Fiammetta's Stratilia to see to the ladies' chambers and to the general cleanliness of the rooms we use. And we wish and command that, if they value our good graces, each member of the servant body should take care, wherever they might go, wherever they might return from, whatever they might hear or see, not to bring us back from the outside world any piece of news which is not a happy one.'

The orders thus summarily given were commended by all present. Pampinea now stood up happily and spoke again.

'There are gardens here,' she said, 'and lawns and other very delightful spots. Let each of us go and savour their pleasures in any way he or she wishes. Then by the time the bell rings for terce,[7] let everyone be back here so that we can eat out of the sun.'

Thus released by the new queen, the happy band, young men and lovely ladies together, strolled away in leisurely fashion, talking of pleasurable matters, through one of the gardens, weaving garlands from the foliage of various trees and singing songs of love. When they had occupied themselves in this way for the space of time allowed by the queen, they walked back to the house, where they found Parmeno had zealously set about his duties. Entering the hall on the ground floor they saw tables set out with gleaming white cloths and goblets that shone like silver, and broom flowers decorating the whole room. After rinsing their hands, in accordance with the queen's wishes, they all took their places, as directed by Parmeno. Exquisitely prepared dishes arrived and choice wines were offered, the three menservants serving at table in silence without need of further orders. That all was so beautifully arranged added to the general gaiety and the meal was a jolly, joking affair.

All the ladies knew how to dance in the round, as did the young men, and some of the party were excellent singers or musicians. Once the tables were cleared away, the queen ordered instruments to be brought. Then, again by royal command, Dioneo took up a lute and Fiammetta a viol, and the two of them started on a melodious dance tune. The queen and the other ladies, together with the other two young men, formed a round and, sending the menservants off for their meal, performed a slow-stepping dance. When that was over they began singing delicate, happy songs. Things went on like this until the queen decided it was time for a sleep. All having been duly dismissed, the three young men went off to their rooms, which were set apart from those of the ladies, and found their beds properly made up and everywhere as full of flowers as the hall had been. The ladies found their rooms similarly ready; they undressed and got into bed to rest.

Nones[8] had not long been rung when the queen rose from her bed and told all the other ladies and the young men to rise from theirs too, declaring that it was unhealthy to sleep too much by day. They then went off into a little meadow in which the grass grew green and high and the sun could not penetrate at all. There, soothed by the breath of a soft breeze, they all sat down in a circle on the green grass as the queen commanded.

'As you see,' she said, 'the sun is high, the day is at its hottest and nothing can be heard but the cicadas up in the olive trees. So going anywhere just now would certainly be folly. This is a lovely cool spot to stay in, with chessboards and gaming tables, and anyone can enjoy themselves in the way that most appeals to them. But if we followed a suggestion I want to make, we wouldn't start gaming, which has to upset one of the players and doesn't give that much pleasure to the other, or to anyone watching. Instead we'd spend this hot part of the day telling stories, which, though just one person speaks, can give delight to everyone listening. You will have all barely finished your stories before the sun will be going down and the heat will have lessened. Then we can go and enjoy ourselves wherever you prefer. So if you like what I'm proposing – though I am ready to follow your wishes in this – let's get on with it. If you don't like it, let everyone do what he or she feels like doing until we hear the bell for vespers.'

Telling stories had everyone's approval, ladies and gentlemen alike.

'Well then,' the queen said, 'if you like the idea, my wish is that this first day, each one of you should be free to speak on whatever subject most appeals to them.'

Turning to Panfilo, who was sitting on her right, she gently told him to begin the storytelling with any story he had ready. The order received and everyone else all ears, Panfilo began immediately as follows:

Ser Cepparello Becomes a Saint

Ser Cepparello tricks a God-fearing friar with a false confession and then dies. After being a terrible man during his life, he is reckoned a saint after his death and called Saint Chaplet.

It is appropriate, dear ladies,[1] for anything that man does to take as its starting point the wondrous and holy name of Him who made everything. Since I am the first speaker and must open the storytelling for you, I propose to start with one of the marvellous things He has done. Hearing it should help us rest our hopes securely in Him as the one being who never changes, and His name should be praised by us for ever.

It is obvious that all temporal things are transitory and mortal, and are troubling, stressful and exhausting in themselves and in everything connected with them, as well as being subject to endless perils. We are involved in these things and are part of them, and we could not put up with them or deal with them without going wrong, if some special grace from God did not lend us strength and insight. It is absurd to believe that our merits have anything to do with it. That grace comes from God's own loving kindness towards us, aided by the prayers of those who were once mortal like ourselves and followed His wishes as long as they were alive, but now enjoy with Him eternal bliss. We ourselves hesitate to address our prayers directly to so great a judge and resort to these intermediaries, believing that they have experience of our human frailty, when we pray for things we think will benefit us.

But the Lord is full of compassionate generosity towards us, though there is something greater still which we can discern in

Him. A mortal eye is not sharp enough to penetrate in any way the secret recesses of the divine mind, and it may sometimes happen perhaps that we are tricked by common opinions and make an intermediary before His majesty one who is exiled from it for all eternity. But nothing is hidden from Him, and He considers more the purity of mind of the person praying than his or her ignorance, or the eternal banishment of the being we pray to, and hears our prayers as willingly as if the latter were blessed in His sight. You will be able to see this clearly from the story I intend to tell, though when I say 'clearly', I am referring to human judgement, not to that of God.

The story begins with Musciatto Franzesi,[2] a grand and wealthy merchant, who was made a knight in France and was obliged to join Charles Lackland, the brother of the French king, on the Tuscan expedition that Pope Boniface had urged on him. He calculated that, as is usually the case in business, his complicated dealings in various places could not be easily or quickly wrapped up and decided to put them in the hands of several different individuals. He managed to make the arrangements, but one problem remained, which was who to get to recover the money he had lent on credit to a number of Burgundians. The reason for the problem was the reputation of the Burgundians for being double-dealing, dyed-in-the-wool troublemakers. He could not call to mind anyone bad enough to be entrusted with countering their perversity.

After a long and careful review of the possibilities, he came up with the name of a certain Ser Cepparello of Prato,[3] who often used to stop over in his Paris house. He was a small, very dapper individual. The French, who didn't realize that his name just meant 'bit of a stump', thought it meant *chapel*, that is, 'garland' in their language, but, since he was a small man, as I've said, they used the diminutive 'Chaplet' for him rather than 'Chapel'. So he was known everywhere as Ser Chapletto and only a few people knew him as Ser Cepparello.

His way of life deserves a few words. As a notary, he was immensely ashamed if any of the few legal documents he drew up was not found to be false in some way. But he would have happily drawn up all the false documents he could have been asked for, and have been readier to do so gratis than many a man charging a fortune. He took the greatest delight in giving false witness, whether he was specifically asked to or not. In those days in France great store was set by formal oaths. Ser Chapletto would insouciantly swear anything and, through sheer wickedness, won all the cases at which he was summoned to swear to tell the truth, so help him God. He took exceeding pleasure in – and put a lot of energy into – creating ill-will, feuding and mayhem between friends, relatives and anybody else. The worse the outcome, the happier he was. If he was invited to take part in a murder or some other violent crime, he would never say no, but eagerly go along with it. Several times he ended up happily wounding or killing men with his own hands. He was the greatest blasphemer of God and the saints, and would swear on the slightest pretext, being one of the most short-tempered men that has ever lived. He never went to church and jeered at the sacraments in the most abominable language, saying it was all rubbish. On the other hand he liked to visit taverns and other disreputable places and did so regularly. He liked women as little as a dog does a stick and revelled in their opposite more than any pervert you can think of. He would thieve and rob with the clear conscience of a holy man giving alms. He was a great eater and drinker, to the point of sometimes making himself disgustingly ill, and he was a gambler and a past master of the crooked dice. But why am I going on like this? He was perhaps the most terrible man who has ever been born, and his evil talents were for a long time one of the props of Messer Musciatto's power and standing. For this reason he was mostly treated with respect by the private individuals who frequently suffered from his criminal acts, and also by the forces of law and order, who suffered from them even more often.

So it was this Ser Cepparello who came to Messer Musciatto's mind. He knew very well what he was like and he decided that he was just the man he needed to handle the twisted Burgundians. He summoned him and explained.

'As you know, Ser Chapletto,' he said, 'I am about to make a complete withdrawal from here. Among the people I'm

dealing with are those tricksy Burgundians, and I can think of
no one more appropriate than yourself to get what is mine out
of them. Assuming you have nothing going on at the moment
and wish to take the job, I propose to arrange for you to oper-
ate with the say-so of the royal court, and then to remunerate
you with an appropriate percentage of the amount you recover.'

Ser Chapletto was very aware that he was currently un-
employed and uncomfortably short of worldly wealth and that
the man who had long been his support and protection was
leaving. Given the circumstances, he made up his mind on the
spot and said that he accepted the commission most willingly.
The terms once agreed, authorization and supporting letters
were obtained from the king for Ser Chapletto. Ser Musciatto
left and Ser Chapletto made his way down to Burgundy, where
he was barely known. There, contrary to his nature, he began
work on the recovery he had come to carry out in a considerate, gentle way, as if keeping rage and fury as a last resort. He
found lodging with two brothers from Florence, who were
lending out money at a profitable rate in the region and who
treated him with great respect out of regard for Messer Musciatto. But it so happened that he fell ill in the course of his
negotiations. The two brothers quickly arranged for doctors
and servants to look after him and for everything to be obtained
that might help him back to health. But all treatment was in
vain. The good man was getting on and had a life of dissipation
behind him. The doctors' opinion was that his condition was
worsening with every day that passed and that the illness
was fatal, all of which was extremely upsetting for the two
brothers.

They were standing one day just outside the room where Ser
Chapletto was lying ill, when they began to talk things over.

'What are we going to do with him?' one asked the other.
'The thing puts us in an impossible situation. Throwing him
out of our house when he is as sick as this would be a serious
blow to our good name and a clear sign of irresponsibility on
our part. People would see us first welcoming him in and then
looking after him and getting medical care for him in such a
considerate way. And now, without his having possibly done

anything to upset us, they'd see us suddenly throwing him out when he's mortally ill. On the other hand, he has been such a wicked man that he will refuse to confess his sins or to take any of the Church's sacraments. If he dies unconfessed, no church will wish to accept his body and it will be tossed into the town ditch like a dead dog. Then, if he does actually confess, his sins are so many and so horrible that the result will be the same. There's not a friar or priest who will want to give him absolution or be able to, and so, not being absolved of his sins, he will still be thrown in the ditch. And if this happens we'll have to deal with the inhabitants of this town. They think our business is not right and constantly grumble about it, and at the same time they want to get their hands on our money. When they see all this happening, there'll be an uproar. They'll be shouting, 'The Church didn't want to take in these Lombard dogs[4] and we won't put up with them any more!' They'll chase us into our houses and it could be they won't just plunder our goods and possessions, but maybe they'll rob us of our lives as well. Whatever happens, we're for it if he dies.'

As I said, Ser Chapletto's bed was near where they were talking and his hearing had sharpened in the way we know often happens with sick people. Having overheard what they were saying about him, he asked for them to be called to his bedside.

'I don't want you to have any worries on my account,' he said, 'nor to suffer loss or damage because of me. I followed what you were saying and I'm very sure that it would all happen just as you say it would, assuming this business goes the way you expect. But it's not going to be like that. I've done our Lord God so many wrongs during my life that doing him another now at the hour of my death will be neither here nor there. So arrange for me to be visited by a good and holy friar, the best you can get hold of, if there are any good and holy friars round here. Then leave it to me. I'm confident I can sort out your problems and mine for the best and leave you two feeling well-pleased.'

Though what he said did not make them particularly hopeful, the two brothers all the same went off to a friary and asked if some wise and holy man were available who would be willing to hear confession from a Lombard lying ill in their house. They were assigned an aged friar, noted for his holiness and virtue, one who was deeply learned in the Scriptures, thoroughly venerable and regarded with particular devotion by local citizens.

They took him back with them and showed him into the room where Ser Chapletto was lying. Taking a seat at his side, he first of all offered him some kindly words of comfort. Then after a while he asked him how long it was since he had last been to confession.

Ser Chapletto, who had never confessed his sins to a priest in his life, replied, 'Father, it has been my habit to go to confession at least once a week, though there are many weeks when it's more than that. But the truth is that I've not confessed my sins since I fell ill, that is, for close on eight days, and that's because I've been so incapacitated by this illness.'

'My son,' the friar said, 'you have done well and I am sure you will do well henceforth. But I deduce that, since you go to confession so frequently, I'm not going to be overworked hearing and questioning you.'

'Don't say that, Friar sir,' said Ser Chapletto. 'No matter how many times or how often I confessed particular sins, I always wanted to make a general confession of all the sins I could remember from the day I was born up to the day I was confessing. So I beg you, my good father, ask me about each thing, point by point, as if I had never made any confession at all. And don't spare me because I'm ill. I much prefer for my flesh to be discomforted than to treat it gently and do something that could mean the perdition of my soul, which my Saviour redeemed with His precious blood.'

The holy man was very pleased to hear these words, which he thought indicated an appropriate attitude of mind. He highly commended Ser Chapletto for this habit of his and then began asking him if he had ever lusted after a woman and sinned with her.

Ser Chapletto gave a sigh.

'My father,' he replied, 'I blush to tell you the truth on this score, since I'm afraid to fall into the sin of vainglory.'

'Speak out and don't be nervous,' said the holy friar. 'No one has ever sinned by speaking the truth during confession or on any other occasion.'

'You reassure me,' said Ser Chapletto, 'and I shall tell you. I am as pure as the day I left my dear mother's womb.'

'The Lord's blessing be on you!' said the friar. 'What a virtuous way to have lived! And you deserve to be rewarded for living like that all the more because, if you had wanted to, you could have chosen to do the opposite, being much freer than people like myself and everyone else who is constrained by the rules of a religious order.'

After this he asked him if he had offended God by indulging in the sin of gluttony. Ser Chapletto gave a heavy sigh and said yes, often. As well as the various fasts that pious people keep over the course of the year, it had been his habit to limit himself to bread and water for at least three days a week. However, he had drunk the water as thirstily and with as much enjoyment as boozers drink their wine, especially after strenuous praying or tiring pilgrimages. Then he had many times felt a longing for the sort of little green side salads that ladies make up when they go and stay in the country. Sometimes he had rated food more highly than he thought was permissible for anyone like himself, who was fasting for religious reasons.

'My son,' the friar said, 'these are natural sins and not serious. I don't want you to let them weigh on your conscience more than is needed. However religious they are, people find themselves enjoying eating after a long period of abstinence and enjoying drinking after an expenditure of effort.'

'Oh,' said Ser Chapletto, 'don't say this just to comfort me, father. You are well enough aware that I know that things which are done in the service of the Lord must always be done with a pure and undefiled heart. If you do them in any other way, you commit a sin.'

The friar was extremely pleased.

'Well, I'm happy with your way of seeing it,' he said, 'and I really approve of your good, clear conscience in this regard. But what about the sin of avarice? Have you ever wanted more money than it's decent to have or held on to more than you should have?'

'Father,' Ser Chapletto said, 'I shouldn't like any suspicious thoughts to cross your mind because I'm staying with these moneylenders. I have nothing to do with their business. In fact, I had come here to upbraid and castigate them, to get them to quit this abominable profiteering. And I think I might have been successful, if God had not visited this tribulation on me. I want you to know that my father left me a rich man, but after his death I gave most of my wealth to charity. I have carried on my own little trading business since then in order to keep myself alive and also to be able to help the poor of the Lord. I did want to make a profit, but I have always divided the profits evenly, keeping half for my own needs and giving half to the poor. My Creator has given me such generous aid that my affairs have just kept on improving.'

'You have done well there,' said the friar. 'But how often have you succumbed to anger?'

'Oh,' Ser Chapletto said, 'let me tell you plainly that that's something I've done very often. Could anyone control himself at the sight of people constantly doing disgusting things with not a thought for God's commandments or any fear of divine judgement? Every day, time and again, I wish I was dead, when I see young people wasting their lives, swearing and cursing, going out drinking, not going to church and generally follow-ing the ways of the world rather than those of God.'

'My son,' the friar said, 'this is righteous anger. As far as I'm concerned there isn't any penitence I'd impose on you. But could it have ever happened for some reason that anger has led you to commit murder or to tell someone they're contemptible or to wrong them in any other way?'

'Oh dear, good sir,' Ser Chapletto said, 'you seem to me to be a man of God and yet how can you say things like that? If I had ever had the faintest inkling of doing any one of the things you mention, do you think God would have sustained me for so long? These are things mobsters and criminals do. And when-ever I've seen one of their sort I've always said, "Go on your way and may God change your heart!"'

'Blessings on you again, my son,' said the friar. 'But now tell me if you have ever given false witness against anyone or spoken ill of anyone or taken another's goods without permission from their rightful owner?'

'I have indeed, sir,' Ser Chapletto replied. 'Yes, I have spoken ill of others. I had a neighbour who would keep on beating his wife, for no reason in the world. So I once said a few negative words about him to his wife's parents, because I felt so sorry for that poor woman. The state he reduced her to once he had had a few too many drinks, God only knows.'

Then the friar asked him, 'Now, tell me this, since you've been a businessman; have you ever deceived someone in the way businessmen do?'

'Yes, in the name of heaven, I have, sir,' said Ser Chapletto. 'But I'm not sure who it was. A man brought me some money that he owed me for some cloth I'd sold him and I put it in a chest without counting it. A month or so later I found there was four pence more than there should have been. I didn't see him again and after keeping the pennies ready for him for a year, I gave them to charity.'

'That was a small thing,' the friar said, 'and you did well to do what you did.'

And so the holy friar went on to ask him many other questions, all of which he answered in this way. The friar wanted to proceed to the absolution, but Ser Chapletto interrupted.

'Sir,' he said, 'there are still one or two other sins I have not told you about.'

When the friar asked him what they were, he replied, 'I recall that I had my manservant sweep the house one Saturday evening and didn't show the reverence I should have showed for the holy day.'

'Oh, dear,' the friar said, 'that's just a trifle.'

'No,' Ser Chapletto said, 'don't call it a trifle. Sunday is a day to be fully honoured, being the day when our Lord rose again from death to life.'

'Well,' the friar said, 'have you done anything else?'

'I have, sir,' said Ser Chapletto. 'I once found myself inadvertently spitting in the house of God.'

The friar gave the beginnings of a smile.

'This isn't anything to worry about, my son,' he said. 'We who are members of religious orders spit there all day.'

'Then you are behaving outrageously,' said Ser Chapletto. 'Nowhere deserves to be kept as spick and span as the holy temple in which sacrifice is made to God.'

All in all he came out with a string of things of this sort, until in the end he began sighing and then was wracked with weeping, being someone who could turn on the tears whenever he wanted.

'What is it, my son?' asked the holy friar.

'Oh dear, oh dear,' Ser Chapletto said, 'there is one sin I have never confessed, because I'm too ashamed to put it into words. Every time I remember it I cry in the way you see. I feel certain that this sin will prevent God from having mercy on me.'

'Come along, my son,' said the holy friar, 'what are you saying? Imagine all the sins ever committed by all mankind, plus all those mankind will commit for the duration of the world, being all rolled up in one man. If that man were as repentant and contrite as I can see you are, God's goodness and mercy are vast enough for Him to give pardon freely to that man, so long as he makes his confession. So trust in Him and say it.'

Ser Chapletto was still wracked with tears. 'Oh, dear, oh dear,' he said, 'this sin of mine is enormous, father. I can barely credit that it can ever be forgiven by God without your prayers working on my behalf.'

'Just trust in Him and say it,' said the friar, 'because I do promise to pray to God on your behalf.'

Ser Chapletto went on weeping and wouldn't come out with it, while the friar went on encouraging him. But after he had kept him on tenterhooks for a long time with his tears, Ser Chapletto finally gave a big sigh and spoke.

'Father, I shall tell you,' he said, 'since you promise to pray to the Lord for me. And what I have to tell you is that when I was a little boy I once swore at my mother.' With that he again burst into tears.

'O my son,' the friar said, 'do you really think that's such a great big sin? Men swear using God's name every day of the

year, and He willingly forgives those who blaspheme against
Him if they repent. Do you not believe He'll forgive you that?
Stop weeping and cheer up. Really, with the contrite heart
you're showing me, He'd forgive you even if you had been one
of those men who nailed Him to the Cross.'

'Oh dear, oh dear, father,' said Ser Chapletto, 'how can you
say that? My sweet, sweet mummy who carried me day and
night for nine months in her body, and then carried me round
hundreds of times on her back! It was a horrible thing to swear
at her, a horrible sin. And I won't be forgiven unless you pray
for me.'

When the friar saw that Ser Chapletto had nothing further
to confess, he gave him absolution and then his blessing, taking
him for one of the devoutest of men and fully believing that
every word he had said was true. But would anyone not have
believed him, given that here was a man making a confession of
his sins in the face of imminent death?

Then, when it was all done, the friar spoke again. 'Ser Chapletto, with God's help you will soon be well again. But if it
should happen that God summons your now blessed and ready
soul to Himself, would you be happy for your body to be buried within our precincts?'

'Yes, I would, sir,' Ser Chapletto replied. 'I shouldn't like to
be buried anywhere else, since you have promised to pray for
me. Besides I have always felt a particular devotion to your
order. For that reason I beg you, once you are back at your
house, to let the true body of Christ which you consecrate in
the morning above the altar be brought to me. I am not worthy
of it, but with your permission I intend to take it. Then let me
receive the holy extreme unction, so that, if I have lived like a
sinner, I might at least die like a Christian.'

The holy man said that he very much approved and that
Ser Chapletto's words were right and proper; he would make
sure that what he requested was brought to him as soon as
possible – which he did.

The two brothers, who had worried that Ser Chapletto
might put one over on them, had stationed themselves behind
a partition dividing the room in which he was lying from

another one. They stood listening and had no difficulty following what he said to the friar. Several times, when they heard
what he was confessing to having done, they felt an almighty
urge to laugh that almost made them burst. They said to each
other once or twice, 'What a card he is! Old age, illness, fear of
death (which he can tell is close), not even fear of God, whose
judgement he's going to face very soon – none of these things
have managed to turn him against his bad old self or stop him
wanting to meet his death in the way he's lived his life.'

But once they knew what he had said would lead to his body
being buried in the church, they couldn't care less about the
rest.

Ser Chapletto took communion a little later and, as his condition was worsening irremediably, received extreme unction.
He died the same day that he had made his virtuous confession,
a little after the evening bell had rung. The two brothers drew
on his funds to make sure he would have an honourable funeral
and informed the friary, asking for some brothers to come and
pass the night chanting and praying over the dead man, and
then to take the body away in the morning, for all of which
they made the appropriate arrangements. Learning that Ser
Chapletto had passed away, the holy friar who had heard his
confession got the agreement of the prior that the bell should
be rung for a meeting of the whole chapter. He then laid before
the assembled brothers all the evidence he had derived from his
confession, that Ser Chapletto had been a truly religious man.
He expressed hopes that the Lord God would perform many
miracles through him, and persuaded them that his body should
be received into their church with the greatest reverence and
piety. The prior and the other friars unsuspectingly gave their
agreement. That evening they all went to the house where Ser
Chapletto's body was lying and held a full-scale, solemn vigil
over it. In the morning they arrayed themselves in their albs
and copes and went to get the body, chanting as they walked,
hymnals in their hands and crosses leading the way. Then they
carried the body with great pomp and ceremony to the church,
followed by almost all the inhabitants of the city, men and
women alike. Once the body was set down in the church, the

same holy friar who had heard the confession went up into the pulpit and began to say marvellous things about Ser Chapletto and how he had lived, his fastings, his sexual purity, his simplicity, innocence and sanctity, including the story of what he had tearfully confessed to him as his greatest sin, and how he had had to struggle to get it into his head that God would pardon him, using this as a chance to berate his audience.

'While you,' he said, 'you are the cursed of the Lord! Let a blade of straw get between your toes and you swear at God, the Virgin Mother and all the saints of Paradise.'

Then he went on to say a great deal more about Ser Chapletto's devotion and purity.

The local population believed every word, and he so convinced and inspired them all that as soon as the service was over there was a stampede to kiss Ser Chapletto's hands and feet, with people ripping his clothes off and thinking themselves blessed if they managed to get hold of a strip of the cloth. The body had to be kept on display all day so that everyone could see and touch it. Then, at nightfall, it was interred with full honours in a marble tomb in one of the chapels. On the following day people began immediately coming to light candles and say prayers. From there it was a short step to making vows and hanging up wax images in accordance with the promises made. The fame of his sanctity and people's devotion to him grew so much that anyone in trouble of any kind wouldn't make a vow to any other saint, and they started calling him St Chaplet, as they still do. People claim that God has performed many miracles through him and continues to perform them for any who commend themselves to him with a pious heart.

So lived and died Ser Cepparello from Prato, becoming a saint, as you have heard. I don't want to deny that it is possible that he is blessed in the presence of God. Though he lived a criminal, morally perverse existence, he could have shown such contrition at the last moment that God may have shown mercy on him and received him into His kingdom. But since this is hidden from us, I draw on the evidence we have and declare that he must be in the clutches of the Devil rather than in paradise. If that is the case, we can recognize the greatness of God's loving kindness to us. When He hears our prayers, He does not consider our error, but the purity of our faith, even if we use as a go-between one who is an enemy of His whom we believe to be a friend. It is as if we had recourse to a true saint to act as the transmitter of His grace. And we here, desiring through that grace to be kept safe and sound throughout our current adversities in this happy company, praise His name as we praised it at our beginning, and hold Him in reverence, commending ourselves to Him amid our needs, certain that we shall be heard.

And with that the storyteller[5] fell silent.

2

The Conversion of Abraham

Abraham, a Jew, under pressure from Jehannot de Chevigny, goes to visit the Roman court. After seeing the churchmen's evil ways, he returns to Paris and becomes a Christian.

Some of Panfilo's story made the ladies laugh and the whole thing won their full approval. It had been heard attentively and, when it was over, Neifile, who was sitting by Panfilo, was ordered by the queen to continue the entertainment now underway by telling another story. Her social graces were as lovely as her looks and she happily replied that she would do so with pleasure. She began as follows:

Panfilo has given us a demonstration in his story of how God's loving kindness does not consider our errors, when these stem from causes that we cannot ourselves perceive. I intend with my story to give you an instance of how this same kindness – through patiently tolerating the flawed behaviour of those who should offer true witness to its nature in their words and deeds, but who do the opposite – may give us clear evidence of its infallible truth and teach us to practise what we believe with greater firmness of purpose.

Gracious ladies, I heard some time ago about a great and good merchant living in Paris called Jehannot de Chevigny. He was exceptionally honest and upright and a major figure in the cloth trade. He was also a particular friend of a very wealthy Jew called Abraham, who was also a merchant and of a similarly honest and upright character. Thinking about his virtues, Jehannot began to feel uncomfortable with the idea that the soul of such a stalwart, shrewd and moral individual would end up being damned because of a lack of Christian faith. So he began begging him in a friendly way to abandon the errors of the Jewish religion and to turn to the truths of Christianity. As he could see for himself, he argued, Christianity was growing stronger and more widespread all the time thanks to its holy and righteous nature. His own, on the other hand, he could surely see, was shrinking and risked disappearing altogether.

The Jew replied that he didn't believe any religion to be righteous or holy apart from Judaism; that was what he'd been born into and he intended to live and die in the Jewish faith and nothing would ever make him reject it. But Jehannot did not give in. Some days later he returned to the subject, setting out in the rough and ready way characteristic of merchants the arguments why our religion is superior to the Jewish one. While Abraham had an advanced knowledge of Jewish doctrine, he was perhaps swayed by his great friendship for Jehannot or perhaps the words that the Holy Spirit put into his uncultured friend's mouth had an effect. In any event he began to find Jehannot's arguments attractive. All the same he held stubbornly to his beliefs and wouldn't let himself be deflected from them.

So things stayed like that for some time, Abraham obstinately resisting and Jehannot never ceasing to go on at him. Eventually the Jew was worn down by the continual pressure.

'Look, Jehannot,' he said, 'you want me to become a Christian and I'm well disposed to the idea. My one condition is that I first to go to Rome. I want to see the man you say is the Vicar of God on earth and assess his behaviour and the sort of life he lives, and similarly with his brothers, the cardinals. If the impression they make fits with what you say and I end up understanding how your religion is better than mine, as you've been working hard to show me, I'll do what I've just said. If I am unimpressed, I shall stay as Jewish as I am now.'

When Jehannot heard this, he felt thoroughly depressed.

'I've wasted my efforts,' he said to himself. 'I thought I was really getting somewhere and that I had converted him. But if he goes to the Roman court and sees what sordid, criminal lives the clerics lead, there's no chance of him changing from a Jew into a Christian. If he were already a Christian, he'd inevitably come back a Jew.'

'Ah, my friend,' he said, addressing Abraham, 'why do you want to go to the enormous trouble and expense of travelling from Paris[1] to Rome? That's not to mention all the dangers on land and sea that a rich man like yourself would be letting himself in for. Don't you think you could find someone here to baptize you? And if you do have any doubts about our religion as I spell it out, where has it greater teachers and savvier experts than those here? They'll be able to clear up any questions you want to put to them. In my opinion, so far as all that's concerned, it's an unnecessary journey. Take it from me that the prelates down there are just like the ones you've been able to see here, only better, since they're closer to our spiritual leader. My advice to you is that you save up this expedition for some time when you want to go on a pilgrimage. Perhaps it'll turn out that I can come along with you.'

'I can well believe, Jehannot,' said the Jew, 'that it's all just as you say. But to put the whole thing in a nutshell, if you want me to do what you've been begging me to do, my mind is completely made up that I must go down there. Otherwise I'm not doing anything about it, ever.'

Jehannot saw he was determined.

'Go on then,' he said, 'and the best of luck.'

He's never going to become a Christian, he thought to himself, when he sees the Roman court. But he wasted no more energy and refrained from further comment.

The Jew mounted his horse and rode off as quickly as he could to see the Roman court. On his arrival he was received as an honoured guest by his fellow Jews. Then, during his stay, without telling anyone why he had come, he began looking into the sort of lives that the Pope, the cardinals, the other prelates and all the members of the court were living. As a shrewd observer he saw for himself what others told him: every one of them from the highest to the lowest was a disgusting practitioner of the sin of lust, not just in the natural way, but sodomitically too. Untrammelled by conscience or shame, they granted whores and rent-boys whatever favours they wanted, no matter how large. Apart from the sex, he saw that they were all gluttons and drinkers, constantly at it and as much the slaves of their bellies as are brute beasts. Taking a closer look, he saw they were all obsessed with keeping or making money, buying and selling human lives – yes, Christian lives – and holy objects of all sorts relating to services and benefices. They did more trading and had more brokers than the cloth trade or any other trade in Paris. And they called blatant simony 'procurement' and gluttony 'sustainment'. Leaving aside the meaning of words, it was as if they thought God didn't know their evil intentions and would let Himself be taken in by names in the way men are. All these – and many other things it's best not to speak about – were extremely distasteful to a sober, modest man such as the Jew. Thinking he had seen enough, he decided to return to Paris, which he did.

When Jehannot heard he was back, he went to see him, expecting anything except that he might have become a Christian. They greeted each other with great warmth and then, after Abraham had had a few days to recover from the journey, Jehannot asked him what he thought of the Holy Father, the cardinals and the other members of the court.

The Jew was quick to reply.

'My view,' he said, 'is that God should make them suffer one and all. I say this because, after due consideration, down there I found no holiness, no devotion, no good works or models of how to live or do anything else in any of the clergy. I just saw them revelling in lust, avarice, greed, fraud, envy, pride and such like – or worse, if any of them could find worse things to do. It's a hotbed of diabolical activity, not good works. So far as I can tell, your pastor, and hence all the rest of them, use all their energy, all their intelligence and all their wits to reduce the Christian religion to nothing and to eliminate it from the world, when they should be its foundation and support. However, I also see that what they are after is not happening. Instead your religion is continually growing and shines forth with ever greater brightness. I deduce that the Holy Spirit is deservedly its foundation and support, being the religion which is truer and more holy than any other. And so, having previously rigidly withstood your appeals and been determined not to become a Christian, I tell you now in all frankness that nothing could stop me converting. Let us go to church and there have me baptized in accordance with the due rite of your holy faith.'

Jehannot was expecting the total opposite of this. He was the happiest man alive to hear what Abraham said. Together they went to the church of Notre-Dame and asked the priests to baptize Abraham. They immediately did as they were requested. Jehannot raised him from the holy font and named him John. He subsequently arranged with some eminent teachers for him to receive instruction in our faith. This he quickly absorbed and went on to live a good and committed Christian life.

3

The Story of the Three Rings

Melchisedek, a Jew, tells a story of three rings and escapes a very dangerous trap that Saladin sets for him.

Neifile's story met with everyone's approval. When she stopped speaking, the queen's choice fell on Filomena, who began as follows:

The story that Neifile has told makes me think of a perilous turn of events to which a certain Jew was once exposed. Since very fine things have been said of God and the truth of our faith, it won't now be out of place to lower our sights and speak of human actions and experiences. I propose to tell you a story which may subsequently make you ladies wary about the answers you give to any difficult questions put to you.

You must be aware, my darling companions, how stupid behaviour often ruins people's happiness and reduces them to an abject condition, but also how practical intelligence can rescue a thoughtful person from enormous dangers and bring them to safety and tranquillity. There are obviously lots of cases of stupidity bringing people down, but I'm not interested in telling you about any of them just now, what with so many new instances coming to our attention every day. Instead the little story I am going to tell will show how – as I have just stated – sharpness of mind can produce beneficial results.

Saladin[1] was a man of enormous ability. He not only rose from very small beginnings to become Sultan of Babylon, but he also won victory after victory over Saracen and Christian kings of the time. But his various wars and lavish generosity consumed all his finances. He suddenly found himself needing a large amount of money with no idea where he could quickly lay hands on the necessary sum. Eventually he recalled a wealthy Jew named Melchisedek, who was a moneylender in Alexandria and was in a position, he thought, to help him out, if he wished. But Saladin knew he was too tight-fisted to do it of his own accord, and at the same time he didn't want to force him. The situation was, however, becoming urgent and he worried obsessively about how he could get the Jew to make the loan. Eventually he decided to apply force, but to give the force the air of being rationally justified.

He sent for the Jew, gave him a friendly welcome and had him sit down by his side. He then addressed him as follows: 'You are an able man, and I have heard from various people that you are also a man of great wisdom with a deep knowledge of divine matters. I am most eager to learn from you which of the three religions – the Jewish, the Saracen or the Christian – you consider to be the true one.'

The Jew, who really was a very perceptive man, realized all too well that Saladin was aiming to catch him out whatever he said and put him in an awkward position. He thought that he couldn't speak more highly of one than of the others without Saladin achieving what he intended. Aware of needing a reply that would let him off the hook, he sharpened his wits and very quickly came up with what he ought to say.

'My lord,' he said, 'the problem you set me is a fine one. If I'm going to give you my opinion, I'm going to have to tell you a little story.

'I recall, if I'm not mistaken, being often told of an important, wealthy man, who had various expensive jewels in his coffers, including a very beautiful and precious ring. Its value and beauty made it a thing to be treated with honour and he wanted it to be handed down through his descendants in perpetuity. Accordingly, he gave orders that the son to whom he left the ring and was found to be in possession of it should be his heir, and should be honoured and revered by all the other sons as their superior. The son who received the ring gave similar orders regarding his own descendants and acted as his predecessor had done. And so, to cut a long story short, the ring was passed on from hand to hand through many generations, until it finally came into the hands of a man who had three fine, virtuous sons, all very obedient to their father, who loved them all equally. The young men knew about the tradition of the ring and were of course all eager to be the one who was most highly honoured. Each of them fervently begged their father (who was now old) to leave the ring to him on his death.

'Being a worthy man with equal love for all three sons, he found himself unable to choose which one he should leave the ring to. He decided to promise the ring to each of them and to devise a way of satisfying all three. He secretly commissioned a skilful craftsman to make two further rings, which were so like the first that he himself, who had commissioned them, could barely tell which was the real one. On his deathbed he secretly gave each of his sons his ring.

'After their father's death, each of them wanted to claim the inheritance and the honour for himself. They all denied the rights of the others and, to support their arguments, they all produced their rings. When they found the rings were so alike that no one could tell the real one from the others, the problem of which of them was the true heir had to be left unresolved, as it still is. And that, I say, is the case, my lord, with the three religions given to the three peoples by God our Father, which was the problem you set me. Each believes it possesses by due right the Lord's bequest and practises His true religion and commandments. But as with the rings, the question of who is correct is still pending.'

Saladin realized that Melchisedek had managed with great skill to avoid stepping into the trap he had set for him. He decided it was best to reveal the state of his finances and to see if he would be willing to make him a loan. He did this, explaining what he had intended to do if he had not been given such a clever reply. The Jew readily supplied the full amount that Saladin asked him for. In due course Saladin repaid him entirely and, in addition, presented him with ample gifts. From then on he treated him as his friend and made him a much honoured member of his court.

DAY TWO

The First Day of the Decameron *ends, and the Second begins, in which, under the rule of Filomena, the members of the party tell stories about people who are beset by misadventures of various sorts, but who emerge from them much more happily than they ever hoped.*

5
Andreuccio da Perugia's Neapolitan Adventures

Andreuccio da Perugia comes to Naples to buy horses and has three misfortunes happen to him in one night, but he emerges safely from all of them and goes back home with a ruby.

Landolfo's finding the precious stones,[1] (began Fiammetta, whose turn it was to be the storyteller) reminds me of another story which contains just as many perilous adventures as the one Lauretta has told, though it is different in one way: the events of that story were spread over a number of years; these all happened in a single night, as you will hear.

I was told some time ago about a young man from Perugia called Andreuccio, the son of a certain Pietro and a horse-dealer by trade. Hearing that horses were selling cheaply in Naples, he put five hundred gold florins in his bag and went off there with some other merchants, never having previously been away from home. He arrived on a Sunday evening, about vesper time, got the necessary information from his innkeeper and was in the market square early the next morning. He saw a lot of horses, many of which met with his approval, and did a good deal of bargaining without being able to agree a price for any of them. But he was keen to show that he was there to do some buying and naively and imprudently pulled out his bag of florins several times before the eyes of people coming and going past him. It was while he was negotiating, his bag in full view, that a young Sicilian woman walked past. She was very beautiful, but ready to give any man what he wanted for a small payment. He didn't see her, but she saw his bag and immediately said to herself, 'Wouldn't I be a lucky one if that money were mine?' Then she went on her way.

There was an old woman with her, who was also Sicilian. As soon as she saw Andreuccio she let the girl go on and hurried over to give him an affectionate hug. The young woman noticed and, without saying anything, stopped and waited for her on one side. Andreuccio, who had turned round and recognized the old woman, greeted her with great warmth. She promised to come and see him at his inn, but didn't keep him talking for too long just then and soon left. Andreuccio went back to his bargaining, though he made no purchases that morning. After seeing first the bag and then the intimacy with the old servant, the young woman began to wonder if she might not get hold of some or all of the money. She asked a few cautious questions about who the young man was, where he was from, what he was doing there and how she came to know him. The old servant gave her all the information she wanted, almost in as much detail as Andreuccio might have supplied himself, being able to do this because she had spent a long time with his father, first in Sicily and then in Perugia. She likewise told her where he was lodging and why he had come to Naples.

Once the young woman was fully informed about his family and their names, she had the basis for playing a clever trick that would bring her what she wanted. Back at her house she made sure that the old woman was busy all day, so that she couldn't go and see Andreuccio. She had a much younger servant girl to whom she had given a very good training in the sort of work she had in mind, and towards evening she sent her to the inn where Andreuccio was staying. When she arrived, she found him by chance standing alone in the doorway. She asked for Andreuccio and he said that he was the very man. At which she drew him to one side.

'Sir,' she said, 'there is a noble lady in this town who would appreciate a conversation with you, if you were so inclined.'

Andreuccio thought carefully for a moment when he heard this. He decided that he was a good-looking lad and deduced that this lady must have fallen for him, as if there were no other fine young men in Naples just then apart from himself. He quickly said that he was up for it, and asked where and when this lady wanted to have a talk with him.

The young servant girl replied, 'She's waiting for you in her house, sir, whenever you feel like coming along.'

'Well, you lead the way and I'll follow on,' Andreuccio said immediately, with no thought of letting anyone at the inn know.

So the girl led him to the Sicilian woman's house, which was in a district called Malpertugio,[2] a name meaning Bad Passage, which gives a clear idea of just how respectable a district it was. But Andreuccio, knowing nothing of this and quite unsuspecting, thought he was going to a most respectable house to see a lady of some standing, and confidently followed the girl into the house. As they were climbing the stairs, she called out to her mistress 'Here's Andreuccio!' and he saw her appear at the top, waiting for him.

She was still young, with a full figure and a lovely face, and her clothes and jewellery were tastefully ornate. When Andreuccio was closer, she came down three steps towards him, her arms wide, and, flinging them round his neck, stayed like that for a while without saying a word, as if too overcome to speak. Then she tearfully kissed his forehead and said in a broken voice, 'O my precious Andreuccio! Welcome to my house!'

Such a heartfelt reception amazed Andreuccio and he replied, quite dazed, 'Well, it's wonderful to meet you, my lady!'

After this she took him by the hand and led him into the main room, and from there, without saying another word, into her private chamber, which was redolent with the scents of roses, orange blossom and other flowers. Andreuccio noticed a splendid curtained bed and an abundance of beautiful dresses arranged on hangers in the south Italian way, and many other fine and costly items. In his inexperience he was fully convinced by all this that the woman could be nothing but a great lady. Once they were seated together on a chest that was at the foot of her bed, she embarked on the following speech.

'I am quite certain, Andreuccio, that you are startled at being embraced and wept over by me in this way. After all, you don't know me and and may never have heard my name mentioned. But in a moment you are going to hear something which will perhaps amaze you even more. The fact is, I am your sister.

And I can tell you that, since God has granted me the enormous grace of letting me see one of my brothers before I die – though, of course, I want to see all of you – I shall not die unconsoled. Perhaps you have never heard a word of this. So I shall happily tell you all about it.

'As I think you may have been told, Pietro – that is, your father and mine – lived for a long time in Palermo. Thanks to his native goodness and appealing character he gained the affections of those who came to know him and he still has a place in their hearts. But among those most attached to him, there was someone who loved him more than anyone else, and that was my mother, who was a noble lady and recently widowed. She loved him so much that she put aside all fears of her father and brothers and any concern for her honour and entered into intimate relations with him. As a result I was born into the world and am now the person you see before you.

'A little later, when a reason arose for Pietro to return to Perugia, he left me, still a very little girl, with my mother. From everything I heard, he never gave me or her another thought. If he had not been my father I would be very critical of him, considering the ingratitude he showed to my mother – and let's leave aside the love he should have felt for me, his daughter, and not by a serving girl or some woman of easy virtue either. My mother was inspired by the truest form of love when – knowing nothing of who he was – she put herself and everything she had in his hands. But there you are. Wrongs of long ago are more easily criticized than put right.

'So he left me a little girl in Palermo. When I had grown into more or less the woman you see before you, my mother, who was a rich lady, married me to a man from Agrigento, an upstanding man of noble rank. Out of love for myself and my mother he moved to Palermo, and there, being very much on the Guelf side,[3] he became involved in plotting with our King Charles. King Frederick got wind of the plot before any of our plans could be acted on and so we had to flee Sicily just at the moment when I was expecting to become the finest lady there had ever been on the island. We took with us what few things we could – I mean few in comparison with all the possessions we had – and, leaving our lands and mansions behind, escaped to this city. We found King Charles very grateful. He partially compensated us for the losses we had suffered on his behalf. He gave us lands and houses and he still gives my husband – your brother-in-law – a substantial pension, as you'll soon be able to see. So that is how I came to be here, and how – thanks to God's grace, though not at all to you – I now see you before me, my sweet brother.'

With this she clasped him to her again and kissed his forehead, still weeping tenderly.

She told her cock and bull story in a supremely coherent and convincing way, with not a hesitation or stutter. Andreuccio recalled that his father really had been in Palermo and he knew from his own experience what young men are like and how prone they are to falling in love. What with the tender tears, embraces and decidedly unamorous kisses, he was convinced that what she said was more than true. When she finished, he made the following reply.

'My lady, you must not be shocked by my own amazement. To be candid, either my father for some reason of his own never spoke about you and your mother or, if he did speak of you, not a whisper reached my ears. So I had no more knowledge of you than if you had never existed. But it's all the more precious to me to have found you, my sister, in this place, because I'm here all alone and this was the thing I least expected. And to tell the truth, I can't imagine your not being precious to the grandest businessman I can think of, let alone to a small-scale merchant like myself. But please, explain one thing for me. How did you come to know I was here?'

'I was told this morning,' she replied. 'And the person who told me is a poor woman who spends a lot of time here with me, the reason being that, from what she says, she was with our father for a long time in both Palermo and Perugia. If it hadn't seemed to me more honourable for you to come here to what is your house than for me to go and see you at someone else's, I would have been with you ages ago.'

After this she started putting precise questions to him about his relatives, identifying each one by name. Andreuccio told her about them all, becoming more and more willing to believe what he should not have believed at all.

Since they kept on talking for a long time and it was very hot, she called for white wine and nibbles and made sure Andreuccio was duly served. He made to leave after this, since it was now dinner time, but she wouldn't allow it. Looking deeply distressed, she flung her arms round him, saying: 'Oh poor me! I can tell I don't really matter to you! To think that you're here with a sister you've never seen before, in her house, where you should have come and stayed when you arrived, and you want to go off and have your dinner in an inn! No, you'll dine with me, and though my husband is not here, I'm very sorry to say, I'll do what little a lady is capable of to see you are treated with some degree of honour.'

Andreuccio could only come up with one reply.

'You do matter to me,' he said, 'as much as any sister should. But if I don't go, I shall keep them waiting for me for dinner all evening, which will be really churlish.'

'Lord in heaven!' she said. 'Do you think I've nobody in the house I can send to tell them not to expect you? Though you would be doing a finer thing – not to say, your duty – if you sent a message to your friends inviting them to come and dine here. Then afterwards, if you were set on leaving, you and all the rest could go off in one big party.'

Andreuccio replied that he had no wish to see his friends that evening, and that, if that was how she felt, she should treat him as she pleased. She then made a show of sending a message to the inn, telling them not to expect him for dinner. After this they talked for a long time, before sitting down to eat. They were served in splendid fashion with a series of dishes, the woman cunningly prolonging the dinner well into the night. When they got up from the table and Andreuccio expressed a desire to leave, she said that she could not possibly allow it. Naples was not a city for anyone to walk through at night, especially a stranger. She had sent a message to say he should not be expected for dinner and then she had sent another regarding where he was staying. He believed everything she said and was delighted, in his deluded state, to stay on.

She made sure that conversation after dinner was prolonged and varied. Late into the night she left Andreuccio in her own chamber with a young servant boy to show him anything he needed, while she herself went off to another room with her maids.

It was very hot and as soon as he saw he was alone Andreuccio removed his jacket and peeled off his leggings, which he left over the bedhead. Feeling nature calling him to lighten his stomach of the excess weight within it, he asked the servant where one did that sort of thing. The boy pointed to a door in a corner of the room.

'Go in there,' he said.

Andreuccio went insouciantly through the door. One of his feet came down on a board, the other end of which was no longer attached to the strut on which it was resting. The result was that the board swung up in the air and then crashed downwards, taking Andreuccio with it. God was kind to him and he did himself no harm in the fall, although he fell from a considerable height, but he was thoroughly covered in the horrible filth that the place was full of. To explain what the arrangement was – to give you a clearer picture of what I've just said and what follows – two struts had been fixed over the sort of narrow alleyway we often see separating two houses, with some boards nailed to them and a place to sit on fitted. It was one of these boards which had fallen with Andreuccio.

When he found himself down below in the alleyway, he was extremely upset at what had happened and began calling out to the boy. But as soon as he had heard him fall, the boy had rushed to tell his mistress. She in her turn ran into the bedroom, quickly looked to see if his clothes were there and found them. With them was the money, which, crazily, the ever suspicious Andreuccio always carried on his person. The Palermo tart who now had what she had schemed for by turning into the sister of the visitor from Perugia, couldn't care less about Andreuccio any more. She went promptly over to the door which Andreuccio had passed through when he fell and closed it.

When the boy didn't reply, Andreuccio started calling more loudly, but to no avail. He was now becoming suspicious and beginning, somewhat late in the day, to have an inkling of the trickery. He climbed on to the low wall separating the alleyway from the street and once down on the other side found his way to the door of the house, which he easily recognized. He stood there for a long time, vainly calling out and shaking and banging on the door. He could now see the full extent of his misfortune quite clearly, which reduced him to tears.

'Oh poor me!' he began saying. 'How little time it's taken for me to lose five hundred florins and a sister too!'

After a lot more of this, he began again beating on the door and calling out. The result was that many people living nearby woke up and then, when the din became unbearable, got themselves out of bed. One of the lady's female servants appeared at a window, looking all sleepy, and called out in an irritated voice, 'Who's banging away down there?'

'Oh, don't you know me?' said Andreuccio. 'I'm Andreuccio, the brother of Madonna Fiordiliso.'

The servant replied, 'My good man, if you've had too much to drink, go and sleep it off and come back in the morning. I don't know anything about any Andreuccio or anything else of what you're gabbling on about. Do us a favour, please go away and let us get some sleep.'

'What?' said Andreuccio. 'Don't you really know what I'm saying? Oh, you must do. But if family relations in Sicily are like that and get forgotten as quickly as this, at least let me have back the clothes I left with you and I'll be glad to go on my way with only the Lord for company.'

The servant almost broke out laughing.

'Good man,' she said, 'I think you're dreaming.'

And even before she finished speaking, she was back inside with the window shut.

Andreuccio was now fully aware of his losses and the pain of the realization made him so angry it almost drove him wild. He could not recover what he had lost through words and he resorted to physical violence. He picked up a big stone and began savagely beating at the door again, only now with much more force. At this, many of the neighbours who had been woken up and were out of their beds started thinking that he was some no-gooder who was inventing the whole palaver to bother the good woman. When the banging got too much for them, they started calling out from their windows, as if they were the neighbourhood dogs barking all together at some stray intruder.

'It's an outrage!' they said. 'Coming at this hour of night to respectable women's houses with all this claptrap. Oh, go away for God's sake and please let us sleep! If you have anything to sort out with her, you can come back tomorrow. Just don't be such a blasted nuisance tonight!'

What they were saying perhaps encouraged the good Sicilian woman's pimp, who was inside the house, though he had not been seen or heard till now by Andreuccio. He came to the window and in his best horrible and savage voice called out loudly, 'Who's that down there?'

Andreuccio looked up when he heard this and saw someone who, so far as he could tell (which was not much), had the air of a man to be taken seriously. He had a thick black beard and was yawning and rubbing his eyes, as if he'd just awoken from deep sleep.

'I'm a brother of the lady of the house,' Andreuccio nervously replied.

The man did not wait for him to go on.

'I can't think,' he said in an even more intimidating voice than before, 'why I'm stopping myself from coming down there and giving you such a thrashing you won't ever move again. An irritating drunk of a donkey, that's what you must be, not letting anyone round here get any sleep tonight.'

With that he turned back inside and bolted the window.

Some of the neighbours knew what sort of a man he was and whispered a few fearful words of advice to Andreuccio.

'For God's sake,' they said, 'go away, good man, don't get yourself murdered down there! Go away for your own good.'

Being already terrified by the ruffian's voice and appearance, Andreuccio saw every reason for accepting this advice, which he felt was motivated by simple goodwill. He was now as dejected as anyone could be and saw no chance of recovering his money. He set off towards the part of the city he had come from following the serving girl earlier that day, aiming to get back to his inn, but with no idea of the way. Then, since the stench he could smell coming from him was disgusting, he decided to go towards the sea in order to wash himself. But he turned left and headed up a street called the Ruga Catalana.[4] This was taking him to the higher part of the city, when he happened to see in front two figures coming towards him with a lantern. He was afraid they might be part of the official watch or else just up to no good. He noticed an open building nearby and quietly crept in to try to avoid them. But it was as if they had been directed precisely to that spot. They, too, entered the building. One was carrying various tools round his neck, which he unloaded, and the two of them began looking them over and commenting on them.

At a certain point in their conversation, one of them said, 'What can it be? I can smell the worst stink I've ever smelt.' And then, lifting up the lantern a bit, they saw the miserable Andreuccio.

'Who's that there?' they asked, astounded.

When Andreuccio said nothing, they came over to him with the light and asked him what he was doing there in such a repulsive state. Andreuccio told them the whole story of what had happened to him. They guessed where it could have been and said to each other, 'It must have all happened at that villain Buttafuoco's.'[5]

'My good lad,' said one of them, turning to Andreuccio, 'you might have lost your money, but you have plenty reason for praising the Lord that you happened to have that fall and then couldn't get back into the house. If you hadn't fallen, you can be sure that you'd have been murdered as soon as you fell asleep, and then you'd have lost your life as well as your money. But what's the point of crying over it at this stage? You've as much chance of getting a penny back as of picking stars from the sky. You're likely to end up dead if that villain hears you've been blabbing.'

Then, after some conferring together, they put a proposal to him.

'Look, we feel sorry for you,' they said. 'So if you want to join us in a certain project we are en route to perform, we are of the definite opinion that your share of the profits will amount to much more than what you have lost.'

Andreuccio, in his desperate state, replied that he was ready and willing.

That day had seen the burial of a certain Archbishop of Naples called Messer Filippo Minutolo.[6] He had been buried in elaborate finery with a ruby ring on his finger worth more than five hundred gold florins. The two of them had in mind to detach it. They explained the scheme to Andreuccio, who let greed override his good sense, and the three of them set off.

Andreuccio still had a strong smell about him, as they proceeded towards the cathedral.

'Can't we find a way,' said one of the two at a certain point, 'for this companion of ours to have a wash somewhere to stop him stinking so horribly?'

'Yes,' said the other, 'we're near a well now. It's always had a pulley and a big bucket. Let's go over and give him a quick wash.'

When they reached the well they found the rope was there, but the bucket had been removed. So they decided to tie Andreuccio to the rope and lower him into the well. Once at the bottom, he would wash himself, and then, when he had done, he would give the rope a shake and they would pull him up.

So they moved into action and lowered Andreuccio into the well. But it so happened that some of the night watch were feeling thirsty because of the heat and also because they had been chasing after someone. They were coming towards the well to get a drink when the other two saw them and at once took to their heels, without any of the company coming after the water seeing them. Down in the well, Andreuccio, having finished washing, shook the rope a few times. The thirsty watchmen, who had now unstrapped their bucklers, their weapons and their overwear, began pulling on the rope, believing that it was attached to a big bucketful of water.

As soon as Andreuccio saw he was near the rim of the well, he let go of the rope and grabbed hold of the rim in his hands. The sight was enough to terrify the watchmen, who immediately, without a word, let go of the rope and ran off as fast as they could. Andreuccio was profoundly startled. If he had not kept a firm hold he would have fallen back into the well and perhaps have hurt himself badly or even finished up dead. Once he was finally out of the well, he found the abandoned weaponry, which he knew his companions had not been carrying, and was even more amazed. Nervous, unclear what was going on, bemoaning his misfortune, he decided to take himself off without touching anything and wandered away with no idea where he was going. He was walking along like this when he bumped into his two companions, who were coming back to pull him up out of the well. They were astonished and asked him who had actually done that. Andreuccio replied that he did not know, but gave them a full account of what had occurred and of what he had found by the well.

His companions realized what had happened and explained, laughing, why they had run away and who the people were who had pulled him up. Then, without wasting any more words, since it was already midnight, they all went off to the cathedral. They got in quite easily and reached the tomb, which was marble and very large. They used their irons to lift the cover, which was enormously heavy, raising it just enough for a single man to get inside, and then they propped it open.

When this was done, one of them asked, 'Who's going to go inside?'

'Not me,' said the other.

'Me neither,' said the first. 'But let Andreuccio go in.'

'I'm not doing that,' said Andreuccio.

Both of them turned on him.

'What do you mean you won't go in?' they said. 'By God, if you don't go in, we'll give you a bashing round the head with one of these iron poles and that'll be the end of you.'

This put the wind up Andreuccio. He went inside, thinking to himself as he did so, 'These two are making me enter the tomb in order to trick me. When I've passed them everything and am getting myself out again, they'll be off and I'll be left with nothing.'

He decided first and foremost to pocket his own share. He remembered the precious ring he had heard them discussing

and, as soon as he was in the tomb, he took it off the archbishop's finger and put it on his own. Then he passed them the
crosier, the mitre and the gloves and stripped the body down to
the shirt, passing them each item, saying that was all there was.
They protested that the ring must be somewhere and told him
to look everywhere. He replied that he couldn't find it and pretended to go on looking, keeping them waiting for some time.
But they were as canny as he was. They continued telling him
to keep looking, and then, picking their moment, they pulled
away the prop supporting the lid of the tomb and ran off,
leaving Andreuccio enclosed within. Anyone can guess how
Andreuccio felt when he heard the lid fall.

He tried many times to push up the lid with his head and
shoulders, but his efforts were useless. He was so overcome
with the anguish of it all that he passed out, collapsing on the
archbishop's dead body. And anyone who had seen the two of
them would have had difficulty deciding which was the more
lifeless, the archbishop or Andreuccio. When he came to his
senses, he broke into a flood of tears, foreseeing that he could
not avoid one of two ends. If no one came to open the tomb, he
was doomed to die of hunger and the stink among the worms
from the corpse. Or else, if people came and found him inside
the tomb, he would be hanged as a thief.

With these bleakly distressing thoughts going round in his
head, he heard movement in the church and many people talking. They were, he gathered, going to do what he and his
companions had already done. This sharply increased his terror. But when they had opened the tomb and propped up the
lid, they began to argue about who should go inside, which
none of them wanted to do. At last, after much dispute, a priest
said, 'What are you frightened of? Do you think he's going to
eat you? The dead don't eat people. I'll be the one to go in.'
With this he leant over the edge of the tomb, turned his head
outwards and swung his legs inside in order to lower himself
down. Andreuccio saw what was going on, jumped up and
seized the priest by one of his legs, and made as if to pull him
down inside. When the priest felt himself being pulled, he let
out an enormous shriek and scrambled out of the tomb as fast

as he could. This terrified the rest of them. Leaving the tomb open, they took off as if they were being chased by a hundred thousand devils.

Seeing them go, Andreuccio clambered out of the tomb, happier than he could have hoped, and left the church by the way he had come in. It was almost daylight as he walked off, trusting to luck, with the ring on his finger. But he reached the seafront and finished up somehow at his inn, where he discovered that the merchants he had come with and the innkeeper had been worrying about him all night. He told them what had happened to him and they all opined that he should take the innkeeper's advice and leave Naples immediately. He hastily did so and returned to Perugia, with his funds now invested in a ring, after having set out to buy horses.

9

The Trials of Madonna Zinevra

Bernabò da Genova, tricked by Ambrogiuolo, loses his money and orders his innocent wife to be killed. She survives and, disguised as a man, becomes the Sultan's servant. She discovers the deceiver and brings Bernabò to Alexandria, where Ambrogiuolo is punished and she resumes female clothing. She and her husband return wealthy to Genova.

Elissa had done her duty with her moving story.[1] Filomena, the queen for the day, and someone with a fine, full figure and a particularly attractive face and smile, now settled herself into position.

'The terms agreed with Dioneo[2] must be kept to,' she said. 'And so, since he and I are the only ones left to tell their stories, I shall tell mine first and he will be the last to speak, which was the favour he asked for.'

With that she began her story:

'He who practises deceit ends up at his victim's feet' is a saying you often hear ordinary people come out with. The truth of it doesn't seem provable by reasoned argument, only by the things that happen in the world. What I find myself wanting to do now, dearest ladies, is to give you a demonstration of how true the saying is, while keeping at the same time to our theme today. And you shouldn't find what you hear valueless, since it will help you to be wary of men who deceive you.

A number of important Italian merchants were once staying in a Paris inn, each one with different business to transact as usual. One evening during their stay, after a cheerful dinner together, they began talking of this and that. One thing led to another and eventually the talk came round to the wives they had left at home.

One of them started joking. 'I don't know what mine's up to,' he said, 'but I do know this: when a young girl I fancy here falls into my hands, I put the love I feel for my wife to one side and have as good a time as I can with the local talent.'

Another agreed. 'I do the same,' he said, 'since, if I start believing that my wife is playing away, she will be, and, if I don't believe she is, she still will be. So it's tit for tat. Do as you will be done by, I say.'

A third joined in with an almost identical opinion. And all in all everyone seemed to agree that the wives they had left behind wouldn't want to waste any time.

Only one of them said the opposite. His name was Bernabò Lomellin[3] and he was from Genova. He declared that by some special grace of heaven he had in his wife a lady with all the best qualities that a lady should have and most of those you might expect in a knight or a squire. In fact, he said, there might well be no one like her in the whole of Italy. She was physically attractive, still very youthful and quick and lithe in her movements. She could do anything a lady was expected to do, such as silkwork and the like, better than anyone else. Besides that, he said, you couldn't find a waiting-man or any sort of domestic servant who could serve at a lord's table as well as she did, or as attentively, since she was so polite, perceptive and discreet. And then he went on to praise her riding ability, her skill with falcons, her reading and writing and the way she could draw up accounts better than if she were a merchant. From there, via much further eulogizing, he eventually came round to the subject under discussion and asserted on oath that it would be impossible to find a truer or purer wife than she was. So he was absolutely sure that if he stayed away from home for ten years or even for ever, she would never start any sort of nonsense with another man.

One of the merchants taking part in the discussion was a youngish man called Ambrogiuolo da Piacenza. This last glorification of Bernabò's wife made him fall about laughing and he mockingly asked him if the Emperor had given him a special privilege over everyone else. Bernabò was slightly irritated and replied that it was not the Emperor who had granted him this grace, but God, whose powers were somewhat greater than the Emperor's.

'Bernabò,' said Ambrogiuolo, 'I have no doubt at all that you believe you are speaking the truth, but in my opinion you have not taken a proper look at the real nature of things. If you had, I can't see you being so dim as not to have noticed a few facts that might make you speak about all this with more caution. The rest of us have said some very frank things about our wives, but you mustn't think that we think our wives are somehow different from yours. It was an awareness implanted in us by nature that made us speak in this way. I want to say a few words to you on the subject.

'I have always been of the understanding that man is the noblest of all the mortal creatures that were created by God. Then after him comes woman. But man is the more perfect being. That is what is generally believed and what the facts seem to indicate is so. Since he has more perfection, it follows, without any chance of error, that he must have more constancy of purpose, and that's what he does have, since women are universally more unreliable. Why this is so could be proved by a whole lot of arguments from natural science. But I intend to leave these out of this present discussion. Just think how a man – in spite of this greater constancy of purpose – still can't stop himself giving in to desire for a woman he finds attractive (and let's leave aside being faced by a woman who simply asks for it) and then how he doesn't stop at desire, but does everything he can to be together with her, and how this doesn't happen once a month, but countless times a day. If all that is so, what hope can you have that a woman – made by nature to be more changeful – will be able to resist the pleading and enticing and giving of gifts and so on and so forth that a male lover with his wits about him will resort to? Do you really believe she'll be able to hold out? You can say it as much as you like, but I don't believe you believe it. And you yourself say that your wife is a woman and made of flesh and bone like the others. If that is so, she must have the same desires as other women and have the

same capacity to control these natural appetites as other
women. Therefore, however true and faithful she is, it is quite
possible that she will do what other women do and it is illogical
to deny anything that is possible or assert its opposite as fiercely
as you are doing.'

'I'm a merchant,' Bernabò responded, 'not a cod intellectual,
and I'll give you a merchant's reply. Of course I recognize that
what you're suggesting can happen with silly women who have
no self-respect. But those with sense are so set on preserving
their good name that they become stronger than the men who
couldn't care less about it. And my wife is one of those.'

'The truth is,' said Ambrogiuolo, 'if every time they went in
for malarkey of this sort they found a horn sprouting out of
their foreheads, which testified to what they had been up to, I
can well believe that not many would go in for it. But forget the
horn. You don't see a print or a mark on those with any sense.
Disgrace and dishonour consist only in what's plain to the eye.
So when they can do it undercover, then they do it, unless
they're witless and just give up. But one thing's indisputable.
The only one who stays pure is the one who was never asked
for it or who asked for it and didn't get it. Now I know the
good, natural reasons why this should be so, but I wouldn't go
on about it as much as I am doing if I hadn't put it to the test
numerous times. Let me tell you that if I found myself near
your ever so saintly lady wife, I'm convinced that in no time at
all I'd have her doing what I've managed with the rest.'

Bernabò was now becoming angry.

'A dispute like this could go on a long time,' he replied.
'You'd say one thing and I'd say another and in the end we'd
have got nowhere much. But since you say that they're all per-
suadable and that you're so good at it, and I want to convince
you that my wife is pure and honest, I'm ready for my head to
be cut off if you can bring her to do the sort of thing you like
doing. And if you can't, all I want you to lose is a thousand
gold florins.'

Ambrogiuolo had already got himself worked up over the
issue.

'Bernabò,' he retorted, 'I've no idea what I could do with your blood if I won. But if you want to see my arguments put to the test, put down five thousand of your own gold florins, which you can't value as much as your head, against a thousand of mine. You haven't stipulated any time limit. But I commit myself now to going to Genova and then, within three months of leaving here, having my way with your wife. As proof I shall bring back some of the most precious things she has and sufficient detailed evidence to make you yourself admit that I'm telling the truth. My only condition is that you promise solemnly not to return to Genova before the three months are up, or to write to her at all about any of this.'

Bernabò said that he was very happy with the proposal. The other merchants, who realized that the outcome could be deeply unpleasant, did what they could to stop them going ahead, but the blood of the two men was up. Ignoring the wishes of the rest, they wrote out and signed a contract of mutual obligation.

Once the contract was in place, Bernabò stayed where he was and Ambrogiuolo went off to Genova as quickly as he could. Within a few days of arriving he had learned from some prudent enquiries the name of the area where the lady was living and what kind of person she was. What he learned was what he had heard from Bernabò, and more, and he found himself thinking that his project was quite crazy. However, he made the acquaintance of a not so well-off woman who often went round to the lady's house and to whom she was much attached. Since he was otherwise stymied, he resorted to bribery and corruption. He had a chest specially made to fit him, which he then got the woman to have deposited in the lady's house and, what is more, in her bedroom. Then, following his instructions, the woman gave the lady the impression that she was going away somewhere and asked her to look after it for a few days.

So the chest stayed in the room and that night, when Ambrogiuolo could tell that the lady was asleep, he opened it with some tools he had equipped himself with and stepped out quietly into the room. There was a light burning and he began taking stock of the arrangement of the room and the pictures and other noteworthy things in it and fixing them in his memory.

Then he crept over to the bed. Checking that the lady and a young girl she had with her were deeply asleep, he gently uncovered her entire body. He saw that she was as beautiful naked as she was clothed, but could not see any distinguishing mark to report on, except for something he made out below her left breast. It turned out to be a mole with a few fine blonde hairs round it that shone like gold. After taking this in, he quietly covered her again, although seeing how beautiful she was he felt a strong urge to chance his life and stretch out at her side. But after what he had heard about her icy hostility to tomfoolery of that sort, he decided not to take the risk. Instead, having spent most of the night doing nothing in particular in the room, he took a purse and an overgown from a strongbox, together with a ring and a belt, and put them all in the chest, before getting back into it himself and locking it shut like before. He spent two nights like this without the lady noticing anything. Early on the third day the nice woman came back for her chest as instructed and had it brought back to the place from which she had originally sent it. Ambrogiuolo climbed out, paid her what he had promised and set off with his booty for Paris as fast as possible, arriving well before the date set.

Once there he called together the merchants who had been present when the bet had been made and the sums stipulated. Then, in Bernabò's presence, he declared that he had won the amount promised, because he had carried out what he had boasted he would do. To show that what he said was true, he sketched out first of all the layout of the bedroom, including the pictures, and then he showed the various things belonging to Bernabò's wife which he had brought with him, stating that he had received them directly from her. Bernabò admitted that the room was as he said and, what's more, that he recognized those things as having indeed belonged to his lady wife. But, he said, Ambrogiuolo could have found out from one or another of the servants what the room was like and obtained the things in a similar way. So unless he had something further to say, he didn't think that there was enough here to show that he had won.

'It should really have been adequate,' said Ambrogiuolo at this. 'But since you want me to say something further, I shall do just that. Let me tell you that your wife, Madonna Zinevra, has under her left breast a neat little mole with around it maybe six fine blonde hairs that shine like gold.'

When Bernabò heard this, he felt the same stabbing pain as if a knife had been plunged in his heart. Though he had not said a word, the change in his face gave a very clear signal that Ambrogiuolo was speaking the truth. 'Gentlemen,' he said after a while, 'what Ambrogiuolo says is true. So, since he has won, he may come whenever he wishes and be paid what he is owed.'

So the next day Ambrogiuolo received payment in full.

Bernabò left Paris and travelled on towards Genova feeling nothing for his wife but destructive fury. Nearing his destination, he decided not to enter the city and stopped off a good twenty miles away at a property he owned. Instead, he sent on a particularly trusted member of his staff with two horses and some letters, informing his wife that he had returned and asking her to come with the man to join him. But he secretly gave instructions to the man that as soon as he and the lady reached what he judged to be a suitable spot, he should quite ruthlessly kill her and then make his way back. The man arrived in Genova, handed over the letters, conveyed his messages as instructed and was given a delighted welcome by the lady. The next morning she and he mounted their horses and set off for Bernabò's property.

They rode along together, talking on various topics, and eventually entered a deep, lonely ravine, hemmed in by high, tree-lined crags. It was, the man thought, a place where he could carry out with impunity his master's instructions. He drew out his knife and seized the lady's arm.

'My lady,' he said, 'commit your soul to God. You are going no further, because you must now die.'

The lady was terrified when she saw the knife and heard him speak like this. 'Have mercy in God's name!' she cried. 'And before you kill me at least tell me what wrong I've done you to make you do such a thing!'

'My lady,' said the man, 'you have not wronged me in any way. How you have wronged your husband I don't know either, but he ordered me to kill you during this ride and not to show you the slightest pity. He threatened to have me hanged if I didn't do it. You know very well how much I'm bound to him and how I can't say no to anything he tells me to do. God knows, I feel really sorry for you, but I can't do anything else.'

The lady was in tears.

'Oh, have mercy in God's name!' she said. 'Don't choose to become the murderer of a person who has never done you wrong, just to oblige a third party. God, who is all-knowing, knows that I have never done anything that justifies my husband rewarding me in this way. But let's now consider this. You can, if you wish to do so, act in a way that will please God, your master and myself. That is, you take these clothes I have on, giving me just your jerkin and your hood, and go back with them to your master, who is also mine, and tell him you have killed me. I swear by the life you will have granted me that I shall simply vanish into thin air and not a word about me will trickle back from wherever I go, either to you or to him or to anyone else round here.'

The man was a very unwilling murderer and easily moved to pity. He took her fine clothing and passed her his old jerkin and hood, leaving her also some coins he had with him. Then, begging her to disappear completely from those parts, he left her standing there in the ravine and rode off to rejoin his master. He told him that not only had his orders been carried out, but that there were wolves around the body when he left. After a while Bernabò made his way back to Genova, where he was strongly criticized once the business became public knowledge.

The lady had been left alone and destitute. When night fell, she made her way in her makeshift disguise to a nearby hamlet. There she obtained from an old woman what she needed to adapt the jerkin to her size, and when that was shortened, to make a pair of mariner's leggings out of her shift. When she also cut her hair short, she looked just like a sailor.

She then found her way to the coast, where she encountered by pure chance a Catalan nobleman called Señor En Cararch. He was the captain of a ship moored a little way out and had come ashore at Albenga[4] to get fresh water at a spring. She entered into conversation with him, which resulted in her being taken on to serve at his table and embarked on the ship under the name of Sicurano da Finale.[5] Fitted out with better clothes by the nobleman, Sicurano proved a virtuous and attentive servant whose talents were greatly appreciated.

Not long afterwards the Catalan sailed with a cargo of goods to Alexandria, including some trained peregrine falcons for the Sultan, which he presented to him. The Sultan gave him dinner several times, during which he observed how well Sicurano, who was always in attendance, carried out his duties. He was so impressed that he asked the Catalan if he could have him. Though the Catalan was not happy about it, he let him go. Before long Sicurano's excellent work had won him as much grace and favour from the Sultan as it had from the Catalan.

Time went by and eventually the moment in the year came round when a great number of Saracen and Christian merchants were due to gather for a trade fair at Acre,[6] which was under the Sultan's lordship. To ensure the safety of the merchants and their goods, the Sultan would always send along (in addition to some other officials) one or other of his senior men with the troops who were to keep guard. He began to think as the date came closer that the man for the job was Sicurano, who by now knew the language very well, and made his decision accordingly. So Sicurano arrived in Acre as lord and captain of the guard of merchants and merchandise. He performed all the duties associated with his position well and with proper attention, and would walk around inspecting what was going on, meeting many merchants from Pisa, Sicily, Genova, Venice and elsewhere in Italy, and gladly spending time chatting with them out of nostalgia for his homeland. On one occasion he happened to have stopped off at a Venetian duty-free warehouse when his eyes fell on some jewels among which he saw a purse and a belt that he quickly recognized as having once been his. He was amazed, but let his face give nothing away and asked in a pleasant voice who was the owner and whether they were for sale.

The fact was that Ambrogiuolo da Piacenza had arrived on a Venetian ship with a whole array of goods. When he heard that the captain of the guard had been asking who the items belonged to, he came forward and announced, laughing, 'Sir, those things are mine and I'm not selling them. But if they've taken your fancy, I shall be glad to make you a present of them.'

Seeing him laugh, Sicurano guessed that he hadn't a clue who he was. All the same his face showed no emotion.

'Perhaps you're laughing,' he queried, 'because you see a man-at-arms like myself asking about this feminine stuff?'

'Sir,' said Ambrogiuolo, 'that's not what makes me laugh. I'm laughing at the way I came by them.'

'Well, God grant you success,' said Sicurano, 'only tell us how you did that, assuming it's something that can be decently talked about.'

'Sir,' said Ambrogiuolo, 'these were given to me with a few other things by a noble Genovese lady called Madonna Zinevra, the wife of Bernabò Lomellin, the night I spent with her. She begged me to keep them out of her love for me. I laughed just now, because I remembered Bernabò's idiotic behaviour. He was so out of his mind that he bet five thousand florins against a thousand that I wouldn't manage to get her to pleasure me. But I did and I won the bet. He should just have punished himself for his mindless stupidity, not her, who just did what all women do, but he came back from Paris to Genova and, as I heard, had her put to death.'

Listening to this, Sicurano instantly understood the reason for Bernabò's anger and realized that the man standing there was the cause of all his troubles. He made his mind up not to let him get away with it. He put on a show of finding the story a good one and took steps to build up a friendship with him. He was so successful that, once the fair was over, he managed to cajole Ambrogiuolo into coming back with him with all his goods to Alexandria. There he set up a warehouse for him and put a fair amount of his own money in his hands. Ambrogiuolo was happy enough to stay on, envisaging great profits for himself. Sicurano could barely wait now to give Bernabò proof of his innocence. He made use of some big Genovese merchants operating in Alexandria, and on some pretext he dreamt up was able to get him to come over. Bernabò's own business was in a poor state and Sicurano had him quietly lodged with some friends until he judged that it was time to do what he had in mind.

He had already arranged for Ambrogiuolo to tell his tale before the Sultan, and amused him with it. But once he knew Bernabò had arrived, he thought it best not to delay things any further. Picking an opportune moment, he got the Sultan to agree to have Ambrogiuolo and Bernabò summoned to appear before him, and then, in Bernabò's presence, to extract from Ambrogiuolo the truth of what he boasted had happened with Bernabò's wife, using force if a softer approach didn't work.

So Ambrogiuolo and Bernabò appeared before the Sultan and a crowd of onlookers. The Sultan, with an implacable air, ordered Ambrogiuolo to tell the truth about how he had won the five thousand florins from Bernabò. Ambrogiuolo felt he could rely most on Sicurano, who was also there, but Sicurano gave him an angry look and threatened him with serious torture if he did not tell the truth. This attack from two sides frightened him and allowed him no room for manoeuvre. So, expecting that the only punishment he would face would be to have to return the articles and the five thousand gold florins, there in the presence of Bernabò and everyone else, he gave a clear account of what had happened.

When he finished, Sicurano, acting on the Sultan's behalf, immediately turned to Bernabò and asked him, 'And what was your reaction to this falsehood about your lady?'

'I was overcome by rage at the loss of my money,' he replied, 'and by the disgrace which I thought my wife had inflicted on me. I had one of my men slaughter her. He reported back that she was immediately devoured by a pack of wolves.'

All this was said in the Sultan's presence. He heard and understood everything, but still did not know what Sicurano, as the one who had requested and organized the interrogation, was driving at. Then Sicurano addressed him as follows:

'My lord, you can see clearly how much that virtuous lady can glory in her lover and husband. The lover dishonours her by ruining her good name with his lies and at the same time reduces her husband to poverty. The husband is more willing to believe lies from someone else than what long personal experience should have told him was the truth and has her killed and eaten by wolves. In addition, the lover and the husband feel such love and concern for her that – in spite of all the time they have spent with her – neither of them recognizes her. I should like you, sir, to be fully aware just what each of these two deserves. But, if you are ready to grant me the special grace of punishing the deceiver and pardoning the person deceived, I shall produce the lady here, in your presence and in theirs.'

It was a matter on which the Sultan was prepared to let Sicurano have his way completely. He agreed to his request and told him to produce the lady. Bernabò, who believed she was dead, was stunned. Ambrogiuolo guessed now that he was in trouble and was frightened that something much worse than paying up was in store. Unsure whether there were grounds for hope or whether he should be even more afraid, he stood waiting for her arrival in an even more bewildered state.

Once the Sultan had granted the request, Sicurano burst into tears, threw himself on his knees before him, cast off his masculine voice and almost simultaneously stopped making any effort to behave like a man.

'My lord,' he said, 'I am that wretched and unfortunate Zinevra! I have spent six years traipsing the world disguised as a man, after being falsely and criminally maligned by this treacherous Ambrogiuolo here, and then handed over to one of his minions by this other paragon of cruelty and iniquity to be murdered and left for the wolves to eat!'

Then she tore open the front of her clothing and showed her bosom, making it plain to the Sultan and everyone else that she was a woman. Turning round, she furiously laid into Ambrogiuolo, demanding that he should say whenever it could have been that he had sex with her, as he had been boasting earlier. He said nothing, having now recognized her and been shamed almost into losing his voice.

Having always taken her to be a man, the Sultan was astounded at what he saw and heard, so much so that more than once he thought he was hearing and seeing things in a dream, rather than in real life. But at last, once he had got over his astonishment and grasped the truth, he had only the highest praise for this Zinevra, who till a few moments ago had been called Sicurano, commending her conduct, her constancy, her manner and all her excellent virtues. He had appropriately fine women's clothes brought for her, and also ladies to act as her companions. Then, in accordance with her request, he did not have Bernabò put to death as he deserved. For his part, Bernabò threw himself in tears at her feet as soon as he recognized her, and begged her forgiveness. And however unworthy he was, forgive him she did in a more than kindly way, drawing him to his feet and enfolding him in a tender embrace that showed he was still her husband.

The Sultan next ordered that Ambrogiuolo should be taken to one of the highest points in the city, tied to a stake and his body smeared with honey, and then not to be untied until such a moment as the stake fell down of its own accord. This was duly carried out. He then ordered that the money belonging to Ambrogiuolo should be assigned to the lady, a sum which added up to something more than ten thousand Spanish doubloons. After that he arranged a superb celebration, honouring Bernabò as Madonna Zinevra's husband and Zinevra herself as a truly redoubtable being, presenting her with an abundance of jewels and gold and silver tableware, plus money amounting to more than another ten thousand doubloons. Then he had a boat fitted out for them, and, once the celebrations in their honour were over, he gave them permission to leave and to sail back to Genova at their own pleasure. They arrived home a very wealthy and happy couple and were received with all possible honours, especially Madonna Zinevra, who everybody had believed was dead. For the rest of her life she was rated someone of outstanding moral worth and strength of character.

Ambrogiuolo died in agony on the very day he was tied to the stake and smeared with honey, tortured to death by the bluebottles, wasps and horseflies that abound in that country and which ate his body down to the bones. Held together by the sinews, the bleached skeleton hung there for a long time without being moved, a testament to his wickedness for all who saw it. Thus it was that he who had practised deceit ended up at his victim's feet.

10

Ricciardo da Chinzica
Loses His Wife

Paganino da Monaco robs Messer Ricciardo da Chinzica of his wife. Finding out where she is, the latter goes and makes friends with Paganino. When he asks for her back, Paganino agrees to let her go if she wishes. She refuses and, after Messer Ricciardo's death, becomes Paganino's wife.

Everyone in the honourable company highly commended the story their queen had told, particularly Dioneo, who was the only one left to speak that day. When he was through praising it, he had this to say:

My lovely ladies, there is something in the queen's story that has made me change my mind. I was intending to tell you one story and have decided to tell you another instead. That something is the bestial stupidity of Bernabò, even if in the end everything turned out well. It's a thing you find also in all the other men who convince themselves of what he was apparently convinced of. They go off on their travels, have fun with one bit of stuff here and another there, and imagine that their wives are sitting at home twiddling their thumbs, as if we who are born among women and grow up among them and live with them, don't really know what they fancy. I'll show you with the story I'm going to tell how silly men like this are and how much sillier still are another lot – those who rate themselves stronger than nature, believing that jiggery-pokery will make them able to do things they can't do at all and struggling to drag others along with them, when the real nature of the person being dragged won't put up with it.

There was once a judge in Pisa with more brains than muscle called Messer Ricciardo da Chinzica,[1] who may have thought that what worked well with his studies would satisfy a wife too. Being very rich, he was able to dedicate considerable time and effort to looking for a good-looking young lady to marry, whereas, if had been able to give himself the sort of professional counsel he gave to others, good looks and youth were just what he should have run away from. And he managed it: Ser Lotto Gualandi[2] gave him one of his daughters in marriage. She was called Bartolommea and she was one of the best-looking and most fanciable girls in Pisa, although admittedly there aren't many there who don't look like hairy spiders. The judge took her home with great razzmatazz and the marriage feast was magnificent.

When he finally geared himself up for the actual consummation, he just about brought it off. But being scrawny, wizened and not exactly spunky, next morning he had to have a glass of fortified wine, some sweet biscuits and other pick-me-ups before he could re-enter the world of the living. The experience gave the judge a better idea of his capabilities than he had had before and he began teaching his wife a calendar of saints' days of the kind that schoolboys pore over looking for holidays and which might have been made in Ravenna.[3] As he now showed her, there wasn't a day that wasn't a saint's day, or rather every day had a multitude of them. Reverence for these demanded, as he demonstrated on various grounds, that man and woman should abstain from acts of congress. Then he threw in fasts, the four Ember days,[4] evening vigils for the apostles and hundreds of other saints, Fridays, Saturdays, the Lord's Day, the whole of Lent, certain phases of the moon and endless other special cases, no doubt assuming that the breaks from court work he enjoyed from time to time applied just as much to women in bed. So this was how he managed things for a long time, with his wife becoming seriously depressed from being given at best a monthly treat, while he always kept a watchful eye on her, just in case someone else gave her lessons about working days like the ones he had given her about saints' days.

Since the next summer was very hot, Messer Ricciardo found himself wanting to go off to a beautiful property he had near Monte Nero,[5] where he could relax and enjoy the air for a few days. With him he took his lovely wife. To give her some entertainment while they were there, one day he organized a fishing trip. The two of them sailed out on small boats to watch the spectacle; he on one with the fishermen, she on the other with some ladies. They were so captivated that they drifted several miles along the coast almost without realizing it. But while they were gazing in wrapt attention, a sloop suddenly came on the scene, belonging to Paganino da Mare,[6] a celebrated corsair of the time. Once it sighted the boats, it set a course straight for them. They were unable to get away fast enough and Paganino caught up with the boat with the ladies in it. As soon as he laid eyes on Messer Ricciardo's beautiful wife, he stopped wanting any other booty and whisked her into his sloop under the eyes of her husband, who was now on shore, and sailed away.

It doesn't take much to imagine how upset the judge was by the sight, given that he was so jealous that he was fearful of the very air she breathed. In Pisa and elsewhere, he started fruitlessly complaining about the criminal behaviour of corsairs, but without discovering who had carried off his wife or where they had taken her.

When Paganino took in how beautiful she was, he felt that things were looking up. Not having a wife, he thought he might hang on to her permanently and began gently soothing her tears, which were copious. He had long ago thrown away saints' calendars and forgot all about feast days and holidays. That night he consoled her with some action, on the grounds that words had not helped much during the day. His consolations were so effective that the judge and his rules had gone entirely out of her head before they reached Monaco, and she began to have the time of her life with Paganino. And once he had got her there, he not only consoled her day and night, but honoured her as his wife.

After a while Messer Ricciardo got wind of the whereabouts of his good lady. Ardently desiring to do something and believing that no one else could manage to do what needed to be done, he made up his mind to go and get her himself, being prepared to pay out any amount of money to recover her. So he set to sea and sailed to Monaco. Once there he caught sight of his wife and she caught sight of him, as she reported back to Paganino that evening, also informing him what her husband's intentions were. When Messer Ricciardo saw Paganino the next morning, he went up to him and quickly started an easy, friendly conversation with him, while Paganino pretended all the while not to recognize him and waited for him to get to the point. When he judged the moment had arrived, deploying his best abilities in the most ingratiating way possible, Messer Ricciardo disclosed the reason why he had come to Monaco, begging Paganino to take as much money as he wanted and give him back the lady.

'Sir,' replied Paganino with a cheerful expression on his face, 'you are very welcome here. My reply in brief is as follows; it is true I have a young woman in my house, though I don't know whether she's your wife or someone else's. I don't know anything about her except what I've gathered from her during her stay with me. If you are her husband, as you say, I'll take you to her, since you seem to me a likeable gentleman and I'm sure she'll recognize you very well. If she says that the situation is as you say and wishes to go away with you, then, since I do love a likeable man such as you, you can give me the amount you yourself decide on for a ransom. But if the situation should be different, it would be indecent for you to try to take her from me, since I've got youth on my side and can hold a woman in my arms as well as any man, particularly one who is more attractive than any girl I've ever seen.'

'She certainly is my wife,' said Messer Ricciardo, 'as you'll soon see if you take me to where she is. She'll fling her arms round my neck straight away. So I won't ask for the terms to be different from those you yourself have proposed.'

'Let's go then,' said Paganino.

So they walked off to Paganino's house and went into a reception-room, from where Paganino sent for her. She appeared from a chamber properly and neatly dressed and went over where Messer Ricciardo was waiting with Paganino. There she addressed only the sort of remarks to Messer Ricciardo that she might have made to any other stranger who had come with

Paganino to his house. The judge, who was expecting to be given a rapturous welcome, was amazed.

'Could it be,' he began to wonder, 'that depression and my protracted sufferings ever since I lost her have altered me so much that she doesn't recognize me?'

'Lady,' he said, 'taking you fishing has cost me dear. No one has suffered as much as I have since I lost you, and here you are seeming not to recognize me, given the unfriendly way you're talking. Can't you see that I'm your Messer Ricciardo, who's come here to pay whatever sum is demanded by this fine gentleman in whose house we find ourselves, so that I can have you back and take you away from here? He's being kind enough to restore you to me for a sum of my own choosing.'

The lady turned to him and gave him a faint smile.

'Are you addressing me, sir?' she asked. 'You should check you've not mistaken me for somebody else. As far as I'm concerned, I don't recall ever seeing you before.'

'It's you who should check what you're saying,' said Messer Ricciardo. 'Look at me properly. If you're willing to do a little serious recalling, you're bound to see that I'm your very own Ricciardo da Chinzica.'

'Sir, you'll forgive me,' said the lady, 'but it's not as right and proper as you imagine for me to give you a lengthy looking over. All the same I've looked at you enough to know that I've never seen you before.'

Messer Ricciardo imagined that she was acting in this way out of fear of Paganino and did not want to admit to knowing him in his presence. So after a few moments, he asked Paganino if he would be so kind as to let him speak with the lady alone in her chamber. Paganino said that he was happy to do so, on condition that he didn't start kissing her against her will. Then he told the lady to go with him into the chamber, listen to what he wanted to say and to give him whatever reply she felt like.

Once the lady and Messer Ricciardo were in the chamber by themselves and had sat themselves down, Messer Ricciardo began entreating her. 'Oh, heart of my life, my own sweet soul, my one hope, don't you recognize your Ricciardo, who loves you more than he loves himself? How can it be? Have

I altered so much? Oh, lovely darling girl, at least give me a little look.'

The lady broke out laughing and wouldn't let him go on. 'You are very well aware,' she said, 'that I've not such a bad memory that I don't know you are Messer Ricciardo da Chinzica, my husband. But you made a poor show of knowing me as long as I was with you. You're not as wise as you want people to think you are, and you never were. If you had been, you really should have had the wit to see that I was young, fresh and frisky, and then have consequently acknowledged that young ladies require something else apart from food and clothing, though modesty forbids them to spell it out. But you know how you managed all that.

'You shouldn't have married, if you liked studying law more than studying your wife. Not that I thought you were much of a judge. You seemed more like a crier calling out holy days and feast days, you knew them so well, not to mention fast days and overnight vigils. Let me tell you, that if you had given as many days off to the labourers working your lands as you did to the one who should have been working my little plot, you'd not have harvested one grain of corn. By chance I've met with this man here, chosen by God, because he shows a compassionate concern for my youth. And I stay with him in this chamber, where no one knows what a feast day is – I mean, those feast days that you celebrated one after another, piously serving the Lord in preference to the ladies. Saturdays don't pass through that door, neither do Fridays, vigils, Ember Days or Lent, which just goes on and on. No, it's all work, day and night, banging away all the time. As soon as the bell rang for matins this morning, there we were back at it, doing the same job again and again, as I know very well. So I intend to stay and work with him while I'm young, and keep feast days and penances and fasts for when I'm old. Get out of here as soon as you can and good luck to you. Go and keep your saints' days as much as you like without me.'

Messer Ricciardo's distress at hearing her speak like this was unbearable.

'Oh, sweet soul of mine,' he said, when he realized she had finished, 'what are you saying? Aren't you bothered at all about your family's honour or your own? Do you want to stay here as this fellow's tart living in mortal sin, rather than be my wife in Pisa? He'll get fed up with you and throw you out in total disgrace. But I'll always hold you dear and you'll always be the lawful mistress of my house, even if I didn't want to be your husband. Oh, please listen. Are you going to let this unbridled, immoral lust make you forget your honour and forget me, when I love you more than my very life? Please, my dear love, don't say things like that any more, just come away with me. Now that I know what you want, I'll really make an effort from now on. So, sweetheart, change your mind, come away with me. I've been so miserable since you were carried off.'

'Now that there's nothing to be done about it,' said the lady, 'I don't see how anyone apart from me can be squeamish over my honour. I just wish my family had been a bit more squeamish when they gave me to you! But since they didn't bother about my honour then, I don't intend to bother about theirs now. If my sin's mortar, I'll stay stuck in it like a pestle. So don't you worry about me. And what's more, let me tell you I feel like Paganino's wife here, while I felt like your tart in Pisa, what with lunar charts and geometric squarings having to align your planet and mine, while here Paganino has me in his arms all night, squeezing me, biting me, and the state he leaves me in God alone can tell you. Then you say you'll make an effort. Doing what? Waiting for something to happen? Straightening it by hand? I can tell you've turned into a redoubtable knight since I saw you last! Go on, do your best to come to life. But you can't manage it. I don't think you belong in this world, you look such a wasted, miserable little wimp. And another thing. If he leaves me – which I don't think he's inclined to do as long I want to stay with him – I've no intention of ever coming back to you. Squeeze you till you squeaked and you still wouldn't produce a spoonful of sauce, which meant that when I was with you I just lost out and paid out. I'm after better returns somewhere else. To go back to where I started, I tell you there are no feast days and no vigils here, where I mean to stay. So leave as quickly as you can and the Lord be with you. If you don't, I'll start shouting that you're forcing yourself on me.'

Messer Ricciardo saw the game was up, recognizing there and then the folly in marrying a young wife without the appropriate wherewithal. He left the chamber in a saddened, suffering state and spoke a lot of waffle to Paganino, which got him nowhere. In the end, he left the lady and returned to Pisa, empty-handed. The blow affected his mind and, when he was walking around the city and someone greeted him or asked him a question, he would only reply, 'A horrid hole hates a holy day.'

It wasn't long before he died. When Paganino heard, knowing how much the lady loved him, he took her as his lawful wedded wife. Thereafter, with no thought for holy days or vigils or Lent, they worked their patch as much as their limbs would let them and had a wonderful time together. So, my dear ladies, that is why I think that friend Bernabò[7] was heading for an almighty tumble when he argued with Ambrogiuolo the way he did.

DAY THREE

The Second Day of the Decameron *ends and the Third begins, in which, under the rule of Neifile, the members of the party tell stories about people who, through their own efforts, acquire something they much desire or recover something they have lost.*

I

Masetto da Lamporecchio Helps Out in the Convent

Masetto da Lamporecchio makes himself deaf and dumb and becomes a gardener in a convent, where the sisters all hurry to get into bed with him.

Lovely ladies,[1] there are many men and many women who are so witless as to be convinced that, once a young woman has a white band on her head and a black cowl round her shoulders, she is no longer female and no longer feels female urges, as if making her a nun had turned her to stone. If they do hear something contrary to their belief, they become as flustered as if some monstrous crime against nature had been committed, forgetting or ignoring how their own freedom to do what they like doesn't mean they are ever sated, not to mention the powerful effects of inactivity and frustration. Then similarly there are many others convinced that hoeing, digging, a stodgy diet and a generally hard life utterly destroy the sexual appetites of those who work the land and make them coarse and sluggish mentally. I now have the pleasure, following the queen's command and not departing from the subject she proposed, of telling you a little story that will make it plain to you just how mistaken are all those with ideas like these.

There is a convent in our region which for years was famous for its sanctity. It still is, though I shan't tell you its name in order not to diminish its reputation in any way. Not so long ago the inhabitants were reduced to eight ladies and an abbess, all of them young. They had a fine vegetable garden and a good-natured little man who looked after it. Since the gardener was not happy with his wages, he got the ladies' bailiff to pay him his due and returned to Lamporecchio,[2] the place he was from originally. Among the people who welcomed him back was a young farm labourer by the name of Masetto, who had a strong, sturdy build and, for a peasant, a personable appearance and attractive features. Masetto asked him where he had been all this time and the old boy, whose name was Nuto, told him. Masetto then asked him what sort of work he did for the convent.

'I looked after a fine, big garden for them,' said Nuto. 'Then I'd sometimes go to the wood for firewood or draw up water or do other jobs of that sort. But the wages those ladies paid me were so mean I could barely buy leggings to work in. What's more, they're all young and it's as if they've the devil in them. You can't do anything right for them. I mean, sometimes when I was working the vegetable garden one would tell me 'Put this thing here' and another one 'Put that thing here' and another one would snatch the hoe from my hands and say 'That's not right!' They'd pester me so much I'd drop what I was doing and walk out of the garden. In the end, what with one thing and another, I decided I'd had enough, and so I left and came back. But the bailiff asked me when I left to send him anyone I thought might be right if any such turned up, and I said I would. But if I do get hold of someone and send them on, God give them a strong back!'

Hearing Nuto talk like this, Masetto felt an immense urge come over him to gain access to these nuns, so much so that he could think of nothing else. He had worked out from what he heard that there was a good chance of getting a bit of what he wanted, but realized that it would all come to nothing if he said anything about it to Nuto.

'Well, you did the right thing to leave!' he said. 'What kind of man sticks with a lot of women? You'd be better off with devils. Six times out of seven they don't know themselves what they want.'

Their conversation over, Masetto set his mind to working out how access was to be achieved. He knew he could do the jobs Nuto had mentioned and had no worries about being rejected on that score. But he was concerned he might be turned down because he was too young and good-looking. After turning over various possibilities, he had an idea. 'The place is quite a way from here,' he said to himself, 'and no one knows me there. What will get me in for sure will be if I put on a show of being deaf and dumb.'

Having settled on this idea, he slung his axe over his shoulder and, without telling anyone where he was going, set off for the nunnery looking like a poor workman. Once there he went in and had the luck to meet the bailiff in the courtyard. Using signs the way dumb people do, he mimed a request to him to show some Christian charity and give him something to eat, in return for which he would chop some wood. The bailiff readily gave him food and then set in front of him some old tree stumps that Nuto had not been able to chop. Being a very strong lad, Masetto chopped them all up in no time. There was work also to be done in the wood. So the bailiff took him along and had him do some woodcutting. Then he stuck an ass in front of him and signalled to him to take the chopped wood back to the house. Masetto did all this well. So the bailiff, who had various jobs that needed to be done, kept him on for several days. At some point during this period the abbess happened to see him and asked the bailiff who he was.

'He is a poor deaf mute, madam,' he replied. 'He turned up a few days back looking for alms. I treated him well and I also got him to do quite a lot of jobs that needed doing. If he knew about garden work and wanted to stay on, I think we'd get good service out of him, since we need a man like him. He's strong and we could use him any way we wanted. What's more, there wouldn't be any worry about him making sly remarks to these young girls of yours.'

'By God, you're right!' said the abbess. 'Check that he can garden and, if he can, use your wits to keep him here. Find him some footwear and an old cape. Flatter him, be nice to him, give him a good meal.'

The bailiff said he would do all this. Masetto was not far away, pretending to sweep the courtyard, but following the whole conversation.

'If you let me into that garden of yours,' he said to himself, his spirits rising, 'I'll give it a working over like it's never had before.'

Once the bailiff had seen that he was a very good worker, he asked him, using signs, if he felt like staying, to which Masetto, also using signs, replied that he was ready to do whatever he wanted him to. So the bailiff took him on, told him to work the garden and showed him what he should be doing. Then he went off to see to other jobs in the nunnery and left him to get on with it. Masetto worked away, day after day, and the nuns began needling him and making fun of him, as people often do with the deaf and dumb, saying to him the most scandalous things in the world under the impression that he didn't understand them. The abbess, who perhaps thought he was as underendowed as he was undervoiced, paid little or no attention to what was going on.

It finally happened. He had worked hard one day and was stretched out, resting, when two very young nuns who were strolling through the garden passed near where he was lying, pretending to be asleep, and began looking him over. The one who was a bit more self-confident said to the other, 'If I thought you could keep it between us two, I'd tell you something that's crossed my mind a few times. It's something that might not do you any harm, either.'

'You know you're safe with me,' said the other. 'Tell me about it. I'm definitely not going to say a word to anyone.'

'I don't know,' said the more confident one, 'if you've thought much about how tightly controlled we are, with not a man ever daring to come in here, except for the bailiff, who's old, and this deaf-and-dumb creature. But I've heard quite a few times from quite a few ladies who've visited us that all the nicest pleasures in the world are a joke compared to the pleasure a woman enjoys with a man. Since I can't do it with anyone else, I've wondered more than once about putting it to the test with our deaf mute. It's got the enormous advantage that he hasn't the ability or the wit to tell on us, even if he wanted to. You know he's a stupid young lump, with a grown-up body and a child's mind. So now I'm very eager to hear what you think of the idea.'

'Good grief!' exclaimed the other. 'What are you talking about? Don't you know we promised our virginity to God?'

'Oh,' replied the first, 'what a lot of things are constantly being promised Him which He never actually gets! If we made Him a promise, let Him find some other girl or girls to carry it out!'

'And what would happen,' asked her friend, 'if we ended up pregnant?'

To which the other rejoined, 'There you go, worrying about troubles before they come. If that did happen, we'd think what to do then. There are thousands of ways of keeping other people from knowing, as long as we don't blab about it ourselves.'

Her friend was actually keener than she was on experiencing what sort of beast the human male was.

'Well then,' she said, when she heard this, 'how are we going to manage things?'

'It's now around one o'clock, you know,' said the first nun, 'and I think all the sisters except us are having a nap. But let's take a look around the garden to see if anyone's here. If there's nobody, all we need to do is take him by the hand and lead him into the hut where he shelters from the rain. One of us can be inside with him, while the other keeps watch outside. He's so stupid he'll just fit in with whatever we want him to do.'

Masetto was listening to the whole conversation, ready to follow instructions and looking forward to being appropriated by one of them. The two of them looked all around and made sure that they couldn't be seen from any angle. Then the one who had started the discussion came over to Masetto and woke him. He stood up at once and the nun, with an inviting simper, took him by the hand and led him, giggling idiotically, into the shed, where, without further encouragement, he gave her what she wanted. Her desires satisfied, she loyally yielded her place to her companion. Still keeping up his show of simple-mindedness, Masetto went along with their wishes, and that meant that, before they separated, each of them got her wish to test out more than once the horsemanship of the deaf-and-dumb rider. Afterwards, they kept on talking about how it really was the nice thing they'd heard it was – or even nicer – and picked various suitable moments when they could go off and have fun with their dumb friend.

It happened one day that another of the sisterhood saw what was happening from the window of her cell and alerted two others. They first discussed making a denunciation to the abbess, but then changed their minds, came to an agreement with the first two and took part-shares in Masetto's farming. Various things happened to draw in the remaining three nuns sooner or later. That left the abbess, who was still unaware of what was going on. She was walking alone in the garden one day when it was particularly hot, and came across Masetto stretched out asleep in the shade of an almond tree, overcome by a little daytime exertion after excessive night-riding. The breeze had blown the front of his smock back and everything was on view. The lady took a look and, checking that there was no one else about, succumbed to desire, just as her young nuns had succumbed before her. She woke Masetto and led him off to her room. Though the nuns complained about the gardener not coming to work the garden, she kept him there for several days, having again and again that nice experience she used to blame others for having.

Though she finally sent him out of her chamber back to his room, she had him return a multitude of times and, what is more, wanted something more than just a normal share of him. Masetto found himself unable to give satisfaction to so many and decided that being deaf and dumb could have seriously harmful consequences if he stayed any longer. So one night when he was with the abbess he suddenly stopped being tongue-tied and began to speak.

'Lady,' he said, 'I've heard it said that one cock is plenty for ten hens, but that ten men can barely satisfy one woman, and then only with an effort. And here I am having to serve nine of them. I couldn't go on like this for anything you gave me in the world. Or rather, with what I've done so far, I'm in such a state I can't even begin again, let alone go on. Either you wish me well and let me go, or you find some way of arranging things better.'

The lady was utterly astounded to hear someone she considered a deaf mute begin speaking.

'What's all this?' she said. 'I thought you were deaf and dumb.'

'So I was, my lady,' said Masetto. 'But I wasn't born that way. I've had an illness that took away my ability to speak. Tonight for the very first time I feel that it's come back, for which I give all the praise to God that I can.'

The lady believed him. She asked him what he meant by saying that he had nine women to serve. He explained and the abbess realized that there wasn't a nun there who was any more respectful of the rules than she was. Being a woman of discretion, she did not let Masetto leave, but decided to come to an arrangement with her nuns to avoid any risk of his casting slurs on the convent. Their bailiff had very recently died and what they had all been up to could be brought into the open. So an agreement was reached over what was to be done, to which Masetto gave his approval. They organized things in such a way as to convince the people roundabout that after a long period of dumbness the power of speech had been restored to him through their prayers and the merits of the saint to whom the convent was dedicated. Then they appointed him bailiff and divided up his workload in a way that was bearable for him. Though he fathered quite a few little monks and nuns, things were handled so discreetly that no one heard anything about it until after the death of the abbess. By then Masetto was getting on and wanting to go back home with money in his pocket. Once his wishes were known, this was easily arranged.

Masetto had left home with just an axe over his shoulder, but he had had the wit to make good use of his younger years. He made his way back in old age, a father and a wealthy man, having been spared the trouble of feeding his children or spending money on them. That was, he declared, how Christ treated the man who had it off with His brides.

4

Brother Puccio's Penance

Don Felice teaches Brother Puccio how to achieve beatitude by performing an act of penance. While he is doing what he is told, Don Felice has fun with his wife.

When Filomena fell silent after finishing her story, Dioneo sweetly and emphatically commended the lady's intelligence and also the prayer Filomena had just uttered.[1] The queen, laughing, turned her gaze on Panfilo.

'Now, Panfilo,' she said, 'keep our enjoyment going with another entertaining little piece.'

Panfilo promptly replied that he would be happy to do so and began as follows:

My lady, there are a good number of people who work hard to get themselves into paradise and inadvertently send someone else there instead. This happened to a woman from our city not long ago, as you're about to hear.

The story I was told regards a well-to-do righteous man called Puccio di Rinieri, who used to live near San Pancrazio. Since he was entirely given over to things of the spirit, he became a proper Franciscan tertiary[2] under the name of Brother Puccio. Living this spiritual life, he managed with no one to help in the house, except a wife and a servant girl, and had no need to practise any sort of a trade. Instead he went constantly to church. He was an uneducated, slow-witted man, who was constantly saying his Our Fathers and going to sermons, who would hear Mass after Mass and never missed a hymn session for the lay public, but went on fasting and giving up things all the time, and was even, so they said, a practising flagellant.[3]

His wife was called Isabetta, a still youthful woman aged between twenty-eight and thirty, as fresh and lovely and plump as a round red apple. What with her husband's holy living and perhaps also on account of his age, she found herself all too often dieting for longer than she would have wished. When she would have preferred to go to bed or perhaps share a bit of rumpy pumpy, he would fob her off with a Life of Christ, the sermons of some Brother Anastasius, the lamentations of Mary Magdalen and other things of that sort.

That was the situation when a monk called Don Felice came back from Paris.[4] He was a member of the fraternity at San Pancrazio and a fine-looking young man, who was also acutely intelligent and profoundly learned. Brother Puccio made him his friend. He resolved all the doubts and queries Brother Puccio put to him extremely well and, once aware of his way of life, gave him an impression of his own utmost saintliness. Brother Puccio began to take him home now and then and to keep him for lunch or dinner, depending on how things turned out. His wife, too, out of her affection for her husband, became equally friendly and willingly did him the honours. So, as the monk went on with his visits to Brother Puccio's and kept seeing such a fresh, plump wife before his eyes, he realized what she must be missing more than anything else. He made his mind up that, if he could, he would help Brother Puccio out and fill the gap.

It took only a few artfully placed glances on a couple of occasions and he had sparked the same desire in her that he himself was feeling. When he realized this was so, at the first opportunity he had, he told her what he would like to do to her. But though he found her willing for the action to begin, it was impossible to see how, since she was unwilling to risk getting together with the monk anywhere in the world except in her own house, and her own house was out of the question, since Brother Puccio never left the city. The monk found all this very depressing. But after a while he dreamt up a way to be with the woman in her house without arousing suspicions, even if Brother Puccio were at home.

One day, during one of Brother Puccio's visits to him, he delivered the following speech:

'There have been many occasions, Brother Puccio, when I've registered how your one desire is to achieve saintliness. It seems to me that you're taking the long way round, when there is one which is much shorter. The Pope and his highest prelates know about it and use it, but don't want it to be known to the general public, because if it were, it would mean the end for the entire clergy, which is almost entirely dependent on charitable donations, given that lay people would no longer provide them with alms or anything else. However, since you are my friend and have often done me proud, I'll teach you this other way, but only if I can be confident that you won't breathe a word to anyone else in the world and that you'll really follow it through.'

Brother Puccio was agog. He first beseeched Don Felice with great insistence to teach him all about it, and then he went on to swear that he would never tell anyone anything he didn't want him to, declaring that, if it was a way he could follow at all, he would put everything he had into it.

'Since you promise,' said the monk, 'then I'll show you what you have to do. The thing you must know is that the Sainted Doctors of the Church hold that one who is desirous of holy bliss must perform the penance that you will now hear me explain. But bear one thing very much in mind. I am not saying that after the penance you will not be the sinner you are now. But what will happen is that the sins you have committed up to the time of penance will all be purged and pardoned through the penance, and those you commit subsequently will not be recorded for the damnation of your soul, but will be washed away with holy water, as happens already with venial sins.

'So, therefore, and most importantly, sins must be confessed in due detail before beginning the penance. Then the penitent must begin a period of fasting and maximum abstinence. This has to last forty days and during it you must abstain not just from touching any woman but from touching your own wife. Furthermore, you must have in your home some place from which you can see the night sky. When the compline bell[5] tolls, you must go to this place, where you will have a broad board set up in such a way that you can stand there, leaning your backside against it, and can stretch out your arms like the crucified Christ, though with your feet on the ground. You can rest your arms on projecting supports if you really want to, but you must stay there in this position looking up to heaven without moving an inch until matins. If you had had any schooling, you would be obliged to recite some Latin prayers that I would give you. But given your lack of education, you will just have to say three hundred Our Fathers and three hundred Hail Marys in honour of the Trinity.

'As you look up to heaven, you must call constantly to mind that God is the creator of heaven and earth, and recall constantly, too, the Passion of Christ, positioned as you are as he was positioned upon the Cross. Then, when you hear the matins bell, you may, if you wish, go and throw yourself, fully dressed, on your bed and sleep. Later in the morning you must go to church, hear a minimum of three Masses, and recite fifty Our Fathers and the same number of Hail Marys. After this you should deal in all simplicity with any matters of your own that come up, have something to eat and be back in the church for vespers, when you will recite certain written prayers I'll pass over to you, without which the whole thing falls apart. Then around compline you restart the whole procedure. If you do all this, as I have done already myself, I am hopeful that even before the penance comes to an end, you will feel the wondrousness of eternal bliss, assuming you have done everything with the appropriate devotion.'

'This isn't anything overly demanding, or too drawn-out,' replied Brother Puccio, 'and it should be quite doable. And so, God willing, I want to start this Sunday.'

Leaving the monk, he went home and, since he had obtained due permission from his instructor, explained the whole thing systematically to his wife. The woman grasped very well what the monk really meant by staying at it without moving until matins. It seemed to her a good way of proceeding and she told him that she was happy with it and with anything else he wanted to do for the good of his soul. She added that, in the hope of God making his penance profitable, she wanted to fast with him, but not to do anything further.

So harmony reigned. When Sunday came, Brother Puccio began his period of penance and Mr Monk made an arrangement with the woman, and started coming over for dinner most evenings at a time when he couldn't be seen, always bringing with him a good supply of food and drink. Then he would stay with her until matins were rung, at which he would get up and go, and Brother Puccio would come back to bed.

The place which Brother Puccio had chosen for his penance was next to the room where the woman had her bed and was separated from it only by a very thin wall. Once when the monk was rollicking uninhibitedly with her and she was responding similarly, Brother Puccio thought he felt the floorboards shaking. So, having already said a hundred of his Our Fathers, he made a pause at this point and, without moving, called out to his wife to ask her what she was up to. She was a witty woman and perhaps at that very moment she was having a saddle-free ride on St Benedict's or St John Gualbert's ass.[6]

'Good heavens, husband!' she replied. 'I'm shaking to my very limits.'

'How are you shaking?' asked Brother Puccio. 'What does this shaking mean?'

The lady laughed, like the merry, spirited woman she was, and perhaps with good reason.

'How can you not know what it's all about? I've heard you say a thousand times, "Going without supper will not do, because you'll shake the whole night through." '

Brother Puccio did not doubt that it was the fasting she pretended to be doing that was stopping her sleeping and making her shake. He replied in all innocence, 'I've told you firmly, woman, don't go without food. But since you had to starve yourself, just don't think about it. Think about getting some rest. You're tossing round in the bed so much that you're making everything in the house shake.'

'Don't you worry about it,' called the woman. 'I know what I'm doing. Just you do properly what you have to do and I'll do my bit properly too, if I can.'

Brother Puccio said no more and went back to his Our Fathers.

After that night, throughout the rest of Brother Puccio's period of penance, his lady and the monk enjoyed themselves in a bed they fixed up in another part of the house. The monk would leave at the same time as the woman returned to her own bed, and a little later Brother Puccio would join her there after he'd finished. So in this way the brother kept up his penance and his wife kept up her enjoyment with the monk. She often joked with him, saying 'You've got Brother Puccio doing the penance by which we've reached paradise.'

Living in this happy state, she became so accustomed to the dishes the monk was serving up after the miserable diet her husband had kept her on for so long that, when the penance came to an end, she was able to find somewhere else for them to dine, and for a long time went on discreetly savouring her pleasures.

So, to confirm what I said to begin with, the result was that whereas Brother Puccio believed he would get himself into paradise through penance, those he actually got in there were the monk, who had shown him the quick means of access, and his wife, who was living with him in great need of what Mr Monk charitably supplied in abundance.

9

Gilette and Her
Supercilious Husband

Gilette de Narbonne heals the King of France of a fistula[1] and asks to be given Bertrand de Roussillon as her husband. Having unwillingly married her, he goes off in a huff to Florence, where he pursues another girl. Gilette impersonates her, sleeps with him and gives birth to two sons. As a result he comes to love her and treats her as a proper wife.

Since she did not wish to infringe Dioneo's privilege,[2] the queen was the only one left to speak, now that Lauretta's story[3] was over. Without waiting for her subjects to press her, she launched herself eagerly into what she had to say:

Who can possibly tell a story that will seem any good after the one Lauretta's just told? It's lucky she wasn't the first, since few of the others would have gone down so well. I'm not optimistic about those left to be told today. All the same, whether it proves a good story or not, I'm going to tell you the one that's come to my mind on our set subject.

There was once in the Kingdom of France a nobleman called Isnard, Count of Roussillon,[4] who suffered from poor health and always had with him a personal physician called Master Gerard de Narbonne. The count had only one small son, a delightful, very attractive boy called Bertrand, who was brought up along with other children of the same age. These included the doctor's daughter, who was called Gilette. She conceived an immense love for Bertrand, a far more passionate one than children of tender years should really feel. On the death of the count, Bertrand became a ward of the king and had to go to Paris, which left the girl utterly disconsolate. When her own father died only a very little later, she would have much preferred to go to Paris to see Bertrand, if she could have found a respectable pretext. But being a rich girl without brothers or sisters, she was carefully supervised and no solution that wasn't scandalous offered itself. She reached marriageable age without ever being able to forget Bertrand, and rejected many possible husbands that her relatives tried to foist on her without giving any hint of why she did so.

When she was told that Bertrand had become a very handsome young man, her love became more passionate than ever. And then she happened to hear an interesting piece of news. The King of France had developed a tumour in his chest which had been poorly treated. He was now left with a fistula that was causing him immense pain and distress. Though many doctors had been tried, it had so far been impossible to find one who could cure him. All had made his condition worse, with the result that the king had despaired and was now refusing advice or assistance from any of them.

The girl felt inordinately cheered by all this. She thought that not only did she now have a legitimate reason for going to Paris, but that – if the trouble was what she thought it was – she could easily manage to obtain Bertrand as her husband. Profiting from what she had learned from her father, she mixed a powder from certain herbs which were an effective treatment for what she guessed was the problem. Then she mounted her horse and rode off to Paris. The first thing she did on arriving was to contrive to catch a glimpse of Bertrand. The second was to find a way into the royal presence. There she asked the king if he would be so gracious as to show her the afflicted part. Seeing this beautiful and charming young woman before him, the king was unable to refuse and allowed her to look.

She was confident she could cure him as soon as she saw it.

'Sire,' she said, 'if it so please you, I trust God that, with no discomfort or effort on your part, I shall within eight days have restored you to good health.'

The king pooh-poohed the girl's claims to himself. 'How can a young woman like this know how to deal with something that's stumped the greatest doctors in the world?' he thought.

He thanked her for her concern and told her he had decided not to follow medical advice any more.

'Sire,' said the girl, 'you spurn my skills because I am young and just a woman. I assure you that I'm not offering treatment merely on the basis of my own knowledge. I treat with God's help and with all the expertise of Master Gerard de Narbonne, who was my father and in his lifetime a famous doctor.'

'Perhaps she is sent by God,' the king thought to himself. 'Why don't I test out what she can do, since she says that she can heal me in a short space of time without causing me any discomfort?'

Having decided to try it, he addressed her again. 'Young lady, if you make us break our resolution and then don't manage a cure, what penalty do you think you should incur?'

'Put me under guard, sire,' the girl said, 'and if I don't cure you in eight days, have me burnt at the stake. But, if I do cure you, what reward can I expect?'

'You look to us as if you are still without a husband,' replied the king. 'If you are successful, we shall arrange for you to marry into the highest and best nobility.'

'Sire,' said the girl, 'I'm truly happy for you to find me a husband, but I want only the husband I shall ask you for, and I shall not ask for one of your sons or for any member of the royal family.'

The king immediately gave his word. The girl began the treatment and quickly restored him to good health even before the specified day arrived.

'Young lady,' said the king, realizing he was cured, 'you really have earned yourself this husband.'

'In that case, sire,' the girl replied, 'I have earned myself Bertrand de Roussillon, who I fell in love with when I was a child and whom I have loved devotedly ever since.'

The king felt he was being asked for a difficult gift. But since he had made a promise and wanted to stay true to his word, he had Bertrand summoned.

'You're a grown man now, Bertrand,' he said, 'and have had all the training you need. We wish you to go back to govern your lands and take with you the young lady we are giving you as your wife.'

'And who is the young lady, sire?' Bertrand asked.

'She is the person whose treatment has restored us to good health,' said the king.

Bertrand had seen her and knew who she was. Though he thought her very beautiful, the fact that she was not from a family appropriate to his own noble rank greatly offended him.

'Sire,' he said, 'so you want to give me a female quack as a wife? God forbid I should ever marry a woman like that!'

'So you want us to go back on our word?' the king said. 'We wanted to recover our health and made a promise to this young woman, who asked for her reward to be marriage to you.'

'Sire,' said Bertrand, 'you can take from me everything I have and give me as your vassal to anyone you choose. But I assure you that I shall never be happy with such a marriage.'

'Oh yes you will!' said the king. 'The young lady is beautiful, has great good sense and loves you enormously. We are confident you will have a much happier life with her than you would have with a lady of higher birth.'

Bertrand said no more and the king ordered lavish preparations to be made for celebrating the marriage. When the due day came, there before the king, Bertrand grudgingly married the young lady, who loved him more than she did herself. Once that was done, with the air of apparently having already worked out his next step, he declared he wanted to return to his family lands and consummate the marriage there. Having obtained the king's permission to depart, he rode off not homewards, but to Tuscany. There he learned that the Florentines were at war with the Sienese and decided to engage himself on their side. He was warmly and honourably received. He was made commander of a company of soldiers and offered a decent salary. So he stayed in their service and flourished.

His new bride was none too happy with the way things were turning out. Hoping some good deeds on her part would bring him back to his domains, she went down to Roussillon, where she was received by all there as the lady in charge. She found everything run down or in chaos, since they had been without a count for so long. She showed she was a very capable lady, patiently and energetically restoring everything to order, which made the count's subjects more than happy. They came to treasure and love her and very strongly criticized the count for not appreciating her.

When his lady had put his domain to rights, she sent two knights to the count to convey as much, and with a plea to let her know if it was because of her that he was refraining from coming back to his lands: if so, she would try to accommodate him by going away. The count was unyielding and gave the knights the following reply: 'Let her do what she wants. As far as I'm concerned, I'll go back to be with her when she has this ring on her finger and has a son of mine in her arms.'

He attached great value to the ring and never separated himself from it, because of the powers he had been given to understand it possessed.

The knights thought these conditions particularly harsh, since the two things were effectively impossible, but saw that nothing they said could persuade him to change his mind. They returned to the lady and gave her his reply. She was deeply upset, but, after mulling things over for a long time, she decided to see if somehow and somewhere the two things might be brought about and she might regain her husband as a result. Once she had worked out an idea of what to do, she called together some of the great and the good of the count's domain and in a clear but moving speech went through all she had done out of love for the count and pointed out the positive results that had ensued. Finally, she announced that it was not her intention that the count should live in permanent exile because of her being there and that she planned to spend the rest of her life going on pilgrimages and doing good works for the salvation of her soul. She begged her hearers to assume the duties of protecting and governing the territory and to convey to the count that she had left possession of it vacant and unimpeded and had forthwith departed with the intention of never more returning to Roussillon. Many tears were shed by the good men during her speech and many pleas made to her to change her mind and stay, but all to no avail.

She commended them to God's protection, told no one where she was going, and set off with a male cousin and a maid, all of them dressed as pilgrims, though with a good stock of money and precious jewels. She didn't stop until she reached Florence, where she happened to find a lodging house kept by a good-natured widow lady, and stayed quietly there as if she were just a poor pilgrim.

She was aching for news of her lord and master, and it so happened that the day after she arrived she saw Bertrand ride by the lodging house with his company. Though she recognized him very well, she asked her good landlady who he was.

'He's a noble foreigner,' the landlady replied, 'called Count Bertrand, an attractive, courtly man who is very popular in this city. He's totally besotted by a lady who lives nearby, a woman of noble birth but without any money. The fact is she's a very virtuous girl and she's not married because she's so poor. She lives with her mother, a good, very sensible lady. Still, if this mother of hers weren't around, perhaps by now she'd have done what this count would love her to do.'

The countess thought over what she'd just heard. After examining in detail all the factors in play and assessing all the implications, she decided on a plan of action. She found out the name and address of the lady and of this daughter who was the count's beloved, and without telling anyone went over there one day in her pilgrim's garb. She found the lady and her daughter living in much reduced circumstances. Once greetings were over, she told the lady that, if she didn't mind, she would like to have a quiet word with her.

The gentlewoman stood up, saying she was prepared to hear her. They went by themselves into a separate chamber and sat themselves down.

'My dear lady,' the countess began, 'I can tell you are suffering as much at the hands of Fortune as I am. But if you were willing, you could perhaps bring comfort both to yourself and to me.'

The lady replied that there was nothing she wanted so much as some honest comforting.

'I need to be able to trust you,' the countess went on. 'If I put myself in your hands and you were to deceive me, you would ruin things for yourself and for me.'

'Tell me everything you want with complete confidence,' the lady said. 'You won't ever find your trust in me misplaced.'

So, beginning with the time when she first fell in love, the countess told her who she was and what had happened to her from that time up until the present. She spoke in such a way that the noble lady, who had got wind of some of the story from other people, believed what she said and began to feel sorry for her.

'So now you've heard all about my troubles,' the countess went on, after telling her story, 'and you know what two things I have to obtain if I want my husband to be mine. I don't know anyone who can help me obtain them but you, assuming that the story I've heard is true and the count is deeply in love with your daughter.'

'My lady,' the other replied, 'I don't know if the count does love my daughter, but he gives all the signs of it. But how does that mean I can help you get what you want?'

'My dear lady,' replied the countess, 'I'll tell you. First, though, I want to explain the benefits I wish to ensue for yourself, if you help me out. I see you have a lovely daughter of marriageable age, but from what I've heard and can also see for myself, not having the wherewithal to marry her means you have to keep her living at home. I intend to reward you for the service you will do for me by immediately settling on her, from my own funds, whatever dowry you yourself reckon is appropriate for an honourable marriage.'

Given her needy state, the lady was attracted to this proposition. But there was nobility in her character too.

'My lady,' she said, 'tell me what I can do for you. If it is a course of action that's honourable for me, I'll do it willingly. Then afterwards you may act as you please.'

The countess explained. 'I need you to get in touch with my husband via someone you trust to tell him that your daughter is ready to let him have his way with her, but only if she can be sure that he's not just putting on a show. The message must be that she'll never be convinced of it, unless he sends her the ring he has on his finger and which she gathers is something he really does love. If he sends it to you, you will then pass it on to me. The next stage is for you to send another message saying that your daughter is ready and waiting for him to come and take his pleasure. You'll let him in without anyone knowing, but you'll secretly put me instead of your daughter by his side in the bed. Perhaps God will grant me the grace of becoming pregnant. In this way, with his ring on my finger and his son in my arms, I shall get him back and live with him as a wife should live with her husband, and it will all be thanks to you.'

It seemed a serious matter to the gentlewoman, who was afraid of some blame attaching itself to her daughter. But she reflected that it was an honourable thing for her to do her bit to help a good lady to get her husband back, and that this lady was working towards an honourable end, motivated by feelings towards her husband that were virtuous and above suspicion. She not only promised the countess her help, but within a few days, acting with the secrecy and circumspection that had been impressed on her, she also gained possession of the ring, which the count reluctantly surrendered, and then, with masterly skill, she put the countess in bed with the count instead of her daughter. God so willed it that these first acts of congress, so passionately sought after by the count, resulted in the lady becoming pregnant with twin boys, as their birth in due course made plain. Nor did the gentlewoman let the countess have the pleasure of her husband's embraces just that one time, but on many other occasions. All was conducted with such discretion that not a word leaked out and the count never stopped believing that he had been with the woman he loved, rather than his wife. When morning was coming and he had to leave, he would present her with some beautiful and precious jewellery, all of which the countess carefully put away and kept.

Once she sensed she was pregnant, the countess decided not to impose any further on her noble friend.

'My dear lady,' she said, 'thanks to God's kindness and your own I have what I desired. It is therefore time for me to do something that will gratify you, so that I can then make my departure.'

The gentlewoman said that it gave her pleasure enough if the countess had obtained something that she herself was gratified by, and that she had not acted in the expectation of any reward, but because she thought it was the right thing to do.

'Dear lady,' the countess said, 'I approve of what you say. And from my point of view I'm not intending to give you anything you ask me for as payment, but in order to do what I think is the right thing.'

So the noble lady, conscious of the pressures of necessity, overcame her deep embarrassment and asked her for a hundred pounds, so as to be able to find a husband for her daughter. The countess could tell how mortified she was and appreciated the delicacy of her request. She made her a gift of five hundred pounds and some precious jewels that were probably worth about the same amount. The noble lady was overjoyed and gave her warmest thanks to the countess, who then returned to her lodging house. In order to stop Bertrand having any further chance of sending messages or coming in person to her house, the other lady went off with her daughter to stay with relatives in the country. A little later Bertrand received a message from his subjects urging him to return home, which he was happy to do, once he learned that the countess had disappeared from view.

The countess was pleased to hear he had left Florence and gone back to his lands. She stayed where she was until the time came for her to give birth. The two little boys she had were both very like their father, and she made sure they were scrupulously nursed and fed. When she thought the time had come, she set off again and travelled with them to Montpellier, unrecognized by anyone. She rested there for a few days, during which she enquired about the count and where he was. When she was told that he was due to hold a great feast for knights and ladies on All Souls' Day in Roussillon, she dressed herself in her usual pilgrim's garb and made her way there.

Having heard that the knights and ladies were gathered in the count's palace getting ready to go and sit at table, she went up into the hall, her clothes unchanged and her little boys in her arms. Making her way through the crowd of men to where she saw the count, she threw herself in tears at his feet.

'My lord,' she said, 'I am your unfortunate wife, the wife who has been wretchedly wandering far and wide, so that you could come back and live in your home. I ask you now in God's name to abide by the conditions you put to the two knights I sent you. Look, I have in my arms not one son of yours but two, and look, here is your ring. It is therefore time for me to be received by you as your wife in accordance with your promise.'

Her words disoriented the count completely. He recognized the ring and the little boys, since they were so like himself. 'How can this have come about?' he asked finally.

The countess astounded the count and everybody else there when she presented the full facts of what had happened and how. The count recognized that she was telling the truth. Taking into account her persistence and intelligence, and also his two lovely little sons, he felt he should stand by what he had promised and give in to the wishes of his men and of the ladies there too, who were all begging him to welcome her now as his lawful wife and pay her due honour. Letting his obdurate hostility evaporate, he raised the countess to her feet, put his arms around her and kissed her, acknowledging her as his lawful wife and the little boys as his legitimate children. He had her change into clothing appropriate for her rank and, to the delight of all present and all the other vassals who heard the news, embarked on a magnificent celebration that lasted the rest of that day and went on for many more days. From then on he always honoured the countess as his true bride and wife, and loved her and held her extremely dear.

10

Putting the Devil in Hell

Alibech becomes a hermit and is taught by the monk Rustico how to put the devil back in hell. She is eventually taken home and marries Neerbale.

Dioneo, who had been listening attentively to the queen's story, realized that now it was over, he was the only one left to speak. Without awaiting the order, he gave a smile and began:

Gracious ladies, perhaps you've never heard how one can put the devil back in hell. So I want to tell you, without digressing, though, from the subject you've all been talking about the whole of today. Perhaps the knowledge will help you save your souls and you may also learn something about Love. It may be more willing to take up residence in fun-loving palaces and luxury bedrooms than in the hovels of the poor. All the same, every now and then, it shows its mettle in the depths of forests, on freezing mountains and in desert caverns. All of which makes you realize how every single thing is subject to its power.

So to get down to business, my starting point is an extremely rich man who once lived in the city of Capsa[1] in Barbary. This man had various children, one of whom was a good-looking, graceful young girl called Alibech. Not being a Christian, but hearing many Christians in the town highly praising their faith and the service due to God, she asked one of them one day how this serving God could be done with the least interference from earthly concerns. She was told that the people who did it best were those who fled the things of this world, for example, those who had gone off into the uninhabited deserts near Thebes.[2] She was a simple girl, perhaps fourteen years old, with no clear idea of what she wanted, but she was full of childish eagerness. The next morning, without telling anyone, she set off secretly all by herself for the Theban desert. It was a very hard journey for her, but her enthusiasm remained undimmed and some days later she reached the wilderness she was aiming for.

Seeing a hut in the distance, she made her way towards it and found a holy man standing in the doorway. He was startled to see her there and asked her what she was hoping to find. She replied that God had inspired her and that she was seeking to give herself over to His service, and also looking for someone who could teach her how best the serving might be done.

The man had strength of character and, seeing that she was young and attractive, felt nervous that the devil might play one of his tricks on him if he kept her with him. He praised her attitude and gave her some roots, crab apples and dates to eat and a drink of water.

'My daughter,' he said, 'not far from here there's a holy man who's a much better teacher of what you want to know than I am. He's the one you must go and see.'

With that he sent her on her way.

She found the second holy man and, having had the same story from him, went on further again, until she reached the cell of a young hermit, a virtuous, deeply religious person called Rustico. She asked him the same question that she had asked the others. And Rustico, in order to put his strength of will to a serious test, did not send her away or further on like the others, but kept her with him in his cell. When night fell, he made her a rough bed of palm leaves along one side of the cell and told her to rest on that.

That done, it was no time at all before the powers of temptation launched a full-scale attack on his forces. He realized he had grossly miscalculated their strength and, after the first few assaults, he turned tail and admitted defeat. He pushed aside religious meditation, prayers and the rigours of penance and began turning over in his mind how young and beautiful the girl was. The next thing was to work out the tactics and attitude to adopt to avoid her thinking he was just a lecher out to have his way with her.

He first of all tested the ground with a few questions, and discovered that her knowledge of men was non-existent, and that she really was as simple as she seemed. Given this, he saw a way of getting her to give in, under the impression that she would be serving the Lord. He first went through a long rig-marole, explaining what an enemy of the Lord God the devil was, and followed this up by giving her to understand that the form of service that was most to God's liking was putting the devil back in hell, to where the Lord God had condemned him.

The girl asked him how this was done. Rustico replied, 'You'll soon see. And you must just do what you see me do.'

With that he began removing the few garments he had on, until he was completely naked. The girl did the same. Rustico then got down on his knees, as if he wished to pray, and set her opposite him in the same position.

In this situation, with Rustico's desires becoming all the more heated at this vision of beauty before him, there came about a resurrection of the flesh. Alibech considered it in amazement.

'Rustico,' she asked, 'what is that thing sticking out of you like that, which I don't have?'

'My child,' Rustico replied, 'this is the devil I spoke to you about. Do you see? He's causing me so much trouble I can hardly bear it.'

'The Lord be praised!' exclaimed the girl. 'I can see that I'm better off than you, because I just don't have this devil at all.'

'You're right,' said Rustico, 'but you have instead something that I don't have.'

'And what's that?' asked Alibech.

'What you have is hellfire,' Rustico replied. 'And let me tell you that I do believe that God has sent you here for the salva-tion of my soul. I can see this devil is going to keep on causing me this distress. If you were willing to take pity on me and could bear me returning him to hell, you will give me immense relief, and you will give pleasure and service to God – assuming that you have really come to these parts to do that, as you say.'

The girl replied in all innocence, 'O my father, since I have the hellfire, just let it happen as soon as you're ready.'

'Bless you, my daughter!' said Rustico. 'Then let's get on with it and let's put him back in his place, so that he'll leave me alone.'

With these words he took the girl over to one of their beds and taught her what the procedure was for imprisoning that spirit that God had cursed.

The girl had never put any devil in hell before and found the first time quite painful.

'My father,' she said, 'this devil must definitely be a bad thing and a real enemy of God, since he doesn't just hurt people but hell too, when he's returned there.'

'It won't always be like that, my child,' said Rustico.

And to stop it happening, they returned the devil to hell about six times before they left the little bed. So for the time being they knocked all the pride out of his head and he was happy to snuggle down in peace.

But his pride came back frequently in the days that followed. The girl was always obedient and ready to help knock it out of him and began to like the game. She started telling Rustico, 'I'm clear now that those nice gentlemen in Capsa were telling the truth when they said that it was such a sweet thing to serve God. I can't remember ever doing anything that has given me as much pleasure and delight as putting the devil back in hell. In my opinion anyone who sets their mind on anything but serving God is an ignorant beast.'

So she would often go up to Rustico and say, 'My father, I came here to serve the Lord and not just sit about. Let's go and put the devil back in hell.'

In the course of doing this she would sometimes say, 'Rustico, I don't know why the devil runs away from hell. If he was as willing to stay there as hell is to receive and hold him, he'd never come out at all.'

Her frequent invitations to Rustico and her encouragement to him to keep on serving God were having an effect. A good deal of his own stuffing had been taken out of him, and instead of hotting up as another man might have done, he started sometimes cooling down. He began telling the girl that the devil should only be punished or returned to hell when pride made him raise his head.

'And by God's grace we've rattled him so much that he's praying the Lord just to be left in peace,' he'd say.

In this way he managed to get the girl to stay quiet for a while. But having seen that Rustico wasn't asking her any more to return the devil to hell, she had a word with him one day.

'Rustico,' she said, 'if your devil is punished and causing you no more trouble, this hell of mine won't leave me alone. You'll be doing a good thing, if you use your devil to calm down the fury tormenting my hell in the same way that I helped you with my hell to knock the pride out of your devil.'

Living on a diet of roots and water, Rustico was a bit short of the necessary resources. He told her that it would need too many devils to calm the hell down, but that he would do what he could. So there were times when he provided satisfaction, but so infrequently that it was like tossing a bean in a lion's mouth. The girl felt she wasn't serving God as much as she wanted, and more often than not ended up grumbling about it.

But something happened while the dispute was dragging on between Rustico's devil and Alibech's hell, with much desire on one side and little capacity on the other. There was a fire in Capsa in which Alibech's father was burnt to death in his own home, together with all his other children and the rest of his family, and Alibech was left as his sole heir. The fact that she was alive came to the ears of a young man called Neerbale, who had lost all his wealth living beyond his means. He began looking for her and managed to locate her, before the courts could seize her father's goods and chattels on the grounds that they had belonged to someone who had died without an heir. To Rustico's great relief and to Alibech's distress, he took her back to Capsa and married her, so becoming entitled to share her enormous inheritance.

Before Neerbale went to bed with her the first time, Alibech was asked by some ladies how she had served God in the desert. She replied that she had served him by putting the devil back in hell and that Neerbale had committed a heinous sin by taking her away from service of that sort.

The ladies asked her, 'How do you go about putting the devil back in hell?' Using a mixture of words and gestures, the girl explained. The ladies broke into endless guffaws of laughter.

'Don't be upset, girl, please don't,' they said. 'It's done here too. Neerbale will do some good service to the Lord God with you.'

The story spread from one lady to another throughout the whole city and it became a common saying that the most pleasing service that could be rendered to God was to put the devil back in hell. The saying crossed the sea and is still in use.

So, you young ladies, who have need of God's grace, learn to return the devil to hell. It is highly pleasing to God and to the parties involved, and much good may come about as a result.

DAY FOUR

The Third Day of the Decameron *ends and the Fourth begins, in which, under the rule of Filostrato, the members of the party tell stories about people whose loves had an unhappy ending.*

Author's Introduction[1]

Dearest ladies, I had reckoned from what wise men have said – and from what I have seen and heard many times for myself – that the fiery blasts of envy strike only tall towers or the highest treetops. But I find I have miscalculated. I have always done my best to avoid fierce assaults from this raging fury and tried to follow a quiet, unobstrusive path in the lowlands or rather down in the deepest valleys. That should be obvious to anyone who takes a look at these little stories here. They're not only written by me in vernacular Florentine and in prose, with no fancy structure, but also in the most unassuming, least elaborate style possible. In spite of this, I haven't been able to stop the winds savagely buffeting me this way and that, and have found myself all but torn up and shredded by envy's teeth. I appreciate now how true is that saying of the wise that the one thing in this world envy keeps away from is utter wretchedness.

There have been, then, discerning ladies, some people who, on reading these little stories, have said that I like you too much, and that it's not decent for me to enjoy pleasing and consoling you, and – what is worse, according to some of them – praising you as I do. Others have made a show of speaking from a more mature perspective, saying that it's unseemly at my age to engage in things of this sort; that is, discoursing about ladies or trying to satisfy them. Then there are those who apparently are full of tender concern for my reputation; they say that I would be a wiser man if I spent time with the Muses on Parnassus,[2] rather than getting mixed up with you and all this nonsense. And there's another group who witter on with more peevishness than understanding, saying it would be more sensible to think where I was going to get my daily bread and not go chasing after trivia and feeding myself on thin air. And still others try to undermine my efforts by making out that the things I recount actually occurred differently from the way in which I present them to you.

So, valiant ladies, here I am, buffeted by so many ferocious blasts of this sort, savaged and bitten to the quick by such vicious pointed teeth, but still soldiering on in your service. I hear it all and take it all in, God knows, with cheerful forbearance; and though it's entirely up to you to defend me, still I don't intend to spare my own forces. No, without replying as fully as I probably should, I intend to sweep my critics out of my hearing with some deft ripostes, and to do so right now. For if these carpers are already so many and so presumptuous when I'm less than a third of the way through my labours, I can envisage them multiplying enormously before I reach the end. Since they won't have been repulsed earlier, I see them needing to make only the slightest effort to scuttle me altogether; and, while your forces are great, ladies, they would not be strong enough to put up much resistance at that point. However, before I come to reply directly to some of my critics, I want to tell a story in my defence – or rather, not a complete story, since I don't want to give the impression of wanting to mix my own stories in with those of such an admirable company of story-tellers as the one I have laid before you. It's just part of a story and its incompleteness should show that it doesn't belong with the others. So here in story form is what I say to my attackers:

A good while back there lived in our city a man named Filippo Balducci.[3] He was of a modest social class, but he was rich and successful, with the sort of worldly expertise that his position required. He was married to a lady he loved as deeply as she loved him, and the two of them led a happy and tranquil life together, thinking of nothing else but how to please each other as fully as they could. Then what eventually happens to all of us occurred and the good lady departed from this life, leaving Filippo nothing of herself but the single son she had borne him, who was then about two years old.

The death of his wife left Filippo as distraught as anyone could be on losing someone deeply loved. Now that he was deprived of the only company he wanted, he decided to withdraw entirely from the world and devote himself to God, making his little son do the same. He gave all his possessions to charity and without any more ado went up on to Mount Asinine.[4] He found a small cell for himself and his son and lived in it together with his son on the alms they were given. He spent his life fasting and praying, taking the utmost care not to discuss the transient beauties of this world with his son, nor to let him see anything of the sort in case it distracted him from serving God. Instead he constantly talked with him about the glory of eternal life and about God and the saints, and taught him nothing but devout prayers. He kept him living like this for many years, never letting him leave their cell or see anyone but himself.

The good Filippo would sometimes come to Florence, where he would be given assistance with basic needs by pious benefactors, after which he would go back to his cell with what he had been given.

One day, when the boy had reached the age of eighteen, he asked his now aged father where he was going. Filippo told him and the boy replied, 'Father, you're old now and you find the effort very tiring. Why don't you take me with you for once to Florence? That way you can introduce me to these God-fearing friends of yours. Then, being a young man and more resilient than you, when you want, I can go down to Florence to get what we need, while you stay up here.'

His worthy father reflected that his son was now grown-up and was so conditioned to serving God that it would be hard for things of this world to distract him.

'He's right,' he said to himself, and, since he had to go, he took his son with him.

When the young man saw the palaces, houses, churches and all the other things we know the city is full of, he was simply amazed, since he had no memory of having seen any of them before. He asked what many of them were and what they were called, and his father told him. When his curiosity about one was satisfied, he would ask about another. So they went along, the son asking questions and the father giving him answers, until they happened to bump into a party of good-looking young ladies coming back in their finery from some wedding. As soon as the young man saw them, he asked his father what they were.

'My son,' said his father, 'lower your eyes and don't look at them. They're a bad thing.'

'Well, what are they called?' asked his son.

His father did not wish to stir the natural inclinations of his son in any but a morally correct direction. He decided not to call them by their proper name, that is, 'women'.

'They're called goslings,' he said.

It is quite amazing! This young man who had never seen such a gosling before, lost interest in palaces, oxen, horses, asses, money and everything else he had seen.

'Father,' he said immediately, 'I beg you, please let me have one of those goslings.'

'Oh dear, son,' said his father, 'be quiet. They are a bad thing.'

'So bad things look like that?' asked the young man.

'Yes,' said his father.

'I don't know what you're on about,' said his son, 'or why they should be a bad thing. So far as I'm concerned, I don't think I've ever seen anything as lovely or as pleasing to the eye as they are. They're more beautiful than the painted angels you've often shown me. Oh, if you care for me at all, arrange for us to take one of these goslings back up with us and I'll give it something to peck!'

'I won't have it. You don't know anything about what sort of pecking they like!' his father said, immediately realizing that nature had more force than his own wits, and now regretting bringing him down to Florence.

That's as far as I want to go with this story. I turn now to those it is addressed to. A good number of my reprovers say that I do wrong, young ladies, to put so much effort into making you like me and that I like you far too much. I openly admit both things: I do like you and I do my best to make you like me.

And I ask them what they find so surprising in that. Let's leave aside the experiences they must have had of loving kisses, pleasurable embraces and delightful unions that, sweetest ladies, are often to be enjoyed with you. Let them just think how they've constantly had before their eyes your refinement, your everchanging loveliness, your delicate elegance and, what's more, your ladylike virtue. And then think how here's someone nursed, reared and grown to manhood on a wild and lonely mountain, in the confines of a little cell, with no company but his father. As soon as he saw you, you were all he desired, all he asked for, all his emotions homed in on. Are they going to tell me off, rip into me and tear me apart, when I've a body made by heaven for loving you, when even in boyhood I decided to lay my soul before you as soon as I sensed the power of your eyes, the softness of your honeyed words and the fire in your compassionate sighs? It is no surprise I like you and strive to please you, the more so if we think how you were more pleasing than anything else to this callow hermit, a boy with no proper feelings, in effect, a wild animal. Without any doubt it's people who don't love you and don't want to be loved by you, people with no sense or knowledge of the pleasures or the positive virtues of natural desire, who are criticizing me like this, and I don't give two hoots for them.

And then there are those who raise the objection of my age. They seem incapable of recognizing that, though the leek has a white head, it keeps a green tail. But putting flippancy aside, I reply to them that I shall never feel ashamed to try to give pleasure to creatures who were honoured by Guido Cavalcanti and Dante Alighieri in their later years and by Cino da Pistoia[5] when he was very old indeed. All of them were delighted that ladies appreciated them. If it didn't mean stepping outside the limits I've been keeping to, I could bring some history to bear and show how it's full of examples of impressive men of antiquity who put their best efforts of their maturer years into pleasing the ladies. If my critics don't know this, let them go and get educated.

As for spending time with the Muses on Mount Parnassus, I admit that they're giving me good advice. However, the fact is we cannot live up there with the Muses, nor can they live down here with us. If it sometimes happens that there's a period of separation from them, one can hardly be blamed for enjoying seeing something that resembles them. The Muses are ladies and although other ladies aren't on a par with them, the resemblance strikes you as soon as you see them. If there weren't other reasons for liking them, this would be good enough for me. That's omitting the fact that ladies have been the reason for my writing thousands of lines,[6] whereas the Muses have never been the reason for writing any, although they really helped me and showed me how to compose all those lines I wrote. And perhaps when I've been writing what I'm writing now, lowly though it is, they've come along a good few times to stand by me, out of a sense of duty and honour, because of the resemblance between our ladies and themselves. So, as I go along stitching these stories together, perhaps I don't stray as far from Mount Parnassus and the Muses as many might think I do.

But what shall we say to those who feel such compassion for my empty stomach that they advise me to go and earn my bread? I really don't know. When I think to myself what sort of reply they'd give if I asked them for bread in my hour of need, I can only imagine they'd tell me, 'Go away, find it in your fables!' Which is fine, since many poets of the past found more riches in their fables than many wealthy men did among their treasures, and many men who went hunting after fables lived a long and full life, whereas looking to earn more bread than they needed brought many others to an early grave. One other thing. I'm not yet so needy, thank God, that they'll have to chase me away for asking them for bread. But suppose the need did arise, I can do as the Apostle[7] said, and bear both abundance and shortage. So let me be the one to worry about me, not anyone else.

Then there are those who say that these events never happened. I'd appreciate it if they would produce the original documents. If there were any disparity with what I write, I'd say their criticisms were justified and do my best to make corrections. But given that so far all that's been produced is words, I'll leave them with their opinion and keep to my own, observing of them what they say about me.

I think I have said enough for the moment, and declare that – armed with God's help and with yours, noblest ladies, and also with patient fortitude – I shall continue to go forward, turning my back to the gale of envy and letting it blow. I can't see how anything can happen to me except what happens to fine dust. When a wind whirls round it, it either doesn't lift it from the ground or, if it does, it carries it high up and many times leaves it there on the heads of men, on the crowns of kings and emperors and sometimes even on high palaces and lofty towers. If the dust falls down again, it cannot descend lower than the place from which it was first raised. If I was determined in the past to use all my strength to give you pleasure, I shall be more determined than ever to do so in the future. For I know that there is nothing that anyone can rightly say, except that I and others who love you are acting naturally. Too much strength is required to go against the laws of nature and it is often not only deployed in vain but with immense harm to the one struggling to deploy it. I confess that I do not have such strength, nor do I want to have it. If I did have it, I'd lend it to someone else rather than use it on my own behalf. So those who want to get their teeth into me can shut up. If they can't manage any warmth of feeling, they can stay frozen. Let them keep to their own enjoyments – or rather perversions – and leave me to do what I enjoy in this short life that is given to us.

But we have strayed enough. It is time, lovely ladies, to return to where we left off and to resume our orderly progress forwards.

The sun had driven every star from the sky and the damp shades of night from the earth, when Filostrato rose from his bed and commanded the whole party to rise too. They went into the lovely garden and entertained themselves there. When the time came, they ate their morning meal where they had dined the previous evening. After resting while the sun was at its highest, they went and sat themselves down as usual by the beautiful fountain. Filostrato ordered Fiammetta to tell the first story. She began with ladylike grace as follows:

Tancredi and Ghismonda

Tancredi, Prince of Salerno, kills his daughter's lover and sends her the heart in a golden chalice. She pours poisonous liquid over it, drinks this and dies.

It is a violent subject that our king wants us to talk about today. He thinks that when we've come here to cheer ourselves up, we should tell stories about people's miseries, which can't be done without both speaker and hearer feeling sorry for those involved. Perhaps he's done this to tone down the happy mood of the last few days. Whatever his motives, it's not up to me to go against his wishes. I shall tell a story about a distressing event or rather about a disastrous one, which well deserves to bring tears to our eyes.

Tancredi,[1] the Prince of Salerno, was a lord with many human qualities and a kindly disposition, except that in old age he stained his hands with the blood of lovers. The only child he had in his life was a daughter, and he would have been a happier man if he had never had her. She was loved with as much tender affection by her father as any daughter could be, and, because his feelings were so strong, he couldn't bring himself to part with her, refusing to find her a husband, even when she was well past the normal age for marriage. Eventually he gave her to one of the sons of the Duke of Capua, but they hadn't been together long before she was left a widow and returned to live with her father.

She had as lovely a face and figure as any woman ever, and was youthful and spirited, as well as perhaps more knowing than a lady should be. In her life with her doting father she enjoyed the many luxuries a great lady might expect, but she saw that his love for her was stopping him from prospecting for another husband for her. She thought it was not proper for her to put a direct request to him and decided that, if she possibly could, she should secretly find herself a valiant lover.

She cast an eye around her father's court, which, as is normal, was frequented by many men, some nobly born, some not, and weighed up the social graces and general behaviour of a large number of them. Her choice settled on a young valet of her father's named Guiscardo, who was of very humble birth but noble in his character and behaviour. Since she saw him often, she developed a fervent, unspoken passion for him and found herself thinking more and more highly of him with every passing moment. The young man, who was no dullard himself, very quickly noticed the change in her. Within a short time he had let her into his heart and could barely think of anything but his love for her.

They went on loving each other secretly in this way, with the young woman wanting only to find a way of being alone with the young man, but unwilling to take anyone else into her confidence. Eventually she came up with a novel stratagem for communicating a plan to him. She wrote a letter in which she explained what he should do the following day in order to be with her. Then she inserted the letter inside a piece of reed and gave the reed to Guiscardo with a joking instruction. 'Tell your serving girl,' she said, 'to blow into this tonight to start the fire going.'

Guiscardo took the reed and went off, aware that she couldn't have given it to him or spoken in this way without some reason. When he got back home, he took a look at the reed and saw that it was split. He opened it up, found the letter and read it. Realizing what was in the offing he felt the happiest man in the world. He now prepared himself to go and join her in the way she explained.

Just by the prince's palace there was a cave that had been dug into the mountainside at some time in the far distant past. It received some light from a shaft that had been laboriously hacked out of the mountain above. Since the cave was no longer used, the shaft had become almost blocked by the weeds and brambles that had grown over it. Although the cave was closed off by a very solid door, it was possible to get into it via a secret stairway leading off one of the ground-floor chambers of the palace that was assigned to the lady. No one gave a thought to it, since it had not been used for so long and almost everyone had forgotten it existed. But nothing is so secret that it will not eventually be seen by the eyes of Love, and Love had jogged the memory of the enamoured lady.

Taking care that no one noticed what was going on, she had spent days struggling with various tools until she was able to open the door. Once it was open she went down by herself into the cave and saw the airshaft above. She wrote in her letter that Guiscardo should contrive to use the shaft as a way down and gave him an idea of the rough height of the hole above the ground. Guiscardo immediately set to work. He got hold of a rope with knots and loops in it that he could use to climb up and down, tied a piece of hide round himself to protect him from the thorns and then, without anyone else perceiving anything was going on, went off the next night to the shaft. He fixed one end of the rope to a robust bush growing at its mouth and lowered himself into the cave to wait for his lady.

The next day the princess pretended to need to sleep and sent away her attendants, locking herself up alone in her chamber. She then opened the door, went down into the cave and met Guiscardo. They greeted each other rapturously. Then they went back to her room and stayed there, enjoying each other for most of that day. After they had worked out how best to organize the affair so as to keep it secret, Guiscardo returned to the cave, while she locked the door and left the chamber to rejoin her attendants. Later on, at nightfall, Guiscardo climbed up his rope and made his exit through the airshaft by which he had entered. Now that he knew the way, he subsequently came back many more times.

Fortune, however, begrudged the two lovers such long-lasting and heartfelt delight and took a disastrous turn that changed their joy to tears and bitterness. Tancredi had the habit of sometimes coming by himself into his daughter's room and staying to talk with her for a while, before leaving again. One day he went down there after eating, while Ghismonda (that was the lady's name) was out in a private garden with all her attendant women. Not wishing to interrupt her enjoyment, he went into the room without anyone seeing or hearing him. Finding the windows closed and the curtains drawn back round the bed, he sat himself down at one of its corners on a low chest, resting his head on the bed and pulling the curtain over himself, almost as if he were deliberately hiding. In that position he fell asleep.

Unfortunately, Ghismonda had told Guiscardo to come that day. So with her father fast asleep like this, she left her attendants in the garden, quietly went back into her room and locked the door, not realizing that anyone might be there. She then opened the other door for the waiting Guiscardo. The two of them climbed on to the bed as they always did and began happily enjoying the pleasures of love, at which Tancredi woke up and saw what Guiscardo and his daughter were doing. He was inordinately upset and his first impulse was to start shouting at them. Then he decided to keep quiet and to stay hidden, if he could, so as to be able to carry out more circumspectly and with less risk to his honour an idea that had already hatched in his mind.

As usual the two lovers stayed together a long time, unaware of Tancredi's presence. When they decided the moment had come, they climbed out of bed and Guiscardo went back into the cave and Ghismonda left the room. In spite of his age, Tancredi managed to climb through one of the windows down into the garden and went back to his own room without being seen by anyone, feeling mortally wounded.

That night, on Tancredi's orders, about the time people would be going to bed, Guiscardo was seized by two men as he was emerging from the airshaft, his movements constrained by the hide he was wearing. He was secretly transported into the presence of Tancredi, who almost broke down when he saw him.

'Guiscardo,' he said, 'my kindness towards you did not deserve to be repaid with the outrage and shame you have inflicted on what belongs to me, as I have seen today with my own eyes.'

Guiscardo said nothing in reply, except this: 'Love has much greater power than either you or I.'

Tancredi then ordered Guiscardo to be put under secret guard in one of the inner rooms, which was duly done.

When the next day came Ghismonda still knew nothing of what had occurred, while Tancredi's mind was plunged in strange and dreadful thoughts. After eating he went to his daughter's room as usual. He called for her and locked himself in with her, before launching himself into a tearful address.

'Ghismonda,' he said, 'I thought of you as a highly virtuous and chaste person. And if I'd not seen it with my own eyes I would never have imagined, whatever anyone said, that you could even think of submitting to a man who was not your husband, let alone actually doing so. The thought will make me suffer every moment I have left of my declining years. I wish to God that since you had to stoop to such a disgrace you could have chosen a man appropriate to your rank. But of all those who frequent my court, you chose Guiscardo, a young nobody, brought up by us in our court since he was a little boy, out of charity, as it were. You have thrown me into turmoil over this and I don't know what to decide about you. As far as Guiscardo is concerned, I had him seized last night as he was emerging from the shaft. I'm keeping him in prison and I have made my decision. But, God knows, I just do not know what to do with you. I'm pulled in one direction by the love I feel for you, which has always been stronger than any father has ever felt for his daughter. And I'm pulled in the other by a quite righteous anger at your immense folly. Love wants me to forgive you, anger wants me to go against my nature and be cruel. But before I make up my mind, I should like to hear what you yourself have to say.'

With this he lowered his gaze, weeping floods of tears like a boy who has been soundly beaten.

Hearing her father made Ghismonda all too aware that her secret love was out in the open and also that Guiscardo had been caught. Her pain was unimaginable and more than once she came close to showing it with the sort of screams and sobs that women are prone to. But she was too proud to yield to any such feebleness and with amazing strength of will kept her composure. Rather than beg any favour for herself, she made up her mind not to remain alive any longer, guessing that her Guiscardo was already dead.

So when she replied to her father it was not in the manner of some wretched woman castigated for going astray, but in a confident, assertive way, looking him in the face with no hint of tears or distress.

'Tancredi,' she said, 'I am not minded to voice denials or make entreaties. Denying would not help me and I have no wish for entreating to help me either. Besides I do not intend in any way to try to turn the tenderness and love you feel for me to my advantage. I intend to confess the truth and first of all to deploy valid arguments to defend my reputation. Then I shall confirm by my actions the greatness of spirit I shall claim as mine.

'The truth is that I have loved Guiscardo, love him still and will continue loving him for what little is left to me of life, and that I shall not stop loving him if there is love after death. It was not feminine weakness that led me to this, more your lack of interest in finding me a husband and the excellent qualities I could see in him. It must have been plain to you, Tancredi, being a man of flesh and blood, that you had fathered a flesh-and-blood daughter, not one made of stone or iron. And you should have remembered and should still remember, however old you are now, what the laws of youth are, and with what force they demand to be observed. You, as a man, spent some of your best years under arms. All the same you should have been aware of what effects leisure and luxury can have on old and young alike.

'Being your offspring, I am then of flesh and blood and I am also still a young woman. For both reasons I very much feel sexual desires, the strength of which had been remarkably re-inforced through having known during my marriage what pleasure it is to have desire satisfied. There were forces at work here I could not resist. So I decided, as a young woman, to follow where they were pulling me and I fell in love. And I certainly used all the powers I could draw on to make sure that what natural sinfulness was pulling me towards should not bring shame on either you or myself. The God of Love took pity on me, Fortune was kind, and the two together found and showed me a covert path by which I was able to reach fulfilment of those desires without anyone having a clue what was happening. I don't know who disclosed it to you or how you know about it, but I deny nothing. Unlike many women, I did not rely on chance. No, I selected Guiscardo in preference to anyone else after careful consideration, consciously planned how to get him into my room, and I have long enjoyed satisfying my desires, thanks to continuing good sense on his part and on my mine.

'Leaving aside the sin of loving, it appears that you hold to the opinion of the vulgar herd rather than the truth, and criticize me all the more bitterly on the grounds that I've let myself down by going with someone of humble status, as if you would have been less upset if it had been someone of noble birth. You don't realize that you are criticizing not me, but Fortune, which often raises the unworthy to the heights and leaves men of great merit far below.

'But let us leave all this aside. Turn your mind to underlying principles for a moment. You must see that all of us are made from the same flesh and blood and have from one single Creator souls with equal powers, equal strength and equal capacities. We are all born equal, as we have always been. It was the quality of virtue that created distinctions between us in the first place. Those who had and displayed more virtue were called the noble, while the rest remained as they were. Though custom later went against this law and concealed it, it has still not been abolished or destroyed, as nature and virtuous behaviour show. For a man who acts virtuously patently shows himself to be noble. If someone calls him something else, the flaw is not in the person spoken of, but in the person speaking.

'Look at all your noble subjects, examine their lives, behaviour and manners, and then look at those of Guiscardo. If you lay aside your prejudices, you will say he is indeed noble and all these so-called nobles of yours are just peasants. And it was the assessment of Guiscardo that you, not anyone else, delivered, and then the evidence of my own eyes that made me believe in his virtues and the excellence of his character. Did anyone else ever praise him as much as you did for all the qualities that a superior man should have and be praised for? You were not mistaken. Unless my eyes deceived me, there was no quality you ascribed to him which I did not see him actually display in his life, and more impressively than your words were able to express. If I should have been deceived at all in this regard, I would have been deceived by you. Will you say then, that I have been with a man of low status? You would not be speaking the truth.

'But perhaps, if you meant with a poor man, that might be granted, to your shame, since that's how well you have rewarded a valiant servant of yours. But poverty does not take nobility from a man, only possessions. Many kings, many great princes were poor in the old days, and it is as true today as it ever was that many of those who dig the earth and watch over sheep were once very wealthy.

'The final problem you raised is what you should do with me. Don't let it bother you. If in your extreme old age you are set on treating me in a way you never did when you were young – that is, with cruelty – then be cruel to me. I am not disposed to beg anything of you, the first cause of this sin, if sin it is. I assure you that if you refuse, my own hands will do to me what you have done – or will do – to Guiscardo. Come on then, go away with the women and cry your tears. Be cruel, strike us both down with a single blow if you think we deserve it. Kill us!'

The prince recognized his daughter's exceptional strength of character. But he did not believe that she was as resolute as she sounded. He left her and, abandoning any thought of hurting her physically, decided to try to cool her ardour by directing his violence at the other party. He ordered the two men guarding Guiscardo to strangle him silently the following night and then to cut out his heart and bring it to him. The two did as they had been ordered.

When day came, the prince had brought to him a large and beautiful gold drinking cup in which he placed Guiscardo's heart. He then sent the cup to his daughter with one of his discreetest servants, with instructions to say on delivery, 'Your father sends you this to console you for the thing you most love, just as you have consoled him for what he most loved.'

Ghismonda's fierce resolve had remained unshaken. When her father left, she had poisonous herbs and roots brought, squeezed the juice from them and mixed it with water to make a potion she could have immediately ready if what she feared happened. When the servant arrived with the gift and the message from the prince, she took the cup in her hands, showing no trace of emotion. As soon as she lifted the lid, saw the heart and heard and understood the words, she realized for certain that the heart had to be Guiscardo's. She raised her eyes to the servant and said, 'A tomb less valuable than gold would not have been fitting for a heart such as this. My father has acted wisely.'

With this she pressed the cup to her lips and kissed it.

Then she said, 'I have always found my father to show the tenderest love for me in everything, right up to these last hours of my life – in fact, now more than ever. And so the final words of gratitude I shall ever offer him will be those you convey to him on my behalf, thanking him for so great a gift.'

With this she turned back to the cup, which she was clasping tightly to her. 'Oh sweet abode of all my delights,' she said, looking at the heart, 'cursed be the vicious cruelty of the one who forces me to see you now with these two eyes! It was enough for me to have you always before the eyes of my mind. Your life has run its course, you have been dispatched in the way Fortune allotted, and you have reached the end that everyone hurries towards. You have left the miseries and troubles of the world, receiving from your enemy himself the tomb that your excellence merited. Nothing was missing for the last rites to be perfect, except the tears of her whom you loved so much during your life. God inspired my pitiless father to send you to me so that you should receive them. I shall give them to you, even though I had intended to die dry-eyed and with no fear in my face. But once they are given, I shall immediately, with your help, take steps for my soul to rejoin the soul that you so cherished and protected. And in what company could I depart for the unknown more happily or more safely? I am sure that soul is still in this room, looking at the places in which we shared our happiness. I am sure that it still loves me and is awaiting my own soul, by which it is supremely loved.'

After this speech it was as if she had a spring of water in her head. Without feminine groans or wails, she bent over the cup and poured out an amazing flood of tears, endlessly kissing the lifeless heart all the while. Her attendants crowded round her with no idea what heart it was or what her words meant. But they were overwhelmed with pity and wept themselves, asking in vain in their distress why she was weeping and even more striving as best they could to comfort her, though to no effect.

At a certain moment Ghismonda felt she had wept enough. She raised her head and dried her eyes. 'Much loved heart,' she said, 'all my obligations towards you have been fulfilled. All that remains is for me to come with my soul to provide company for the soul that was yours.'

With this she asked for the little jug containing the potion she had concocted the day before. She poured this into the cup in which lay the heart, bathed by all the tears she had shed over it. Showing no sign of fear she put it to her lips and drank its contents to the last drop. Once she had finished, holding the cup in her hand, she climbed up on to the bed, arranged herself as decorously as she could and put the heart of her dead lover near her own. Saying nothing further, she waited for death to come.

The attendants who had been watching and listening did not know what the liquid was that she had drunk. But they sent a message to Tancredi telling him everything that had happened. With a fearful premonition he rushed down to his daughter's room, arriving just as she lay down on her bed. It was too late, but he leaned over her, trying to soothe her with some tender words. When he saw how far gone she was, the pain was too much and he burst into tears.

'Tancredi,' said Ghismonda, 'store up these tears for some twist of fortune that is less desired than this and do not waste them on me, since I do not want them. Has anyone but you been known to weep at getting what he wanted? Yet, even if any of the love you once had for me survives, grant me a last gift. Since you baulked at the idea of my living my life secretly and quietly with Guiscardo, at least let my body be laid out in public with his, wherever you had his corpse thrown.'

The prince's sobs were too anguished for him to reply. Feeling that she had reached her end, the young woman clasped the lifeless heart to her and spoke again. 'God be with you,' she said, 'for I now take my leave.'

With that her eyes clouded over and she lost consciousness and departed from this life of pain.

So the love of Ghismonda and Guiscardo came to its unhappy end, as you have now heard. Tancredi wept and wept. Then, regretting too late his cruel behaviour and with all Salerno plunged in grief, he arranged for the two lovers to be buried honourably together in a single tomb.

2

Friar Alberto Becomes
the Angel Gabriel

Friar Alberto convinces a lady that the Angel Gabriel has fallen in love with her and, disguised as the angel, beds her numerous times. In terror of being caught by her relatives, he flees her house and finds refuge in the home of a poor man, who next day leads him, dressed as a wild man of the woods, to the main piazza, where he is recognized and seized by his brother friars and imprisoned.

Fiammetta's story had more than once brought tears to the eyes of the other ladies. But the king showed no emotion when it was over and had only this to say: 'I'd think it a small amount to pay with my life for half the pleasure that Ghismonda enjoyed with Guiscardo. That shouldn't surprise you at all, since my life is just a thousand deaths one after another with not an atom of pleasure in return. But let's put my own affairs to one side for now. I want Pampinea to speak next and to keep up the cruel theme with which I so readily identify. If she follows where Fiammetta has led, I'll doubtless begin to feel some cooling dew start to fall on the flames burning inside me.'

When Pampinea heard herself being ordered to go next, she intuitively grasped what her female friends were feeling and thought that this was more important than what the king's words said about his state of mind. She felt inclined to cheer them up, rather than doing anything to please him, beyond obeying his primary commandment, and decided that she would keep to the set subject, but tell a story that would make them laugh.

The people have a saying (she began) which goes: 'Give a crook a name for virtue and you don't believe it when he's hurt

you.' That gives me ample material for what I want to talk
about. It will also let me demonstrate once again just how
hypocritical the clergy are. They walk about in long, flowing
robes, their faces made artificially pale, with voices that are
humble and gentle when they ask for alms, but turn loud and
brutal when they lay into people for having the vices they have
themselves; and they try to prove how they attain salvation by
taking, while others attain it by giving. They're not like us normal humans, who have to make an effort to reach Paradise, no,
it's as if they're its lords and owners, who decide how high up
or low down a person's going to be, depending on how much
he leaves them on his deathbed. That's how they work to trick
themselves in the first place – if they believe any of this – and
then to trick those who credit a word they say. If it was up to
me to spell it out as it deserves, I'd soon show many a poor
simpleton what horrors they've got lurking under their great
big cowls. I wish it were God's will for them all to have their
lies and deceits exposed in the way it happened to one of the
Friars Minor, who hadn't the excuse of youth and who was
rated in Venice one of the greatest products of Assisi.[1] I am
delighted to tell you his story in the hope that some fun and
laughter might lift the pall of pity and distress that descended
on you with the death of Ghismonda.

So, my valiant ladies, let's turn to Imola, where there was
once a twisted, criminal individual called Berto della Massa.
His appalling conduct was no secret to the inhabitants and had
reached the point of no one crediting a word he said, whether
true or false. He realized that there was no room there for his
manoeuvres any more and in desperation he moved to Venice,
which takes in all the scum that comes its way.[2] Here he decided
to adopt a style of wickedness unlike that which he had practised elsewhere. It was as if he had become conscience-stricken
at the thought of his past misdeeds. He seemed suddenly overwhelmed by an attack of humility, became exceptionally
religious, and went off and became a Friar Minor, calling himself Friar Alberto da Imola.

Once in his friar's robes he began living a life of apparent
austerity, constantly commending penitence and abstinence,

never eating meat, never drinking wine, at least not when a wine he liked was unavailable. Without anyone quite realizing, he suddenly changed from thief, pimp, forger and murderer into a great preacher, although without quitting his vices whenever he had the chance to practise them surreptitiously. He went on to become a priest and, when celebrating Mass before the altar, he would weep over the Passion of our Saviour if he had a good congregation watching, being a man who found it easy to turn on the waterworks when he wanted. What with his sermons and his tears, he soon had the Venetians so much under his spell that he became the executor and depository for almost all the wills that were made there, the guardian of many people's money, plus the confessor and adviser for the greater proportion of the male and female inhabitants. Thus he turned from a wolf into a shepherd and won a higher reputation for sanctity around Venice than St Francis had in Assisi.

One day it happened that an empty-headed, silly young lady called Madonna Lisetta, who belonged to the Querini family[3] and was the wife of a merchant grandee who had sailed off with the trading galleons to Flanders,[4] went with some others to confess her sins to this holy father. Once she was kneeling at the friar's feet and had babbled away (as all Venetians do) about stuff she had done, he asked her if she had a lover.

She gave him an offended look. 'Heavens, Mr Friar!' she said. 'Haven't you eyes in your head? Do my looks seem like those of these others? I could have masses of lovers if I wanted. But my beauties aren't available for loving by any man I can imagine. How many women do you see around with looks like mine? I'd be counted a beauty even in Paradise.'

And then she went tediously on and on about how attractive she was.

Friar Alberto immediately took on board the witlessness radiating from her and saw an opening for a resourceful man like himself. He straight away conceived an inordinate passion for her, but decided to postpone any fancy talk to a more appropriate moment. To keep up his holy air for now, he started reproaching her, saying that this was vaingglorying and so forth. This drove the young lady to call him an ignorant beast who couldn't see how one beauty was better than another. Friar Alberto didn't want to irritate her and, having heard her confession, let her go on her way with the others.

After a few days had gone by he took one of his trusted cronies and went to Madonna Lisetta's house. He took her aside in one of the reception rooms, so no one else could see them, and fell on his knees before her.

'Madam,' he said, 'I beg you in God's name to forgive me for what I said to you last Sunday when you spoke to me about your looks. I was so fiercely beaten up for doing so the following night that I have only managed today to get back on my feet.'

'And who beat you up like that?' the lady dimwit asked.

'I'll explain,' said Friar Alberto. 'I was kneeling in prayer that night, as I always do, when I suddenly became aware of a great brightness in my cell. Before I could turn round to see what it was I found a handsome young man standing over me with a big stick in his hand. He grabbed my cowl, pulled me to my feet and gave me such a beating that he almost broke every bone in my body. When he finished I asked him why he'd done it and he replied, "Because today you had the gall to find flaws with the heavenly beauties of Madonna Lisetta, whom I love above all else, barring God Himself." At which I asked, "Who are you?" And he replied that he was the Angel Gabriel. "Oh my lord!" I cried. "I beg you to forgive me!" To which he gave this reply: "I forgive you on these terms. You must go and see her as soon as you possibly can and ask her pardon. If she won't pardon you I'll come back here and give you a beating you'll regret for the rest of your life." I dare not tell you what he said next, if you don't pardon me first.'

The lady had the wits of an empty pumpkin. Simpering with pleasure and believing every word she heard, she let a moment or two pass before replying.

'I did tell you, Friar Alberto,' she said, 'that my looks were just heavenly. But, God help me, I'm sorry for you. To stop you having to suffer any more I pardon you here and now – that is, as long as you tell me what the Angel Gabriel said next.'

'Madam,' said Friar Alberto, 'now that you've pardoned me, I'll be glad to tell you. Just one thing though. Whatever I say, you must be careful not to pass it on to anyone else in the world, if you don't want to ruin things for yourself as the luckiest woman on earth today. This Angel Gabriel told me to tell you that he is so attracted to you that many's the time he has wanted to come and stay the night with you, only he didn't want to frighten you. Now he has me acting as his messenger and telling you that he wants to come and see you one night and spend time with you. He's an angel and if he came in his angelic form you wouldn't be able to touch him. So he says that for your enjoyment he's ready to come in the form of a man. He says you must send a message saying when he's to come and in whose form and then he'll be there. So you have more reason than any other woman alive for considering yourself beatifically blessed.'

The gormless one said that she was very pleased to be loved by the Angel Gabriel, since she really loved him too. There was never a time that she didn't light a costly candle to him when she saw a painting with him in it. He would be welcome to visit her if he wanted to come, since he would find her all by herself in her room. Her one condition was that he shouldn't forsake her for the Virgin Mary. She gathered that he was very attached to her, since everywhere she saw him he seemed to be down on his knees in front of her. Apart from this, he could come to her in any form he wanted, so long as he didn't frighten her.

'Madam,' said Friar Alberto, 'those are very sensible words. I'll convey very clearly to him what you say. But you can do me a great favour which won't cost you anything. The favour is this: that you should have him come to you in this body of mine. And listen how your favour to me will work: he will draw my soul from my body and take it to Paradise. He will then enter into me and I shall stay in Paradise all the time he is with you.'

'That's splendid,' said our pea-brained one. 'I should like you to have a nice experience like that to make up for the beating he gave you on my account.'

'Now what you have to do,' said Friar Alberto, 'is to make sure he can open the door of your house in order to get in.

Since he'll be coming in a human body, he'll only be able to enter through the door.'

The lady replied that it would be arranged. Friar Alberto went away and she was left wriggling with such gleeful anticipation that her bottom and her shift parted company. She felt it was taking a thousand years for the Angel Gabriel to make his appearance.

Calculating that he was going to have to be a knight of the saddle that evening, not an angel, Friar Alberto set about building himself up with sweetmeats and other delicacies to avoid any risk of being prematurely unhorsed. He obtained permission to go out and went off at nightfall with a crony of his to the house of a woman he was friendly with, which he'd used as a base on other occasions when he'd had young mares to ride. When he guessed the moment was right, he left in disguise for the lady's house. Once inside he used the bits and pieces he'd brought with him to transform himself into an angel, then went upstairs and entered the lady's chamber.

As soon as she saw this white thing appear she fell on her knees before it. The angel made the sign of the cross over her, raised her to her feet and signalled to her to get into bed. She was eager to obey and quickly did so. The angel followed his devotee and lay down at her side. Now Friar Alberto had a good, stout body, with more than adequate equipment, and finding himself in bed with Madonna Lisetta, who was a soft and juicy young woman, he was able to give her a quite different treatment from that which her husband gave her. He enjoyed many a flight that night, though he had no wings, which made her cry out how happy she was, and he also told her a great deal about heavenly glory. With the approach of daylight, he fixed up to come back again, left the house with his gear and went off to find his crony, who had enjoyed the friendly company of the good woman of the house, she not having wanted him to be frightened through sleeping alone.

Once the lady had had her morning meal, she went with some attendants to see Friar Alberto. She told him all about the Angel Gabriel, explaining what she'd learned from him about the glory of eternal life and what he was like, with additions of further mind-blowing piffle.

'Lady,' Friar Alberto said, 'I don't know how you and he got on. I only know that when he came to see me last night and I gave him your message, he immediately carried away my soul and placed it amid a profusion of roses and other flowers such as has never been seen this side of the grave. I remained in one of the most delightful places there has ever been until morning came. I simply do not know what became of my body.'

'Shall I tell you?' asked the lady. 'Your body passed the whole night in my arms with the Angel Gabriel. If you don't believe me, take a look under your left breast. That's where I gave the angel a great big kiss. The mark's going to show for quite a few days.'

'Today then,' said Friar Alberto, 'I'm going to do something I haven't done for ages. I'll take my clothes off to see if you're telling the truth.'

They chatted for some time before the lady returned home. There followed many occasions when Friar Alberto went back to see her in the form of an angel without any problems arising.

However, a day came when Madonna Lisetta started talking with a neighbour she was close to about questions of female beauty and wanted to parade the superiority of her own attractions in her usual empty-headed way.

'If you knew who has taken a fancy to me,' she said, 'you really wouldn't mention anyone else's looks in the same breath.'

The neighbour was curious, since she knew her well.

'My lady,' she said, 'you may be right, but if people don't know who it is, they're not going to be persuaded that easily.'

It never took much to get Madonna Lisetta to open up.

'My dear,' she said, 'I shouldn't say it, but my beau is the Angel Gabriel, who loves me more than himself and, going by what he says, he thinks I'm the most beautiful woman in the whole world and hereabouts too.'

The friend wanted to laugh, but contained herself in order to get her to say more.

'In heaven's name, my lady,' she said, 'if the Angel Gabriel is your beau and says that to you, then it must be so. But I didn't think angels did these things.'

'My dear,' said the lady, 'you are mistaken. As God is my witness, he's better at it than my husband and he says that it's something they do up there too. But since he thinks I'm more beautiful than any soul in heaven, he's fallen in love with me and comes to be with me really often. Now do you see what I mean?'

The neighbour left Madonna Lisetta, aching to find somewhere straight away where she could spill the beans. She joined up with a large company of ladies at a party and gave them the full version of what she'd been told. These ladies told their husbands and other ladies, who passed it on further, and in less than two days the whole of Venice was full of it. Among those whose ears it reached were Madonna Lisetta's brothers-in-law. They said nothing to her, but they were determined to find this angel and see if he could fly. They spent several nights lying in wait for him.

Some inkling of what had happened reached the ears of Friar Alberto. He went to see the lady one night with the intention of reproaching her. He had barely undressed, before her relatives, who had seen him arrive, were at the door about to force an entry. Friar Alberto heard the noise, guessed what was afoot and sprang out of bed. Seeing no other way of escaping, he opened a window that gave on to the Grand Canal and threw himself down into the water. Since the water was deep and he was a good swimmer, he didn't hurt himself. He swam across the canal and darted into a house that happened to be open, begging the nice man inside to save his life for the love of God and concocting some rigmarole to explain how he came to be there at that time without a stitch on. The nice man felt sorry for him and, since he had to go out to deal with a few things of his own, let him have his bed, telling him to stay there till he got back. He then locked him in and went about his business.

When Lisetta's relatives entered her room they found that the Angel Gabriel had left his wings behind and flown away. They were outraged and poured out their bile on the lady, eventually leaving her there all disconsolate, while they went back home with the angel's equipment. Day dawned as all this was going on and the nice man, who was by then on the Rialto,[5] heard how the Angel Gabriel had gone that night to sleep with Madonna Lisetta, but on being discovered by her brothers-in-law had thrown himself in terror into the canal, no one having any idea what had become of him after that. The nice man quickly guessed that his guest had to be the angel in question. He went back home and established that it was so. After lengthy negotiations he reached an agreement with Friar Alberto that if he didn't want to be handed over to the brothers-in-law, he would arrange for him to receive fifty ducats.

Friar Alberto did this and then wanted to leave.

'There's no way you can,' said the nice man, 'unless you're ready to try this one trick. We're having a festival today and people take along someone else all dressed up – say as a bear or as a wild man of the woods or something like that – and then in Piazza San Marco there's a sort of hunt. When that's finished, the festival is over and everyone goes on their way with whoever they brought. If you want, I'll take you along in one of these disguises before anyone sniffs out that you're here. Then I'll be able to lead you off where you want to go. I don't see otherwise how you can get out of here without being recognized. The lady's relatives are pretty sure you're somewhere hereabouts and they've posted guards everywhere to look out for you.'

Though Friar Alberto found the idea of escaping like this hard to swallow, he was frightened enough of the brothers-in-law to talk himself into it. He told the man where he wanted to be taken and said he was happy with any way he chose to do it. The man then smeared him all over with honey, pasted his upper body with feathers and put a chain round his throat and a mask over his head, giving him a big stick to hold in one hand, while to the other he tied two large dogs he'd brought back from the slaughterhouse. He then sent someone off to the Rialto to shout to the public that anyone wanting to see the Angel Gabriel should go to Piazza San Marco. Thus it was that he kept faith, Venetian-style.

After waiting a little while he led Friar Alberto out of the house and set off with the friar in front and himself holding him by the chain behind. Noisy crowds of people surged round calling out 'What's that then? What is it?' as he led him towards Piazza San Marco. What with those who followed behind and others who had heard the Rialto announcement, the piazza was soon seething with people. Once there, the man chose a prominent, raised spot and tied his wild man of the woods to a column, giving the impression of waiting for the hunt to start. Since he was coated in honey, the wild man was in agonies from gnats and horseflies.

When he saw that the whole piazza was full, the man pretended to be about to unchain his wild man and removed Friar Alberto's mask.

'Gentlemen,' he announced, 'since the pig is staying away, the hunt is cancelled. But I do not want you to have come here to no purpose. Cast your eyes on the Angel Gabriel, who descends by night from heaven to earth to console the ladies of Venice.'

Once the mask was off, everyone immediately recognized Friar Alberto. They all started yelling and bawling, calling out the foulest and vilest names they knew for swindlers and throwing handfuls of muck or slime at his face. They kept at him for a long time, but finally the news reached his brother friars. Six of them hurried to the scene, where they flung a cape round him and untied him. Then, with the clamour still raging behind them, they led him off back to their monastery and locked him up. It is believed he died there after living out the rest of his days in total misery.

Thus a man who was thought virtuous and whom no one could believe was really a villain, had the nerve to make himself into the Angel Gabriel, after which he was changed into a wild man of the woods and finally ended up vilified, as he deserved, weeping empty tears over his past sins. May it please God that the same thing happens to all those who are like him.

5

Lisabetta and the Pot of Basil

Lisabetta's brothers murder her lover. He appears to her in a dream and shows her where he is buried. She secretly digs up the head and puts it in a pot of basil, which she weeps over for hours every day. Her brothers take it from her and soon afterwards she dies of grief.

When Elissa's story was over, the king said some positive words about it and then imposed on Filomena the task of speaking next. She was still feeling very sorry for the wretched Gerbino and his lady[1] and gave a piteous sigh before starting.

Gracious ladies (she began), my story is not about such high-ranking people as those Elissa has spoken of. But it will, perhaps, be no less moving. It came to my mind because of the mention a few moments ago of Messina, since it was there that the events took place.

There were once living in Messina three young merchants, three brothers who had been left very well off after the death of their father, who was originally from San Gimignano.[2] They also had a sister, a lovely and delightful girl, for whom they were being slow in finding a husband for some reason. The brothers had, though, working for them in one of their warehouses a younger man from Pisa called Lorenzo, who looked after all their business for them. He was good-looking and stylish and, after casting her eyes over him a few times, Lisabetta began to find him unusually attractive. Noticing more than once how she was reacting, Lorenzo set all his other love interests on one side and turned his attentions to her in a similar way. So, since the attraction was mutual, before long they were sure of each other's feelings and did what each of them was longing to do.

So their affair went on, to their mutual pleasure and satisfaction. But they did not manage to keep things completely hidden. One night, unbeknown to her, the eldest of Lisabetta's brothers caught a glimpse of her making her way to the room where Lorenzo was sleeping. He was a judicious young man and, though deeply troubled by the discovery, he decided honour was the main issue and did not create a rumpus or say anything, spending the time until morning turning over the problem in his mind. Once it was daylight, he informed his brothers of what he had learned that night of Lisabetta and Lorenzo's relationship. After much discussion, he and they concluded that the way to avoid any disrepute attaching itself to their sister or themselves was to say nothing at all and give no sign of having seen or learned anything, until such time as they felt able to wipe out the disgrace without risk of harm or disturbance to themselves and so stop it going any further.

They kept to their plan, chatting and joking with Lorenzo as they always had. Then one day the three of them made a pretence of going out of the city on a pleasure jaunt and took Lorenzo with them. Once they reached an isolated and remote spot, they seized their opportunity to catch Lorenzo completely off guard and killed him. They buried his body there and then, and there were no witnesses. On their return to Messina they told people they had dispatched him somewhere on business, which was easily believed, since they often sent him to places thereabouts.

When there was no sign of his returning, the delay began to weigh heavily on Lisabetta, who kept anxiously asking her brothers what could have happened to him. One day, when she was particularly insistent, one of the brothers rounded on her.

'What is all this?' he asked. 'What is it with Lorenzo that makes you keep on pestering us like this? Any more questions and we'll give you the sort of answer you deserve.'

This upset and depressed the girl, who began to feel afraid without knowing quite why, but asked no more questions. Again and again during the nights that followed she made piteous appeals to Lorenzo, begging him to come back, and there were times when she burst into floods of tears and complained about his long absence. Nothing could raise her spirits and all she did was wait.

One night, when she had cried and cried over Lorenzo's failure to return and had finally fallen asleep, still crying, Lorenzo appeared to her in a dream. He was pale, his hair awry, and his clothes torn and dirty.

'O Lisabetta,' he seemed to say, 'all you do is call me and make yourself miserable over my long absence. You reproach me so violently with all the tears you shed, but I want you to know that I can never return. On the last day you saw me I was murdered by your brothers.'

He then described where they had buried him, told her not to call for him or wait for him any longer, and disappeared.

The girl awoke, feeling that the vision had to be true, and cried bitterly. When she got up later that morning, she dared not say anything to her brothers, but she decided to go to the place she'd been told about and see if what had appeared to her in her sleep was actually the case. She obtained permission to go for a walk some way out of town and set off as soon as she could, taking with her a female servant who had helped the two of them in the past and knew all about their affair.

Once they reached the spot, she brushed away the dry leaves that had accumulated and dug down where the ground seemed less hard. But barely any digging was needed before she found the body of her poor lover, with no trace as yet of decay or decomposition, which clearly demonstrated the truth of the vision. No woman could have been more unhappy, but she knew it was not the time or place for tears. She would have liked, if it were possible, to carry away the entire body and give it a more fitting burial, but, realizing this was impossible, she used a knife to cut the head away from the trunk as best she could and wrapped it in a napkin, throwing earth back over the rest of the body. Giving the parcel to her servant to carry in her lap, she left the spot and walked back home, unseen by anyone else.

She closeted herself with the head in her room and wept long and bitterly over it, bathing every inch of it in tears and kissing it all over a thousand times. Then she found a fine, large pot of the sort used for growing parsley or basil and put the head inside wrapped in a lovely piece of cloth. On top she spread some soil in which she planted some seedlings of the best Salerno basil.[3] These she watered only with rose water or orange-blossom water or else with her tears. It became her habit to stay always sitting by the pot and gazing at it fondly and longingly as the place where her Lorenzo lay hidden. And after she had gazed and gazed, she would lean over it and begin to weep. She would weep for so long that the whole basil plant would be drenched in tears.

The plant benefited from both her unbroken and prolonged attentions and also from the richness added to the soil by the decaying head, and became a lovely, sweet-smelling plant. But the girl's behaviour, being constantly like this, came to the attention of the neighbours. 'We've noticed how she does this every day,' they said to her brothers, who were themselves shocked by her wasted looks and by the way her eyes had almost disappeared into her head. They reacted first of all by telling her off, which had no effect. So they secretly had the pot removed. Not being able to find it, she asked again and again with the greatest insistence where it was. When it was not given back to her, her sobbing and weeping continued and she fell ill, still begging for nothing else but her pot. The young men were deeply puzzled by her constant requests and decided to take a look at what was in the pot. They turned out the soil, found the cloth and inside it the head, which was not yet so decayed that they could not identify it from the curly hair as the head of Lorenzo. They were stunned and worried that the story might get out. Saying nothing to anyone, they buried the head and made a discreet exit from Messina. Then they closed down their business there and moved to Naples.

The girl, who couldn't stop weeping and asking for her pot, cried herself to death and thus her unhappy love came to an end. In the course of time the story became widely known and someone composed that song which is still sung today:

> Who was it with an evil heart
> who stole away my vase, etc.[4]

DAY FIVE

The Fourth Day of the Decameron *ends and the Fifth begins, in which, under the rule of Fiammetta, the members of the party tell stories about lovers who go through disasters and misfortunes, but whose love has a happy ending.*

4

Catching a Nightingale

Messer Lizio da Valbona discovers his daughter with Ricciardo Manardi. Manardi marries her and is reconciled with her father.

Elissa fell silent to a chorus of approval for her story from her female companions. The queen indicated to Filostrato that he was now to speak. He gave a laugh and began:

I've had so many of you ladies tell me off so many times for setting you such a harrowing subject and reducing you to tears[1] that I guess I should make up for all that pain by telling you something that will make you laugh. So I intend to tell you quite a short story about a love that was disturbed only by sighs of longing and then by a moment of fear and embarrassment, before it reached a happy conclusion.

Not long ago then, valiant ladies, there lived in Romagna a well-off, respectable knight called Messer Lizio da Valbona.[2] He was getting on a bit in years, when, out of the blue, his wife Madonna Giacomina bore him a daughter, who then grew into the loveliest and most attractive girl in the area. She was the only surviving child of her father and mother, and was loved and treasured by them, and also guarded by them with the utmost attentiveness, since they had in mind to marry her eventually to some grandee.

Now a frequent visitor to Messer Lizio's house and one who spent a lot of time with him was a fine-looking, lively young man from the Manardi da Brettinoro[3] family called Ricciardo. Messer Lizio and his wife took no more precautions with him than they would have done with their own son. For his part he kept seeing a young girl who was very good looking and engaging, with the sort of manners and behaviour people complimented and who was already of marriageable age. He fell wildly in love with her, although he took the utmost care to keep his love concealed. The girl noticed, however, and, making no effort to take evasive action, fell similarly in love with him, much to Ricciardo's satisfaction.

Many times he felt a compulsion to say something to her, but nervously kept quiet. At last what seemed like the right moment came. He gathered his courage, seized his opportunity and spoke.

'Caterina,' he said, 'please don't make me die of love.'

The girl immediately replied, 'Would to God you weren't making me die a worse death than you.'

The reply added to Ricciardo's satisfaction and emboldened him further.

'I'll never be the cause of anything to displease you,' he said, 'but it's up to you to find a way to save your life and mine.'

'Ricciardo, you know how well guarded I am,' she replied. 'I myself can't see how you can come and visit me. But if you can think up something I can do that won't ruin my good name, tell me what it is and I'll do it.'

Ricciardo had already been through various possibilities in his mind.

'My sweet Caterina,' he replied immediately, 'the only way I can see is for you to sleep on the balcony overlooking your father's garden or maybe to come out on to it. If I knew that you were there during the night, I promise I'd work out how to climb up there, even though it is very high.'

'If you're ready to follow your heart and climb up,' Caterina replied, 'I really think I can arrange for me to sleep there.'

Ricciardo said he was ready, after which they exchanged a single fleeting kiss and separated.

It was now close to the end of May and the next day the girl began complaining to her mother that she hadn't been able to sleep the night before, because it was so hot.

'What do you mean "hot", daughter?' said her mother. 'No, no, it wasn't hot at all.'

'My dear mother,' said Caterina, 'you ought to say "in my opinion" and then perhaps you might be right. But you should bear in mind how much more prone to heat young girls are than ladies of a certain age.'

'That's true, daughter,' said her lady mother, 'but it won't turn hot or cold at my say-so. We just have to put up with whatever temperatures the seasons settle on. Perhaps tonight will be cooler and you'll sleep better.'

'Please God that happens,' said Caterina, 'but it's not usual for nights to cool down as we get closer to summer.'

'Well, what do you want us to do?' asked the lady.

'Assuming you and my father agreed,' Caterina replied, 'I'd really like to have a couch set up on the balcony next to his room over his garden. I could sleep there. Hearing the nightingale sing and being in a cooler spot, I'd be much more comfortable than I am in your room.'

'Well, don't fret, daughter,' said her mother. 'I'll speak to your father and we'll do what seems best to him.'

When Messer Lizio heard about the idea from his wife, he proved rather uncooperative, perhaps because of his age.

'What's this nightingale bird she wants to help her sleep?' he said. 'I bet she'll sleep just as well to the chirping of cicadas.'[4]

The next night, having heard what he had said, more out of pique than because of any heat, Caterina not only did not sleep a wink herself, but, with her constant moaning about how immensely hot it was, didn't let her mother sleep either. Her ears full of it, her mother went at once next morning and accosted her husband.

'Messer Lizio,' she said, 'you don't really care about the girl. What difference does it make to you if she sleeps on that balcony? She hasn't managed to feel cool anywhere all night. Besides, are you surprised that she likes hearing the nightingale sing? She's only a wee girl. The young are fond of things that are young like themselves.'

Messer Lizio heard what she said.

'All right,' he said, 'have a bed that will fit there set up for her with a serge[5] curtain round it and let her sleep in it and listen to the nightingale as much as she wants.'

As soon as the girl heard, she straight away set up the bed. Now she was due to sleep on it the next night, she waited until she saw Ricciardo and then gave him their agreed signal telling him he should act.

When Messer Lizio heard the girl go to bed, he locked the door from his room on to the balcony and went to bed himself. Ricciardo waited until all seemed quiet. Then he climbed up on to one wall with the help of a ladder and from there, holding on tight to pieces of masonry protruding from another wall, he made a laborious and perilous ascent to the balcony. The girl gave him a silent but ecstatic welcome. After numerous kisses they lay down together on the bed and spent almost the whole night in mutual pleasure and delight, making the nightingale sing its song many times. It was the season of the year when nights are short and enjoyment goes on and on, and so, although they did not realize it, day was already near when they fell asleep, still hot from the warm night and their pleasant exertions. Caterina lay there, embracing Ricciardo just below his neck with her right arm and holding him in her left hand by that thing that you ladies feel far too modest to mention in male company.

They were sleeping like this, not waking even with the onset of daylight, when Messer Lizio got up. Remembering that his daughter was sleeping on the balcony, he quietly opened the door, saying, 'Let me see how well the nightingale made Caterina sleep last night.'

He went out and, gently lifting up the coverlet over the bed, beheld Ricciardo and his daughter lying asleep stark naked in the position I have described. Having taken in that it was indeed Ricciardo, he left the balcony and hurried to his wife's room.

'On your feet, lady!' he called. 'Get up and come and take a look! Your daughter was so keen on the nightingale that she set a trap for it and caught it, and now she's holding it in her hand!'

'How can that be?' asked the lady.

'You'll see if you're quick about it,' said Messer Lizio.

His lady hurriedly got dressed and quietly set off after Messer Lizio. When the two of them reached the bed and lifted the coverlet, Madonna Giacomina was able to see quite plainly how her daughter had caught the nightingale she had so longed to hear sing and had now hold of it.

She felt Ricciardo had played a very dirty trick on her and wanted to shout out and tell him what a swine he was. But Messer Lizio intervened.

'My lady wife,' he said, 'you'll take care not to say a word if you value my love for you. Since she's caught it, it's going to stay hers. Ricciardo is well-born and a wealthy young man. It can only be a good match as far as we're concerned. If he wants to leave here intact, he's going to have to commit himself to marrying her first.[6] That way he'll find he's put his nightingale in his own cage, not someone else's.'

This cheered his good lady, who became quiet. She could see that her husband wasn't seriously outraged by what had happened and reflected that her daughter had had a good night, resting extremely well and catching the nightingale too.

Their conversation was barely over when Ricciardo woke up. He saw that it was fully daylight and thought himself a dead man. He cried out to Caterina, 'O soul of my life, what are we going to do? The day's dawned and it's caught me here!'

It was Messer Lizio who replied, coming out and pulling back the curtain.

'You'll do the right thing!'

When Ricciardo saw him, he felt as if his heart had been torn from his body.

'My lord,' he said, sitting up in the bed, 'I beg you for mercy in God's name! I know that I've been wicked and disloyal and deserve to die. So do with me whatever you want. But I really beg you, if it's at all possible, spare my life and do not put me to death.'

'Ricciardo,' Messer Lizio replied, 'what you've done wasn't worthy of the love and trust I showed you. Yet, since that's the way it is and it is youth that has led you to commit such an error, let's take steps to avoid you losing your life and me my good name. Before you a move an inch, you must take Caterina to be your lawful, wedded wife, to be yours as long as she shall live, just as she has been yours this night that has just passed.

Do this and you'll have my pardon and your life. If you refuse, commend your soul to God.'

While this exchange was taking place, Caterina had let go of the nightingale. Covering herself and bursting into floods of tears, she started begging her father to forgive Ricciardo, and then, turning to Ricciardo, begging him to do what Messer Lizio wanted, so that they could go on having other nights of the same sort together for a long time in total safety. But not too much begging was needed. Ricciardo felt the shame of having done wrong and a wish to make amends, plus terror of dying and the desire to escape alive. He was also passionately in love and longed to make his beloved his own. It was all enough to make him declare freely and without any hesitation that he was ready to do whatever Messer Lizio wanted. Messer Lizio immediately had Madonna Giacomina give him one of her rings, and there and then, without the two of them leaving the bed, Ricciardo formally took Caterina to be his wife. Once that was done, Messer Lizio and his lady left, saying, 'Rest now, since you probably need more to rest than to get up.'

When they had gone, the two young people fell again into each other's arms and, since they had not travelled more than six miles during the night, they managed another couple before they eventually got up and made an end of travelling for their first day. Once up, Ricciardo had a more comprehensive discussion with Messer Lizio and a few days later married the girl again in a more fitting way in the presence of relatives and friends, after which he led her home amid general rejoicing and gave a splendid wedding feast. He then lived many untroubled and happy years with Caterina, organizing nightingale events night and day to his heart's content.

6

The Narrow Escape of Gianni di Procida and His Beloved

Gianni di Procida is discovered with a young woman whom he loves, but who has been given to King Frederick. The two are bound together at the stake and are waiting to be burnt, when he is recognized by Ruggiero de Loria. He is spared and becomes the girl's husband.

The ladies liked Neifile's story a great deal. When it was over, the queen intimated to Pampinea she should get ready to tell a story next. She looked up, her eyes clear and shining, and immediately began:

The force of love, charming ladies, is enormous. It makes lovers ready to face great difficulties and extraordinary, unthought-of dangers, as we've gathered from many of the events we have heard about today and on other days. All the same, I want to demonstrate again what it can do with this account of the sheer boldness of one young man in love.

Ischia is an island close to Naples and some time ago its young female inhabitants included a lovely, laughing girl whose name was Restituta and who was the daughter of one of the island's noblemen called Marin Bolgaro.[1] She was loved more than life itself by a young man called Gianni[2] from the little island just by Ischia called Procida, and she felt the same about him. He would not just come over from Procida to Ischia during the day to see her, but when he couldn't find a boat he would swim all the way between the two islands by night, so that, if nothing else, he could at least see the walls of her house.

Their love was at its most intense, when, one summer day, the girl went walking along the seashore all by herself, going from rock to rock, prising off shellfish with a small knife. At a certain point she found herself in a secluded place among the rocks. But some young Sicilians sailing out of Naples had landed there from a sloop, wanting to take advantage of the shade and of a cold-water spring nearby. They saw this lovely girl appear, unaware of them as yet and all alone, and decided to seize her and carry her off. It was no sooner said than done. Though she screamed and yelled, they took hold of her, carried her to their boat and sailed away.

When they arrived in Calabria, they began debating who was going to have the girl for himself. The trouble was, every one of them wanted her. Since they couldn't reach an agreement and were frightened of the argument becoming serious and of their operations being ruined on account of a girl, they eventually agreed to present her to King Frederick of Sicily,[3] who was a young man at the time and enjoyed having a good-looking girl. So they went on to Palermo and did that. The king saw how beautiful she was and took a real fancy to her. But his health was giving him cause for concern and he decided to hold back until he was stronger. He ordered her to be lodged and looked after for the time being in some lovely apartments in one of his parks called La Cuba.[4] This was duly done.

There was a great outcry on Ischia at the girl having been carried off like this. What most upset people was that they had no idea who had taken her. But Gianni, who was more distressed than anyone else, didn't wait for news to filter back to Ischia. He found out the direction the sloop had taken and had a sloop of his own rigged out in which he sailed off at full speed, exploring the whole coast from the Cape of Minerva to Scalea in Calabria,[5] and enquiring everywhere about the girl. He was finally told in Scalea that some Sicilian sailors had carried her off to Palermo. Gianni had his boat sail there as quickly as possible. He discovered after much searching that she had been given as a present to the king and was being kept under guard for him in La Cuba. This threw Gianni into turmoil, and he almost despaired of seeing her again, let alone of getting her back.

However, love kept its hold. He sent his sloop away and stayed on, knowing that no one knew who he was. He would often walk by La Cuba and one day by pure chance he happened to see the girl at a window and she saw him too. They were both elated. Since there was no one about, Gianni got as near as he could and managed to have a conversation with her. Having learned from her what he would have to do if he wanted the conversation to become more intimate, he made a careful survey of the whole place before leaving. He then waited until long after night had fallen before going back. There were places in the wall where a woodpecker would have lost its hold, but he clambered up and dropped into the garden. There he found a pole and leant it against the window which the girl had pointed out to him and then shinned up it without much difficulty.

The girl, who had previously been chary about safeguarding her honour, now felt it was lost anyway. She thought that there was no one more worthy to give herself to than Gianni and guessed she could induce him to carry her away. So she had decided to surrender to him completely and had left the window open, so that he could immediately get inside.

When Gianni found the window open, he silently went in and lay down beside the girl, who was not asleep. She explained what she had in mind, before they settled down to anything else, begging him fervently to get her out of there and carry her away. This, said Gianni, was what he most wanted and that truly, as soon as he left her, he would make all the arrangements so that he could take her away the next time he came back. That sorted, they fell delightedly into each other's arms and enjoyed that pleasure which is the greatest that love can offer. After several repetitions they inadvertently fell asleep, each still in the arms of the other.

The king had been very taken by the girl the first moment he set eyes on her. He was feeling much better physically and he now thought of her again. Though it was close to daybreak, he decided to go and spend some time with her. He quietly set off for La Cuba with a few servants. Once inside the apartments, he had the door softly opened to the chamber where he knew the girl was sleeping and went in, preceded by a large blazing candle. There on the bed he saw her and Gianni lying asleep, naked in each other's arms. He was violently put out. He said nothing, but his rage became so intense that he only just stopped himself from killing the two of them there and then with a dagger he was wearing at his side. His second thought was that it was totally improper for any man on earth, let alone a king, to slaughter two naked people in their sleep. He controlled himself and decided to have them executed in public by being burnt at the stake.

Turning to the one companion he had with him, he asked him, 'What do you make of this immoral tart of whom I had so many hopes?'

He then asked him if he knew the identity of the young man who had dared to come into his house and commit such an outrageous and offensive act. The man replied that he had no memory of ever having seen him.

The king left the chamber in a state. He gave orders that the two lovers, naked as they were, should be seized and bound, and that, as soon as it was fully daylight, they should be taken to Palermo, where they were to be left tied to the stake, back to back, until the bells rang for terce,[6] so that everyone had time to see them. Then they were to die by burning, as they deserved. Having given his instructions, he went back to Palermo and shut himself in his chamber, still in a fury.

As soon as the king had left, his men broke in on the two lovers, waking them and ruthlessly seizing and binding them. As you would expect, the young people were distraught, fearing for their lives, crying bitterly and blaming themselves. In accordance with the king's orders they were taken to Palermo and bound to a stake in the main square. There, before their eyes, the wood for the fire was piled up ready, so that they could be burnt at the time the king had commanded.

The whole of Palermo immediately hurried to see the two lovers, all the men coming to look at the girl, whom they praised as thoroughly lovely and beautifully formed, and the women all running to see the young man, whose looks and figure were given their highest approval. The two unfortunate lovers, ashamed at the way they were exposed, hung their heads, weeping at the disaster that had overtaken them and expecting at any moment to die horribly by fire.

While they were held there, waiting for their destined hour to arrive, the whole city was full of the crime they had committed and some wind of what was going on reached the ears of Ruggiero de Loria,[7] a figure of immense importance and ability, who at that time was admiral of the king's fleet. Feeling curious, he walked over to the place where they were tied up. On arriving, he first looked the girl over and commented approvingly on her beauty. Then, when he transferred his attentions to the young man, it took little effort for him to recognize who he was. He pushed closer and asked him if he was Gianni di Procida.

Gianni raised his eyes and recognized the admiral.

'Sir,' he said, 'I was indeed once the man you ask about, but I won't be him for much longer.'

The admiral asked him what had reduced him to this state. 'Love and the king's rage,' Gianni replied.

The admiral had him fill out the story. When he had heard every detail and turned to go, Gianni called him back.

'Oh, my lord,' he said, 'if it is possible, obtain a favour for me from the person responsible for my being here like this.'

Ruggieri asked him what the favour was.

'I know that I must die,' Gianni replied, 'and very soon too. I am here, back to back, with this girl I have loved more than my own life, as she has loved me. The favour I ask is for us to be turned round, face to face, so that I may die looking into her eyes and have that consolation as I leave this world.'

Ruggieri laughed.

'I'll arrange it you'll see so much of her you'll be sorry you spoke,' he said promptly.

As he left, he gave orders to those in charge of the business not to proceed any further without additional orders from the king. He himself went to see the king straight away. He could tell that he was angry, but didn't give him time to say what was on his mind.

'King,' he said, 'how have those two young people you've ordered to be burnt at the stake offended you?'

The king explained.

'The crime they committed,' said Ruggieri, pressing on, 'does indeed deserve to be punished, but not by you. And just as crimes deserve punishment, so good deeds deserve reward, not to mention grace and compassion. Do you know who those people are you want burnt?'

The king said he didn't.

'Well,' said Ruggieri, 'I want you to know, so that you realize just how sensible you're being to let yourself be carried away by attacks of rage. The young man is the son of Landolfo di Procida, blood brother of the estimable Gian di Procida, whose actions led directly to your being king and lord of this island of Sicily, and the young woman is the daughter of Marin Bolgaro, whose power and influence is the reason you still haven't lost control of Ischia. Apart from all that, they are young people who have loved each other for a long time. It was love, not some desire to affront your authority, that drove them to commit this sin, if what young people do for love is to be called a sin. So why do you want to have them executed, when you ought to honour them and shower them with gifts and things they could enjoy?'

Hearing all this, the king realized that Ruggieri was right. He regretted what he had done already and even more that he might go on to do worse. He immediately gave orders that the two young people should be untied from the stake and brought before him. This was done. Having learned all the details of their families' positions and status, he resolved to present them with honours and gifts to make up for the wrong done to them. He had them dressed in honourable robes and, after checking they were of one mind, formally married the girl to Gianni. He then made them some magnificent gifts and sent them contentedly home. They were welcomed with great rejoicing and went on to live long years of pleasure and happiness together.

8

Nastagio degli Onesti
and the Infernal Chase

Nastagio degli Onesti spends all his wealth out of love for a girl from the Traversari family, without winning her love in return. He goes away to Chiassi, as his friends and relatives beg him to do, and sees there a knight hunting down a young woman, killing her and letting his hounds devour her. He invites his relatives and the lady he loves to a meal, during which she sees the savaging of this young woman. Fearing that the same fate is in store for herself, she accepts Nastagio as her husband.

As soon as Lauretta[1] fell silent, the queen's command fell upon Filomena, who began:

Loveable ladies, any pity we display is commended, and correspondingly any cruelty is severely punished by God's divine justice. To give you a demonstration of this fact and also to encourage you to drive all cruelty from your hearts, I want to tell you a story that you will find deeply disturbing, but which is also very enjoyable.

Ravenna is one of the oldest cities in Romagna, and some time ago it had many noble and wealthy men living in it. One of these was a young man called Nastagio degli Onesti,[2] who had been left incalculably wealthy after the deaths of his father and one of his uncles. Being unmarried, he fell in love, as young men do. The girl was one of the daughters of Messer Paolo Traversaro,[3] who was from a much higher-ranking family than his own. He hoped that his actions would make her love him and he did all sorts of fine things for her on a grand and praiseworthy scale. But they were of no help. If anything they seemed to damage his case, since the behaviour towards him of his beloved remained cruel, hard and unforthcoming. Whether it was on account of her exceptional beauty or else because of her nobler birth, she became so superior and contemptuous as to find him and everything about him distasteful.

It weighed very hard on Nastagio. More than once, after a lengthy bout of self-pity, he felt depressed enough to want to take his own life. While he stopped himself going as far as that, he made frequent resolutions to let go of her completely – or else (if he could) to develop the same loathing for her as she felt towards him. But he was wasting his efforts; it seemed that the less room for hope there was, the more his love grew.

Since the young man went on both loving the girl and spending his money in such an exaggerated way, some of his friends and relations became worried that he was going to ruin his health and at the same time reduce himself to beggary. They repeatedly pleaded and argued with him to leave Ravenna and to go and stay somewhere else for a while, saying that both his love and his spending would that way be lessened. Nastagio mocked the idea at first, but eventually, when they kept on pressing him, he was unable to continue saying no and finally gave in. Having put together the sort of vast baggage train he might have needed for a journey to France or Spain or somewhere else far away, he mounted his horse and left Ravenna, accompanied by a great host of his friends. The place he went to was called Chiassi,[4] and is about three miles outside the city. There he had tents and pavilions erected and then told the friends who had come with him that he wanted to be alone and that they should go back to Ravenna.

Once properly encamped, Nastagio embarked on a life of unparalleled splendour and magnificence, inviting one party of guests after another to join him for an evening or a midday meal, as he had done in the past.

One Friday, just before the beginning of May, the weather was particularly beautiful. Finding his thoughts turning to his cruel lady, Nastagio ordered his servants to leave him so that he could think about her undisturbed. He then wandered off, letting his feet carry him in his self-absorbed state wherever they would, and finally entering the pine forest of Chiassi. By the time midday was approaching, he was a good half-mile into the forest, oblivious to thoughts of food or anything else, when he suddenly seemed to hear a female voice wailing and shrieking loudly. Shaken out of his reverie, he raised his head and saw to his amazement that he was in the forest. He looked ahead and saw running towards the place where he was, through a tangle of shrubs and thornbushes, a lovely looking young woman, naked, dishevelled and scratched all over by the branches and thorns, crying and screaming for mercy. Then he made out two big, fierce mastiffs running hard after her, one on each side, and biting her savagely whenever they got hold of her. Behind her he saw a black charger ridden by a dark knight. His face was a mask of fury and he had a rapier in his hand with which he threatened in fearsome, offensive language to kill her.

The spectacle first shocked and frightened Nastagio, but then made him feel compassion for the unfortunate lady, and hence to want to rescue her and save her life, if he could. Being unarmed, he resorted to breaking a branch from a tree to use as a cudgel and advanced with that against the dogs and the knight.

The knight saw what he was doing and called out to him before he could get close. 'Don't meddle, Nastagio!' he shouted. 'Let the dogs and me give this wicked woman what she deserves!'

He was still speaking when the dogs got hold of the young woman's flanks and stopped her going any further. The knight caught up with them and dismounted.

'I don't know who you are, though you clearly know who I am,' Nastagio said, when he got near. 'I only say this: it's utterly despicable for an armed knight to want to kill a naked woman and to set his dogs on her as if she were some wild animal. I shall protect her with all the strength I have.'

'Nastagio,' said the knight, 'I was from the same town as you, but you were still a little boy, when I – my name is Guido degli Anastagi[5] – fell even more in love with this woman here than you are today with your Traversari girl. Her fierceness and cruelty made everything go wrong for me, and one day I took the sword you see me holding now and in despair killed myself. I am now damned to the pains of hell for all eternity. She was indecently happy at my death, but not much later she died herself. Since she did not repent of her cruelty, nor of her pleasure in my sufferings, regarding her behaviour as not sinful but meritorious, she too was damned to suffer the pains of hell.

'She had no sooner arrived than a special torment was set up for the two of us. She has to run away from me, who once loved her so much, and I have to pursue her as my mortal enemy, not as my beloved lady. Each time I catch up with her I take this sword with which I killed myself and use it to kill her. I then cut her back open and, as you will now see, I rip from her body that hard, cold heart that never felt any trace of love or pity, together with the rest of her innards, and throw the lot to these dogs to eat. After a while, as is willed by the justice and power of God, she is resurrected, as intact as if she had never died, and the torture of the flight, with the dogs and myself in pursuit, begins again. Every Friday I catch up with her around this time and tear her apart, in the way you will see. And don't think we have the other days off. I catch up with her in other places, where she indulged in cruel thoughts or actions towards me. Now that I've turned from lover into enemy, as you can see, I'm going to be pursuing her a whole year for every month she behaved cruelly towards me. So let me execute what divine justice decrees and dismiss any thought of opposing a power you could not possibly withstand.'

His words left Nastagio quaking with fear and with barely a hair on his body not standing on end. He drew back and, with his eyes fixed on the wretched girl, waited fearfully for the knight to set to work. His explanations over, the knight became like a mad dog and launched himself, sword in hand, at the girl, who was on her knees, held down by the two mastiffs and screaming at him for mercy. He rammed the sword through her breast and out the other side. The impact threw her face down on the ground, still wailing and calling, while the knight produced a knife and slit her back open. He pulled out her heart, with all the bits round it, and threw it to the mastiffs, which straight away devoured everything ravenously. After a little while the girl suddenly got to her feet, as if none of this had happened, and ran off in the direction of the sea, with the dogs behind again, tearing at her. The knight remounted, took his sword in his hand once more and set off in pursuit. In a few moments they were far away and Nastagio could no longer see them.

What he had witnessed left him standing there for a good while, torn between fear and pity. Eventually it dawned on him that this was something he could make good use of, since it happened every Friday. He marked the spot and went back to join his servants. Somewhat later, choosing his moment carefully, he got various friends and relatives to come and see him.

'You have been pressing me for ages to leave off loving this woman who loathes me and to stop spending all my money,' he said. 'I am ready to do what you want, as long as you do me one favour, which is this: next Friday you must bring Messer Paolo Traversaro, his wife, his daughter and all other ladies in their family to eat their morning meal here with me. Why I want you to do this will become clear to you then.'

His listeners thought it was a small thing he was asking and promised to do it. They went back to Ravenna and in due course transmitted the invitation to the people Nastagio had specified. It was hard to get the girl that Nastagio loved to join in, but in the end she came along with the rest. Nastagio organized a magnificent lunch with the tables set up under the pines around the spot where he had seen the cruel lady torn apart. In assigning seats to his guests, he arranged things in such a way that the girl he loved was sitting directly opposite the place where everything would happen.

The last course had just been served when the desperate sounds of the hunted girl reached everybody's ears. They were all puzzled, asking each other what was going on and nobody being able to say, then getting to their feet and looking to see what it could be. Suddenly they saw the wretched girl and the knight and the dogs and within moments they were all there in their midst.

People started shouting at the dogs and the knight and many of the men rushed forwards to try to help the girl. But the knight said to them what he had said to Nastagio, making them draw back in terror and astonishment. When he began doing what he had done the previous time, all the ladies there – and many of them were related either to the girl being tormented or to the knight, and recalled his passion for her and his death – broke down in tears, as shattered as if what they were watching was being done to each of them.

Once the spectacle was over and the girl and the knight had gone on their way, everyone started giving their different views about what they had seen. But one of those who had been most frightened was the cruel young woman who was Nastagio's beloved. She had heard and seen everything with perfect clarity and realized that this all applied to her more than to anyone else, given the cruelty with which she had always treated Nastagio. She already could see herself fleeing from his rage with the mastiffs snarling at her sides. So intense was the fear this generated that she seized the first opportunity she had to counter any risk of it really happening. That very evening, her loathing now transformed into loving, she secretly sent a trusted maidservant to Nastagio to beg him to be so good as to visit her, since she was ready to do anything he desired. Nastagio sent a message back that this was very pleasing news, but that, subject to her agreement, he wanted his pleasure to be combined with her honour – that is, he wanted to take her to be his wife.

The young woman knew that she had been the only one stopping the marriage and said in her reply that she was glad to accept. She herself put it to her father and mother that she was happy to be Nastagio's bride, which made them very happy in their turn. The following Sunday Nastagio formally married her and celebrated the wedding, after which they lived a long and happy life together.

It was not the only good thing to emerge from that terrifying scene. All the ladies of Ravenna became fearful of what might happen and showed much greater willingness to give men what they wanted than they had before.

9

Federigo degli Alberighi and His Falcon

Federigo degli Alberighi loves a lady, but his love is not returned. He spends all his money on courtship and has just a single falcon left. This is all he can offer her to eat when she comes to visit. Learning what he has done, the lady has a change of heart, marries him and makes him a wealthy man.

Filomena had now finished. The queen knew that no one else was left apart from Dioneo, with his privilege of telling the last story,[1] and, with a happy look on her face, began to speak:

It's my turn now and I'll gladly do my duty, dearest ladies, by telling you a story which has some resemblances with the preceding one. It's a story which should make you appreciate the power your charms can exert over noble hearts and which should teach you to make yourselves the givers of the rewards you can appropriately give. It shouldn't all be left to Fortune, which acts without sense and usually bestows its gifts in an indiscriminate way.

Let me start with Coppo di Borghese Domenichi.[2] I'm not sure if he's still alive, but he was someone whose virtues and conduct, rather than any nobility of birth, made him one of the most deeply revered figures of our time, a truly illustrious man, whose name deserves to live for ever. One of his regular pleasures in his later years was talking with neighbours and others about things that had happened in the past. It was something he was exceptionally good at, since his memory was excellent and he could tell a story eloquently and coherently.

One of his best stories was about a young man called Federigo, the son of Messer Filippo degli Alberighi, who stood out among the young men of Tuscany aspiring to knighthood for his chivalry and courtliness. Like most noblemen, he fell in love with a noble lady. She was called Madonna Giovanna and in her time she was held to be one of the loveliest and most attractive ladies in Florence. To win her love, Federigo took part in jousts and other displays of arms, held feasts and sent her generous gifts, spending what he had with no restraint whatsoever. She was as mindful of her honour as she was beautiful and showed no interest in him or anything he did for her.

As you might expect, spending far more than he could afford and getting nothing in return meant that Federigo consumed all his wealth. He was left a poor man with only a small farm, which produced just enough for a very frugal existence. Otherwise he had nothing but one of the best falcons ever bred. His love being as strong as ever and feeling unable to live in the city in the way he wanted, he went away to live in Campi,[3] where he had his farm. There he went hunting with his falcon whenever he could, not asking anyone for assistance and patiently resigning himself to a life of poverty.

His circumstances had reached a very low ebb when there was a new development. The husband of Madonna Giovanna fell ill and, realizing that he was close to death, made a will. He was a very wealthy man and he named his son, who at this stage was a growing boy, as his sole heir, with the proviso that if his son were to die without a legitimate heir of his own, Madonna Giovanna, to whom he was devoted, should inherit everything. Soon afterwards he died.

Now a widow, Madonna Giovanna followed the custom of Florentine ladies by going into the country in the summer each year with her son, staying in a property she owned near to Federigo's farm. As a result the boy made friends with Federigo and came to enjoy hawks and hounds. Having seen Federigo's falcon fly many times, he became singularly captivated by it and would have dearly liked to have it. But he couldn't bring himself to ask for it, since he could see how much it meant to Federigo.

That was how things stood when the boy fell ill. His mother was deeply distressed, since she had no other children and loved him with all her might. She stayed all day with him, trying to raise his spirits. She would often ask him if there was anything he wanted and beg him to tell her what it was, saying she would certainly get it for him if it were at all obtainable.

'Mother,' said the boy, hearing all these promises, 'I think I'll get better quickly if you can arrange for me to have Federigo's falcon.'

The lady felt at a loss to hear this and wondered what she should do. She knew that Federigo had loved her for a long time and had never received so much as a glance from her.

'How can I send someone or go myself to ask him for this falcon?' she said to herself. 'I gather it's the best that has ever flown and it's also the thing that keeps him going. How can I be so insensitive as to want to deprive a noble-hearted man of the one thing he has left that gives him pleasure?'

She said nothing at first to her son, but stood there perplexed by such considerations, though feeling sure she would be given the falcon if she asked for it.

Her love for her son won out in the end. She decided to try to make him happy, whatever the consequences, and not to send someone else but to go personally to obtain the bird and to bring it back for him.

'My son,' was her eventual reply, 'try to cheer up and concentrate on getting well again. I promise you that the first thing I'll do tomorrow morning is to go and ask for it and I'm sure I'll come back with it.'

At this the boy's spirits lifted and that very day his condition showed some improvement.

The following morning, with another lady to accompany her, his mother set off on a casual-seeming stroll that actually brought her to Federigo's cottage, where she asked if he were free. The weather wasn't right for hawking, as it hadn't been for some days, and Federigo was in his vegetable garden sorting out a few things. When he was told that Madonna Giovanna was at the door asking for him, he was immensely surprised and hurried happily to greet her.

Seeing him appear, and having received from him some
reverential words of welcome, she advanced towards him with
the grace of a perfect lady.

'I wish Federigo well!' she said and went on, 'I have come to
repay you for the privations you have endured on my behalf
through loving me more than you really should. The repayment is this. I should like, with my friend here, to enjoy with
you this morning an informal, friendly meal.'

'My lady,' replied Federigo humbly, 'I do not recall ever
suffering any privation on your account, only good. If I've ever
been worth anything at all it's on account of your own excellence and the love I have borne you. Let me assure you that I
value your generous visit here much more than if I were granted
the possibility of spending again all the money that I spent in
the past, though it is a poor man's hospitality that you will be
given.'

With that he received her with some embarrassment into his
house and then led her into his garden, where, however, he had
no one he could ask to keep her company.

'My lady,' he said, 'since there's nobody else, this good
woman, who is the wife of the workman here, will stay with
you while I go and arrange the table.'

Although he was poor in the extreme, he hadn't realized as
fully as he should have how inordinately rash he had been with
his wealth. But it was brought home to him this morning. After
having lavishly entertained hosts of people to impress the
woman he loved, he now found he had nothing he could
decently set before her. Totally distraught, cursing his misfortune to himself, he rushed round the house like a madman,
looking vainly for money or something to pawn, with time
pressing and aching to find some way of entertaining the lady
properly, although he rejected any idea of asking his workman
or anyone else for a loan.

Then his eyes lighted on his precious falcon, there in a small
room on its perch. With no other possible solution coming to
mind, he picked it up and found it quite plump. It would make,
he decided, a dish worthy of such a lady. Without further hesitation he wrung its neck and gave it to a young servant girl he

had, to be plucked, cleaned and then put on a spit and duly roasted. Having spread on the table the beautifully white cloths that he still had, he rejoined the lady in the garden with a happy look on his face, announcing that such a meal as he had been able to manage was now in train. The lady rose to her feet and she and her companion went to sit at the table. Without realizing what they were eating, together with Federigo, who waited on them with the utmost attention, they polished off the precious falcon.

After rising from the table, the ladies engaged in pleasant chit-chat with Federigo for a while, until the lady thought the moment had come to tell him why she was there.

'Federigo,' she said, addressing him with a considerate air, 'I don't doubt you will be amazed at my presumption when you hear the main reason for my coming here, since you'll recall your own past life and my virtuous conduct, which you may well have thought hardness and cruelty. But had you ever had any children, you would know how powerful is the love one feels for them, and I am sure you would excuse me to some extent. But while you have no children, I do have one son and cannot help but obey the laws that apply to all mothers. Since I am bound to observe them in all their force, I am obliged to exceed the limits of what I myself would wish, and also the limits of all decency and duty, and to ask you to make me a gift of something I know is particularly dear to you. And rightly so, for your extreme ill-fortune has left you no other pleasure, amusement or consolation. The gift I ask for is your falcon, which my little boy is obsessed with. I am afraid that if I don't return to him with it, his illness will be aggravated to the point of my running the risk of losing him. I am not begging you to make me this gift out of the love you feel for me, which puts you under no obligation at all, but out of the exceptional nobility of heart that you have shown in all the courtly deeds you have performed. Then I may be able to say that through this gift I have kept my son alive and thus left him in your debt for ever.'

Listening to the lady's request, Federigo became more and more aware that he could not oblige her, given what he had served her to eat. He began weeping openly in front of her before he could manage a word of reply. At first the lady thought that the tears stemmed more than anything from the idea of having to separate himself from such a good falcon, and was on the point of saying that she didn't want it. But she restrained herself and waited until Federigo had finished crying and gave her an answer.

'My lady,' he said, 'ever since it pleased God that you should be the one I should love, I have judged Fortune to be against me in a multiplicity of ways and have often railed against her blows. But all are trivial compared to the blow she has just delivered. I shall never be reconciled to her again, when I consider how you have come here to my poor home, never having deigned to visit me when it was a rich one, and how, when all you want is a small gift from me, she has so arranged things that I cannot give it.

'I shall briefly explain why. When I heard you being so kind as to say you wished to dine with me, I thought I had to take account of what an excellently superior person you are. I felt it only right and fitting that, so far as my means allowed, I should honour you with a more splendid dish than visitors usually receive. So I thought of the falcon you are asking me for and of what a good bird it was and I judged it was food worthy of you. This morning it was put roasted before you on a trencher, which I thought I was making the best imaginable use of. Now I see that this wasn't how you wanted the bird at all. I am so distraught at being unable to oblige you that I don't think I'll ever put my mind at rest again.'

After this speech he had the feathers, feet and beak tossed down in front of her as evidence of what he had said. The lady's first reaction to what she saw and heard was to reproach him with having killed a falcon of such quality to feed a silly woman, but then she found herself admiring the greatness of his spirit, which poverty had not been able to dent in the slightest.

With no hope now of obtaining the falcon, she began to be worried about her son's well-being. Thanking Federigo for the honour he had done her and for his eagerness to help, she returned, now totally despondent, to her son. Perhaps it was despair at not being able to have the falcon or perhaps it was the disease taking an inevitable course, but not many days went by before the boy departed from this life, to the immense distress of his mother.

For some time she could do nothing but weep and feel bitter. But she was very wealthy and still young. Her brothers kept urging her to marry again. Though she would have preferred not to, their pestering began to affect her. She recalled the admirable qualities Federigo had displayed and his final generous gesture of killing such a falcon in her honour.

'If I had your approval,' she said to her brothers, 'I would happily stay as I am and not marry again. But since you're set on my taking a husband, I'm definitely never marrying anyone other than Federigo degli Alberighi.'

Her brothers laughed her to scorn.

'Idiot,' they said, 'what are you talking about? How can you want him? He hasn't a thing to his name.'

Her reply was this: 'My brothers, I know well enough that you're right. But I put a man who needs money before money that needs a man.'

Her brothers appreciated her spirit and were also aware of Federigo's admirable qualities. Poor though he was, they gave her to him as she wanted, with all her wealth. So he found himself married to the remarkable lady he had loved so much, and a very rich man too. He learned how to manage his affairs better and lived happily with her for the rest of his days.

DAY SIX

The Fifth Day of the Decameron *ends and the Sixth begins, in which, under the rule of Elissa, the members of the party tell stories about people who got themselves out of trouble with a smart turn of phrase, or escaped loss, danger or humiliation through some quick retort or stratagem.*

I

Madonna Oretta's Put-down

A knight tells Madonna Oretta that he will give her a ride on a story he has ready, but he makes such a mess of it that she asks him to put her down.

Young ladies,[1] on bright clear nights stars adorn the skies, and in springtime there are flowers in the green meadows and bushes once more clothed in leaf on the hills. In the same way a well-turned witticism is a further adornment to admirable manners and fine conversation. The fact that witticisms must be concise makes them more suited to ladies than to men, given that speaking at length is less appealing in a woman than in a man. It's true that for some reason, perhaps because of some perversity in the way our minds work or on account of the peculiar hostility of the heavens to our times, there are few ladies left – perhaps none – who know how to pick the right moment and cut in with a telling remark, or if someone else comes out with one, to grasp its meaning properly. It's something we ladies in general should be ashamed of. However, I shall say no more on the subject, since Pampinea has already said quite enough.[2] I shall simply bring home to you how beautiful the right remark at the right time can be by telling you how one noble lady courteously reduced a certain knight to silence.

It's likely that many of you ladies have heard about a certain noble lady who lived in our city until not long ago, or else knew her personally. She had many social graces, spoke extremely well and all told was someone whose name doesn't deserve to be passed over in silence. She was called Madonna Oretta[3] and she was the wife of Messer Geri Spina.

She once happened to be in the countryside, much as we are, and was enjoying a stroll from one place to another with a party of knights and ladies she had had to lunch at her house that day. When the distance from where they had set out to where they were intending to walk started looking a little long, one of the knights in the company came out with a proposal.

'Madonna Oretta,' he said, 'if you're willing, I'll make a good portion of the way we have to walk fly by, by telling you one of the best stories that's ever been told. You'll feel as if you're on horseback.'

'Sir,' replied the lady, 'yes, please do tell the story. I should really like that.'

The knight, who was maybe no better at using the sword at his side than at getting his tongue around a story, took her up and embarked on his tale, which really was in itself a very good one. But he kept repeating words three or four times or more, or else he would go back over something he'd said, and sometimes he would say 'I didn't put that right' or lose track of the names and mix them up, all of which spoilt the story terribly. And that's leaving out how poorly he adapted his way of telling the story to characters and events.

Listening to him, Madonna Oretta started perspiring and felt her heart flutter, as if she'd fallen ill and her end was nigh. At last, when she could bear it no more, she realized that the knight had blundered into a mess he wasn't going to get himself out of, and gently intervened.

'Sir,' she said, 'this horse of yours is a very bumpy trotter. I beg you, please set me down.'

The knight may have been a poor storyteller, but it turned out he wasn't stupid. He saw the point of her quip and took it in good part, trying his hand with other stories and leaving the one he'd begun and made a muddle of without an ending.

9

Cavalcanti among the Tombs

Guido Cavalcanti uses a clever remark to deliver a courteous rebuke to certain Florentine gentlemen who have caught him by surprise.

The queen saw that Emilia had finished her story and that she was the only member of the company left to speak, apart from the one with the privilege of speaking last.[1] So she began as follows:

Pretty ladies, I've been robbed by you of more than two stories I had it in mind to tell. Still, I have one story left, the conclusion of which contains a clever remark that has more subtlety to it than any we've heard so far.

Let me remind you that, in days gone by, many fine and laudable customs were observed in our city, of which none have survived, thanks to increasing wealth being accompanied by increasing avarice, which has caused all of them to lapse. One custom was for noble citizens of the various districts to meet together in different parts of the city. Setting a limit to numbers in the company and taking care to include only people who could adequately cover the expenses involved, they would take it in turns to entertain all the others, each one playing host on a particular day. They would also often honour noble visitors from elsewhere with invitations, as well as other Florentine citizens. And at least once a year, on some significant day, they would all get dressed up in the same way and ride together through the streets. Sometimes they would organize jousts too, especially on the principal feast days or when news of a victory or some other happy event reached the city.

One of these companies was headed by Messer Betto Brunelleschi.[2] He and his companions did everything they could to
draw in Guido,[3] the son of Messer Cavalcante de' Cavalcanti,
and with some justification. For he was superbly skilled in
logical argument and was an excellent natural philosopher.[4]
The company cared very little for all that, but he was also stylish, sophisticated, good with words, and could do with more
ease than anyone else all the things that he wanted to do and
that he felt were appropriate for a noble gentleman to do.
Besides that he was extremely rich and knew how to entertain
on the most lavish scale anyone he felt deserved such an
honour.

But Messer Betto had never managed to get him to join
them. The reason, he and the others believed, was that Guido's
speculative habits made him chary of human company. Since
he had taken up some Epicurean ideas,[5] popular opinion had it
that these speculations of his were directed solely towards finding a way of proving that God doesn't exist.

It happened one day that Guido set off from Orto San
Michele[6] and walked along Corso degli Adimari to the church
of San Giovanni, which was a route he often took, past the
great marble tombs now in Santa Reparata, and the many
other tombs around San Giovanni. He had reached the porphyry columns there, between the tombs and the locked doors
of San Giovanni, when Messer Betto and his company rode up
through the piazza in front of Santa Reparata and saw Guido
among the graves.

'Let's go and harass him,' they said.

Spurring their horses into a pretence charge, they were on
top of him before he realized.

'Guido,' they said, 'you refuse to join our company, but
what will you have achieved when you prove God doesn't
exist?'

Seeing himself hemmed in by them, Guido immediately
replied, 'Sirs, you can say anything you like to me in your own
home.'

With that he pressed a hand down on one of the tombs,
which were indeed big, and vaulted over it on to the other side

with characteristic nimbleness and went on his way, having extricated himself from them completely.

They were left there, looking at each other, saying he had lost his wits and that what he had said didn't make sense, since they had no more say-so over the place where they were than any other Florentines, nor did Guido have any less of a say-so than they had.

But Messer Betto turned to them and said, 'It's you who've lost your wits, if you don't get it. With those few words he's paid us the worst possible compliment in a very polite way. If you think about it, these tombs are the houses of the dead, since that's where they're put and where they stay. He says that this is our home. He's letting us know that we and all the others with no reading or education behind us are worse than dead men in comparison with himself and other men of learning. If that's the case, then being here means we really are in our proper home.'

They all now grasped what Guido had meant and felt put to shame. From then on they stopped harassing him and considered Messer Betto a knight with a subtle and perceptive mind.

10

Friar Cipolla and the Coals

Friar Cipolla promises to show some country people one of the feathers of the Angel Gabriel. When he finds some bits of coal have been put there instead, he tells them they're from the fire on which St Lawrence was roasted.

The rest of the company having all delivered their stories, Dioneo knew at once that it was now his turn to speak. So without waiting for a formal order, he told those who were still praising Guido's telling riposte[1] to be quiet and began:

Dainty ladies, though I enjoy the special privilege of being able to tell a story about anything I like, I do not intend today to depart from the subject you have all spoken on with such aplomb. So I shall follow in your footsteps. I aim to show you how cannily and adroitly a friar in the order of St Anthony[2] managed to escape the humiliation which two young men had set up for him. I want to tell the full story properly and you must not feel alarmed if I speak at some length. If you look up, you'll see that the sun is still high in the sky.

You have perhaps heard of Certaldo,[3] a fortified township in the Val d'Elsa in our territory. Though it's a small place, at one time it had members of the nobility and other people of means living in it. There was, though, a friar belonging to the order of St Anthony who found it fertile territory and would regularly visit once a year to gather in the alms that the gullible were happy to hand over. His name was Friar Cipolla[4] and perhaps it was the name 'Onion' as much as any religious fervour that made his appearances welcome, since the land there produces onions that are famous throughout Tuscany. He was small,

red-haired and cheery-faced and the best man in the world to
have a drink with. He had no real education, but he had such
a ready skill with language that if you didn't know anything
about him, you'd think he was more than just a trained orator,
perhaps Cicero incarnate or else Quintilian.[5] He was on the
friendliest terms with almost everyone in the district and very
close to some.

On one occasion he arrived, as he usually did, sometime in
August. When Sunday came round, all the good men and
women from the outlying hamlets came to Mass in the parish
church. Choosing his moment, Friar Cipolla stepped forward.
'Gentlemen and ladies,' he said, 'as you know, it is your custom
to send a portion of your wheat and oats every year to the poor
servants of his lordship St Anthony, some giving more, others
less, depending on the giver's capability and devotion to the
saint, in order that the blessed St Anthony will be a guardian to
your oxen and asses, your pigs and your sheep. You are also
accustomed, especially those of you who are enrolled in our
confraternity, to pay that small additional sum that falls due
just once each year. I have been sent to collect all these contri-
butions by my superior, that is, my lord abbot. Therefore, with
God's blessing, when you hear bells ringing after nones,[6] you
will gather here outside the church, where I shall preach a sermon as usual and kiss the cross. As well as preaching, since I
know that you are all devoted to his lordship St Anthony, I
shall bestow on you the special grace of showing you a really
holy and splendid relic, which I myself brought back from the
Holy Lands across the seas. This relic is one of the feathers of
the Angel Gabriel, which he dropped in the Virgin Mary's room
when he came to Nazareth to do the Annunciation.'

After this speech he went back to the Mass.

Among the crowd in the church listening to Friar Cipolla say
these things, were two very fly young men, one called Giovanni
della Bragoniera, the other Biagio Pizzini.[7] They had a good
chuckle to each other over Friar Cipolla's relic. Then, although
they were good friends with him and two of his drinking
companions, they decided to play a trick on him with this
feather. They found out that Friar Cipolla was dining in the

morning with a friend of his up in the town citadel. As soon as they heard he had sat down to eat, they went down to the main road and then to the inn where the friar was staying. Their plan was that Biagio would keep Friar Cipolla's servant in conversation, while Giovanni would search his things for the feather, whatever sort of feather it was, and remove it. They would then see what he had to say to the people when he found out.

Now Friar Cipolla had a servant called Guccio,[8] who was known to some people as Gucky Whaleblubber and to others as Mucky Gucky or Guck the Pig. He was even more of a goon than Lippo Topo[9] ever managed to be and Friar Cipolla would often joke about him with his drinking mates.

'My servant,' he would say, 'has nine things about him. If Solomon, Aristotle or Seneca had just one of these, any goodness in them, any sense, any religion, would be completely wrecked. Just think then what sort of a man he is, with all these nine things and not a trace of goodness, sense or religion.'

He would sometimes be asked what these nine things were and he would reply with a rhyme he had concocted. 'I'll tell you,' he would say. 'He's sluggish and sloppy and lying, he's feckless, malicious and trying, and he's dopey and loutish and mentally dying. That's forgetting a few other blemishes better not mentioned. What's particularly absurd about him is that anywhere he goes he tries to find a wife and a house to rent. He has a big, black, greasy beard, but he thinks he's so wonderfully attractive that all the women who see him fall for him. Given the chance, he would chase blindly after them all and not realize his trousers had ended up round his ankles. Truly, he's a big help to me, because he won't let anyone have a private conversation with me and not listen in. If I happen to be asked about something, he's so frightened I won't know how to reply that he butts in with the yes or the no he thinks fit.'

When Friar Cipolla left Guccio at the inn, he gave him orders to make sure no one touched his things, especially his saddlebags, since his sacred objects were in them. But Mucky Gucky felt happier in a kitchen than a nightingale on its greenwood perch, particularly if he noticed that there was a servant girl around. He had now seen one in the innkeeper's kitchen, one who was squat, fat, bulgy and badly put together with a pair of bosoms like two manure baskets and a face like one of the Baronci[10] and a generally sweaty, greasy and soot-stained air. Leaving Friar Cipolla's room open and his things in a complete mess, he dived down to the kitchen, like a vulture swooping on carrion. Though it was August, he took a seat by the fire and started chatting to the girl, who was called Nuta.

He told her he was an accredited gentleman who was bursting with florins – not including those he owed, which made them more, not less – and that he was a speaker and doer who outspoke and outdid his master himself. He ignored the grease and fat on his hood, which would have been enough to spice up the monastery cauldron at Altopascio,[11] and the tears and patches in his jerkin, which was stiff with grime around the neck and under the arms, and stained more colours than a drape from Tartary and India, not to mention the holes in his shoes and his tattered stockings. Instead, he spoke as if he were a French grandee, telling her he wanted to dress her in new clothes, see she was all right and get her away from slaving for others: he said he couldn't make her a great landholder, but he'd improve her prospects enormously. And so he went on, speaking with great feeling, but, as usual with his grand designs, it was all wind with no chance of anything coming of it.

The two young men, then, found Guck the Pig completely taken up with Nuta. Happy that half their work was unnecessary, they went unimpeded into Friar Cipolla's room, which they found open. The first thing they picked up to have a look at was the saddlebag containing the feather. They opened it and found a little casket wrapped in a roll of silk. When they opened the casket, they found a parrot's tail feather, which they deduced was the one he had promised to show the people of Certaldo.

And no doubt in those days he could easily have put one over on them, since Egyptian luxuries had reached Tuscany only in dribs and drabs, and the flood of such stuff that later ruined the whole of Italy was still to come. If some people were in the know, they weren't the people living around there, who still had the honest-to-goodness roughness of days gone by.

The great majority had never heard mention of a parrot, let alone seen one.

The duo were pleased with their discovery. They removed the feather, and in order not to leave the casket empty, filled it with some bits of coal they noticed in a corner of the room. Then they closed it up, arranged everything as they had found it and went cheerfully off without anyone seeing them. Then they waited to see what Friar Cipolla would say when he found bits of coal instead of a feather.

When the simple men and women who were in church had heard that after nones they were going to see the Angel Gabriel's feather, they went home at the end of Mass and the men told their neighbours about it and the women the women they knew. As soon as the midday meal was over, so many people of both sexes, all eager to see the feather, congregated inside the citadel that there was barely room for them all.

Friar Cipolla had dined well and had a good nap. When he got up a little after nones, he saw just how great a multitude of the local people had come for the feather-viewing. He told Mucky Gucky to go up there with his little bells and to take his bags, too. The latter managed to tear himself away from the kitchen and Nuta, and walked slowly up with the items requested, arriving out of breath, because his body was swollen with all the water he had drunk. At an order from Friar Cipolla he went to the church door and began to ring the bells loudly.

Once the people were all assembled in front of him, Friar Cipolla, unaware that his things had been tampered with, began his sermon and said a great deal to prepare the ground. When he was due to display the Angel Gabriel's feather, he first recited the Confiteor[12] with great solemnity and ordered two torches to be lit. Then, pushing back his friar's cowl, he delicately unwrapped the silk covering to produce the casket. After a few words praising and commending the Angel Gabriel and his relic, he opened it. When he saw that it was full of bits of coal, he immediately discounted any thought of Gucky Whaleblubber having played such a trick on him, since he knew he was not up to it, nor did he curse him for his sloppiness in letting someone else get their hands on the casket. Instead, he silently swore at himself for putting his things in the care of someone he knew was feckless and trying, dopey and mentally dying. Nevertheless, his face as unperturbed as ever, he raised his eyes and his hands to heaven and said, loudly enough for everyone to hear him, 'O God, may Your power be for ever praised!' Then he closed the casket again and turned to the people.

'Gentlemen and ladies,' he went on, 'I must inform you that, while I was still very young, I was sent by my superior to parts of the world where the sun comes out, under an express order to search and search until I found the Porcine privileges,[13] which, though they are stamped and sealed free of charge, profit others much more than ourselves. And so, setting on my way, I departed from Venice[14] via Greekly, and rode on through the realms of Garble and Ballyhoo all the way to Alesfree, from where I went on, not unthirsting, to arrive somewhat later in Sardinee. But what am I doing telling you of all the countries my search took me through? Past St George's Arms I went and arrived in Fiddlia and Diddlia, both populous countries with many inhabitants, from which I went on to the Land of Lie, where I found many members of our order and of other orders too, all shunning unease for the love of God, careless of others' labour if they glimpsed profit on the horizon and spending nothing in those lands but the currency of pardon.

'From there I travelled into the wilds of Abruzzi,[15] where men and women walk the mountains in clogs with sausages on full display. A little further on I met people with outsize baguettes and skinfuls of wine, and from there I journeyed to the Basque Mountains,[16] where all waters flow in descending order. To be brief, I penetrated deep into Parsneep India[17] and there, I swear by this habit I am wearing, I saw feathery creatures flying by, which anyone who hadn't seen them would find incredible. But I wouldn't be allowed to invent such things by Maso del Saggio,[18] who I found had become a great trader there by cracking nuts and selling off the shells piecemeal.

'Still, I was unable to find what I was seeking, because from there on it is water, water all the way. So I turned back and came to those holy lands where in summer bread costs fourpence cold and you get the hot stuff free. There I met the venerable father, the Lord High Shurrup Orelse, the most worthy Patchwork of Jerusalem, who, out of reverence for the St Anthony habit which I have always worn, wanted me to see all the relics he had in his purview. There were so many of these that it would take me miles to lay them out.

'However, I'll tell you a few to waylay your disappointment. First of all he showed me a finger of the Holy Spirit, as firm and juicy as it ever was, then a tuft of hair from the Seraph that appeared to St Francis, then one of the Cherubim's fingernails and some ribbing from the Word-made-flesh, then some vestments of the Holy Catholic faith, and then there were some rays of the star that the Three Wise Men saw in the East, and a little jar of the sweat of St Michael from when he fought with the Devil, and the jawbone of the Lady Death, who knocked out St Lazarus,[19] and much else besides.

'Since I let him make free with my vernacular version of Mount Morello's[20] bottom, and threw in a Capretius touch or two[21] that he'd been after for ages, he let me have a portion of his holy relics. So he presented me with a tooth our Holy Cross had lost, a tiny bottle with the tinkle of Solomon's temple bells in it, and the Angel Gabriel's feather which I mentioned. Then there was one of the clogs of St Gherardo di Villamagna, which I passed on not long ago to Gherardo di Bonsi[22] in Florence, because he is one of his greatest devotees. And he also gave me some of the coals over which the blessed martyr St Lawrence[23] was given his grilling.

'I brought all these things back with me and I have them all still. It's true that my superior wouldn't allow me to show them in public until he had proper certification. But he's now been certified by certain miracles they have worked and by letters he has received from the Patchwork, and he has given me an official display licence. Since I am nervous of entrusting them to others, I always carry them with me. The fact is that I keep the feather of the Angel Gabriel in one casket to stop it getting damaged and the coals from St Lawrence's grilling in another. The two caskets are so alike that I often take one for the other. And that is what has happened this time. I thought I had brought here the casket with the feather in it and instead I've brought the one with the coals.

'But I do not consider there to have been any error. No, it seems to me sure that it was the will of God, and that He Himself put the casket of coals in my hands, since I have recalled just this very moment that it will be the Feast of St Lawrence in two days' time. God willed me, by showing you the coals over which the saint was given his roasting, to rekindle in your souls the devotion you should feel for him. So He made me bring, not the feather, but the blessed coals whose flames were extinguished by the melting liquids of that most holy body. Therefore, my blessed children, bare your heads and in all piety come closer, so that you may see them. But first I want you to know that, whoever is marked by these coals with the sign of the cross, may rest secure all year in the knowledge that no fire will burn him that he will not feel.'

After all this, singing one of the hymns of praise to St Lawrence that he knew, he opened the casket and let the coals be seen. The foolish multitude gaped at them in reverent wonder for a while, and then they all converged on Friar Cipolla in a great throng, everyone offering larger donations than usual and begging to be touched with the coals. Taking a handful, Friar Cipolla began to mark the white smocks and jerkins of the men and the veils of the women with the biggest crosses that he could find space for, proclaiming, as he did so, that all the coal worn away by making the crosses grew back again in the casket, as he had witnessed many times.

So it was that with great personal profit he put crosses on all the people of Certaldo and by his quick thinking turned the tables on those who aimed to make a fool of him when they stole his feather. Those two were present at the sermon and heard him coolly get himself out of trouble with his inventive quick-thinking. All of which made them laugh so much that they thought they would dislocate their jaws. Once the populace had dispersed, they went over to him and, with tremendous jollity, confessed what they had done. They then returned his feather to him. It proved as effective the next year as that day the coals had been.

DAY SEVEN

The Sixth Day of the Decameron *ends and the Seventh begins, in which, under the rule of Dioneo, the members of the party tell stories about the tricks which ladies have played on their husbands for reasons of love, or else in order to get themselves out of trouble, whether or not the husbands have realized what was going on.*

2

Peronella and the Jar

Peronella hides a lover in a storage jar when her husband comes home. He says he has sold the jar, but she says that she has already sold it to the man who is now inside the jar, checking it is sound. Jumping out, the man gets the husband to scrape the jar clean, then carry it home for him.

Emilia's story was heard with a great deal of laughter and the prayer[1] was declared by everyone to be a virtuous and holy one. When she reached her conclusion, the king ordered Filostrato to speak next:

My dearest ladies (he began), you have so many tricks played on you by men, especially husbands, that when it does happen that some lady plays a trick on her husband, you shouldn't just be glad to know it has happened or to hear about it. No, you should go around spreading the word, so that men learn that if they know how to be canny, so too do the ladies. That has to be to your advantage, since if someone realizes that someone else knows what they themselves know, they think twice before trying to trick them.

So can anyone doubt that any man who hears what we're going to be saying today on the subject will feel mightily inclined to curtail his operations, since he will have learned that you are capable of similar things when you want to be? This being so, it's my intention to tell you what a young woman, in spite of her being from the lower classes, did to her husband almost on the spur of the moment to get herself out of trouble.

Very recently in Naples a poor man took as his wife a good-looking, winsome girl called Peronella. What with his work as a builder and her spinning, they managed to keep themselves alive, although their earnings were pretty meagre. One of the cocksure lads about town happened to see this Peronella one day. He thought she was attractive and developed a real passion for her. He pestered her so much in one way or another that he managed to start a relationship with her. They worked out a system of what to do in order to be together. Since her husband got up early every morning to go out on a job or to find piecework, the lad would position himself in a place from where he could see him leaving. As there was never anyone about in Avorio, the district where they lived, he could go and enter the house as soon as the husband left. This arrangement worked well a good many times.

However, one morning was different. The good man had gone out and Giannello Scrignario[2] (as the young beau was called) had gone in and had been some time there with Peronella, when the husband, who usually never came back all day, returned home. He found the door locked from the inside and gave it a couple of loud knocks.

'O Lord, may Your name be praised for ever!' he said to himself. 'Though You made me a poor man, You have consoled me with a young wife who's good and virtuous! Just see how quickly she locked the door inside as soon as I left, so that no one could come in and cause her any trouble!'

Peronella realized that it was her husband from the way he knocked.

'Oh no, my precious Giannello!' she cried. 'I'm a dead woman! That's my husband, God damn him, who's come back! I've no idea what it means, since he's never come back at this time. Perhaps he saw you come in! Whatever it is, for the love of God, get into that big storage jar you see over there! I'll go and let him in, and let's see what's behind him coming home so soon this morning.'

Giannello quickly got himself into the jar, while Peronella went to the door and opened it for her husband to come in.

'What's all this then?' she said, putting on a disgruntled expression. 'What are you doing back home so soon this morning? It looks to me like you don't want to do any work today, since I see you've come back with your tools in your hands. If you carry on like this, what are we going to live on? How are we going to get our bread? Do you think I'm going to let you pawn my best skirt and petticoats? All I do is spin, day and night. My nails are falling out, just so we can get enough oil to light our lamp. Husband, husband, every woman around here is shocked. They all laugh at me for putting up with it, while you come back home with nothing for your hands to do, when you should be off working.'

With that she burst into tears, before starting all over again.

'Oh poor, miserable me!' she wailed. 'I was star-crossed from birth, yes, when I came into the world, they were all lined up against me! I could have had a decent young man, and I turned him down and ended up with someone who doesn't appreciate what a treasure he brought home! Other women enjoy themselves with their lovers – and they've all got them, maybe two or three at the same time. There they go having fun, persuading their husbands that black is white, while here I am, miserable, suffering, a victim of fate, because I'm a good person with no interest in stuff of that sort. I just don't know why I don't get me a lover boy like everybody else. Get this straight, my dear husband, if I wanted to step out of line, I'd have no trouble finding someone worth having. There are lots of smart lads who fancy me and like me and have let me know they'd be generous with the money or with jewels or dresses, if I wanted. But my heart wouldn't let me, since I'm not the daughter of a lady of that sort. And then what happens? Here you are coming back home when you should be out working.'

'Listen, woman,' said her husband, 'don't get so upset, for God's sake! You have to believe that I do know what kind of a person you are, and this morning I've had further evidence of it. It's true that I set off for work, but it looks like you don't know something that I didn't know, either. It's St Galeone's Day[3] today and nobody's working, and that's why I've come home at this time. But I've found a way to make sure we have bread for more than a month. You see this chap here with me? I've sold him the enormous storage jar that you know has been cluttering up the house for ages. He's giving me five silver ducats.'

'This gets worse and worse!' said Peronella. 'You're a man and you get out and about and you ought to know how things work. You've sold the jar for five ducats. I'm a housewife who's barely ever had her head out of the door, but I was fed up with it getting in the way and I've sold it to an honest chap for seven ducats. He'd just climbed into it to check it was sound when you came back.'

The husband was more than pleased to hear this.

'You'd better go, mate,' he said to the man who'd come back with him. 'You heard my wife say she's sold the thing for seven pieces, when you were offering only five.'

'Well, the best of luck to you then!' said the man, leaving.

'Come on in then,' said Peronella to her husband, 'since you're here, and sort out this business with him directly.'

Giannello had been waiting with his ears pricked in case he sensed danger brewing or he had to take counter-measures. When he heard what Peronella had just said, he immediately jumped out of the jar, pretending to have no idea her husband was back.

'Where are you, good lady?' he called.

The husband was by then coming towards him.

'Here I am,' he said, 'what's the problem?'

'Who are you?' Giannello asked. 'I'd like to speak with the lady who agreed to sell me this jar.'

'Don't worry, you can deal with me,' said the good man. 'I'm her husband.'

'The jar seems to me to be a sound one,' said Giannello. 'But it strikes me you left some wine lees in it. It's caked with dried gunge I can't scrape off with my nails. I can't take it unless I see it properly cleaned first.'

'Oh no, that's not going to make the deal fall through,' said Peronella. 'My husband will clean out the whole thing.'

'Very well then,' said the husband, putting down his tools and unfastening his jacket. He had his wife light a candle and pass him a scraper. Then he clambered in and began scraping, while Peronella gave the impression of wanting to see what he was doing. Sticking her head in the mouth of the jar, which wasn't very wide, and one arm and a whole shoulder too, she started telling him 'Scrape this bit and that one and this bit over here' or 'Look there, there's a smidgeon you've missed.'

So there she was giving instructions and suggestions to her husband, when Giannello, who had not quite achieved total satisfaction when the husband came home, decided to do the best he could under the circumstances, seeing that he couldn't get what he wanted quite in the way he wished. He closed in on Peronella standing there, filling the whole opening of the jar. You may know how the stallions that run wild and rampant over the steppes assail the mares of Parthia.[4] Just so did Giannello bring the desires of youth to their natural effect. A perfect ending was achieved and the jar was scraped clean almost at the same moment, after which Giannello backed away, Peronella withdrew her head from the jar and the husband climbed out.

'Take this candle, good man,' Peronella said to Giannello, 'and check the cleaning has been up to what you had in mind.'

Having taken a look inside, Giannello said that it was fine and he was happy with it. After which he handed over the seven silver ducats, and had the husband carry the jar round to his house.

4
Tofano, His Wife and a Well

Tofano shuts his wife out of their house one night. When her pleas to be allowed in again have no effect, she pretends to throw herself down a well, but drops a large stone into it instead. Tofano comes out and rushes over. She runs in, locks him out of the house and ridicules him as loudly as she can.

As soon as the king perceived Elissa's story was over, he turned briskly to Lauretta and signalled to her that he would like her to speak next. She began without hesitation:

O Love, how great and varied are your powers! What stratagems and ruses you devise! What philosopher or artist, past or present, could ever show the resources, the nimbleness of mind, the powers of argument that you instil from the start in anyone who follows in your tracks? There's no schooling that can compete with yours, as the examples set before us so far have amply demonstrated. My loving ladies, I will now add a further instance of a solution to a difficult problem being found by a quite unsophisticated lady, which I think can have been shown to her only by Love.

There was once living in Arezzo a rich man called Tofano, who ended up marrying a very beautiful lady named Ghita. Very quickly, for some reason he didn't know himself, he began to act the jealous husband. His wife perceived what was happening and thought his behaviour offensive. She asked him various times what was behind his jealousy and, when he could give her only vague, unsatisfactory explanations, she took it into her head to give him a lethal dose of the very thing he was so irrationally afraid of.

She was aware of having caught the eye of a young man of whom she had a very favourable opinion and began discreetly to build up an understanding with him. Things between the two reached the point when the only thing left to be done was to translate words into action, which the lady also set her mind to bringing about. She had found out that one of her husband's bad habits was a fondness for drink. She began not just to express her approval of this, but skilfully to encourage him to indulge himself again and again. She became so good at it that she got him to drink himself stupid almost every time he felt like a glass or two. When she saw he was totally drunk, she would put him to bed. In this way she was able to meet her lover alone for the first time and then safely go ahead with a succession of further meetings. Being so confident about her husband's drunken state, she not only had the nerve to let her lover into her own house, but sometimes she went off to spend most of the night with him in his house, which was not far away.

She was a woman in love and she was able to go on like this for some time. However, it eventually registered with the unfortunate husband that, while she encouraged him to drink, she never drank at all herself. He began to suspect what was really going on – that is, that his lady was getting him drunk in order to do what she pleased while he was asleep. Wanting to test whether this was really the case, he came back one evening, not having tasted a drop all day, but speaking and behaving like a complete inebriate. His wife was taken in and put him straight to bed, judging that he needed no more drink for a good night's sleep. That done, following her established practice, she left the house and went off to her lover's, where she stayed until midnight.

As soon as Tofano could tell that his lady was no longer there, he got up and went to the house door, which he bolted on the inside. He then stationed himself at the window, so that he could see her coming back and make it plain to her that he'd cottoned on to her game. Eventually the lady did return. When she reached the house and found herself locked out, she was extremely distressed and tried first of all to force open the door. Tofano let her go on trying for a while.

'Madam,' he said at last, 'you're wasting your efforts. You won't be able to get in. Go on back to where you've been until now and rest assured that you're not returning here until I can pay you the honours that you deserve for this behaviour in the presence of your relatives and the neighbours.'

The lady started begging him for the love of God to relent and open up, saying she wasn't coming from where he thought, but had been staying up a few hours with one of the neighbours, since the nights were long and the neighbour couldn't sleep all through them or face staying up by herself in the house. Her pleas were useless. The idiot was set on his dishonour, which, so far, no one knew anything about, becoming public knowledge throughout Arezzo.

Realizing that begging was a waste of time, the lady tried threatening.

'If you don't open the door for me,' she said, 'I'll make you the most miserable man alive!'

To which Tofano retorted, 'And what could you possibly do?'

But she was a lady whose wits had been sharpened in the school of Love.

'Before I'm willing to suffer the shame you wrongly want to expose me to,' she replied, 'I'll throw myself in this well that's just by. When they find my corpse, every single person will believe it was you who threw me down it in a drunken fit. Then you'll have to run away and lose everything you have and live the life of a wanted criminal. Or else you'll have your head cut off as my murderer, which in reality is what you'll be.'

Her words made no impression on Tofano's stupid obstinacy.

'Well, look,' she went on eventually, 'I can't bear your obnoxious attitude any longer. May God forgive you! Please put away my spindle, which I'm leaving here.'

The night was pitch-black and two people meeting in the street would barely have been able to make each other out. After this last speech the lady went over to the well and picked up a very large stone that was by it. With a cry of 'God forgive me!' she let it fall into the well.

The stone hit the water with a tremendous splash. Tofano heard and felt sure that she had thrown herself in. He seized the bucket and rope and, flinging himself out of the house, rushed over to the well to help her. The lady had hidden herself by the door and, as soon as she saw him running to the well, she dived into the house, barred the door and went over to the window.

'Wine's to be watered when you're drinking, not in the middle of the night when you've finished!' she called out.

Hearing her, Tofano realized he'd been made a fool of. He went back to the door and, when he couldn't get in, started telling her to open up.

The lady stopped keeping her voice down, as she had done up to this point. 'By the crucified Jesus,' she called out, now almost shouting, 'you're not coming in here tonight, you drunken creep! I can't stand you behaving like this any more! The only thing I can do is to let everyone see what you're like and what time of night you come home!'

Tofano was furious and began calling her names and shouting. Hearing the din, the neighbours, men and women, got out of bed and went to their windows to ask what was up.

'It's this villain coming home to me drunk of an evening or else falling asleep in taverns and then getting back at this time,' the lady said, tearfully. 'I've put up with it for long enough and told him off in no uncertain terms. But it's done me no good and I can't bear it any longer. I made my mind up to shame him like this and lock him out of the house to see if that'll make him mend his ways.'

Tofano went on being a fool, explaining what had really happened and making violent threats.

Meanwhile, the lady was saying to her neighbours, 'So you see what sort of a man he is! What would you say if I was in the street instead of him and he was in the house instead of me? In God's name, I can't imagine you not believing he was telling the truth. You can see from this how his mind works. He claims that I've done what I'm sure he's done himself. He thought he'd frighten me by throwing something or other down the well. I just wish to God he had really thrown himself in and drowned, and then all that wine he's drunk too much of would have been properly watered down.'

The neighbours, men and women alike, began telling Tofano off, saying he was the one at fault and laying into him for criticizing his lady wife. In a short while the uproar had spread through the whole neighbourhood and reached the ears of her relatives. They came round and, having listened to various people's versions of the story, they got hold of Tofano and gave him a thorough beating. Then they went into the house, picked up the lady's things and returned home with her, threatening Tofano with worse to come.

Tofano recognized he was in a mess and that his jealousy was responsible. Being a man who loved his wife dearly, he persuaded some friends to act as intermediaries. Eventually he achieved a reconciliation and got his wife home again. He promised never to be jealous in the future, granting her in addition the freedom to do whatever she liked, on condition that she acted discreetly and nothing came to his attention. He was like the proverbial bumpkin[1] who goes mad and then makes peace, having lost what he had. Long live love, meanness go to hell and let's all enjoy ourselves.

9

Lydia, Nicostratos and a Pear Tree

Lydia, the wife of Nicostratos, loves Pyrrhus, who asks her to do three things to convince him she is serious. She does all three and, in addition, makes love with Pyrrhus in the presence of her husband. She then convinces Nicostratos that what he has seen never happened.

Neifile's story had gone down so well that the ladies couldn't stop laughing and talking about it, although the king told them repeatedly to be quiet, since he had given the order to Panfilo to tell his story. They finally fell silent and he was able to begin:

I don't believe, revered ladies (he said), that there is anything, no matter how difficult and dangerous, that someone fervently in love won't be courageous enough to face. This has been demonstrated various times in a good few stories. But I think the story I intend to tell you will ram the point home. You will hear about a lady who was helped to success more by the hand of Fortune than by the application of reason. Hence, I wouldn't advise any other woman to follow in her footsteps. Fortune doesn't always keep to one pattern and not all the men in the world can have the wool pulled over their eyes in one and the same way.

Argos[1] is an ancient Greek city more famous for its past kings than for its size and importance. There was once among its inhabitants a nobleman called Nicostratos, whose luck it was to marry, somewhat late in life, a fine lady, as feisty by nature as she was beautiful to look at, by the name of Lydia. Being a rich nobleman, her husband kept a large household, plus hounds and falcons, since his greatest pleasure was hunting. One of his household staff was an engaging, well-turned-out young man with an attractive physique and the capacity to bring off anything he set his mind to. He was called Pyrrhus and he was a particular favourite of Nicostratos, who trusted him more than anyone else. Lydia fell passionately in love with him and couldn't get him out of her mind day and night. But Pyrrhus – either because he wasn't aware of this passion or because he wanted nothing to do with it – gave no sign of being in the slightest bit interested, which was all unbearably distressing for the lady.

She made a firm decision to let him know how she felt and summoned one of her maids – a girl called Lusca, in whom she had complete confidence – and spoke to her as follows:

'Lusca, you've received a lot of kindnesses from me in the past which should make you my obedient and loyal servant. So take care that what I'm going to say to you reaches the ears of no one except the person I specify. As you can see, Lusca, I'm a young woman in the prime of her life and I have in great abundance all the things that a woman could want. To put it briefly, there's only one thing I can complain about. And that's my husband's age, which doesn't tally with my own. Consequently, I find myself out of sorts regarding that activity which gives young women most pleasure. I want to participate in it as much as anyone else and decided a while back that, if it was an unfriendly act on the part of Fortune to give me such an elderly husband, I shouldn't turn into my own worst enemy and give up on any prospect of pleasure and well-being. I want to feel as fulfilled in this part of my life as in all the others and have made my mind up to look for satisfaction in the arms of our Pyrrhus, who I consider a more worthy choice of lover than anyone else. I've conceived such a passion for him that I don't feel at all well when I don't see him or think about him. I'm sure I'll die if I can't be alone with him at the soonest possible moment. If my life means anything to you, find the best way you can to let him know about my love and just beg him on my behalf to agree to come and see me, when you go back and give him the word.'

The maid said she would be glad to help. As soon as she saw her opportunity she got Pyrrhus on one side and did all she could to deliver her mistress's message properly. Pyrrhus appeared stunned to hear what she said, as if he really had been unaware of anything until that moment. He wondered whether the lady had set up the maid in order to test his loyalty and so gave a quick, off-hand reply.

'Lusca,' he said, 'I can't believe that what you've said comes from my lady. Just think what you're saying. And supposing it does come from her, I can't believe she meant it. And even granted that she meant it, my master does me more honour than I deserve and I wouldn't do him such a disservice to save my life. So make sure you don't raise the subject with me ever again.'

Lusca was not to be put down by his stark refusal.

'Pyrrhus,' she said, 'I'll speak to you about this and anything else my lady wants me to speak to you about as many times as she tells me to. And I don't care whether you like it or loathe it. Because you're a cretin!'

So she went off in a huff to report what Pyrrhus had said to her lady, who immediately felt that all she wanted was to die. After a few days she spoke with the maid again.

'Lusca,' she said, 'you know it takes more than one blow to bring down an oak tree. So I think you should go back and start again. He's someone who does incline in my direction in some peculiar way. Find the right moment to lay out the full extent of my passion before him and use all your wits to get things moving. If it all stutters to a halt at this point, it would be the death of me and he'd believe he has just been led on. We're trying to make him love me and instead he'd end up hating me.'

After consoling her lady, the maid went looking for Pyrrhus and found him in a cheerful, receptive mood.

'Pyrrhus,' she said, 'I told you clearly enough a few days ago the state your lady and mine has reduced herself to out of her love for you. Now I want you to really get it into your head this time that if you go on being as unresponsive as you seemed the other day, you can be absolutely sure that she won't stay alive for long. That's why I'm begging you to give in and let her have what she wants. I had you down as a sensible man, but if you must keep up this pig-headed resistance I'll rate you a total fool. What a fabulous thing it could be for you to be loved more than anything by a lady like this, one who's so beautiful, so noble and so rich! You should thank Fortune for offering you something as good as this, something that fits so well with the fancies of a young man like you and will also supply some of the support you need. Do you know anybody in your position who will be better off than you, if you're sensible and just take the path of pleasure? Will you find anyone else who'll be able to compete with you in terms of armour, horses, clothing and cash if you're willing to give your love to her?

'Take my words to heart and come to your senses. Remember the rule that it's a once-in-a-lifetime event for Fortune to present herself with a smiling face and her lap full of gifts. If a man won't accept them, the time will come when he's down and out with only himself to blame, not Fortune.

'Anyway, relations between servants and masters aren't based on the same sense of loyalty you'd expect between friends and equals. As far as they can, servants have to treat their masters in the way their masters treat them. Suppose you had a good-looking wife or mother or daughter or sister that Nicostratos took a fancy to. Could you have a hope he'd show you any of the loyalty that you want to show towards him regarding his lady wife? You're a fool if you think like that. Take it from me that if the sweet talk and pleading didn't work, he'd use force. Let us treat them and what's theirs in the same way as they treat us and what's ours. Make the most of Fortune's kindness. Don't chase her away, go and meet her, welcome her in. If you don't, it's not just that your lady is going to die, as she certainly will, but you'll end up feeling so sorry that you'll want to die yourself.'

Pyrrhus had already reflected at various times on what Lusca had said to him before and had made up his mind to give her a different reply if she came back to him again, and to do what he could to comply fully with the lady's wishes. He only wanted to be sure that he wasn't being tested in some way.

'Look, Lusca,' he replied, 'I know that everything you say is true. On the other hand I also know that my master is very clever and very shrewd. Since he's put me in charge of all his affairs I have a nagging fear he may have planned all this with Lydia in order to test me. There are three things I want her to do to convince me. If she does them, I'll definitely do straight away anything she wants. The three things I'm asking for are these: first, to kill Nicostratos's best hawk before his very eyes; second, to send me a tuft of hair from Nicostratos's beard; and lastly to let me have one of the healthiest teeth he's got in his mouth.'

None of these things seemed easy to Lusca and even less so to her lady. But Love, the good companion and the great teacher of ways and means, gave her the resolve she needed. She sent a message via her maid that she would carry out to the letter his requests and do so soon. What's more she added that, since he thought so highly of Nicostratos's intelligence, she would make love with Pyrrhus in his presence and make him believe it never happened.

So Pyrrhus waited to see what the noble lady would do. A few days later Nicostratos had some high-ranking gentlemen to one of the splendid lunches he often gave. The tables had been carried away, when Lydia, decked in her full finery and wearing a robe of green velvet, came out of her room and entered the hall where the party were gathered. In full view of Pyrrhus and everyone else she walked over to the perch where Nicostratos's favourite sparrowhawk was tied and unfastened it, as if she intended to carry it away, perched on her wrist. Then she took hold of the fastenings on its legs, swung it against the wall and killed it.

'Good grief, lady! What have you done that for?' shouted Nicostratos at her. Making no reply, she turned to the noblemen who had dined with him and said: 'Sirs, I'd be hopeless at obtaining redress from a king who did me wrong if I hadn't the nerve to obtain it from a sparrowhawk. Let me tell you something: for ages this bird has been taking away from me all the hours that men should dedicate to giving pleasure to their ladies. It is barely dawn before Nicostratos is up and riding off into the country with his hawk on his wrist, to watch it fly. And there I am, just as you see me, left miserably alone in bed. I've often thought of doing what I've just done. I only held back because I wanted to wait until I could do the deed in the presence of men who would be fair judges of my case, as I believe you will be.'

The listening noblemen, who took it that she was voicing feelings she genuinely felt for Nicostratos, all found themselves laughing. Nicostratos was beside himself, but they started saying to him, 'Oh, the lady's done well to punish the wrong done to her by killing that hawk!'

And they kept on making wisecracks on the subject well after the lady had returned to her room, until they finally calmed Nicostratos down and made him join in the laughter.

'That's an impressive first step that the lady's taken towards improving my love life!' said the watching Pyrrhus to himself. 'God help her keep going!'

Not many days after Lydia had killed the hawk, she and Nicostratos were together in her room. She started stroking him and generally fooling about. When he joined in and gave her hair a playful tug, she seized her chance to carry out the second of Pyrrhus's demands. She quickly grabbed a little tuft of Nicostratos's beard and, still laughing, gave it such a sharp jerk that she tore it out of his chin completely, which Nicostratos much resented.

'Now come on,' she said, 'why such a miserable face, just because I've pulled out maybe six hairs of your beard? You didn't feel what I felt when you were pulling my hair about just now!'

Joking exchanges like this continued for some time, with the lady taking care to safeguard the tuft of beard which she had pulled out and which she sent to her beloved the same day.

She was more concerned about the third thing. But being naturally highly resourceful and made even more so by Love, she had already worked out a way of dealing with the problem. At their fathers' request Nicostratos had taken in two youths of noble birth to teach them the basics of courtly behaviour. So, when he was eating, one would cut up the food on his plate and the other would see to his drink. Lydia summoned the two of them and gave them to understand that their breath smelled, instructing them to hold their heads as far back as they could when they were serving Nicostratos, but not to say a word about it to anyone. The young men believed her and began behaving in the way she had told them.

In due course Lydia raised the issue with Nicostratos.

'Have you noticed what these boys do when they serve you?' she asked.

'I certainly have,' he replied. 'And I was going to ask them why they do it.'

'Don't bother,' said his lady, 'I can tell you myself. I've kept quiet about it for a while so as not to upset you. But now I see other people noticing it, I can't keep it from you any longer. The only reason this is happening is that your breath stinks horribly. I don't know why it should, since it used not to. But it's a terrible thing, given that you have to mix with people of a certain class. We should see what we can do to deal with it.'

'What could it be?' Nicostratos asked. 'Could I have a tooth somewhere in my mouth that's got something wrong with it?'

'Maybe that's it,' said Lydia.

She led him to a window and got him to open his mouth.

'Oh Nicostratos,' she exclaimed, after examining one side and then the other, 'how on earth have you put up with it for so long? You have a tooth on this side which, as far as I can tell, isn't just damaged, it's completely rotten. Really, if you keep it in your mouth much longer, it's going to ruin the teeth on either side. My advice is to have it out before things go any further.'

'That's fine by me, if that's how you see it,' Nicostratos said. 'Let's call in a doctor to pull it out.'

'A doctor coming here! God forbid!' Lydia said. 'My view is that the way it's positioned I can pull it out very well myself. Besides, these doctors are so ham-fisted that my heart wouldn't be able to stand it if I saw and heard you being treated by one of them. So I really do want to do it myself. Then if it hurts too much, I'll stop pulling straight away, which is something a professional wouldn't do.'

So she had appropriate tools brought and sent everyone out of the chamber, keeping back only Lusca. With the door now locked, she made Nicostratos lie down on a table. Then she inserted pincers in his mouth and took hold of one of his teeth.

He yelled with pain, but while Lusca held him firmly down, Lydia applied all her strength and managed to yank out the tooth. They put it on one side and produced another horrendously decayed one that Lydia had hidden in her hand, which they showed to the aching, half-dead Nicostratos. 'Look what you've had in your mouth all this time!' they said. He was taken in, though he had suffered immense pain and was not at all happy about it. Still, now the tooth was out, he thought he felt much better. They soothed and mollycoddled him and when the pain had subsided he left the room. The lady picked up the tooth and immediately sent it to her lover, who was now convinced she loved him and let her know he was ready to do whatever she wanted.

The lady wanted him to have no doubts whatsoever. Although every hour that passed before she could be alone with him seemed like an age, she was determined to keep the promise she had made. She pretended to be unwell and one day after lunch received a visit in her room from Nicostratos. Seeing no one with him but Pyrrhus, she asked if the two of them might help her down to the garden, since she thought she would feel somewhat better there. So, with support from Nicostratos on one side and from Pyrrhus on the other, she was conveyed to the garden and set down on a stretch of lawn at the foot of a fine pear tree.

After they had been sitting there for a while, the lady put a request to Pyrrhus, whom she had previously instructed what he was to do.

'Pyrrhus,' she said, 'I have a great yen for some of those pears. So climb up the tree and throw a few down.'

Pyrrhus quickly climbed up and began throwing pears down. Then, while he was still throwing, he started calling out.

'Oh sir, what are you up to? And, my lady, haven't you any shame at letting him do that in front of me? Do you think I'm blind? You were so unwell just now. How is it you've got better so quickly you start doing something of that sort? If you really do want to, you have lots of lovely bedrooms. Why don't you go and do it in one of those? It'll be more decent than doing it in front of me.'

The lady turned to her husband.

'What's Pyrrhus saying? Is he raving?' she asked.

'I'm not raving, no, my lady,' called Pyrrhus. 'Don't you think I can see?'

Nicostratos was bewildered.

'Pyrrhus,' he said, 'I really think you're dreaming.'

'I'm not dreaming one little bit, sir,' said Pyrrhus. 'And you're not dreaming, either. No, you're shaking yourself about so much that if this pear tree moved like that it wouldn't have a single pear left on it.'

'What can it be?' said the lady. 'Could it be that he thinks that what he's saying is the truth? God save me, if I was as well as I was a little while ago I'd climb up that tree to see what these weird things are that he says he can see.'

Since Pyrrhus was still calling from up in the pear tree and going on in the same vein as before, Nicostratos now called out to him to get out of the tree.

'What do you say you've been seeing?' he asked him once he was down.

'I think you're taking me for a halfwit or a fantasist,' said Pyrrhus. 'I saw you at work on top of your lady, since you force me to tell you. Then, when I was climbing down, I saw you get up and plonk yourself there where you're sitting.'

'You definitely did have a witless moment,' said Nicostratos. 'We've stayed just as we are, not moving an inch since you climbed the pear tree.'

'What is there to argue about?' said Pyrrhus. 'I did actually see you. And if I saw you, what I saw was you giving her your all.'

Nicostratos became more and more puzzled.

'I really want to see if this tree is bewitched,' he said, finally, 'and whether anyone who climbs up it sees extraordinary things.'

So up he climbed, at which Pyrrhus and the lady began to make love. Nicostratos reacted to the sight with a shout.

'You dirty slut! What are you doing? And you, Pyrrhus, the person I've trusted more than anyone?' he called out, starting to clamber down the tree.

'We're just sitting here,' Pyrrhus and the lady said. And, seeing him climbing down, they resumed the sitting positions he'd left them in. When he was on the ground and saw they were where he'd left them, he began to rail at them loudly.

Pyrrhus interrupted him.

'Nicostratos, I fully confess now that what you said before is correct and that I saw something untrue when I was up the pear tree. I acknowledge this only because I know that you saw something that wasn't true either. All you have to do to be convinced I'm telling the truth is to reflect a moment and decide whether your lady, who is the most blameless and sensible woman there is, could bring herself to commit an outrage like that before your very eyes, assuming she had any inclination of that sort. The only thing I'll say about myself is that I'd rather let myself be cut in pieces before I'd allow such a thought to cross my mind, let alone bring myself to do the act in your presence. The blame for seeing things in this distorted way must lie with the pear tree. Nothing in the whole world would have persuaded me that you hadn't, right here and now, enjoyed sexual relations with your lady, except for the fact that I've just heard you say that it seemed to you that I was doing something that I know for sure I'd never thought of, let alone ever actually done.'

It was then the lady's turn. She had got to her feet in total fury.

'The Devil take you,' she cried, 'if you think I'm just a paltry bitch who – if she'd a mind to do such sordid things as you say you saw – would come and do them right in front of your eyes. You can be sure that if I felt any such urge I'd know how to make good use of one of our bedchambers, and I'd be so discreet about it that I'd be staggered if you got the slightest hint of what was going on.'

Nicostratos began to think that what they were both telling him was true and that they couldn't possibly have brought themselves to do such a thing in his presence. He became quieter and stopped berating them and instead started talking about the strangeness of it all and the supernatural effect on the eyesight of anyone who climbed the tree.

But the lady continued to seem distressed by the poor opinion of her that Nicostratos had come out with.

'Truly this pear tree is not going to play its shameful tricks on any other woman, not on me nor on anyone else, if I've got anything to do with it,' she said. 'So, Pyrrhus, run and fetch an axe and pay it back in one go for what it has done to you and me by chopping it down, even though it would be far better to chop off Nicostratos's head, since he refused to think things through and allowed the eyes of his mind to be blinded by what he saw. What you say appeared true to the eyes you've got in your head, but there's no way you should have let your rational judgement be fooled into understanding or accepting that it was really the case.'

Pyrrhus hurried off for an axe and with it cut down the pear tree. When the lady saw it was fallen, she addressed these words to Nicostratos. 'My anger has evaporated now that I see the enemy of my good name brought low.'

In response to his pleas, she graciously bestowed her forgiveness upon him, with the injunction never again to presume such a thing of one who loved him more than she loved herself.

So the poor bamboozled husband went back with the lady and her lover to the palace. There, many times in the days that followed, Pyrrhus and Lydia shared their pleasure and delight in a more relaxed way. May God show the same kindness to us!

DAY EIGHT

The Seventh Day of the Decameron *ends and the Eighth begins, in which, under the rule of Lauretta, the members of the party tell stories about the tricks which ladies are always playing on men or men on ladies or men on other men.*

2

Mrs Rosie and the Priest

The priest of Varlungo gets Mrs Rosie into bed and lets her keep his cloak in lieu of payment. He then borrows a mortar from her, which he sends back with a request to return the cloak deposited with her. The good lady gives it back, but lets him know what she thinks of him too.

Men and ladies alike were still voicing their approval of Gulfardo's treatment of the avaricious Milanese woman,[1] when the queen turned to Panfilo and smiled at him to signal he should speak next:

Lovely ladies (he began), I'm taking the opportunity to tell you a little story targeting a class of persons who continually wrong us without our having any chance of getting our own back, that is, the priesthood. They've embarked on a crusade against our wives and think they've gained as much remission of sins and penances when they can get one into bed as if they'd dragged the Sultan in chains from Alexandria to Avignon.[2] Poor laymen can't do the same to them. At best they can take it out on the mothers, sisters, women friends and daughters of the priests and torment them with the sort of harassment that's practised on their wives. So I intend to tell you a story about some rustic malarkey. It's a short story, but it has a very funny ending, with also a useful moral for you, namely, that not everything a priest says is to be trusted.

So, to begin, there's a village not far from here called Varlungo,[3] which each of you either knows about or may have heard people mention. It once had a valiant priest, a fine figure of a man who served the ladies well. He was not much of a

reader, but every Sunday he would spout wholesome holy ver-
biage beneath the churchyard elm to refresh the spirits of his
parishioners. When the men were off somewhere he would
come visiting their wives more solicitously than any priest
they'd had before, sometimes bringing religious bits and pieces,
holy water or candle ends to their houses and giving them his
blessing.

Now among the women of the parish he took a fancy to,
there was one he particularly liked called Mrs Rosie. She was
the wife of a labourer by the name of Willy Welcome and she
really was a lovely ripe country girl, tanned, sturdy, with lots of
grinding potential. She was also better than any girl around at
playing the tambourine, singing songs like 'The Water's Running Down My River', and dancing reels and jigs, when she
had to, waving a pretty little kerchief in her hand. With all
these talents she reduced the good priest to a quivering wreck.
He would wander around the village all day trying to catch
sight of her. When he realized she was in church on a Sunday
morning, he would launch into a Kyrie or a Sanctus and struggle to come over as a virtuoso singer, although he sounded
more like an ass braying; whereas, when he didn't see her there,
he barely bothered to sing at all. All the same he was clever
enough not to arouse the suspicions of Willy Welcome or any
of his neighbours.

From time to time he would send Mrs Rosie presents in an
effort to win her over. Sometimes it was a bunch of fresh garlic,
since he grew the best in the region in a vegetable garden he
worked with his own hands; sometimes it was a basket of ber-
ries and now and then a bunch of shallots or spring onions.
When he saw his chance, he would give her a hurt look and
mutter a few gentle reproaches, while she acted cold, pretending not to notice and looking all supercilious. So the estimable
priest was left getting nowhere.

Now it happened one day that the priest was kicking his
heels in the noontime heat out in the countryside with nothing
much to do when he bumped into Willy Welcome driving an
ass loaded with things on its back. He greeted him and asked
where he was going.

'To tell the truth, sir Father,' Willy replied, 'I'm off to town on a bit of business. I'm transporting these materials to Notary Bonaccorri da Ginestreto[4] to get him to aid and assist with a fiddle-faddle on the legal side that the assessor is officializing to put the whole house in order at last.'

'That, my son, is a good thing to do,' said the priest, full of glee. 'Go with my blessing and come back soon. And if you should happen to see Lapuccio or Naldino, don't let it slip your mind to tell them to bring me those straps for my threshing flails.'[5]

Willy said he would do that and went off towards Florence, while the priest decided the time had come for him to go and try his luck with Rosie. He strode out vigorously and did not stop until he reached her house. He went in, calling out 'God be with us! Is anyone here?'

Rosie was up at the top of the house. Hearing him, she shouted, 'Father, you're very welcome. What are you doing all fancy free in this heat?'

'God help me,' said the priest, 'I've come to spend a little time with you, having just met your man on his way to town.'

Rosie was downstairs by now. She sat down and began cleaning some cabbage seeds her husband had sifted out a short time before.

'Well, Rosie,' said the priest, 'must you go on being the death of me like this?'

Rosie began to laugh.

'Well, what am I doing to you?' she asked.

'You're not doing anything to me,' said the priest, 'but you don't let me do what I'd like to do to you, which is love my neighbour as God commanded.'

'Oh get on with you!' said Rosie. 'Do priests do things of that sort?'

'Yes,' said the priest, 'and better than other men. And why shouldn't we? I tell you we do a much, much better job. And do you know why? It's because we let the pond fill up before the mill starts grinding. And truly I can give you just what you need, if you'll just stay quiet and let me do the business.'

'What do you mean just what I need?' said Rosie. 'You priests are all tighter-fisted than the Devil himself.'

'I don't know,' the priest said. 'Just ask me. Maybe you need a nice little pair of shoes or a headscarf or a pretty woollen waistband or maybe something else.'

'That's all very well, Brother Priest,' said Rosie. 'I've enough of that stuff. But if you're that keen on me, you can do me a particular favour and then I'll do what you want.'

'Tell me what you're after and I'll be glad to do it,' said the priest.

'I have to go to Florence on Saturday,' said Rosie, 'to give in the wool I've been spinning and get my spinning wheel mended. If you let me have five pounds (which I know you've got) I'll get the pawnbroker to give me back my purple skirt and the decorated Sunday belt I wore when I got married. You know not having it has meant I can't go to church or anywhere respectable. And after that I'll be up for what you want for ever more.'

'God help me,' the priest said, 'but I haven't the money on me. But trust me, I'll make sure you have it before Saturday.'

'Oh yes,' said Rosie, 'you're all great at making promises. And then you don't keep any of them. Do you think you can treat me the way you treated Nell the Belle, who was left with just a big bass tum to play with? You're not going to do the same to me, by God. She ended up a common tart because of you. If you haven't got it here, go and get it.'

'Oh please,' the priest said, 'don't make me go all the way back to the house. You can tell my luck is up and there's no one about. It could be that when I came back someone would be here to get in our way. I don't know when it might next stand up as well as it's standing up now.'

'That's all very fine,' she said. 'But if you're willing to go, go. If not, you'll just have to manage.'

He saw that she was only going to agree to his wishes when a contract was signed and delivered, whereas he was hoping for a bit of free access.

'Look,' he said, 'you don't believe I'll bring you the money. What about if I leave you this blue cape of mine as a guarantee? It's a good one.'

Rosie gave him a haughty look.

'This cape,' she said, 'how much is it worth?'

'What do you mean how much is it worth?' the priest asked. 'Let me tell you it is Douai cloth,[6] double, maybe triple-ply, and there are even people here who say it's got some foreply in it. I paid seven pounds at Lotto's second-hand clothes shop less than two weeks ago. It had five shillings knocked off, so it was a bargain, according to Buglietti d'Alberto, who you know is a bit of an expert in blue cloths.'

'Oh yes?' said Rosie. 'God help me, I'd never have believed it. But give it to me first.'

The good priest, who was feeling hard-pressed by his loaded weapon, unfastened his cape and passed it over.

'Well, Mr Priest,' she said, when she'd put it away, 'let's go down here to the shed. It doesn't get visitors.'

So off they went. And there he covered her in the sloppiest kisses in the world, introduced her to God's holy bliss and enjoyed himself generally with her for a good while. He finally left in the uncaped state priests normally appear in only at weddings and went back to the church.

There he reflected how all the candle ends he picked up from his parishioners in the course of a year weren't worth half a fiver and felt he had made a mistake. Now regretting leaving the cape behind, he started thinking how to get it back at no cost to himself. Since he was quite crafty minded, he worked out a good way of doing so. And it worked.

The next day being a feast day, he sent the son of a neighbour of his to Rosie's house, with a request for her to be so kind as to lend him her stone mortar, since Binguccio dal Poggio and Nuto Buglietti were dining with him that morning and he wanted to make a sauce. Rosie sent it back with the boy. As soon as it got to around lunchtime, the priest guessed when Willy Welcome and Rosie would be eating. He called his curate and said to him, 'Pick up that mortar and take it back to Mrs Rosie. Tell her, "The Father is immensely grateful and would like to have back the cape the boy left with you as a guarantee."'

The curate went to Rosie's house with the mortar and found her and Willie at the table, eating their meal. He set down the mortar and gave them the priest's message.

Rosie was all set to give her reply to this request for the cape. But Willy's brow darkened.

'So you need guarantees from our estimated father, do you?' he said. 'I swear to Christ, I could really give you a clout up the bracket. Go fetch it right now and get yourself a cancer while you're at it. And watch out for him wanting anything else of ours. He'd better not be told no. I don't care what it is, I tell you, even if he wants our ass.'

Rosie got up, grumbling to herself, and went over to the linen chest. She took out the cape and passed it to the curate.

'You must give that priest a message from me,' she said. 'Say, "Mrs Rosie vows to God that you'll never again be sauce-pounding in her mortar. That last time you didn't do yourself any credit."'

The curate went off with the cape and relayed Rosie's message to the priest, who burst out laughing.

'You can tell her next time you see her,' he told him, 'that if she won't lend out the mortar, I won't lend her the pestle. The one goes with the other.'

Willy believed that his wife had spoken as she did because he had told her off and gave the matter no further thought. But coming off worst made Rosie fall out with the priest and she refused to speak to him until the grape harvest, when he terrified her by threatening to have her stuffed into the mouth of the biggest devil in hell. She made her peace with him over fermenting must and roasting chestnuts, and after that the two of them had a good guzzle together on various occasions. To make up for the five pounds, the priest had her tambourine re-covered and a dinky little bell attached, which made her very happy.

3
Calandrino and the Heliotrope

Calandrino, Bruno and Buffalmacco go into the Mugnone Valley in Tuscany, looking for heliotropes, which Calandrino thinks he finds. He returns home with a load of stones. When his wife upbraids him, he flies into a rage and gives her a thrashing, after which he tells his friends something they know better than he does.

The ladies had laughed so much during Panfilo's story that they couldn't stop, even when it was over. When the queen ordered Elissa to tell the next one, she was still laughing when she began:

I'm not sure, my charming lady friends, if I'll manage to make you laugh as much as Panfilo did when I tell you this story of mine, which is a true one and at the same time an amusing one. Anyway, I shall do my best.

There has always been an abundance of curious and unusual individuals in our city. Not long ago there was a painter called Calandrino,[1] a simple-minded man with some odd habits, who spent a great deal of his time with two other painters called Bruno and Buffalmacco.[2] They were a very amusing pair, and quick-witted and shrewd with it, who liked Calandrino's company, because his cluelessness often let them enjoy themselves at his expense. There was also in Florence at the time a smooth-talking and very clever young man called Maso del Saggio,[3] who brought off every caper he tried with wonderful bravado. Having heard a few things about Calandrino's gullibility, he decided it would be fun to play a trick on him and make him believe something absurd.

Happening one day to find Calandrino in the church of San Giovanni, he saw that he was gazing intently at the paintings and reliefs of the tabernacle[4] that had been recently erected above the church's altar. He thought this was the time and place to put the idea into action. He told a friend who was with him what he had in mind and the two of them walked over to near where Calandrino was sitting by himself. They pretended not to have seen him and began discussing the powers of different stones, Maso speaking with the solemn air of an accredited expert.

Calandrino overheard the conversation and, after a while, feeling that there was nothing confidential in it, he got up and joined them, which was just what Maso wanted. He continued speaking and was eventually asked by Calandrino where the stones with these remarkable powers were to be found. Maso replied that most were in the land of Cod, a Basque region, in a part of Cockaigne where vines are tied up with sausages and you can get a goose for a penny with a gosling thrown in. There was a mountain there, he said, of grated Parmesan, with people on it who did nothing but make gnocchi and ravioli and cook them in cock-a-doodle broth, after which they'd toss them down and if you caught a lot, then a lot you had. And just nearby was a stream with not a drop of water in it, just the best Vernaccia[5] you've ever drunk.

'Oh,' Calandrino said, 'that sounds a really good place. But tell me, what do they do with the cock-a-doodles they cook?'

'The Basquards eat the lot,' Maso said.

'You ever been there?' Calandrino asked.

'You're asking me if I've ever been there?' replied Maso. 'If I've been there once, I've been there a thousand times.'

'And how many miles is it to get there?' Calandrino asked.

'If I counted all night, I'd not count them right,' replied Maso.

'So it must be way past the Abruzzi,' said Calandrino.

'Of course it is,' said Maso. 'Just a bit.'

Maso spoke with a set, unsmiling face. Being slow on the uptake, Calandrino reacted to what he said as if he'd been given the unvarnished truth and believed every word.

'It's too far off for me,' he said. 'If it were nearer, let me tell you, I'd like to go once with you to see those gnocchi come tumbling down and get myself a bellyful. But just tell me, if it's not too much trouble, do you find any of these powerful stones in these parts?'

'Yes,' Maso replied, 'you find two kinds of stones hereabouts, which are pure power. First, there are Settignano and Montisci[6] gritstones. Once they're made into millstones they have the power to produce flour, and that's why in places far from here they say that grace comes from God and millstones from Montisci. But we have such a quantity of boulders that we value them as little here as they value emeralds there. And they've mountains of emeralds that are bigger than Mount Morello[7] and which glitter all through the night, God help us. And let me tell you, anyone who strung the finished millstones together before they had holes put through them and carried them off to the Sultan, would get anything he wanted. The other kind of stone is one that we lapidary people call a heliotrope.[8] It's a stone with remarkable powers, because anyone who's got it on them is not seen by anyone else in some place where they don't happen to be, so long as they have it, that is.'

'Impressive powers, those,' Calandrino said. 'But where do you find this second stone?'

Maso said they could be found regularly down in the valley of the Mugnone.[9]

'And how big is this stone?' Calandrino asked. 'And what colour is it?'

'It comes in various sizes, some larger and some not so big,' Maso said, 'but the colour is always a sort of black.'

After making a mental note of everything he'd heard, Calandrino left Maso with the excuse of having other things to do. He made up his mind to go in search of this stone, but decided not to do so without informing Bruno and Buffalmacco, the two friends he was particularly attached to. He went off to find them, so they could start looking at once, before anyone got a start on them. He spent all the rest of that morning trying to find them. Finally, some time after noon, he remembered that they were working in the nunnery in Via Faenza. Though it was immensely hot, he dropped everything else and almost ran there.

'Listen, chums,' he said, calling them over, 'we can be the richest men in Florence, if you'll just believe me. I've been told by a trustworthy chap about a stone that's found by the Mugnone. Anyone carrying it on them can't be seen by anyone else. So my idea is that we go off and find it straight away, before anyone else gets to it. And we'll definitely find it, because I know what it's like. Once we've found it, all we have to do is put it in our knapsacks and go round to the money changers' tables. You know they always have piles of silver shillings and gold florins on them and we'll take as many as we want. No one will see us and suddenly we'll be rich and can stop spending the whole day smearing stuff over walls like snails.'

Hearing this, Bruno and Buffalmacco began tittering to themselves. They exchanged glances and assumed an air of intense astonishment. They then voiced their approval of Calandrino's idea, although Buffalmacco asked what the name of the stone was.

It had already gone completely out of Calandrino's thick head.

'What do we want with the name,' he said, 'if we know about what it can do? My view is that we just go and find it and not hang about any longer.'

'All right,' said Bruno, 'what's it like?'

'They come in all shapes and sizes,' said Calandrino, 'but they're all sort of black. So I think we collect up all those that look black to us, until we hit on the right one. So let's not waste any time, let's just go.'

'Hang on,' Bruno said, turning to Buffalmacco. 'Myself I think Calandrino's got it right, but I'm not sure that this is the best moment, since the sun's high and shining full on the Mugnone and all the stones are dried out. So there'll be some stones there that look white now, which look black in the morning before the sun has dried them. And what's more, this being a working day, there are lots of people down by the Mugnone for one reason or another. They might see us and guess what we're after, and maybe they'll start looking for themselves and the stone could end up in their hands, in which case we'd have been on a hiding to nowhere. In my opinion, which I hope you will agree with, this is work for the early morning when we can better tell the black ones from the white ones, and it's to be done on a holy day, when there's no one about to see us.'

Buffalmacco supported Bruno's view and Calandrino was won over. They arranged that all three of them would set off the next Sunday morning to look for this stone. Calandrino begged the others not to say a word of all this to anyone else in the world, since he had been told about it in confidence. He also told them what he'd heard about the land of Cod, swearing, hand on heart, that it was all true. Once he had left them, the other two worked out between them a plan of action.

Calandrino waited impatiently for Sunday morning. When it finally came he was up at dawn calling for his companions. They left the city by Porta San Gallo[10] and descended into the Mugnone Valley, which they followed downstream, looking for the stone as they went along. As the keenest of the three, Calandrino led the way, jumping hither and thither and flinging himself on any black stone he saw, scooping it up and stuffing it down his shirt. His friends followed behind, now and then picking up the odd stone. Calandrino hadn't gone far before his shirt was full. So he hoisted up the ends of his long smock, which was loose, and not in the Hainault style,[11] and tied them firmly into his leather belt to create a sort of large pouch. In a short while he had filled that. So a bit further on he made another pouch out of his cloak. That, too, he filled with stones. Seeing that he was thoroughly laden and it was almost time to eat, Bruno and Buffalmacco put their plan into action.

'Where's Calandrino?' Bruno asked Buffalmacco.

Buffalmacco, who could see him there next to him, turned all round, looking this way and that.

'I don't know,' he replied, 'but just now he was right here in front of us.'

'Don't give me that "just now" stuff!' Bruno said. 'I bet you for certain that he's home having his dinner and has left us two lunatics wandering about by the Mugnone looking for black stones.'

'The clever so-and-so!' Buffalmacco said. 'To fool us and leave us here, after we were daft enough to believe him! Can you credit it? Could anyone but us be foolish enough to believe that you could find a stone with such powers down by the Mugnone?'

Hearing this, Calandrino imagined that he had ended up with the right stone and that its powers had stopped them seeing him, although he was there by them. Overjoyed at his luck, he decided to say nothing and to go back home. He turned round and set off.

'What do we do?' Buffalmacco asked Bruno, seeing him do this. 'Why don't we just go?'

'Let's go then,' said Bruno. 'But I swear to God that Calandrino's not going to pull another fast one like this on me. If I got as near to him as I've been all morning, I'd give his heels such a knock with this pebble I'm holding that he'd remember his little caper for close on a month.'

As he said this, he drew his arm back and sent the pebble flying at Calandrino's heels. The pain made him hop and give a great puff. But he stopped himself from saying anything and kept on walking.

Buffalmacco picked out one of the stones from his own collection.

'See this stone?' he said to Bruno. 'I'd love it if it made contact with Calandrino's kidneys!'

With that he paused a moment and then sent it hurtling into the small of Calandrino's back. So, to the accompaniment of remarks of this kind, they went on stoning him all the way up the Mugnone until they reached the Porta San Gallo. There they dropped the stones they'd collected and stopped for a while with the watchmen, who had been primed by them earlier and let Calandrino go past, pretending not to see him and laughing fit to burst. So Calandrino walked on without stopping all the way to his house, which was near Canto alla Macina. Throughout, Fortune was on the side of the tricksters. For no one addressed a word to him on his way up the river and through the city, though in fact he encountered only a few people, since most were at home eating.

Calandrino came into his house all weighed down by his stones. His wife, a good-looking, spirited woman called Tessa, happened to be at the top of the stairs. She was feeling somewhat put out by his being so late and when she saw him come in she began to berate him.

'So, friend and husband, the Devil's finally brought you home!' she called. 'Everybody else has finished eating and you come back ready to start!'

Hearing her and realizing he was visible, Calandrino was overcome with rage and disappointment.

'You horrible woman!' he shouted. 'What are you doing there? You've ruined me! But by God I'll make you pay for it!'

With that he hurried up into their living room and dumped all the stones he'd brought back. Then, in a vile fury, he rushed over to deal with his wife. Seizing her by the hair, he flung her on the floor and, with arms and legs flailing, kicked and punched her all over until every bit of her was black and blue, while clasping her hands together and pleading for mercy did her no good at all.

Having had a good laugh with the watchmen on the gate, Buffalmacco and Bruno slowly followed on at a distance behind Calandrino. When they reached his doorstep, they heard the ferocious beating being given to his wife and called out to him, with the air of having only just arrived. Calandrino appeared at the window, red-faced, sweating and out of breath and asked them to come up. They went up, still looking irritated, and found the room full of stones, with the wife crying miserably in one corner, her hair a mess, her clothes torn and her face a mass of cuts and bruises, and Calandrino slouched on the other side, dishevelled and panting from his exertions.

'What's this, Calandrino?' they asked, after they had taken in the scene. 'A bit of wall-building with all these stones?' Nor did they stop there. 'And what's up with Mrs Tessa?' they added. 'It looks like you've given her a beating. What is all this then?'

Carrying the stones and raging at his wife, plus the pain of losing the gift he'd been lucky enough to be given, had left Calandrino panting and he couldn't get enough breath to articulate a reply. Buffalmacco waited a moment and then began again.

'Calandrino,' he said, 'if you were peeved with us for some reason, you still shouldn't have made fools of us like that. You talked us into going looking for some precious stone with you and then, with not a word of goodbye or good riddance, you left us like a pair of idiots by the Mugnone and came back home. We've taken it very badly. This is definitely the last time you'll pull a fast one on us.'

Calandrino made a great effort and managed a reply.

'Don't get all irate, chums. It's not what you think. I'm unlucky because I'd found the stone. Do you want to know what actually happened? When you two first asked each other where I was, I was ten yards from you. When I saw you going on and still not seeing me, I went in front and kept just a bit in front of you all the way back.'

He then told them everything they'd said and done from beginning to end and showed them his back and heels, so they could see the bruises from their stones.

'I tell you,' he said, 'that when I came through the gate loaded up with all these stones you see here, not a word was said. And you know how pestering and bothersome the watchmen are, since they want to see everything. And on the way I met a good few friends and people I know who always like to stop for a chat or suggest a drink. Not one of them said a single word, not even half a word. And that's because they couldn't see me. But then I finally got home and this damned diabolical woman appeared in front of me and saw me. And that's because, as you know well, women ruin the power of every single thing. I could have called myself the luckiest man in Florence and instead I'm the unluckiest. That's why I've beaten her with all the strength in my arms. I don't know why I should stop myself from cutting her throat. I curse the moment I first set eyes on her and the day she came to live in this house!'

His rage now rekindled, he began struggling to his feet, in order to start beating her again.

Buffalmacco and Bruno reacted with apparent amazement to what Calandrino said. Though they could barely control their laughter, they agreed that his story had to be true. When they saw him stand up in a fury with the intention of beating his wife again, they went over and restrained him, observing that he was to blame, not his good lady. He knew that women caused things to lose their power, but he hadn't told her to take care not to show herself in front of him that day. God had deprived him of the wit to do so, either because that piece of good fortune was not due to be given him or because it was his intention to deceive his mates, who should have been let in on the secret as soon as he realized he'd found the stone. It took a lot of time and effort, but eventually they achieved a reconciliation between Calandrino and his suffering wife. Then they made their departure, leaving him the glum owner of a houseful of stones.

8

Zeppa Sorts Out an Adulterous Situation

One of two close friends has an affair with the wife of the other. Discovering what is going on, the second has his own wife lock his friend in a chest, and on it, while he is still inside, makes love to the friend's wife.

The ladies had found the story of Elena's misfortunes[1] seriously disturbing. Still, the thought that there was some justification for her punishment had somewhat diminished their compassion, even though they considered the scholar to have been aggressively severe, even brutal, throughout. Once Pampinea had finished, the queen ordered Fiammetta to speak next. She was more than ready to obey:

Amiable ladies (she began), I think you have had your hearts wrenched by the severity with which the scholar took his revenge. I consider it appropriate, therefore, to soothe your distress with a more pleasurable story. I intend to tell you about a young man who took the wrong done to him in a gentler spirit and exacted his revenge in a more moderate way. From this story you'll learn that it should be enough for each one of us, if what's given back corresponds to what's given out, and that there's no need to push retaliation beyond appropriate limits, once someone sets out to exact retribution for a wrong done to him.

My story takes place in Siena and concerns two young men I've been told once lived there. They were both well off and from good merchant families. One was called Spinelloccio Tavena, the other Zeppa di Mino,[2] and they lived near each other in the Cammollia district. They always spent a lot of time together and gave every impression of loving each other like two brothers, if not more. Each of them also had a very beautiful wife.

Spinelloccio was often in Zeppa's house. Since Zeppa was sometimes there and sometimes not, Spinelloccio got to know his wife very well and ended up having an affair with her. This went on for some time without anyone noticing. But finally one day Zeppa's wife didn't realize her husband was at home when Spinelloccio came to call for him. The lady said he wasn't in, at which Spinelloccio quickly went up and joined her in the main room. Seeing there was no one else there, he put his arms around her and started kissing her, as she did him. Zeppa saw this happening, but said nothing and stayed out of sight, waiting to see what the outcome of their game would be. After a little while he saw his wife and Spinelloccio go into the bedchamber with their arms around each other and lock the door.

He was immensely put out. But he realized that creating a scene or doing anything else wasn't going to make the wrong done to him any the less; if anything, it would make the disgrace worse. So he started trying to work out a form of revenge which would satisfy him, without people around becoming any the wiser. He stayed hidden all the time Spinelloccio was with his wife and eventually came up with a possible solution.

As soon as Spinelloccio left, Zeppa went into the bedchamber, where he found his wife still pinning up the veils around her head, which Spinelloccio had knocked down in the course of their loveplay.

'What are you doing, madam?' he asked.

'Can't you see?' she replied.

'I can see all right,' said Zeppa, 'and I've seen something else I'd prefer not to have seen.'

With that he launched into the matter of what had just happened. Terrified, she first tried to talk herself out of trouble, but in the end she confessed to what she could not decently deny regarding her intimacy with Spinelloccio and started begging tearfully to be forgiven.

'Listen, madam,' said Zeppa, 'you have done wrong. I'm going to give you some instructions which you must carry out to the letter, if you want me to forgive you. What I want you to do is this. I want you to tell Spinelloccio to find some excuse tomorrow morning, around nine, for leaving me and coming over to see you. Once he's here, I shall come back. As soon as you hear me, get him to hide in this chest and lock him in it. Then, when you've done that, I'll tell you the rest of what you've got to do. But you mustn't be nervous. I promise I'm not going to harm him in any way.'

Wanting to placate him, the lady agreed and did as she was instructed.

Zeppa and Spinelloccio met in town the following morning. Around nine, in accordance with the promise he had given the lady to go and see her about that time, Spinelloccio said to Zeppa, 'I'm eating this morning with a friend and I don't want to keep him waiting. So God be with you and I'll be off.'

'It's not time to eat for a while yet,' said Zeppa.

'That doesn't matter,' said Spinelloccio. 'I've also got to speak with him about a bit of business. So it's better if I'm early.'

So Spinelloccio left Zeppa, circled around and was soon in Zeppa's house with his wife. They were barely in the bedchamber before Zeppa returned. As soon as his wife heard him, she made a show of being terrified, had Spinelloccio climb into the chest that her husband had spoken of, locked it and left the room.

'Is it time to eat, lady?' Zeppa asked, coming up into the room.

'Yes,' she replied, 'by now it must be.'

'Spinelloccio's gone to eat with a friend of his,' said Zeppa, 'and he's left his wife by herself in the house. Go to the window and call her. Tell her to come and eat with us.'

Being fearful for her own safety had made his wife very obedient and she did what her husband told her. Hearing that her husband wasn't going to dine at home, Spinelloccio's wife eventually yielded to her insistent invitations and came over. Zeppa greeted her with great affection when she arrived. Taking her by the hand in a familiar way and quietly asking his wife to go and attend to things in the kitchen, he led her into the bedchamber. Once inside he turned round and locked them in.

'Good grief, Zeppa!' said the lady, seeing him lock the door. 'What does this mean? So you've got me here for this? Now is this the way you show your love for Spinelloccio? Where's your loyalty to him gone?'

Keeping a tight hold on her, Zeppa edged towards the chest enclosing her husband.

'Madam,' he said, 'before you start complaining, listen to what I want to tell you. I've loved Spinelloccio like a brother and still do. But yesterday, though he doesn't know it, I discovered that the trust I had in him had come to this, that he is going to bed with my wife, just as he goes to bed with you. Now since I love him, the only revenge I intend to take on him matches the offence. He has had my wife and I intend to have you. If you refuse, my one course of action is to catch him in the act, and since I do not intend to leave this wrong unpunished, I'll make sure that you and he will never be happy again.'

The lady listened and, after many further assurances from Zeppa, believed what he was saying.

'Zeppa, my friend,' she said, 'I am content to submit to this act of revenge, since it has to be inflicted on me, but only so long as you make sure that what we must do doesn't cause a rift between myself and your wife. In spite of what she's done to me, I intend to remain on the best of terms with her.'

'I shall certainly do that,' said Zeppa. 'And in addition I shall give you a jewel which is more beautiful and more costly than any other you have.'

After this he took her in his arms and started kissing her. Then he stretched her out on the chest in which her husband was locked, and there on top of it, wholeheartedly enjoyed her, as she did him.

Spinelloccio, enclosed in the chest, had heard everything that Zeppa had said and how his wife had replied, and after that he had listened to the in-and-out dance that they performed above his head. He lay there for much of the time in mortal agony. If it hadn't been for his fear of what Zeppa might do, he would have called his wife a few choice names, despite being shut in as he was. But then he began reflecting that the unacceptable behaviour had begun with him and that Zeppa was right to do what he was doing and had behaved towards him like a rational human being and a true comrade. He said to himself that he would henceforth be a better friend to Zeppa than ever, if he so wanted.

After having had as much of the lady as he wanted, Zeppa got down from the chest. When the lady asked him for the jewel he had promised, he unlocked the room and let his wife in. All she said was, 'Well, my lady, you've given me cake in return for the bun I gave you.'

And as she said this, she laughed.

'Open this chest,' said Zeppa to her.

She did so and Zeppa revealed her dear Spinelloccio to his lady wife. It would be hard to say who was the more embarrassed, Spinelloccio on seeing Zeppa and knowing that he knew what he himself had done, or his lady seeing her husband and knowing that he had heard and listened to what she had done to him just above his head.

'Here's the jewel I'm giving you,' said Zeppa to her.

Spinelloccio climbed out of the chest without making too much fuss.

'Zeppa,' he said, 'we're quits. And so, as you were saying before to my lady wife, it'll be a good thing if we stay the friends we used to be, and, since the only thing we keep separate is our wives, we'd better share them too.'

Zeppa was happy with this and the four of them ate their meal together in perfect harmony. From then onwards each of the ladies had two husbands and each of the husbands had two wives, without any dispute or disturbance ever arising between them as a result of this arrangement.

DAY NINE

The Eighth Day of the Decameron *ends and the Ninth begins, in which, under the rule of Emilia, each member of the party is allowed to choose to tell a story on any subject he or she wishes.*

2

An Abbess is Caught Out

An abbess gets up hurriedly in the dark to confront a nun she has been told is in bed with her lover. The abbess has a priest with her and puts his pants on her head instead of her veils. The nun accused of misconduct points this out, after which she is released and is free to be with her lover from then onwards.

Filomena fell silent. Everyone commended the skill with which the lady dispensed with the men she had no wish to love. Equally, they all declared the instrusive presumption of the lovers to be insanity, not love at all.[1] At last the queen intervened with a gentle request to Elissa to follow on, and she promptly began:

Dearest ladies, it was very judicious of Madonna Francesca to escape from a troublesome situation in the way we have heard. But I want to tell you about a young nun, who, with some help from the goddess Fortune, freed herself from pressing danger by coming out with a neat turn of phrase. As you know there are lots of total fools about who like telling others what to do and telling them off too. You'll see from my story how Fortune sometimes puts them to shame as they deserve. This happened to the abbess who was mother superior to the nun in my story.

The setting for the story is a convent in Lombardy that was famous as a pious and holy establishment. Among the nuns there was a young noblewoman of extraordinary beauty called Isabetta. One day she came to the lattice grill to speak with a visiting relative. He had an attractive young man with him and she fell in love at once. The young man saw how beautiful she was, intuited her feelings and was himself immediately enraptured. To the great distress of both of them they had to bear not bringing their love to fruition for a long time. Still, they were both equally determined and eventually the young man worked out a way of secretly going to see his nun. She was delighted and he subsequently visited her not once but many times, to the great satisfaction of them both.

So the affair went on, until one night, without either of the lovers realizing it, the young man was seen leaving Isabetta and going out of the convent by another of the resident ladies. She shared the news with some of the others. Their first thought was to denounce Isabetta to the abbess, a certain Madonna Usimbalda, a virtuous, pious lady in the eyes of the nuns and of everyone who knew her. Then they decided not to leave any room for a straight denial and to arrange for the abbess to catch Isabetta in the act with the young man. So they said nothing and secretly organized a rota of lookouts and sentries, so as to be ready to pounce.

Isabetta remained happily ignorant of what they were up to. So when one night she had her young man come round, the committee of nuns was immediately on to her. They let a few hours go by and then, at what they judged was a good moment, they split their forces. One group stayed on guard outside the door of Isabetta's cell. The other scurried off to the abbess's room and banged on her door. When they heard her beginning to reply, they called out, 'Get up, Madam! Get up quickly, because we've found Isabetta with a young man in her cell!'

That night the abbess was enjoying the company of a priest, whom she often arranged to be transported to her room in a chest. Hearing the noise, she was afraid that the nuns might force the door open in their haste and excitement. She jumped out of bed and put on her clothes in a complete flurry. Thinking she'd got hold of the folded veils, called psalteries,[2] that nuns wear on their heads, she picked up the priest's underpants instead and, being in such a rush, inadvertently plonked these on her head. In which state she went out, quickly bolting the door behind her and exclaiming, 'Where is this girl cursed of the Lord God?'

Then she hurried off to Isabetta's cell with the others, who were all so fired up and obsessed by the thought of catching Isabetta in the wrong that they did not notice the abbess's head-dress. With their aid, she was able to break the door down. They all rushed in and saw the two lovers lying in bed in each other's arms, so stunned by the sudden incursion that they didn't know what to do and just lay still. The young woman was immediately seized by the other nuns and dragged off on the orders of the abbess to the chapter house. Left to his own devices, the young man dressed and decided to wait and see how things turned out. He was determined, however, to make all the nuns he got hold of pay for it if anything untoward was done to his young lady, and then to take her away with him.

The abbess seated herself in the chapter house before all the nuns, who just stood there, staring at the miscreant. Then she launched into the most vicious tirade a woman could be sub-jected to, saying that her disgusting and abominable behaviour would besmirch the sanctity, honour and good name of the convent if the world outside got wind of it, and supplementing this vilification with threats of terrible punishment.

The young woman, being guilty as charged, looked ashamed and fearful. She could find nothing to say in reply, although her very silence made the others begin to feel sorry for her. As the rant continued, the young woman happened to raise her eyes and see what the abbess had on her head, with the strings hang-ing down on either side. She recognized what the item was and felt deeply relieved.

'The Lord help you, Madam,' she said, 'but please tie up your bonnet and then you can say whatever you want to me.'

Not catching on, the abbess retorted, 'What bonnet, you slut? Are you trying to be clever now? Do you think you've done something you can make quips about?'

The young woman repeated what she had said.

'Madam, I beg you to tie up your bonnet. Then say anything you like to me.'

At this many of the nuns raised their eyes to look at the abbess, while the lady herself felt her head with her hands. They all realized now why Isabetta had spoken as she had.

The abbess, all too aware now that she was also at fault and that all the nuns knew it, saw that she had no chance of covering things up and changed her tone. She now started talking in a quite different way and eventually concluded that it was impossible to defend oneself against the urgings of the flesh. So, she said, everyone should enjoy themselves when they had the chance with the same quiet discretion they had shown in the past. After releasing the young woman, she went back to bed with her priest and Isabetta went back to bed with her lover. She subsequently arranged for him to make many more visits, to the envy of the other nuns, who were short of lovers, although they secretly managed to find satisfaction in one way or another.

6

Confusion in the Bedroom

Two young men stay overnight in a man's house. One goes to bed with his daughter, while his wife mistakenly gets into bed with the other. The one who had been with the daughter, now gets into bed with the father and, thinking he is his friend, tells him everything. There is a furious argument, but the wife realizes her mistake, slips into her daughter's bed and delivers from there a short speech that restores peace.

Calandrino[1] made the party laugh this time as much as he had on other occasions. Once the ladies had stopped talking about his antics, the queen gave the order to Panfilo to speak next:

Laudable ladies (he began), the name of Calandrino's beloved, Niccolosa, has brought to my mind the story of another Niccolosa, which I'd like to tell you. In this story you'll hear how the quick-wittedness of a good lady averted an enormous scandal.

There lived not long ago in the valley of the Mugnone[2] a decent man who made his living by providing travellers with food and drink. He was poor with a small house, but sometimes, when it was really necessary, he would also put people up, not everyone, but people he knew. He had a wife, who was a very good-looking woman, and two children. One was a winsome fifteen- or sixteen-year-old girl, still unmarried, the other a baby boy of less than a year, who was being fed on his mother's milk.

The girl had caught the eye of a well-born, nice-looking, amiable boy from our city, who spent a lot of time out in the country. He fell passionately in love with her and she gloried in having a lover of his calibre. She made an effort to keep his passion aflame by giving him fond looks and ended up falling in love with him too. There were various times when their passion might have had the outcome they both wanted, if Pinuccio (that was the name of the boy) hadn't wanted no disrepute to attach itself to the girl or to himself. However, with their ardour growing more intense every day that passed, Pinuccio felt he just had to find a way of being alone with the girl and came up with the idea of arranging with her father for him to stay overnight. Knowing the set-up of the girl's house, he thought that if he managed this, he could find a way for the two of them to get together without anyone knowing. Once the idea had taken shape, he immediately acted on it.

He had a trusted friend called Adriano, who knew all about this love of his. One evening the two of them hired a couple of packhorses, put two cases on their backs, with maybe only straw inside them, and left Florence. They took a long way round and eventually rode into the Mugnone Valley late at night. There, they swung around to make it seem as if they were coming back from the Romagna and headed for the hamlet where the good man lived. He readily opened up when they knocked at his door, since he knew them both well.

'Look,' said Pinuccio, 'you just have to put us up tonight. We thought we'd be able to get back into Florence, but, as you see, we've not managed even to reach here before this time.'

'Pinuccio,' replied the innkeeper, 'you well know what sort of lodging I'm in a position to provide for gents like yourselves. Still, given that you've turned up at this hour and it's too late to find anywhere else, I'm willing to do the best I can for you.'

The two young men dismounted and entered the inn. Once their horses were settled, they sat down with their host and ate with him the good things they'd brought with them for dinner.

Now the innkeeper had only one small bedchamber, into which he'd fitted three cramped beds as best he could. There were two down one side of the room and the third against the wall opposite, with just about enough room between them to squeeze past. The innkeeper had the least uncomfortable bed set up for the two friends and saw them settled in it. After a while, when the two of them seemed to have fallen asleep (although neither had), he put his daughter in one of the remaining beds and himself and his wife in the other, his wife setting the cradle with the baby boy in it by the bed's side.

Pinuccio had observed every detail of the arrangements. He let some time go by and then, when he judged that everyone was asleep, he quietly got up and tiptoed over to the bed where his beloved was lying and got in with her. He was given a delighted – if nervous – welcome and began to enjoy with her the pleasures that both of them had ardently looked forward to.

While Pinuccio was so engaged with the girl, some things were knocked over somewhere by a cat. The noise woke the wife, who began worrying what it might be. She got out of bed and made her way in the dark to where she thought the noise had come from. Adriano, with whom the noise had not registered, happened just then to get up to answer a basic need and en route bumped into the cradle in the place where the lady had put it. Not being able to get past without moving it, he picked it up from where it was and put it down by the bed where he was sleeping. When he had done what he got up to do, he came back and slipped into bed forgetting all about the cradle.

After discovering that whatever had fallen wasn't what she thought it might be, the lady didn't bother to light a candle to take a proper look, but, having given the cat a piece of her mind, went back to the bedchamber and felt her way directly to the bed where her husband was sleeping. Then, not finding the cradle, she muttered to herself, 'Oh silly me! Look what I was doing! Lord Almighty! I was going straight for the bed where my guests are!'

She felt her way forwards a little more and, finding the cradle, lay down in the bed by it, alongside Adriano, thinking she was lying down next to her husband. Adriano, who had not yet fallen asleep again, felt her arrive and gave her a warm and happy reception. Without saying a word, he took her on more than one trip round the bay, which she much enjoyed.

While this was going on, Pinuccio began to fear he might be overcome by sleep in his girl's bed. His desires satisfied, he got up from beside her to return to his own bed. When he bumped into the cradle, he thought he was by the innkeeper's bed. So he went on a little further and lay down next to the innkeeper, who was woken up by his arrival.

'Let me tell you,' Pinuccio said, thinking he had Adriano next to him, 'there's never been anything as good as that Niccolosa! God almighty, I've had the best time in her bed that a man's ever had with a woman! I tell you I've been up the junction six times and more, since I left you here.'

Their host was not exactly pleased to hear this. He first of all asked himself, 'What the devil's this lad doing here?' and then anger overcame his better judgement.

'Pinuccio,' he said, 'you've behaved in a really vile way. I don't know why you have to do this to me, but by God's body I'll pay you back!'

Pinuccio, who was not the sharpest young man in the world, realized he'd made a mistake, but didn't immediately do what he could to make amends.

'What do you mean pay me back?' he said. 'What can someone like you do to me?'

The innkeeper's wife, still thinking she was with her husband, said to Adriano, 'Oh dear, listen to our guests having some sort of argument!'

'Let them be,' Adriano said with a laugh, 'and the Devil take them! They drank too much last night.'

The lady was already beginning to think that it was her husband she'd heard losing his temper. Once she heard Adriano's voice she immediately realized what bed she'd got into and with whom. Being a sensible person, she immediately got up, without saying a word. She took hold of her baby son's cradle and, although there was no light at all in the room, she was able by guesswork to put it down by the side of the bed where her daughter was sleeping. Getting in beside her, she called out to her husband, as if the noise he was making had woken her up and asked him what he was arguing about with Pinuccio.

'Didn't you hear what he said he's done tonight to our Niccolosa?' he replied.

'He's lying through his teeth,' said the lady. 'He's never been in our Niccolosa's bed. I went and got in with her and haven't slept a wink since. You're a numbskull if you believe him. You lot drink so much in the evening that you dream all night and wander about without waking up, thinking you're doing all sorts of incredible things. It's just a pity you don't fall and break your necks! But what's Pinuccio doing over there? Why isn't he in his own bed?'

Adriano realized that the lady was shrewdly concealing her own disreputable conduct and that of her daughter.

'Pinuccio,' he chimed in, 'I've told you a hundred times not to go wandering about. You've a very bad habit of getting up in a dream and then speaking of what you dream about as if it were true. It's going to land you in trouble sooner or later. Come back here, damn you!'

Hearing what his wife said and then what Adriano said, the innkeeper allowed himself to be convinced that Pinuccio was dreaming. He grabbed him by the shoulder and shook him.

'Wake up, Pinuccio!' he told him. 'Go back to your own bed!'

Pinuccio had taken in everything that had been said. He started going on nonsensically, as if he were still in a dream, which made the innkeeper burst into raucous laughter. Then he made a show of having been woken up by all the shaking.

'Is it daylight already?' he called to Adriano. 'Is that what you're telling me?'

'Yes,' said Adriano, 'come over here.'

Pretending innocence and looking all sleepy, Pinuccio finally left the innkeeper and went back to the bed where Adriano was. When day came and they all got up, the innkeeper started laughing and making fun of him and his dreams. So, with quips and digs coming thick and fast, the two young men saddled their horses, loaded their bags on to them, had a drink with their host, remounted and rode off to Florence, as happy with the manner in which things had proceeded as with their eventual outcome. Pinuccio subsequently found other ways of being alone with Niccolosa, who assured her mother that he definitely had been dreaming. The good lady, however, remembered what Adriano's embraces were like and told herself (and no one else) that she at least had been wide awake.

10

A Wife Almost Becomes a Mare

At the insistence of Compar Pietro, Don Gianni recites a spell to turn his wife into a mare, but when it comes to attaching the tail, Compar Pietro declares that he doesn't want one and ruins the spell.

The queen's story[1] provoked a few murmured comments among the ladies and some mirth among the young men. Once the comments subsided, Dioneo began his story:

Charming ladies, a flock of white doves is made more beautiful by the addition of a black crow rather than the whitest swan. In the same way, in a gathering of the wise, their sagacity will be enhanced and embellished by the presence of someone less wise, and not only that, but an element of pleasure and enjoyment might thereby make itself felt too. Therefore, since all you ladies are so discreet and controlled and I myself radiate witlessness, I shall add lustre to your virtues by my defects. That should make you feel more warmly towards me than you would if I displayed merits that put your virtues in the shade. It follows that I should have more latitude to show you myself as I really am, and that, when you hear the story I have ready, you will bear it more patiently than you would if I were a wiser man. I shall tell you, therefore, a quite short story, but from it you will learn how diligently all the instructions from those who practise magic must be carried out and how making just a small mistake can ruin the magician's whole operation.

A few years back there was in Barletta[2] a priest called Don Gianni di Barolo. Since his church was poor, he started supporting himself by travelling around the fairs of Puglia on a mare laden with merchandise of various sorts that he bought and sold. In the course of his travels he became friendly with a certain Pietro da Tresanti, who practised the same trade but with a donkey. A sign of his affection and friendship was that, in the Apulian manner, he would call him only Compar Pietro.[3] Every time he turned up in Barletta, he would lead him off to his church and put him up and entertain him the best he could. Vice versa, every time Don Gianni turned up in Tresanti, Compar Pietro – who was desperately poor and had a little house with just enough room for himself, his good-looking, young wife and his donkey – would take Don Gianni home and do his best to return the honours out of gratitude for the way he was treated in Barletta. However, so far as lodgings were concerned, Compar Pietro had only the one little bed in which he slept with his lovely wife, and thus could not treat him as well as he wished. Don Gianni had to bed down on a pile of straw in the cramped stable by his mare, which was tethered next to Pietro's donkey. His wife knew how well the priest looked after her husband in Barletta and various times when the priest appeared she proposed going and sleeping with one of her neighbours – Zita Carapresa di Giudice Leo by name – so that Don Gianni could share the bed with her husband. She had often put this to him, but he would have none of it.

'Comar Gemmata,'[4] Don Gianni said to her on one of these occasions, 'don't worry about me, because I'm fine. When I feel like it, I turn this mare of mine into a beautiful girl and pass the time with her. Then, when I want to, I turn her back into a mare. So I don't want to be separated from her.'

The young woman was amazed, but she believed him. She told her husband, with an addition of her own.

'If he's such a close friend of yours as you say he is,' she said, 'why don't you get him to teach you the spell? Then you could make me into a mare and you'd have both a mare and a donkey for business-use. We'd make twice the money and then when we got home, you could turn me back into a woman again, just as I am now.'

Compar Pietro was a bit thick. He believed the thing was possible and agreed to her proposal. He started pressing Don

Gianni in his clumsy way to give him the appropriate lesson. Don Gianni did what he could to put this nonsense out of his mind, but made no progress.

'Look,' he said in the end, 'if you're really set on it, we'll get up before dawn tomorrow morning as we usually do and I'll show you how it's done. The fact is, though, that the most difficult part of the business is sticking on the tail, as you'll see.'

Compar Pietro and Comar Gemmata were all agog and barely slept a wink that night. Towards dawn they got up and called Don Gianni. He arrived in Compar Pietro's bedroom still in his shirt.

'I don't know anyone else in the world I'd do this for except you two,' he said. 'However since it's something you really want, I'll do it. But you must do exactly what I tell you if you want it to work.'

When they said they would do that, Don Gianni took a candle and put it in Compar Pietro's hand.

'Watch carefully what I'm going to do,' he said, 'and hold what I say firmly in your mind. Assuming you don't want to ruin everything, beware of saying a single word, no matter what you hear or see. Just pray to God that the tail sticks on properly.'

Compar Pietro, candle in hand, said he would duly follow his orders.

Don Gianni then got Comar Gemmata to strip herself as naked as the day she was born. He then had her bend over with her hands and feet on the ground, on all fours like a mare, instructing her similarly not to say a word, whatever happened.

He then began touching her face and head with his hands, saying, 'Be this a fine mare's head.'

He next touched her hair, saying, 'Be this a fine mare's mane.'

Moving on to her arms, he said, 'Be these the mare's fine legs and feet.'

Then he touched her breast and found it firm and round. At this someone who had not been called awoke and rose from where he had been lying.

'And be this a mare's fine breast,' the priest said.

And so he went on with the back and the belly and the hips and the thighs and the legs. Finally, with nothing left to fix but the tail, he lifted up his shirt, took the dibber for people-planting in his hand and put it in the furrow made for it, and said, 'And be this a beautiful mare's tail.'

Compar Pietro had been watching everything intently up to that moment, but when he saw this final move, something didn't seem to him quite right.

'O Don Gianni,' he said, 'I don't want no tail, I don't want no tail.'

The essential liquid which ensures that all plants take root had been expelled when Don Gianni drew out his instrument.

'Oh dear, Compar Pietro,' he said, 'what have you done? I told you not to say a word, whatever you saw happen. The mare was on the point of being finished, but you opened your mouth and spoilt everything. There's no doing it again today.'

'It doesn't matter,' said Compar Pietro. 'I didn't want that tail, no, I didn't. Why didn't you say to me "You do it"? And besides you were sticking it on too far down.'

'I didn't tell you to do it,' said Don Gianni, 'because this first time you wouldn't have known how to stick it on as well as I can.'

Hearing this exchange, the young woman got to her feet and said to her husband, in all good faith, 'Cor, what a stupid beast you are! Why have you ruined things for both of us? What mare have you ever seen without a tail? God help me, you're poor, but you deserve to be poorer still.'

Since there was no longer any way of turning her into a mare, because Compar Pietro had opened his mouth, the young woman gloomily and forlornly put her clothes back on and Compar Pietro resigned himself to plying his old trade with a donkey as he had done before. He went off with Don Gianni to the fair at Bitonto[5] and never asked a similar favour of him again.

DAY TEN

The Ninth Day of the Decameron *ends and the Tenth and last begins. Under the rule of Panfilo, the members of the party tell stories about people who act with generosity or magnificence in regard to love or anything else.*

5
The Problem of the Magic Garden

Madonna Dianora asks Messer Ansaldo to give her a beautiful May garden in January, which he manages by employing a wizard. The lady's husband agrees to her yielding to Messer Ansaldo's desires. But on learning of the husband's generosity, Messer Ansaldo releases her from her promise and is himself released from payment for his services by the wizard.

Every member of the happy band had praised Messer Gentile[1] to the skies by the time the king ordered Emilia to speak next. She began with great confidence and eagerness:

Tender ladies, no one could reasonably argue that Messer Gentile didn't act magnificently, but to say that he couldn't be surpassed can be shown to be mistaken without too much difficulty. You'll see what I mean from the brief story I'm going to tell you.

Friuli[2] is a cold region, but blessed with fine mountains, many rivers and clear springs. One of its cities is called Udine and in Udine there once lived a beautiful noble lady called Madonna Dianora, who was married to a very wealthy man called Gilberto, a cheerful man with a pleasant disposition. The lady's qualities had inspired a deeply felt passion in a great nobleman named Messer Ansaldo of Grado, a man with much influence who was famous for his military prowess and his courtly qualities. Being fervently enamoured, he did everything he could to make her love him in return and often sent messengers to plead with her on his behalf. But all his efforts were in vain. The lady found his pleading totally wearisome, but saw that none of her rejections were making him stop loving or pestering her. Therefore, she decided to get him finally to leave her alone by making a strange and, to her mind, impossible demand.

There was a woman who came frequently to see her on Ansaldo's behalf. One day she said to her, 'My good woman, you've often assured me that Messer Ansaldo loves me more than anything else in the world and you've offered me marvellous gifts on his behalf. I've always wanted him to keep them, since they can't make me love him or give in to him. But if I could be really certain that he loves me as much as you say, I could honestly bring myself to love him and to do as he desires. So if he could give me proof of his love by doing what I'm going to ask, I would be ready to obey his commands.'

'What is it, my lady, that you desire him to do?' the good woman asked.

'What I desire is this,' the lady replied. 'Next January I want here in this city a garden full of green grass, flowers and leafy trees, no different from what it might be in May. If he can't manage this, tell him not to send you or anyone else to see me ever again. I've so far kept my husband and relatives completely in the dark, but if he were to start up again, I'd do my utmost to get him off my back by complaining to them about him.'

On being told of the demand and the offer, the knight recognized that the lady was asking him to do something difficult or, more likely, impossible, with the sole intention of thwarting his hopes once and for all. But he decided to try everything he could. He sent enquiries to various places in the world in search of help and advice and they produced a result: a man who offered to do the job by magical means, provided he was amply remunerated. Messer Ansaldo agreed to pay out an enormous sum and, feeling much encouraged, waited for the time of year specified to come.

So January came and the night before the calends,[3] when the cold was intense and there was snow and ice everywhere, the magician set to work with his secret arts in a lovely meadow near the city. According to witnesses who saw it with their own eyes, there appeared the following morning one of the most beautiful gardens anyone had ever seen, with grass and trees and fruits of all kinds. Messer Ansaldo was overjoyed at the sight and ordered some of the finest fruit and flowers to be picked. He then had these secretly presented to his lady, together with an invitation to view the garden she had requested, his intention being that she should thus recognize that he did indeed love her and that then, when she recalled the promise made to him under oath, she should act as a true lady, ready to keep her word.

The lady had already heard talk of the marvellous garden. At the sight of the fruit and the flowers she began to repent of having made her promise. Her regret didn't stop her wanting to see something so extraordinary and she went along with many other ladies from the city to take a look. She was amazed and admitted that the garden was quite remarkable, but she returned home in total misery, brooding on what she had committed herself to. Her distress prevented her from completely hiding her feelings and, when they became apparent, her husband noticed and demanded a full explanation. The lady said nothing for a long time, feeling too ashamed to speak. Then, when forced to it, she finally opened up and told him everything.

Gilberto was initially deeply angered by what she said. Then, reflecting on his wife's pure intentions, he thought again and overcame his rage.

'Dianora,' he said, 'a sensible, virtuous lady does not listen to the sort of addresses you received or make her chastity the object of any sort of agreement with anyone. Words that pass through the ears to the heart have more force than many people think and for lovers almost anything is possible. So you did wrong first to listen and secondly to agree to terms. But I know the purity of your heart. In order to release you from that binding promise, I'll allow you to do something probably no other man would agree to, although I am also worried about the necromancer; Messer Ansaldo could have him make us regret it, if you made a fool of him. So I want you to go and see him and then, in any way you can, try your hardest to get yourself released from this promise with your honour intact. But if there should be no alternative, on this one occasion you may yield your body to him, but not your heart and mind.'

The lady listened in tears to her husband and said she couldn't accept such exceptional kindness from him. But although she was insistent, Gilberto had made up his mind. Around dawn the next morning, dressed relatively plainly, with two manservants in front and a maid behind, the lady set out for Messer Ansaldo's house.

Messer Ansaldo was astounded when he was told that his lady had come to see him. He got up and called the necromancer. 'I want you to see what a prize your art has brought me,' he told him.

Then the two of them went to meet her and Messer Ansaldo gave her an honourable and respectful welcome, betraying none of the desire consuming him. The three of them went into a beautiful chamber where a great fire was burning and he invited her to be seated.

'My lady,' he said, 'I beg you, if the love I have borne for you for so long deserves any reward, be so kind as to disclose to me the true reason for your coming to see me at this hour of the day and with a retinue of this sort.'

'Sir,' the lady replied, full of shame and with tears in her eyes, 'it is not any love I feel for you, nor any wish to keep my promise that brings me here, but the order of my husband. He compelled me to come, showing more respect for all the efforts your uncontrolled passion has driven you to than for his honour and my own. At his command I am ready on this occasion to submit to every one of your desires.'

If Messer Ansaldo had been startled before, hearing what the lady said now completely amazed him. He was stirred by Gilberto's generosity and felt his fervour begin to change into compassion.

'My lady,' he said, 'may it never please God that – given what you say – I should besmirch the honour of a man who shows sympathy for the love I feel. For as long as you choose to remain here, you will be treated as if you were my sister and you are free to leave whenever you wish. My only conditions are that you should convey to your husband the thanks you believe appropriate for such great courtesy as he has shown, and that in the future you should always consider me your brother and your servant.'

The lady was overjoyed to hear these words.

'If I had paid due regard to your high standards of behaviour,' she said, 'nothing should ever have made me believe that I would take away from my visit here anything but what I see you now proposing. I shall be for ever obliged to you.'

With that she took her leave and, as honourably attended as before, returned to Gilberto, to whom she explained what had happened. From then onwards he and Messer Ansaldo were joined together in close and true friendship.

Messer Ansaldo was all set to give the necromancer his promised reward, but the latter was impressed by Gilberto's generous behaviour to Messer Ansaldo and by that of Messer Ansaldo to the lady.

'Gilberto has been generous as regards his honour,' he said, 'and you have been generous as regards your love. God forbid I shouldn't be similarly generous with regard to my payment! I know you could well use the money and I intend you to keep it.'

The knight felt ashamed and did all he could to make him take all or part of his fee, but to no effect. When three days later the necromancer swept away his garden and made ready to leave, he sent him off with his blessing. His lustful passion for the lady had now evaporated and he felt only a chaste, Christian affection for her.

What shall we say about this, loving ladies? In the previous instance[4] the lady was close to death, hopes were exhausted and love had lost its fire. Shall we set that above this generous behaviour of Messer Ansaldo, who was more passionately in love than ever, whose passions blazed as his hopes grew, who held the prey so long pursued in his grasp? I think it would be silly to believe the two cases are at all comparable.

6

King Charles Becomes Wiser

King Charles the Old, with his victories behind him, falls in love with a young girl, but comes to feel ashamed of his mad passion and arranges honourable marriages for the girl and her sister.

It would take too long to do full justice to the variety of views among the ladies as to whether it was Gilberto, Sir Ansaldo or the necromancer who showed most generosity in the Madonna Dianora affair. After the king had let them debate the issue for a while, he looked over at Fiammetta and commanded her to put a stop to the arguing by telling her story. She began without hesitation:

Splendid ladies, I've always been of the opinion that with parties of people such as ours it is best to spell things out openly, rather than say them so economically that people end up arguing over the intended meaning. Debates of that sort are all very well for scholars in university schools, but much less so for us who can just about manage to deal with distaffs and spindles. I was thinking of telling a somewhat open-ended story, but seeing you all squabbling about the story we've just heard, I'm going to abandon that one and tell you another. It's not about just anybody, but rather about a valiant king and how he behaved like a true knight and maintained his honour unblemished.

Each of you may well have heard many stories about King Charles the Old or Charles the First, whose magnificent campaigns culminated in the glorious victory over King Manfred and led directly to the Ghibellines being chased out of Florence and the Guelfs coming back.[1] In the light of these events, a certain knight, Messer Neri degli Uberti[2] by name, who had had to leave Florence with his entire household and much of his wealth, decided that the only safe place for him would be under the king's protection. He settled on Castellammare di Stabia[3] as an isolated spot where he could live out the rest of his days in peace and tranquillity. There, a good stone's throw away from the other houses in the town, amid the olive trees, walnut trees and chestnuts which are abundant in the area, he bought himself a property, on which he built a fine, comfortable house with a delightful garden on one side. Given that fresh water was plentiful, he created a lovely, limpid fish pond in our Florentine style in the middle of the garden and easily found the fish to fill it.

It was while he was spending the whole of every day making his garden more beautiful that King Charles happened to come to Castellammare to relax for a while during the hottest part of the year. He heard about the beauties of Messer Neri's garden and wanted to see it. He had also heard whose garden it was and, since the knight belonged to the faction opposed to his own, he decided to avoid too much formality. He sent a message saying that he would like to come along with four companions the following evening and have a quiet dinner with him in his garden. Messer Neri was delighted. Having arranged for a magnificent feast to be prepared and given his servants due instructions, he welcomed the king into his lovely garden with all the cheer he could muster. Once the king had looked round the whole garden and the house and complimented Messer Neri on both, he washed his hands and sat down at one of the tables that had been set up beside the fish pond. He ordered Count Guy de Montfort,[4] who was one his companions, to sit on one side of himself and Messer Neri to sit on the other, telling the other three who had come with him to serve at table, taking their orders from Messer Neri. The food was exquisite, the wines excellent and the organization of high quality, without fuss or bother, to all of which the king gave his warm approval.

While he was enjoying the food and appreciating the seclusion of the place, two young girls, both about fifteen years old,

came into the garden. Their hair shone like spun gold, the loose
ringlets tumbling down from beneath dainty garlands of peri-
winkle flowers, and their faces made you think of angels rather
than any other creature, so delicate and lovely were they. Each
wore a dress of fine-spun linen, as white as a dusting of snow
on their skin, close-fitting around their upper bodies and
spreading in a loose bell shape from their waists to their feet.
The girl in front carried two fishing nets over her shoulder in
her left hand, while in her right she was holding a long stick.
The girl following carried a frying pan over her left shoulder
with a small bundle of twigs under her arm and a tripod in her
hand. In her other hand she held a small vase of oil and a
lighted taper. The sight of all this startled the king and he
waited with some curiosity to see what it all meant.

The girls came forward, chastely and modestly, and curtsied
to the king. Then they walked over to a slope leading into the
pond. The girl with the pan put it down, followed by the rest of
what she was carrying, and took the stick from the other. Then
the two of them entered the pond, the water of which came up
as far as their breasts. One of Messer Neri's servants promptly
lit the fire and put the pan on the tripod with some oil in it,
after which he waited for the girls to throw him some fish. One
of them began poking around in the places where she knew
the fish were hiding, while the other blocked their escape
with the nets. Watched intently by the king, who was delighted
by the spectacle, they soon caught a good number of fish. Some
they threw to the servant, who flicked them into the pan, still
more or less alive. The more beautiful ones they picked out, as
they had been instructed, and tossed them on to the table before
the king, Count Guy and their father. These fishes wriggled and
jumped on the table, providing wonderful amusement for the
king, who started similarly picking them up and courteously
tossing them back to the girls. The game continued until the
servant had finished cooking the fish he had been given. Messer
Neri ordered these to be set before the king, more as a rarebit
between courses than as some special gourmet dish.

Once the girls saw the cooked fish, they felt they didn't need
to catch any more and emerged from the pond, their thin white

dresses clinging close to their flesh and barely concealing any part of their delicate bodies. Having recovered the things each had brought, they passed modestly in front of the king and disappeared back into the house. The king, the count and their companions who had been serving at table had given these girls their full attention and all had been impressed by the beauty of their faces and figures, as well as by the pleasing but decorous way in which they had conducted themselves. The king was particularly struck by them. He had been so absorbed in examining every part of their bodies as they came out of the water that if someone had stuck a pin in him, he wouldn't have felt it. The more he thought about them, without knowing who they were or where they came from, the more he felt a fervent desire awakening in his heart to make himself pleasing to them. He realized that he was risking becoming enamoured, if he didn't take care, and he didn't know how to choose between them, so alike were they in every way.

After being absorbed in such thoughts for some time, he turned to Messer Neri and asked him who the two girls were.

'My lord,' Messer Neri replied, 'they are my daughters, born together on the same day. One is named after Ginevra the Fair and the other after Isotta the Blonde.'[5]

The king was lavish in his praises and encouraged him to find husbands for them. Messer Neri replied that to his regret such a thing was now beyond his means.

Meanwhile, with only the fruit course remaining to complete the dinner, the two girls reappeared in extremely lovely gowns of exotic silk and carrying two large silver trays laden with fruits of the season, which they set down on the table before the king. Then, drawing back a little, they began to sing a song, which begins:

> The state I've come to be in, Love,
>   would take too long to tell.

They sang so sweetly and pleasingly that the king, who was watching and listening in delight, felt as if all the angelic hosts had come down there to sing. When they finished, they sank to their knees and reverently asked the king for permission to take their leave. He found it hard, but put on a cheerful expression and let them go. At the end of the dinner the king and his companions remounted their horses and, leaving Messer Neri, rode back to the royal residence, talking of one thing or another.

The king concealed his feelings, but, despite all the great affairs of state that came up to claim his attention, he could not get the beauties and charms of the fair Ginevra out of his head, feeling much the same, too, about the sister, who was so like her. After a while he became so enmeshed in the toils of love that he could barely think of anything else. He found various pretexts for developing close ties with Messer Neri and made numerous visits to his lovely garden in order to catch sight of Ginevra. Eventually he couldn't bear it any more and, since he was unable to envisage any other solution, he ended up thinking he should deprive their father not of just one of the girls but of both of them. He revealed his passion and what he was intending to do about it to Count Guy, who was a man of strong views and character, and had this to say:

'My lord, I am amazed by what you tell me, more amazed than anyone else could be, since I've a better knowledge of your character than anyone else, I'd say. I have known you from your boyhood days right through to this present time and I don't recall you suffering any such passion in your youth, which is when love most easily gets its talons into a man's heart. Now I hear you talking like this, when you're on the verge of old age. It is so unexpected and bizarre that you should have fallen prey to a love of such intensity that it seems to me to be almost against the laws of nature. If it were my place to reproach you, I know very well what I would say, taking into account that you're still under arms in a kingdom you've recently acquired, among a people you don't know, who are all set to trick and betray you, with enormous, far-reaching problems to deal with and so far no chance of a moment's rest. And in the middle of all this you seem to have found room for the beguilements of love. A king with any magnanimity of spirit wouldn't do that, only some feeble-spirited youth.

'What's worse is that you say you've decided to deprive the poor knight of his two daughters. This is a man who has paid you honours beyond his means in his own home and, in order to honour you all the more, has shown those two girls to you almost completely naked, as evidence of how great a trust he has in you and of how he believes you to be a king, not a ravenous wolf. Has it gone so quickly out of your head how Manfred's violence to women[6] made it easier for you to acquire this kingdom? What treachery more deserves the eternal torments of hell than the one you will commit if you dishonour a man who honours you and deprive him of his future hope and consolation? What will be said of you if you do this? Perhaps you think it's sufficient excuse to say, "I did it because he's a Ghibelline." Now is that the justice a king dispenses, to treat in this way those who take refuge with him, whoever they are? I remind you, king, that it's a great glory to have overwhelmed Manfred and defeated Conradin,[7] but it is a much greater glory to have conquered oneself. You have rule over others. Now conquer yourself and suppress your baser appetite; do not risk staining and spoiling what you have gloriously attained.'

His words pierced the king to the quick, hurting him all the more because he knew them to be true.

'Count,' he said, after more than one heartfelt sigh, 'a trained warrior certainly finds any enemy, however strong he is, much weaker and more easily defeated than his own desires. However great the torment, whatever unimaginable efforts are needed, your words have spurred me into action. Before many days have gone by I shall perform deeds that will demonstrate to you that I can master myself, just as I can overcome others.'

A few days after this discussion the king returned to Naples. His aim now was to avoid any further occasion for behaviour that was beneath him and at the same time to reward the knight for the honours he had paid him. Hard though it was to let another possess what he desired more than anything else, he resolved nonetheless to arrange marriages for the two girls, treating them as if they were not Messer Neri's daughters but his own. With Messer Neri's consent, he immediately settled magnificent dowries on the girls and married Ginevra the Fair to Messer Maffeo da Palizzi and Isotta the Blonde to Messer Guiglielmo della Magna, two noble knights with great baronial power.[8] Once the girls were handed over to their husbands, he left for Puglia, still in unthinkable agonies, and by giving himself over to sheer hard work he gradually sapped his rampant lust of its force. The chains were eventually shattered and he spent the rest of his life free from any such passion.

Some people will perhaps say that it's a small thing for a king to have married off two young girls. And I agree. Still, I would call it a great achievement – no, a very great one – for a king who is passionately in love to have done this, marrying off the girl he was enamoured of, without ever having picked a single leaf, flower or fruit from the tree of love. This was the action of a magnificent king, who amply rewarded a noble knight, laudably honoured both desirable young girls and achieved a powerful victory over himself.

Patient Griselda

Pressed to marry by his subjects, the Marquis of Saluzzo does so in his own way, choosing the daughter of a peasant. He makes a show of killing the two children he has by her and then of being tired of her. He pretends to take another wife, bringing his daughter back home as if she were his bride, and driving his wife outside in nothing but her shift. Finding she bears all this with great patience, he holds her dearer than ever. He brings her back home, presents her with the grown-up children, and has her honoured as his marchioness by himself and everyone else.

The king's long story was over and everyone gave the impression of having liked it. 'The good man who waited till the following night to get the phantom's rigid tail to go down,' Dioneo said, laughing, 'wouldn't have given two pennies for all the praises you lavish on Messer Torello.'[1] And then, being aware that he was the only one still left to tell a story, he began as follows:

My gentle ladies, from what I can see, today has been given over to kings, sultans and the like. In order not to differ too much from the rest of you, I want to tell a story about a marquis, not a story of magnificent conduct, however, but of crazed animality, although the final outcome was happy for him. I don't advise anyone to imitate his behaviour, since it was outrageous that he came out of it so well.

Years ago a young man called Gualtieri inherited the marquisate of Saluzzo[2] as the eldest son of the family. Being unmarried and childless, he spent all his time hunting birds and

beasts, without giving a thought to marriage or future offspring. He should have been considered a very wise man, but
his subjects disapproved. They kept begging him to get himself
a wife, so that he should not die without an heir and they
should not be left without a lord. They kept offering to find
him one with a suitable father and mother, who would satisfy
their hopes and who would make him very happy.

Gualtieri's response was as follows: 'My friends, you are forcing me into something I had been completely set on never ever
doing, given how difficult it is to find someone with the right
character and habits, how plentiful are the inappropriate candid-
ates, and how hard life becomes for the man who ends up with
someone he doesn't get on with. You claim you can tell the
daughters' characters from how the fathers and mothers
behave, and argue on that basis that you can provide me with
a wife I'll be pleased with. That is rubbish. I don't see how you
can know the fathers properly or the mothers' secrets for that
matter. Besides, even if you could, daughters are very often
unlike their fathers and their mothers. But since you like the
idea of tying me up in these chains, I'll try to satisfy you, and,
so as not to end up blaming anyone else if things should go
wrong, I want to do the finding myself. But I tell you that if you
don't honour and respect whoever I choose, you'll learn to
your cost how hard it has been for me to take a wife against my
will, just because you begged me to.'

His valiant subjects replied that they would be happy, just so
long as he could bring himself to get married.

Gualtieri had been impressed for a good while by the behaviour of a poverty-stricken young woman from a village near his
family home. Since he also judged her to be beautiful, he calculated that life with her could be very pleasant. He looked no
further and made up his mind to marry her. He had the father
summoned and entered into an agreement with this complete
pauper to take the girl as his wife.

That done, he called together all his friends in the area he
ruled.

'My friends,' he said to them, 'you have been eager for me to
make up my mind about a wife for some time. Well, I have

made a decision, more out of wanting to comply with your wishes than from any desire to be married on my part. You know what you promised me – that is, to be content with the woman I chose, whoever she was, and to honour her as your lady. The time has come when I am about to keep my promise to you and when I expect you to keep yours to me. I have found very near here a young woman after my heart. I intend to make her my wife and to bring her into my house in a few days. So arrange for the marriage feast to be a fine one and to give her an honourable welcome. In that way I'll be able to say I'm happy with how you have fulfilled your promise and you'll be able to say the same about me.'

His trusty subjects all replied that they were happy with this, and that no matter who she was they would treat her as their lady and would honour her as such in every way. Then they all set about organizing a suitably grand and joyous celebration. And Gualtieri did his part too, arranging for a sumptuous and splendid marriage feast, to which he invited a multitude of friends, relations, great nobles and other people from the surrounding area. In addition he had beautiful, expensive dresses made to fit a young woman who he judged had the same measurements as the girl he had decided to marry. Not only that, but he ordered belts, rings and a lovely, costly tiara, plus everything else a new bride should have.

Soon after sunrise on the day appointed for the wedding, Gualtieri mounted his horse and all those who had come to honour him did the same. Everything needed was now in order and he called out, 'Gentlemen, it is time to go for the new bride!'

After which he set off along the road to the village with the whole company. When they reached the girl's father's cottage, they found her hurrying back from the spring with some other women in the hope of catching sight of Gualtieri's bride. When he saw her, he called out to her by her name – that is, Griselda – and asked her where her father was.

'My lord,' she replied bashfully, 'he is in the house.'

Gualtieri dismounted and, telling everyone to wait, entered the poor cottage. Inside he found the father, a man called

Giannucolo, to whom he said, 'I have come to make your Griselda my wife, but first I want to learn something from her own lips in your presence.'

What he asked her was whether, when he took her as his wife, she would do everything she could to please him, would not be upset by anything he might say or do and would be obedient, together with many other questions of this sort. She replied 'yes' to everything. Then Gualtieri took her by the hand and led her outside, where, in the presence of his whole company and everyone else, he had her stripped naked. He ordered the clothing he had had made to be brought and immediately had her dressed and shoes put on her and a tiara placed on her hair, unkempt though it was. Everyone was amazed.

'Gentlemen,' he said, 'this is the person I intend should be my wife, if she wishes to have me for her husband.'

Then he turned to her, standing there, bashful and awkward, and said, 'Griselda, do you want me for your husband?'

'Yes, my lord,' she replied,

'And I want you for my wife,' he said.

With that, before everyone present, he formally married her. Then he had her set on a charger, with attendants to do her honour, and took her home. The marriage feast was grand and fine and the festivities no different from what they would have been if he had married the daughter of the king of France.

The young wife's character and behaviour seemed to change with her change of clothing. As I said earlier, she had a lovely face and figure. And now to her natural good looks she added enough charm, attraction and refinement to make you think she could not possibly have been Giannucolo's daughter and a shepherd girl, but the daughter of some noble lord. Everyone who had known her before was astounded. What is more, she was so ready to obey and serve her husband that he considered himself the most contented and satisfied man in the world. She was similarly so gracious and kindly towards her husband's subjects that every one of them loved her wholeheartedly and spontaneously honoured her in every way, asking God in their prayers to give her health, prosperity and still greater glory. If they used to say that Gualtieri had acted ill-advisedly in taking such a wife, now they said he was a paragon of wisdom and insight, arguing that no one else could have perceived the exceptional virtues concealed beneath the poverty of her peasant dress. All in all, before much time had passed, she had people speaking of her good qualities and virtuous deeds throughout the marquisate and beyond, and completely turning around any negative comments about her husband that had been made when he married her.

She had not been with Gualtieri very long when she became pregnant and in due course she gave birth to a little girl, much to Gualtieri's delight. But a little later a strange idea came into his head. He felt a need to test her patience by inflicting unbearable torments on her over a prolonged period of time. First of all he made cutting remarks and gave an impression of being angry with her. He said that his men were badly put out by her lowly origin, all the more now that she was having children. The girl child was a particular source of resentment, and they wouldn't stop muttering about her.

When his lady heard this, she kept her composure and gave no sign of being thrown off the virtuous course she had set herself.

'My lord,' she said, 'treat me in the way that most accords with your honour and your happiness. I shall be content with anything. I am aware I'm less than they are and that I didn't deserve the honour you have had the generosity to bestow on me.'

Her response was warmly received by Gualtieri, who recognized that any honour that he or anyone else had paid her had not made her feel in the slightest bit superior.

A little while later, after giving his wife the general impression that his subjects couldn't stand the little girl she had borne him, he had a word with one of the household staff and sent him to her. The man addressed her with a distressed air.

'My lady,' he said, 'I am obliged to do something my lord commands me to do, if I do not wish to die. He has ordered me to take this daughter of yours and . . .'

He stopped there. Hearing his words and seeing his face, the lady recalled what her husband had been saying and deduced

that he had orders to kill the child. She quickly took her from
her cradle, kissed her and blessed her. For all the immense pain
in her heart, she again kept her composure and put the child in
the man's arms.

'Take her,' she said, 'and carry out to the letter what your
lord and mine has ordered you to do. Only do not leave her for
animals and birds to devour, unless he told you to.'

The servant took the child away and passed on what his wife
had said to Gualtieri, who was astounded by her constancy. He
then sent the servant off with the child to a female relative of
his in Bologna, with a request to bring her up and educate her
with the utmost care, but not to let anyone know whose daughter she was.

The next thing to happen was that the lady became pregnant
again. In due course she gave birth to a male child, which
pleased Gualtieri immensely. But what he had done already
was not enough for him. His criticisms became sharper and
sharper, and one day, his face contorted with rage, he said this
to her:

'My lady, ever since you had this boy child I haven't been
able to live with these men of mine. They are bitterly against
some grandson of Giannucolo ending up their lord after me. If
I don't want to be hounded out of here, I'm afraid I'm going to
have to do what I did the other time, and then in the end I'm
going to have to leave you and take another wife.'

The lady listened without flinching.

'My lord,' was all she replied, 'think only of contenting
yourself and following your own inclinations, and don't worry
at all about me. Nothing matters to me except whatever I see
pleases you.'

A few days later Gualtieri sent someone for his son, much as
he had done as regards his daughter. After a similar show of
having him murdered, he dispatched him to Bologna to be
brought up there, like the little girl. What the lady said and
showed in her face was no different from before, which stunned
Gualtieri. He declared to himself that there wasn't a woman
anywhere capable of behaving like that. If he hadn't seen her
visceral attachment to the children as long as she had his

approval, he would have thought she was glad to see the back of them, but he knew that there was sense and wisdom in her.

His subjects, believing he had had his children killed, strongly condemned him for his cruelty and felt nothing but compassion for the lady. When other ladies sympathized with her for having lost her children in this way, she said only that what pleased her was precisely what pleased the man who had fathered them.

Some years after the little girl's birth, Gualtieri decided it was time to put his wife's capacity for endurance to the ultimate test. He told many of his men that he just could not bear Griselda being his wife any more, and that it was clear to him that marrying her had been a bad juvenile error; he was now going to do all he could to obtain a special dispensation from the Pope to take another wife and leave Griselda. Quite a few of his good men took him to task, but he replied only that that was how things had to be. When his lady heard the news, she found herself having to face the idea of going back to her father's house and perhaps tending the sheep, as she had done in the past, with the added prospect of some other lady taking possession of the man to whom she had given all the love she had. She was devastated. But she had borne all the other wrongs that Fortune had done her and she set herself to bear this one with similar fortitude.

A little later Gualtieri arranged for some counterfeit letters to be sent from Rome and gave his subjects to believe that in these the Pope had given him dispensation to marry again and leave Griselda. He had her summoned and addressed her before a crowd of onlookers.

'My lady,' he said, 'thanks to a special concession granted to me by the Pope, I can take another wife and leave you. Since my ancestors were from the high nobility and the lords of these lands, whereas yours have always been labourers, I intend that you should no longer be my wife and should go back to Giannucolo's house with the dowry you brought me. After that I shall marry someone I've found who will be appropriate for my station.'

Hearing this the lady had to make an immense effort – one beyond women's natural capacities – in order to keep back her tears.

'My lord,' she replied, 'I always knew my lowly origins in no way accorded with your own nobility. I was glad to attribute to God and to yourself the position I have enjoyed with you. I have never thought it something I had been given or treated it as anything more than a loan. Your wish is to recover it. I must make it my wish to let you have it and I am happy to do so. Here is the ring with which you married me. Take it. You order me to carry away with me the dowry I brought you. That's not something for which you'll need a banker or for which I'll need a bag or a packhorse. It does not escape me that you took me in naked. If you consider it decent for that body in which I carried the children you fathered to be seen by all and sundry, I shall go away naked. But I beg you that you let me have some payment for the virginity that I brought here and do not take away again, by allowing me, over and above my dowry, to have a single shift to wear.'

Gualtieri wanted only to burst into tears. But his face stayed as hard as ever.

'So you go off with a shift then,' he said.

Everyone there begged him to make her the gift of a robe and not let the woman who had been his wife for thirteen years or more be seen leaving his house penniless and utterly humiliated, which was what leaving in just a shift would mean. But their requests came to nothing. So it was in a shift, barefoot and bareheaded, that the lady commended them to God's care and walked out of her husband's house and back to her father's, amid the weeping and wailing of all who saw her.

Giannucolo had never been able to believe that Gualtieri really wanted his daughter as his wife, expecting every day something like this to happen, and had kept the clothes she was wearing on the morning Gualtieri married her. He brought them out and she put them on. Then she gave herself over to the menial tasks around her father's house that she used to do in the past, valiantly bearing the savage assault that hostile Fortune inflicted on her.

Gualtieri's next step was to pretend to his subjects that he had found himself a daughter of one of the Counts of Panago.[3]

In the course of grandiose preparations for the marriage ceremony, he sent for Griselda to come and see him.

'I'm bringing here as my bride,' he said to her when she
arrived, 'this lady I've very recently promised to marry. My
intention is to receive her with due honour when she comes
here for the first time. You're aware that I don't have ladies in
the house who can spruce up the rooms and do all the things
required for a festive occasion of this sort. Since you know better than anyone else how this house works, sort out what needs
to be done and also invite a welcome party of ladies you think
suitable, and receive them as if you were the lady in charge.
Then once the marriage feast is over, you can go back to your
own house.'

His words were so many knives in Griselda's heart. She had
never been able to abandon the love she felt for him in the way
she had let go of her good fortune.

'My lord, I am willing and ready,' she said.

And so, in a makeshift dress of thick, rough cloth, she went
back into the house she had left in just her shift not long before
and began sweeping the chambers and tidying them up, fixing
hangings and drapes in the halls and getting the kitchen ready,
doing every single thing with her own hands as if she were
nothing but a mere servant girl. Nor did she stop until she had
everything as neat and orderly as the occasion required.

Once she had arranged for invitations to be sent out on
Gualtieri's behalf to all the ladies in the area, all that was left
for her to do was to await the coming festivities. When the day
of the marriage feast arrived, in spite of the poor clothes she
had on, she gave every one of the ladies who came a joyful and
dignified welcome.

Gualtieri had taken care that the children should be properly
brought up in Bologna by his female relative, who had married
into the house of the Counts of Panago. The girl was now
twelve and the prettiest creature ever, and the boy was six.
Gualtieri had written to the relative's husband, asking him to
be so good as to bring his daughter and son to Saluzzo, accompanied by an appropriate guard of honour, and to tell everyone

that he was bringing the girl to be Gualtieri's wife, with no hint to anyone of who she really was.

This gentleman did as the marquis asked and set off with the girl, her brother and the guard of honour. After some days, around the time of the morning meal, they arrived in Saluzzo, where they found all the local people and many others from round about waiting for this new bride of Gualtieri. The girl was greeted by the ladies and entered the hall where the tables were laid out. Griselda, dressed just as she was, went towards her happily enough, saying, 'My lady is welcome.'

The other ladies, who had repeatedly but fruitlessly begged Gualtieri either to let Griselda stay in one of the chambers or to lend her one of the robes that were once hers, so that she would not appear before the visitors looking as she did, were now assigned their places at the tables and began to be served. The girl was the object of everybody's attention and the general view was that Gualtieri had made a good exchange. One of those who was most lavish with her praises, both of the girl and her little brother, was Griselda.

Gualtieri thought he had now had all the proof he could want of the patience of his lady. He could tell that it was not at all affected by events, no matter how bizarre they were, and, given the wisdom he knew was in her, he was sure that dullness of mind was not a factor. He decided it was time to release her from the tortures he judged she must be suffering beneath her calm and steady exterior. He had her come forwards and, before everyone there, gave her a smile and asked:

'What do you think of our bride?'

'My lord,' replied Griselda, 'I can only think very well of her. If her good sense is equal to her beauty, as I believe it must be, I have no doubt that living with her will make you the most contented lord in the world. But I beg you with all my heart not to inflict on her the sort of wounds you inflicted on the other one, the one who was your wife before. I can't really believe that she could stand it. She's younger and what's more she's been brought up in luxury, whereas the other had spent her childhood doing hard physical work.'

Gualtieri could see that she firmly believed the girl was going to be his wife and yet still said nothing he could disapprove of. He sat her down at his side and then spoke.

'Griselda,' he said, 'it is now time for you to taste the fruit of your steadfast patience and for those who judged me cruel, unjust and inhuman to acknowledge that what I did had a deliberate purpose. I wanted to teach you to be a wife, to teach my critics how to take a wife and to keep one, and to bring about for myself unbroken peace and quiet for as long as my life with you might last. This was something I was very afraid wouldn't happen when I first took a wife. It was to test if it were possible that I inflicted on you all the wounds and torments you are all too aware of.

'Since I have never perceived you going against my wishes in anything you have said or done, I judge that I do indeed have from you that contentment which I desired. I therefore intend to restore to you in one single moment what I took from you over the years and to apply the sweetest possible medicine to the wounds I inflicted. So now, with joy in your heart, receive this girl you think is my bride, and her brother too. These are our children that you and many others have long thought I had brutally murdered. And I myself am your husband, who loves you more than anything else. I think I can rightly and honestly boast that no other man alive can be as happy with his wife as I am.'

After this speech he put his arms round her and kissed her. He then raised her to her feet and led her, weeping for joy, over to where their daughter was sitting, astounded by what she was hearing. They tenderly embraced the two children and then told the girl and many other people there the truth of the situation. The ladies were delighted to get up from the tables and go with Griselda into one of the chambers. Expressing hopes of a better outcome this time, they helped her out of her rough clothing and dressed her in one of her noble robes. Then they led her back into the hall a courtly lady, which even in her rags she had retained the air of being. There followed a moment of marvellous celebration with the children and everyone showed their joy at the way things had turned out. Then they plunged into feasting and merrymaking, which went on for days.

Everyone judged Gualtieri to have shown great wisdom, though they considered the tests inflicted on his lady to have been too severe, indeed intolerable. Griselda they held to have shown more wisdom than anyone.

After some days the Count of Panago returned to Bologna and Gualtieri took Giannucolo away from his work. From then he was treated as a proper father-in-law and lived very happily and much respected until a ripe old age. After finding a noble husband for his daughter, Gualtieri himself lived a long and happy life with Griselda and treated her with all possible honour.

What can be said here except that divine spirits descend from heaven even into poor houses and into royal houses come spirits which more deserve to look after pigs than be lords over men? Who else but Griselda could have borne the callous, unprecedented tests Gualtieri subjected her to, not just without tears but with what looked like cheerfulness? Perhaps it would have served him right if the woman he landed on had let another man shake her muff[4] when she was driven from home in her shift, and that way got herself a decent dress.

The Author's Conclusion

Most noble young ladies, it was to console you that I first embarked on such a lengthy and laborious task. I believe that I have been aided by the divine grace that your compassionate prayers – and not, I would say, my own merits – obtained for me, and have now completed the project I committed myself to at the start of this work. With thanks first of all to God and then to yourselves, it is now time for my pen and weary hand to rest. Before I put down either of them, I intend briefly to take up a few small points, as yet largely unvoiced, that some of you or other people might raise, since I fully acknowledge that these stories have no special privilege exempting them from criticism, as I recall stating at the beginning of the Fourth Day.[1]

There may be some among you who will say that, writing these stories, I have allowed myself too much freedom, making the ladies sometimes say, and very often making them hear, things that decent ladies shouldn't say or hear. I simply deny that: there's nothing so indecent that – if the words used are decent – doesn't become acceptable. I think that I've been very successful in keeping up standards in this regard.

But let's assume it's a valid objection – for I don't want to get into a dispute with you, since you would come out the winners. However, I can very quickly produce many reasons for doing what I've done. First of all, if there are things in some places that could be picked on, they're there because they're demanded by the kind of stories these are. It will be obvious to any intelligent person who casts an unprejudiced eye over them that unless I'd been prepared to alter their form radically, they couldn't have been told in any other way. If they should contain some particle, some little word that's more free than maybe you'd expect on the lips of a nit-picking bigot who pays more attention to words than facts and puts her efforts into appearing more virtuous than she really is, I say that it shouldn't be any more inappropriate for me to write these words than it is generally for men and women to come out all day with words like 'hole', 'tube', 'mortar', 'pestle', 'sausage', 'titbit' and a host of other words of that sort.

Besides, my pen should be granted the same freedom of action as a painter's brush. A painter is not criticized, not justly anyway, if he paints St Michael wounding the serpent with a sword or with a lance, or has St George spearing the dragon in whatever spot he chooses. Those examples aside, a painter paints Christ as male and Eve as female, and, when he's tackling Him who gave Himself to die on the Cross for the salvation of mankind, sometimes he nails his feet up with one nail and other times with two.

Then it should also be taken into account that the stories were not told in church, where both feelings and utterances should be utterly chaste, although many stories more dubious than mine can be found in ecclesiastical histories. And they weren't told in the schools of the philosophers, where propriety is as much required as it can be anywhere, nor for that matter in any gathering of clergymen or philosophers. The storytelling took place in gardens, in places of pleasure and relaxation, among people who were young in years but mature in judgement, and not to be led astray by stories, at a moment when the most respectable people were ready to go around with their breeches on their heads[2] if they thought it would save their lives.

Whatever sort of stories they are, they can do good or do harm like anything else, depending on the listener. Who doesn't know that wine is a real benefit to the healthy, according to Drinkhard and Glugg and many other authorities, but harmful to anyone with a fever? Are we to say that it's a bad thing because the feverish are harmed by drinking it? And what about fire, which is useful, or rather essential for mortal beings? Shall we call it a bad thing because fire can burn down houses, villages and whole cities? Weapons similarly ensure the well-being of those who want to live in peace, but they often kill people, not on account of any wickedness in the things themselves, but because of the wickedness of those who use them to an evil end.

No word has ever been understood in a wholesome way by a corrupt mind. And virtuous words do not change the corrupt for the better, any more than words that are not so virtuous pervert a mind that is morally sound, just as mud does not pollute the rays of the sun, or the dirt of earth the beauties of heaven. What books or words or letters are more sacred, more worth their while, more to be revered than those of the Holy Scriptures? Yet there have been many who interpreted them perversely and led themselves and others to perdition.

Everything is in itself good for a particular purpose, but if abused, may cause many different forms of harm. That's what I say of my stories. If someone wants to take from them a lesson in immoral thought or immoral conduct, the stories themselves won't stop them doing so – and whether they contain any element of that sort or not, they'll be twisted and pulled about until they do. But anyone who wants moral benefit and improvement from them, won't be refused either. In fact, no one could think or say that they are anything but beneficial and virtuous if they are read at the times and to the people they were intended for. But women who reel off Our Fathers or bake chestnut cakes and the like for their precious confessors, should leave them alone. They're not going to chase after anyone to get themselves read, although sanctimonious ladies say twee-sounding things that are just as bad – and do them too, if they have the chance.

Some of you will likewise say that some of the stories included would have been better left out. That's all very well. But I could only do my duty and write down the stories that were told. Those who told them should have told good ones and then I'd have written down good ones. But supposing I had been their originator as well as the one who who wrote them down, which I wasn't, I can say that I would not be ashamed if they weren't all good stories, because there's no master craftsman, barring God, whose creations are all perfect in every way. Charlemagne, who first created the paladins,[3] could not make enough of them to form an army by themselves.

If you have a multitude of things, you'll inevitably find differences in quality. There's never been a field, no matter how well-cultivated, where there wasn't a nettle or a thistle or a thornbush growing somewhere among the good plants. Besides, since the intention was to tell stories to simple young women, as most of you are, it would have been silly to spend time and effort trying to find highly refined material or taking great care to give a proper form to the way things are expressed. All the same, anyone picking out stories to read should ignore those that seem disagreeable and read those that seem enjoyable. They have no deceitful intent and all carry inscribed on their forehead an indication of what they hold concealed within their bosom.[4]

There again, I suppose some among you might say that some stories are too long. I say that any lady with other things to do would be crazy to read them, even if they were short. A lot of time has passed between when I began writing and this moment when I'm approaching the end of my labours, but I haven't forgotten that I offered my efforts only to ladies with time on their hands. For those who read to pass the time nothing can be too long, if it does what it's intended for. Short things are much more suited to scholars straining to use time profitably rather than to make it go by, whereas for you ladies time is all empty, apart from what you spend in the pleasures of love. What's more, since none of you go away to study in Athens, Bologna or Paris,[5] it's better to spin things out for you, which is not the case when addressing minds sharpened by study.

I don't doubt at all that there will also be some ladies who will say that the stories are too full of joking and jesting, and that it's unbecoming for a man of any weight and gravity to have written such stuff. I'm bound to thank these ladies, and I do so, because they have the best of intentions and are concerned about my good name. But this is what I say in response to their criticism: I confess to having weight and to having been weighed very often in my time. But, speaking to those who have not weighed me, I declare that my gravity is nil – no, I'm so light that I float on water. And considering that the sermons the friars deliver in order to strike the hearts of men with remorse for their sins are mostly full of jokes, jests and jocularity nowadays, I thought that sort of thing wasn't out of place in my stories, written as they were to help women feel better. However, if they should make them laugh too much, they can easily cure themselves with Jeremiah's lamentations,[6] our Saviour's Passion and the moanings of Mary Magdalen.

There again, let's acknowledge that there will be ladies who say I've a malicious, poisonous tongue because in some places I tell the truth about friars. Those who say this deserve to be forgiven: it's impossible to believe that their motives are anything but fair, since the friars are good people who leave behind discomfort for the love of God and grind away when their ponds are full,[7] and tell no one. If they didn't all have a goatish whiff to them,[8] they'd be very pleasant to deal with.

Nevertheless, I confess that the things of this world have no stability whatsoever and are in a state of constant change, and that this may have happened with my tongue. I don't trust my own judgement, which I discount as much as I can in anything I do, but a lady who's a neighbour of mine told me very recently that I have the best and sweetest tongue in the world. And the fact is that, when she said this, only a few of the stories in question were still to be written. Since those other ladies are so hostile, what I have said will have to do as a reply to them.

I now leave each lady to say and believe what she pleases. It's time to bring my words to a close, humbly thanking Him who, after so long a labour, has led me through His aid to the desired end. And you, delightful ladies, live on in peace and attended by His grace, and remember me, should any of you benefit in any way from your reading.

Here ends the Tenth and last day of the book called Decameron, *whose other name is* Prince Galahalt.[9]

Acknowledgements

I am particularly grateful to three friends. Priscilla Sheringham and Christopher Faram read drafts of the translations of the stories and supplied encouraging feedback and perspicuous suggestions and corrections. Without them the translations would have been much worse than they are. I am also much indebted to David Robey for comments on the first draft of my Introduction. My warm thanks go too to Jessica Harrison and to Ian Pindar for their discreet and sympathetic editorial work, which included many amendments to phrasing that I was only too happy to accept, and also to Anna Hervé for gentle but sure shepherding of the publishing process. But my biggest debt is to Jane Hainsworth, without whose love and support the whole project would have collapsed long ago.

Notes

+ placed before a number indicates a story in the *Decameron* not
included in this selection

PROLOGUE

1. *Decameron*: The title is based on an uncertain Greek 'ten days'
   (*deka hemeron*).
2. *Prince Galahalt*: In stories about Sir Lancelot and his love for
   Queen Guinevere, a certain Sir Galahalt (not the famous Sir
   Galahad) acts as an intermediary, furthering the cause of Lancelot with Guinevere as much as he can. So the *Decameron*, it is
   implied, will serve the cause of love with its women readers.
3. *an exalted, noble love*: For Boccaccio's invented love for Fiammetta or Maria d'Aquino, see Introduction, p. xiv.
4. *fables, parables, histories*: See Introduction, p. xxv.

DAY ONE

1. *the author explains . . . to tell stories*: For the events described in
   Boccaccio's Introduction and the members of the party, see
   Introduction, pp. xvi–xviii.

Introduction

1. *If the extreme limit of happiness is pain*: From Proverbs 14:13:
   'Even in laughter the heart is sorrowful; and the end of that
   mirth is heaviness.'
2. *biers*: Stretchers for carrying bodies, rather than coffins.

3. *Galen, Hippocrates and Aesculapius*: The three canonical fig-
    ures of ancient medicine for medieval writers. Aesculapius (or
    Asclepius) was the god of medicine, Hippocrates (*c.* 460–*c.*
    377 BC) its human inventor, and Galen (AD 129–*c.* 199) its
    greatest practitioner.
4. *Pampinea . . . Elissa*: For the names given to the members of the
    party and their servants' names, see Introduction, pp. xvii–xviii.
5. *the man is the woman's head*: Taken from St Paul: 'For the hus-
    band is the head of the wife, even as Christ is the head of the
    church' (Ephesians 5:23).
6. *vespers*: About 6 p.m. Like other medieval authors, Boccaccio
    indicates the time of day by the canonical hours of service (mat-
    ins, lauds, prime, terce, sext, nones, vespers and compline).
7. *terce*: About 9 a.m.
8. *Nones*: About 3 p.m.

I
Ser Cepparello Becomes a Saint

1. *dear ladies*: The young men of the party are always ignored in
    these openings. See Introduction, p. xxix.
2. *Musciatto Franzesi*: A Florentine merchant who had extensive,
    deeply corrupt dealings in France and became an adviser to the
    French king Philippe le Bel (1268–1314). The king's brother
    Charles de Valois (1270–1325) invaded Italy in 1301 at the
    request of Pope Boniface VIII (1235–1303), one consequence of
    which was the exile from Florence of Dante Alighieri (1265–
    1321). Charles had little land of his own before the invasion,
    hence his nickname, Charles Lackland.
3. *Ser Cepparello of Prato*: This man existed and is known to have
    collected taxes on behalf of the French king and the Pope,
    although he was not a notary and he probably died in Italy early
    in the fourteenth century.
4. *Lombard dogs*: The Lombards were the Italians most involved
    in banking in France and England, and the term was often used
    to refer to Italians generally.
5. *the storyteller*: Panfilo.

2
The Conversion of Abraham

1. *Paris*: Medieval Paris was perhaps the major centre in Europe for theological and philosophical studies. Rome was relatively insignificant.

3
The Story of the Three Rings

1. *Saladin*: Salah ad-Din Yusuf ibn-Ayyub (1137–93), Sultan of Egypt and Cairo (1174–93), who invaded the Holy Land and reconquered Jerusalem from the Christians in 1187, appears in much medieval European literature as an embodiment of courtliness, nobility and sagacity. He is also a protagonist of *Decameron* +10.9.

DAY TWO

5
Andreuccio da Perugia's Neapolitan Adventures

1. *Landolfo's . . . stones*: The previous story, told by Lauretta, was about a merchant adventurer called Landolfo Rufolo, who, after various dramatic ups and downs, loses everything in a shipwreck, but saves his life by hanging on to a chest on which he floats ashore. A woman finds him and gives him food and shelter, after which he discovers that the chest contains jewels and returns home a wealthy man.

2. *Malpertugio*: An area near the port of Naples, well known for its inns and brothels.

3. *the Guelf side*: The two main factions in thirteenth-century Italy were the Guelfs (who supported the Pope) and the Ghibellines (who supported the Holy Roman Emperor). The Guelfs also supported the French Angevins, who, with papal support, had established themselves as rulers of southern Italy after the invasion of Charles I of Anjou (1226–85) in the mid-1260s. His son Charles II (1254–1309), who is referred to here and ruled in Naples from 1285 to his death, was in constant conflict with King Frederick II of Aragon (1272–1337), the Ghibelline-supported ruler of Sicily from 1296 to his death, whom

various Guelf conspiracies of the type mentioned here tried to dislodge.

4. *Ruga Catalana*: One of the main streets of Naples running from the port area up into the higher part of the city. Many of the Catalans who joined the Angevin court in the early fourteenth century established themselves in this part of town.

5. *Buttafuoco's*: Medieval documents mention a Sicilian called Buttafuoco, who fought in the Angevin army and lived in Naples in the 1330s.

6. *Filippo Minutolo*: An important figure in the kingdom, as well as being Archbishop of Naples. He died in October 1301 – that is, when the heat is unlikely to have been as intense in reality as the story has it.

9
The Trials of Madonna Zinevra

1. *her moving story*: Elissa had recounted the touching story of the Count of Antwerp who was exiled after being falsely accused of attempted rape, but was eventually reinstated when the princess who accused him confessed to her crime on her deathbed.

2. *The terms agreed with Dioneo*: At the end of the First Day Dioneo had been granted the privilege of telling the last story each day from then onwards and of departing from the subject of the day if he wished. See Introduction, p. xx.

3. *Bernabò Lomellin*: The Lomellin were a well-established family of Genovese merchants with considerable business in France.

4. *Albenga*: A port on the Ligurian coast to the south-west of Genova.

5. *Finale*: Now Finale Ligure, a port in Liguria, not far from Albenga.

6. *Acre*: A former Christian stronghold in Syria, which fell to Islamic forces in 1291.

10
Ricciardo da Chinzica Loses His Wife

1. *Chinzica*: A district of Pisa.

2. *Gualandi*: One of the noblest Pisan families.

3. *Ravenna*: Reputedly, this city had enough churches (and therefore enough saints' days) for every day of the year.

4. *Ember days*: Four short periods of fasting spread throughout the Christian calendar at roughly three-month intervals.
5. *Monte Nero*: A promontory jutting into the sea south of Livorno, not far from Pisa.
6. *Paganino da Mare*: Although this individual is unknown, the da Mare were a noble family, originally from Genova.
7. *Bernabò*: He and Ambrogiuolo are the male protagonists of the previous story.

DAY THREE

I

Masetto da Lamporecchio Helps Out in the Convent

1. *Lovely ladies*: Filostrato is speaking, having been designated as the first storyteller at the end of the Introduction to this day.
2. *Lamporecchio*: A small village in Tuscany, south of Pistoia.

4

Brother Puccio's Penance

1. *the prayer Filomena had just uttered*: Filomena had ended her story of two lovers finally being able to spend nights together with a prayer that God might likewise show pity on herself and all Christian souls wanting something similar.
2. *Franciscan tertiary*: A lay brother, subject to some monastic rules.
3. *a practising flagellant*: Some lay brothers performed self-flagellation to demonstrate their piety and self-abasement.
4. *Don Felice came back from Paris*: The implication is that he had been studying at the University of Paris.
5. *compline bell*: Rung for the prayers said at compline, the last of the canonical hours of the day, marking bedtime. Matins are the early morning equivalent, rung just before dawn.
6. *St Benedict's or St John Gualbert's ass*: The two saints were often shown riding asses in paintings.

9
Gilette and Her Supercilious Husband

1. *fistula*: A particularly deep and unpleasant ulcer.
2. *Dioneo's privilege*: That is, of telling the last story of the day. See Introduction, p. xx.
3. *Lauretta's story*: A tale about a man who is tricked into believing he is dead and in Purgatory by his wife's lover, an abbot, who also manages to foist his love child on to him as the man's own.
4. *Isnard, Count of Roussillon*: Isnard and the other main characters do not seem to be based on historical figures.

10
Putting the Devil in Hell

1. *Capsa*: A Tunisian city, now Gafsa.
2. *Thebes*: A city in ancient Egypt, famous for all the hermits who withdrew into the desert thereabouts from early in the Christian era.

DAY FOUR

Author's Introduction

1. This is the sole intervention that Boccaccio makes in his own person within the body of the *Decameron*.
2. *the Muses on Parnassus*: In Greek mythology Mount Parnassus in central Greece is the seat of the Muses and therefore the metaphorical home of poetry, literature and the arts.
3. *Filippo Balducci*: The Balducci were a not very well-off Florentine family, some members of which are known to have worked for the Bardi bank, as did Boccaccio himself.
4. *Mount Asinine*: Monte Asinaio in the original, a distortion of the name of a mountain near Florence called Monte Senario, which at one time did have hermits living in its caves.
5. *Cino da Pistoia*: (*c.* 1270–*c.* 1336) A love poet like Guido Cavalcanti (?1259–1300) and the younger Dante. All three are generally associated with what Dante called the 'sweet new style' (*dolce stil novo*).

6. *thousands of lines*: Boccaccio wrote some love lyrics, and much of his narrative work in prose and verse claims to be inspired by love. See Introduction, pp. xiv–xv.

7. *the Apostle*: St Paul: 'every where and in all things I am instructed both to be full and to be hungry, both to abound and to suffer need' (Philippians 4:12).

I

Tancredi and Ghismonda

1. *Tancredi*: Tancredi (or Tancred) was the name of various Norman princes and rulers in southern Italy, but not of any prince of Salerno of the time.

2

Friar Alberto Becomes the Angel Gabriel

1. *Assisi*: St Francis's home town was the centre of the Franciscan order, often called the Friars Minor.

2. *Venice . . . comes its way*: Boccaccio is scathing about the Venetians in various places in his works, probably, at least in part, because of the trading and political rivalry between Venice and Florence.

3. *the Querini family*: One of the oldest and most illustrious Venetian families.

4. *Flanders*: Trade between Flanders and Venice was strong in the early fourteenth century.

5. *the Rialto*: The central island and business centre of Venice.

5

Lisabetta and the Pot of Basil

1. *Gerbino and his lady*: In the previous story (told by Elissa) the young prince Gerbino had attempted to rescue the Saracen princess he was in love with, but in the end both had met violent deaths.

2. *San Gimignano*: Various merchant families from the small Tuscan town of San Gimignano had business branches in Messina in the thirteenth and fourteenth centuries.

3. *Salerno basil*: Salerno is not particularly famous for its basil and the text may be corrupt at this point.

4. *Who was it . . . my vase, etc.*: A version of this song has survived, although its date is uncertain.

DAY FIVE

4
Catching a Nightingale

1. *reducing you to tears*: As ruler for the Fourth Day, Filostrato had imposed unhappy love as its theme.
2. *Messer Lizio da Valbona*: A thirteenth-century lord of Valbona on the border between Tuscany and the Romagna.
3. *Manardi da Brettinoro*: This family existed, but Ricciardo may well be an invention.
4. *to the chirping of cicadas*: That is, in the middle of the day.
5. *serge*: A fine, silky, woollen fabric.
6. *commit himself to marrying her first*: Lizio wants a formal betrothal with an exchange of rings, which does indeed happen. The marriage ceremony will be held later.

6
The Narrow Escape of Gianni da Procida and His Beloved

1. *Marin Bolgaro*: An important shipbuilder for the Angevin kings and a personal friend of Boccaccio's. The daughter Restituta is unknown.
2. *Gianni*: Neither Gianni di Procida nor his father and uncle, mentioned later, have been identified as historical characters.
3. *King Frederick of Sicily*: Frederick II of Aragon. See note 3 to 'Andreuccio da Perugia's Neapolitan Adventures' on p. 297.
4. *La Cuba*: This Moorish palace in the Sicilian city of Palermo still exists.
5. *Cape of Minerva to Scalea in Calabria*: Roughly speaking, from near Naples to northern Calabria.
6. *terce*: That is, about 9 a.m.
7. *Ruggiero de Loria*: (*c.* 1245–1305) An admiral of Frederick II's, highly praised elsewhere by Boccaccio, and also by other fourteenth-century writers.

8
Nastagio degli Onesti and the Infernal Chase

1. *Lauretta*: The teller of the previous story.
2. *Nastagio degli Onesti*: The degli Onesti were a noble family in Ravenna, although Nastagio is unknown.
3. *Messer Paolo Traversaro*: The head of one of the most prestigious families in Ravenna, celebrated by various writers of the thirteenth and fourteenth centuries. He died in 1240.
4. *Chiassi*: On the coast near Ravenna and famous for the pine forest that figures in this story.
5. *Guido degli Anastagi*: The family is again a noble one, although Guido is unknown. The close echo of Nastagio's name suggests a degree of identity between the two figures.

9
Federigo degli Alberighi and His Falcon

1. *his privilege of telling the last story*: Granted to Dioneo at the end of the First Day. See Introduction, p. xx.
2. *Coppo di Borghese Domenichi*: A prominent and apparently slightly eccentric Florentine, somewhat older than Boccaccio himself. Fiammetta is unsure whether he is still alive because of the Black Death raging in Florence.
3. *Campi*: Campi Bisenzio, not far to the north-west of Florence.

DAY SIX

1
Madonna Oretta's Put-down

1. *Young ladies*: The storyteller is Filomena.
2. *Pampinea has already said quite enough*: Introducing her first story (+1.10), Pampinea had made similar comments on the limitations of contemporary ladies.
3. *Madonna Oretta*: The daughter of the Marchese Obizzo Malaspina and the wife of the prominent Florentine politician Geri Spina, who died sometime before 1332 and is mentioned again in the next story (+6.2). She was apparently well known for her clever remarks.

9

Cavalcanti among the Tombs

1. *the one . . . speaking last*: Dioneo. See Introduction, pp. xx.
2. *Betto Brunelleschi*: Brunelleschi was from a noble family and a friend of Cavalcanti and Dante, until he joined the Black Guelf party, of which he became one of the leading figures after Dante's exile in 1301. He was eventually murdered by members of the rival Donati family.
3. *Guido*: The poet Guido Cavalcanti (?1259–1300) was a friend of the young Dante and famous for his intellectual interests, which bordered on the heretical.
4. *natural philosopher*: What we would call a physical scientist.
5. *Epicurean ideas*: That is, ideas associated principally with atheism and a lack of belief in the immortality of the soul, as in Dante's *Inferno* 10.13–15. One of the souls that Dante meets in this circle of unbelievers (heretics) is Guido's father Cavalcante de' Cavalcanti.
6. *from Orto San Michele*: Guido's route takes him from the district of Orto San Michele, named after the old church of San Michele (demolished in the early fourteenth century), up Corso degli Adimari (now via de' Calzaioli) to the Baptistery (the church of San Giovanni) and the Church of Santa Reparata, which stood where the cathedral now stands. The tombs referred to were probably ancient sarcophagi, removed in 1296 after work was begun on the cathedral in 1294. The porphyry columns by the doors of the Baptistery are still there.

10

Friar Cipolla and the Coals

1. *Guido's telling riposte*: See the previous story.
2. *order of St Anthony*: A mendicant order which became notorious for greed, named after the founder of western monasticism, St Anthony (*c.* 251–356).
3. *Certaldo*: The small township ruled by Florence, about thirty kilometres to the south-west, and the home of Boccaccio's family. Boccaccio spent his last years there. See Introduction, p. xxxii.
4. *Friar Cipolla*: Brother Onion.
5. *Cicero . . . Quintilian*: The two ancient Roman authors Cicero (106–43 BC) and Qunitilian (AD *c.* 35–*c.* 100) represented the

pinnacles of the art of oratory for the Middle Ages and the Renaissance.

6. *nones*: About 3 p.m.

7. *Giovanni della Bragoniera ... Biagio Pizzini*: Both families lived in Certaldo. Biagio Pizzini was a friend and neighbour of Boccaccio's father.

8. *Guccio*: This figure seems actually to have existed and to have had the kind of nicknames mentioned here, if not these precise ones.

9. *Lippo Topo*: A hack painter of the time, known for his witlessness.

10. *the Baronci*: A Florentine family much mocked for being ugly and dim-witted.

11. *Altopascio*: A monastery near Lucca known for the cauldrons of soup the monks boiled up for the poor.

12. *Confiteor*: Literally, 'I confess', the prayer traditionally recited at the beginning of Mass.

13. *Porcine privileges*: Perhaps alluding to the greed and filthy tendencies attributed to the monks of St Anthony.

14. *Venice*: This and others that follow in the original are names of streets or districts in Florence, presented as if they were far-off realms that the people of Certaldo have barely heard of. I have adapted the names slightly.

15. *the wilds of Abruzzi*: The Abruzzi were notorious for their remoteness and wildness. They are cited also in 8.3. The references to clogs and to pigs (perhaps literally to pork sausages) may have homosexual undertones.

16. *Basque Mountains*: Famous as a remote wilderness.

17. *Parsneep India*: A deliberately confusing distortion of 'parsnip'.

18. *Maso del Saggio*: A contemporary Florentine prankster, who appears also in 8.3 and +8.5 and is mentioned in +8.6.

19. *St Lazarus*: Lazarus, brought back to life by Jesus in the Gospels, here becomes a saint.

20. *Mount Morello*: Monte Morello is a high mountain near Florence, but apparently was also slang for the male rear. See also 8.3.

21. *a Capretius touch or two*: Capretius is an invented authority: again there are homosexual innuendos.

22. *Gherardo di Bonsi*: A prominent Florentine, who founded the Hospital of St Gherardo di Villamagna (1174–1267), one of the earliest disciples of St Francis.

23. *St Lawrence*: A famous third-century Christian martyr, reputed to have been roasted on a gridiron. His feast day (mentioned towards the end of the speech) is 10 August.

DAY SEVEN

2
Peronella and the Jar

1. *the prayer*: Emilia's story had ended with a mock-prayer addressed to an invented ghost.
2. *Giannello Scrignario*: The Scrignario family lived not far from the Avorio district. Giannello may be the Giovanni Scrignari mentioned with his brother in a document of 1324.
3. *St Galeone's Day*: There was a chapel dedicated to an obscure St Eucalion (San Galeone in Neapolitan) again not far from the Avorio district.
4. *the mares of Parthia*: The artfully incongruous image is taken from Ovid or Apuleius.

4
Tofano, His Wife and a Well

1. *the proverbial bumpkin*: Various proverbs of the time assume the ignorance and stupidity of the peasantry.

9
Lydia, Nicostratos and a Pear Tree

1. *Argos*: The story is set in a medievalized version of antiquity. Boccaccio's source is a comic Latin poem attributed to the twelfth-century French author Matthew of Vendôme.

DAY EIGHT

2
Mrs Rosie and the Priest

1. *the avaricious Milanese woman*: Neifile's story was about a married woman who attempted to extract money from her lover, but was thwarted by him.
2. *Avignon*: The seat of the papacy for most of the fourteenth century.
3. *Varlungo*: A village just outside Florence, now in the suburbs.

4. *Bonaccorri da Ginestreto*: This and the various other names that come up a little later in the story seem to be invented and serve only to add local colour.

5. *threshing flails*: There is probably some sexual innuendo here.

6. *Douai cloth*: Cloth from Douai in Flanders was finely woven and expensive.

3
Calandrino and the Heliotrope

1. *Calandrino*: The nickname of Giovannozzo di Perino, a painter more famous for his simple-mindedness than for his art. He appears also in +8.6, +9.3 and +9.5, as well as in stories by Boccaccio's younger contemporary Franco Sacchetti (*c.* 1332–*c.* 1400).

2. *Bruno and Buffalmacco*: Also painters. They appear again as tricksters in other Calandrino stories (as well as independently in +8.9) and again in stories by Sacchetti. Some of Buffalmacco's work survives.

3. *Maso del Saggio*: A notorious joker, mentioned already by Friar Cipolla in his speech in 6.10. He reappears or is also mentioned in +8.5 and +8.6.

4. *the tabernacle*: This gives a notional date for the events of the story, since the decoration was carried out in 1313.

5. *Vernaccia*: A Tuscan white wine.

6. *Settignano and Montisci*: Two hills near Florence.

7. *Mount Morello*: A mountain near Florence, but it probably also has homosexual overtones. See above, 'Friar Cipolla and the Coals', note 20.

8. *heliotrope*: An emerald-like stone speckled with red, reputed to have magical powers.

9. *Mugnone*: A small river that joins the Arno, very close to Florence.

10. *Porta San Gallo*: At the north end of the old city.

11. *not in the Hainault style*: Not in the short, tight-fitting style of jackets manufactured in Hainault in Flanders, which was then in fashion.

8
Zeppa Sorts Out an Adulterous Situation

1. *the story of Elena's misfortunes*: In the previous story a scholar
    had taken extremely cruel vengeance on Elena for making a fool
    of him.
2. *Spinelloccio Tavena ... Zeppa di Mino*: Both men existed and
    were from notable Sienese families.

DAY NINE

2
An Abbess is Caught Out

1. *insanity, not love at all*: In the previous story Madonna Francesca
    sets her two importunate lovers undignified tasks to carry out if
    they are to win her love. They fail and she is able to be rid of them.
2. *folded veils, called psalteries*: The triangular shape of the veils
    resembled that of a stringed instrument called a psaltery.

6
Confusion in the Bedroom

1. *Calandrino*: The simple-minded protagonist of the previous story
    and others. See above, 'Calandrino and the Heliotrope', note 1.
2. *Mugnone*: See above, 'Calandrino and the Heliotrope', note 9.

10
A Wife Almost Becomes a Mare

1. *The queen's story*: Emilia, the queen, had told a story which
    depicted a good beating as the best way of controlling an unruly
    wife.
2. *Barletta*: A city in Puglia. This is the only story set in the region.
3. *Compar Pietro*: A *compare* was literally a 'godfather', but the
    word was (and is) used in the south to indicate a close friend or
    neighbour.
4. *Comar Gemmata*: A *comare* is the female equivalent of a
    compare.
5. *Bitonto*: A city in the province of Bari. The fair was famous.

DAY TEN

5
The Problem of the Magic Garden

1. *Messer Gentile*: The protagonist of the previous story restores the lady he loves (who had been assumed dead and buried) to her husband, who had lost all hope of seeing her again.
2. *Friuli*: A region of north-east Italy.
3. *calends*: The first day of the month in the ancient Roman calendar.
4. *In the previous instance*: See above, note 1.

6
King Charles Becomes Wiser

1. *the Guelfs coming back*: Charles I of Anjou invaded Italy in 1266 at the instigation of Pope Clement IV (1195–1268). At the Battle of Benevento he defeated Manfred (1231–66), the last of the Hohenstaufen kings who had ruled southern Italy since the late twelfth century. The result was that the Guelfs returned to Florence and other cities and drove numerous Ghibellines into exile. See above, 'Andreuccio da Perugia's Neapolitan Adventures', note 3.
2. *Messer Neri degli Uberti*: The Uberti were a prominent Ghibelline family in Florence. The most famous member, Farinata, who appears in Dante's *Inferno* (canto 10), was one of those who were exiled (see above note). However, Neri degli Uberti is unknown.
3. *Castellammare di Stabia*: A resort on the Bay of Naples, where the Angevin rulers built themselves a summer palace in 1310.
4. *Count Guy de Montfort*: (1244–88) The son of Simon de Montfort and one of the most important – and ruthless – figures in Charles's court.
5. *Ginevra the Fair ... Isotta the Blonde*: Guinevere la belle and Iseult la blonde are heroines in the romances of Lancelot and Tristan.
6. *Manfred's violence to women*: King Manfred had the reputation of being a violent, unprincipled womanizer.
7. *Conradin*: The last of the Hohenstaufen princes, whose defeat at Tagliacozzo in 1268 marked the end of German power in southern Italy.

8.   *two noble knights with great baronial power*: The two families certainly existed and included members with these names.

10
Patient Griselda

1.   *Messer Torello*: The protagonist of the previous story. He is magically reunited with his wife at the moment when she is about to remarry after she believes him to be dead. Dioneo refers jokingly also to another comic story (+7.1) with a magic theme in which a wife persuades her husband that her lover knocking at their door is a werewolf and exorcizes it.
2.   *Saluzzo*: A town to the south of Turin and independent from the twelfth to the sixteenth century.
3.   *Panago*: (Pànico) near Bologna.
4.   *shake her muff*: This unexpected descent into crudeness is clearly present in the original.

THE AUTHOR'S CONCLUSION

1.   *the beginning of the Fourth Day*: See the introduction to that day, p. 123ff.
2.   *with their breeches on their heads*: That is, people would do anything to ward off the plague, however indecorous and silly.
3.   *the paladins*: A select body of heroic knights, including Roland and Oliver, at the court of the Holy Roman Emperor Charlemagne (742–814).
4.   *an indication of what they hold concealed within their bosom*: That is, in the summaries preceding each story.
5.   *Athens, Bologna or Paris*: Cited as the quintessential centres of learning.
6.   *Jeremiah's lamentations*: The only one of the three references here to a book of the Bible; 'our Saviour's Passion' and 'the moanings of Mary Magdalen' may refer to any number of poems on these subjects in Latin and Italian.
7.   *grind away when their ponds are full*: This image has already appeared in 8.2, p. 227.
8.   *a goatish whiff to them*: Suggesting an inclination both to dirt and to homosexuality.
9.   *Prince Galahaltd*: See above, Boccaccio's Prologue, note 2.

PENGUIN CLASSICS

LA VITA NUOVA (POEMS OF YOUTH)
DANTE

> 'When she a little smiles, her aspect then
> No tongue can tell, no memory can hold'

Dante's sequence of poems tells the story of his passion for Beatrice, the beautiful sister of one of his closest friends, transformed through his writing into the symbol of a love that was both spiritual and romantic. *La Vita Nuova* begins with the moment Dante first glimpses Beatrice in her childhood, follows him through unrequited passion and ends with his profound grief over the loss of his love. Interspersing exquisite verse with Dante's own commentary analysing the structure and origins of each poem, *La Vita Nuova* offers a unique insight into the poet's art and skill. And, by introducing personal experience into the strict formalism of Medieval love poetry, it marked a turning point in European literature.

Barbara Reynolds's translation is remarkable for its lucidity and faithfulness to the original. In her new introduction she examines the ways in which Dante broke with poetic conventions of his day and analyses his early poetry within the context of his life. This edition also contains notes, a chronology and an index.

Translated with a new introduction by Barbara Reynolds

PENGUIN CLASSICS

PARADISO
DANTE

'And so my mind, held high above itself,
looked on intent and still, in wondering awe'

Leaving Hell and Mount Purgatory far behind, Dante in the *Paradiso* ascends to heaven and crosses the planetary spheres that circle round the Earth, now guided by his beloved Beatrice. Here Dante encounters spirits, from Thomas Aquinas to Saint Peter, who engage him in passionate conversation about history, politics and Christian doctrine. Ascending finally to a sphere beyond space and time, Dante miraculously sees the faces of human beings with greater clarity than ever before and prepares to contemplate the face of God. The *Paradiso* is an account of the order, harmony and beauty of the universe in which Dante offers a deeply personal and unfailingly inventive exploration of divine truth and human goodness.

Robin Kirkpatrick's new translation captures the sublime imaginative power of the final sequence of the *Commedia* and the vigour of the original Italian, which is printed on facing pages. This edition includes an introduction, a map of Dante's Italy and a plan of Paradise. Commentaries on each canto explain the work's ethical, theological and political subtexts.

Translated and edited with an introduction, commentary and notes by Robin Kirkpatrick

---

THE STORY OF PENGUIN CLASSICS

Before 1946 ... 'Classics' are mainly the domain of academics and students; readable editions for everyone else are almost unheard of. This all changes when a little-known classicist, E. V. Rieu, presents Penguin founder Allen Lane with the translation of Homer's *Odyssey* that he has been working on in his spare time.

1946 Penguin Classics debuts with *The Odyssey*, which promptly sells three million copies. Suddenly, classics are no longer for the privileged few.

1950s Rieu, now series editor, turns to professional writers for the best modern, readable translations, including Dorothy L. Sayers's *Inferno* and Robert Graves's unexpurgated *Twelve Caesars*.

1960s The Classics are given the distinctive black covers that have remained a constant throughout the life of the series. Rieu retires in 1964, hailing the Penguin Classics list as 'the greatest educative force of the twentieth century.'

1970s A new generation of translators swells the Penguin Classics ranks, introducing readers of English to classics of world literature from more than twenty languages. The list grows to encompass more history, philosophy, science, religion and politics.

1980s The Penguin American Library launches with titles such as *Uncle Tom's Cabin*, and joins forces with Penguin Classics to provide the most comprehensive library of world literature available from any paperback publisher.

1990s The launch of Penguin Audiobooks brings the classics to a listening audience for the first time, and in 1999 the worldwide launch of the Penguin Classics website extends their reach to the global online community.

The 21st Century Penguin Classics are completely redesigned for the first time in nearly twenty years. This world-famous series now consists of more than 1300 titles, making the widest range of the best books ever written available to millions – and constantly redefining what makes a 'classic'.

The Odyssey continues ...

The best books ever written

PENGUIN ⟨🐧⟩ CLASSICS

SINCE 1946

Find out more at www.penguinclassics.com